THE HIGH COST OF FLOWERS

CYNTHIA KRAACK

CALUMET EDITIONS

Minneapolis, Minnesota

**CALUMET
EDITIONS**

Minneapolis, Minnesota

FIRST EDITION DECEMBER 2014

THE HIGH COST OF FLOWERS.
Copyright © 2014 by Cynthia Kraack.
All rights reserved.

Printed in the United States of America.

10 9 8 7 6 5 4 3 2 1

ISBN: 978-939548-21-4

For Tom

THE HIGH COST
OF FLOWERS

CYNTHIA KRAACK

Chapter 1

Katherine turned her face away from the family room windows. Late afternoon sun settled harshly across the fine creases of her face. Art rose to close the blinds and placed his hand on top of her head. Beneath soft, thinning white hair, he felt her warm scalp. One hair came away on his fingers and he shook it to the floor. There was a time her hair was multi-hued golden and thick as the grass outside their windows, a time when he carried three or four strands in his wallet as his secret treasure.

Boys tossed a baseball across two neighbors' backyards. He watched, admiring one tall kid's easy bending and throwing. Art flexed one shoulder, itching to feel the ball in his own hands, to have just one afternoon of play. The need to be anywhere but in this room on a beautiful September day exhausted his patience.

"Those boys should be quiet. They're not the only people in the neighborhood." Katherine made a sucking sound through her teeth, one of her most annoying behaviors. "They ought to go to the park. Tell them I'm not well and they need to be quiet."

"They're just doing what kids do. Todd played catch all summer when he was their age."

"Where are our kids? They don't care about anybody but themselves."

"I told you this morning that Carrie is in New York with her husband and Todd is on a business trip." He said nothing about Rachel.

"Why did Todd go away when Carrie is out of town? What if I need help?" Again the sucking sound followed this time by clucking her tongue in the back of her throat.

He tried to humor her with shared favorite memories, but Katherine appeared to be through interacting and turned back toward the window. Her eyes, large in a nearly expressionless face, scanned the now closed blinds. Art moved about the room, fussing with empty drink glasses, clinking remaining ice fragments. Restlessness kept him on his feet.

He held out a glass and tried an old favorite joke. "Nothing planned tonight. We could tie one on. Want another, Katherine?"

"You want me to be an alcoholic, don't you, Art? Always filling those glasses with ice and vodka and that other thing. Why can't we have a cup of milk and some pretzels?"

They talked about the damn pretzels almost every day. The woman who used to fill time with stories of the grandchildren or redecorating now owned only a short string of conversation topics.

She crushed what was left of the sticks with bent fingers still tipped by deep red nails. He drove her to the salon every two weeks to keep the polish intact, to give her time with other ladies.

"I don't want pretzels that you bought when you were with that woman." Her voice flattened. "You bought cheap ones so there'd be money for her lunch. I smell that eating place on your sweater. I want the little squared kind with more salt. Not these chintzy sticks."

"I brought you and me sandwiches home from the deli." Her favorite Italian place, even though he preferred the cheaper chain sub shop. "That story is in your head." He jingled change in his pocket, impatient with her and this life. "Why don't you come with me?"

"You don't ask me."

"I do errands every day. It would do you good to get out of that chair."

"Then when would you meet with that woman?"

"Chris' sake, I can't talk with you." Art lost energy as the bickering began. He dropped his head, blew out air through his mouth instead of the stinging words he wanted to say.

Tears welled in Katherine's eyes behind lenses as thick as old magnifying glass. Art could see smudges from her continuous fussing with the frames and left for a towel and cleaner.

In the kitchen, he fantasized about escaping these responsibilities by walking out the back door for just a few hours of his old life—puttering in the garage, meandering the yard, scratching the ears of the collie next door, talking to those kids. The crazier she acted, the more he hungered for what had been. But he choked down his impatience. For better or worse, in sickness and health, he reminded himself. "Till death us do part," he prayed.

Standing at Katherine's side Art asked for her glasses then looked away from the blank interior of her eyes. She stared in the direction of his hands.

He'd loved her eyes, all green and sassy, across the production line where they first met over five decades ago. Even when she was not part of a discussion, her eyes took in everything. She knew how things connected and could put in a snappy comment. He was a manager in training who fell head over heels in love with the prettiest and smartest girl on the floor.

Katherine was special, kind of aloof, not really the type to engage in plant gossip, off color jokes or rowdy laughter. She wore deep red lipstick and snazzy clothes—a lady that made him feel like a lucky guy. He'd give up some of his health to bring back that woman.

She slid the glasses on and performed a little ritual of patting her hair back into place over each ear. Right hand fluffing, then patting first the left side of her head, then the right. Sometimes she'd run her fingers through the short hair on her neck, then shake her entire head just once.

They watched the television screen for a moment, a commercial about some auto repair place led into the news. Another afternoon over.

"How about supper? Hungry for anything?" Art tried avoiding the pretzel conversation trap by inviting Katherine to name her dinner choice.

She seldom expressed a preference and cooking bored him. While she stared at the television, he fantasized about driving alone to the new fast food place near the grocery store to have a paper-wrapped hamburger with onion rings. Just hang out in a booth and watch the young families and their kids, the teenagers working behind the counter, other adults.

"I didn't think you'd be hungry after eating out with your lady friend." Katherine's voice rasped. He could see spittle bubble with each word. "That was a late lunch. Where did you take her?"

"I'm not going there again." He walked back to the kitchen. "We got pork chops or left over chili." Hoping her mood would improve he called, "Why don't you come help me cook?"

But she turned up the volume on her murder mystery show like she was hard of hearing instead of almost blind. He knew her game, ignoring what she didn't want to hear. The phone rang. He answered using the kitchen wall telephone; the one Katherine refused to take down when he bought wireless models.

"Hi, Art. Janie here. Didn't see you come out to get your mail. Everything all right?"

Art appreciated their neighbor's calls. Janie and Katherine had been queens of the neighborhood, getting their hair done together, planning holiday parties, swapping recipes. After the stroke, Katherine got the idea that her widowed friend was his secret lady. Just the thought made him uncomfortable around the woman he still thought of as Ole's wife.

"Nope, nothing going on here. Same old same old." He wouldn't tell tales out of school.

"Just heat up the chili, Art, and grind a sleeper in her bowl. Give yourself the night off."

"Katherine can't help that she's not that sharp these days. We're all getting older. Either of us could be sitting in her chair."

"But we're not. Live wild, Art. Come out and play cards in the garage. I can find another hand or two. She'd never have to know." Art took a breath, started to respond, but couldn't talk faster than Janie could offer advice.

"What kind of life do you have, Art? Sitting and watching television for hours, sneaking off to the grocery store, waiting on her hand and foot. I've known Katherine for over thirty years and would say she's playing you for the fool."

"It's our life, Janie. The life Katherine and I have now." He cleared his throat and changed the receiver to his better ear. Why older women felt everyone deserved a helping of their supposed wisdom eluded him. "By the way, I did check the mail. Anything else?"

"I'm having a birthday party Sunday night for my sister Mary. Katherine knows her. Nothing big, just cake and coffee. Why don't the two of you join us? Like old times."

Art thought about it. Janie made wonderful cakes. She'd have the table decorated. He'd grab a beer and shoot the breeze about baseball or cars with Jim and Larry. Then he thought about the box of adult diapers sitting on their bedroom floor and Katherine's tantrums.

"We'll see. I can't predict how Katherine will feel, but thanks for the invite."

Janie was quiet on the other end before lowering her voice and responding. "Try a little sour cream or melt some cheese on the chili. If you don't have those things, give me a call and I'll put whichever you want on your front step so Katherine doesn't have to know. I pray for both of you."

Art hung up. Reheating chili would make for an easy meal. He couldn't sit in that blasted recliner for another hour without going nuts. He grabbed two soup bowls, placed them on the counter with more emphasis than necessary, turned to search for lids.

"Did something break?" Katherine's voice carried strong above the television. She was always concerned that he was mistreating her things. The stuff she liked to collect when she still shopped.

Art didn't answer, just mentally challenged her to walk to the kitchen if she was really worried about her precious junk. He leaned into the refrigerator for the chili and removed the plastic tub with one hand then switched it to his other hand to place it on the counter. There was resistance to his blind placement and he turned.

Katherine stood between the counter and his hands. She held a soup bowl upside down in her hands but stared directly at him. "That's not one of our containers. Did that woman make that food? Are you going to eat out of it or is it poisoned just for me?"

"Yes, Janie made it. It's the chili we had for lunch yesterday. You liked it then."

"Janie this, Janie that. Why don't you just move in with her? She's so perfect. You don't even notice she's got it in big time for me. She took my diamond when I was at stroke school and you brought her here. I won't let you sleep with me because I smell her everywhere."

Carrying bags of water softener salt all his waking hours would be easier than sharing the weight of Katherine's insecurity. Unlike that emotional ache, a different pain began in his chest.

"It's in the safety deposit box. Janie cleaned up the place and changed the sheets so things looked nice when you got home. We've been over this a hundred times."

"No, she took my diamond. It was in my mirror dish and it's gone. Probably melted into one of those big rings for her fancy painted fingers."

"Janie's been your best friend for decades. She knows the inside of our cupboards better than me. Do you sit in that chair and think up these wild stories. With all our friends' kindness, can you really think most people in this goddamn world want to do you wrong 'cause you had a stroke?"

She drew in her breath with a hitchy, choking kind of gurgle. Her pale face began blooming with deep pink blotches that meant trouble. Maybe she'd stroke again. He knew he should slow down, but felt his emotions building like the energy a pitcher gathers before even raising his throwing arm. Closing the refrigerator with his hip, he turned from her to give himself time to calm down though she might see his gesture as indifference.

"Don't talk about my mind, Art. You have no right to talk about my mind. You could look for someone to make me better, but you like it this way. You like finally being smarter than me and keeping me stuck stupid."

"Don't pick a fight with me, Katherine. I've had more than enough for one day."

Art jumped as she crashed a soup bowl hard on the end of the granite counter. Shards flew in all directions. She howled and hopped from one bare foot to the other. He watched her dance pieces of white glass into her toes and wondered how she had removed her shoes and socks. Maybe Janie was right, maybe she played him for the fool. He looked into her face to look into her eyes, to call her bluff.

A china triangle stuck out of her chin, blood pushing out around the edges. His words stuck. Katherine's rage escalated, tying the two of them in a circle knot of new and old emotions.

She grabbed the other dish, smashed it down then picked up pieces to throw at his face, screaming with a voice sounding like wood siding being removed with a crowbar and brute force. They'd fought like this a long time ago, when they were equals. Now keeping so much anger alive required too much energy from two old folks.

"The witch was in my room. The witch is wearing my diamond."

He ducked but not quite fast enough. A dish fragment caught him in the left temple before falling to the floor on the growing cluster of china debris.

"Katherine, what the hell are you doing?"

She picked up pieces and dug them into her arms, across her face. "I'm trying to make you ugly so women won't want you. So you won't put me away. I want you to bleed. Like me." She cried, reached for him. For a few minutes he struggled with her, but she had that strength born in her rages. The ache in his chest turned sharp, took his breath away. He stopped.

"I've had it, Katherine." He repeated himself louder, his voice breaking, but she kept yelling. Throwing in the towel, he picked up the phone and dialed 911. "My wife has dementia. She's in a fit, cutting herself up. Got me, too. My chest hurts bad. You got to send someone real fast."

She lunged at him while he spoke, grabbed for the phone. He held her off. She came at him with another china chunk, slashing at his arms. She'd go for his face next, maybe pull off his glasses. She'd tire eventually, not remember her craziness. Maybe not remember him.

One slash burned through his arm, then another. In a moment of pure self-protection, he swung the phone receiver at her. It caught her in the side of the head knocking her glasses caterwauled on her face.

"My God, Katherine," was all he could say after committing the most damning sin of his life. She roared, dragged her glasses off, then grabbed for the receiver and yanked the phone from the wall.

He knew he should stay with her, calm her before the ambulance crew arrived, but the pain in his chest now burned through his back so he slowly moved around her, picked up her glasses. Taking one last look at the chaos surrounding his wife, Art opened the door and escaped to the garage. He tried to take a breath, frightened at how his hand shook while pulling the door closed.

"Don't you leave me," Katherine screamed from the other side. She never left the house when she was worked up. Never had stepped outside the house in a lather in all the decades they were married. The whole family knew Katherine's top cardinal rules--appearances matter and keep family dirt in the family house.

He placed her glasses on the old fridge, took out a cold can of pop for the bump above his eye, then grabbed another to drink. Sinking to the step, he flexed his shoulders, trying to ease his chest. Blood dripped from both arms to the welcome mat at his feet. No one outside the family came to visit the Kempers anymore. Even certain family members were not welcomed.

Each shallow breath required concentration. Even with wooziness coloring what happened in the last hour, he knew a critical invisible barrier had been crushed.

The chest tightness ebbed then returned. His shirt felt clammy, blotches of blood stained his slacks. He leaned against the door, watched an approaching ambulance and squad car. Great weariness kept him on his butt when he should stand up and walk to the curb to greet the professionals. Gathering his breath demanded full attention.

"Mr. Kemper?"

"I'm the one who called. My wife's inside." His voice came out whispery. He tried clearing his throat. "She'll need her glasses." He pointed, taking care as he lifted an arm.

One EMT opened the kitchen door. The other stayed at Art's side. "Having problems breathing, sir? Do you use nitroglycerin?"

Strong fingers lay on Art's wrist. "My heart's racing like wild. It's a mess in there. I should have cleaned up before you got here but I couldn't." His voice stayed reedy, cold sweat started forming under his shirt. "She cut me."

A young police officer appeared. "Mr. Kemper. I'm Officer Chandler. We met when Mrs. Kemper was transported in spring. I see you at church. Seven o'clock Mass on Sundays."

"Stay with him, Chandler." The medic moved away. "I'm going for nitro and oxygen."

The officer squatted in front of Art. "Tell me what happened."

The armed forces taught Art respect for anyone in uniform. He appreciated Chandler's efforts to gather just the facts. "I was making dinner and Katherine thought I broke a dish. She's not herself any-more and today was a bad day."

Art edited the story, keeping details like Katherine's search for her mother that morning out of the telling. "Before I knew it, she started breaking bowls then just went nuts jumping on the glass and cutting herself. She hit me, got my arm pretty good." He realized he'd called his wife 'nuts' to a stranger and paused.

"Sounds like she was too much for you to handle?"

With a sinking feeling, Art saw that calling 911 might have given control of their situation to others. They'd figure out he'd hit her and could take Katherine away. He didn't volunteer anything about the phone, hoping maybe if Katherine said something the EMTs would take into account her state and not believe her.

"I didn't think I'd ever say that. I just want her to get better. She's been sick so long." Art let his eyes meet the young officer's. He didn't see pity, just a competent man doing a difficult job.

The officer clamped a hand on his shoulder. "Can we call some-one to follow the two of you to the hospital? A relative or friend? Maybe Father Christopher?"

"I gotta live here and don't want people thinking I tried to hurt Katherine. Can't you take care of me here?" A voice like a wild cat wailed on the other side of the door. "Maybe you take her to the hospital, and I'll follow when I catch my breath? She'll quiet down if I talk to her."

Art pushed himself up from the step; the garage floor's concrete surface turned wavy with the effort. Katherine's screech scared the piss out of him. Maybe he couldn't shelter her from the outside world.

Pain dragged him back down to the cement step. "Holy Jesus." He clutched one hand to his chest. "Jane Gertzen. She's three doors over and across the street." The EMT appeared, offering a nitroglycerin tablet. Art accepted it as he would a Communion wafer, praying while the medicine melted under his tongue.

Time moved slowly, the nitro doing magic, Katherine's voice lowering. Art flexed each hand and drew in each breath, testing his body's limits. "I got to get my keys and wallet from the desk. The insurance information's in there." He heard his voice drain away. His body refused to straighten. He tipped to the left.

Somewhere he heard a male voice calling, "Hold on, Art." He closed his eyes to say a prayer, not for Katherine, but for himself. He wasn't ready to die at seventy.

* * *

As loud as she screamed, Art didn't come to help. He sent a stranger through the kitchen door, betraying her when she needed him the most. Such a weasel, leaving when she wasn't doing well.

"Look what he did to me," Katherine screamed and waved her bloody fingers at the young man. "I'm bleeding. My heart's busted open and I'm losing my blood. He did this." She gestured across the floor. "Now he doesn't have the courage to come in here and face you." For emphasis, she spat on the floor. "My husband is a coward. Did you take him away? He should be in jail. God will send him to hell."

"My partner's taking care of him. Let me take care of you, Mrs. Kemper."

"I don't care if he dies. Don't you understand? MY HUSBAND TRIED TO KILL ME. He hit me with something and busted my brains to make me stupid."

She mouthed the words carefully so the stranger would understand the difficult situation of her life.

"Look at this place. My blood is everywhere. He broke my china and threw all that poisoned food at me because I figured out what he was up to with that woman across the street. And he busted my phone. My phone. Look at this."

Hands steady, she offered the phone to the stranger; put her foot down cautiously, now avoiding china shards.

"She stole my diamond and he's still sniffing around her arse."

Rattling wheels approached from the garage service door. Katherine stood still, feeling the hot sting of each cut on her body and the cooling lines of blood and chili on her skin. She lifted a hand to cautiously lick, wondering if blood would taste like tomatoes.

The noise could mean one of the kids was home and dragging that old red wagon into the house. She didn't want any of them to see her with a strange man or the kitchen's horrid mess.

"Before the kids walk in I need to wash up. Can someone help me to the sink?"

"Don't worry, Mrs. Kemper. We'll clean you on the way to the hospital. The gurney's here. Follow me so you don't step on anymore of this glass."

A young man swept debris to one side of her kitchen floor with her blue broom. He'd destroy the bristles. It was her favorite broom, but this person wouldn't understand that she'd bought that broom when she came back home. He wouldn't know how difficult it was to clean this house when she came back.

Katherine watched the sweeping man speak with his partner. She couldn't decipher their comments. Another crisis had passed. Art needed to take charge of these people before they did more damage.

"Where's Art?" She used her polite voice, not demanding, but inquiring. For a moment she thought she saw a body bag rolled out of their driveway. If Art died she knew these young men wouldn't tell her. Without him to cook and give her medicine, she might never see her house. She stood straighter to show the strangers that she wasn't weak.

The man next to her looked up from his radio unit. "He's on the way to the hospital, Mrs. Kemper. Chest pains."

"Did you tell me that already?"

"There's a lot going on here, Mrs. Kemper. You probably didn't hear me."

Katherine tried focusing on his voice as her legs began weakening. That awful confusing, sick feeling surged up from her stomach and her bowels loosened. Shaking, she extended a hand to the kitchen island but grabbed the young man's sleeve instead. He held her so she didn't sink to the floor. The room swirled and dipped as they tucked her onto a gurney. She closed her eyes, hating the feel of straps across her legs and middle. Tears rolled from the corners of her eyes but she kept her head straight on the pillow. How she hated her old-lady body and its constant leaking fluids.

While they rolled the gurney down the driveway, Katherine saw lights glowing from every front window of the house. Through blurry eyes, she looked for the living room's silk roses silhouette to be sure Art was keeping up appearances. Her vision cleared, much improved without those awful glasses.

She expanded her view to include the front door, storing details of the potted geraniums on the porch and the metal "Kemper" nameplate. Out of the corner of her eye she saw that woman from across the street coming up the driveway with one of the police officers. Katherine hissed gently, wiggled against the restraints. Words wouldn't come as that witch showed a house key to the officer.

Chapter 2

A long-sleeved jersey kept Rachel semi-comfortable during a late afternoon run along Chicago's Lake Shore Drive. Sunshine gave Lake Michigan a friendly, inviting glimmer, but wind blew across the water reminding Rachel of fall maintenance projects. Another summer had passed without her finding time to finish a long list of tasks. Heading toward home, wind at her back, she opened her stride and took advantage of long legs.

The sticky back door demanded use of both hands and some luck. Once inside, the deadbolt slid easily into its slot after other locks were engaged. Without her son and dog, home felt like a favorite movie without sound. Almost nine months after separating from David, loneliness still denied her total comfort of being in the place they'd created. She considered calling to find out who won Dylan's soccer match, but stopped.

Tonight would be work time. She showered and changed. A hat ridge ruffled through her hair exposing the highlights and lowlights mastery of a New York colorist. She couldn't really name her hair color anymore, but had been assured it brought out the best in her eyes. She tried a wet brush to create a smooth look, gave up, tucked her hair behind her ears.

Their house cleaner left the kitchen clear of rubble. Granite counter tops and stainless steel appliances shone. Red-orange glass pendant lights, chosen by David, glowed over the breakfast bar. Rachel assembled a chicken and avocado sandwich to eat while working. Then she grabbed three of the chocolate squares Dylan loved and filled a large glass with water.

Her office wasn't spacious, cobbled together by sacrificing a butler's pantry, two closets and space below the staircase. Buying something as small as a framed photo, she had to consider displacing books or art within the angled room. Before sitting down, Rachel picked Eric Clapton's blues from her music collection and cranked up the volume. She started on her sandwich and hoped the music's rhythm might thump out worry about David's recent decision to move to Minneapolis. Nothing could be resolved at the moment, but decision time about their relationship could not be postponed much longer.

What demanded attention tonight was paperwork, the most hated task of a psychotherapist. Reviewing clinical notes, completing problem insurance forms, making notes for her office manager kept her busy while daylight dimmed. Beyond the computer screen, Rachel noticed a lamp turn on in the front foyer then wrote a note for Dylan to adjust the lamp timers for shorter days. The phone on her desk rang with caller ID displaying an unknown Minnesota telephone number.

"Rachel Kelsey here."

"Dr. Kelsey, this is Dr. John Wagner, your parents' physician."

It was a call Rachel never expected to receive. Her parents' emergency contacts included her siblings, Carrie and Todd, then a neighbor—in that order.

"Yes, Dr. Wagner. We met last spring when my mother was in the hospital," she said while checking the time on her computer screen. "You're calling at six-fifty in the evening so something must be wrong."

"There was an incident at their home late this afternoon that resulted in both being admitted to St. John's. Your father asked me to call you."

"Is he okay? I mean I know he's not okay or you wouldn't be calling, but how is he? Did anyone call Carrie or Todd?" She struggled to find control. "I'm sorry, I'm not making sense."

"Your father says both your sister and brother are out of town." His voice seemed to pick up speed, or maybe a surge of adrenalin changed how she listened. Rachel sat back in her tall-backed desk chair and concentrated on Dr. Wagner. She seldom relaxed into the chair, but had worked with a decorator to be sure the wine-colored upholstered headrest would be comfortable.

"Your father's in the cardiac unit, resting comfortably while we assess his condition. He's on oxygen and may have had a mild heart attack."

These last words slowed Rachel's world for three or four seconds. Her eyes looked to a framed photo on her desk of David, his father and Dylan taken months before her father-in-law's death from a massive heart attack. Three generations of athletic guys with dark eyes and straight, thick hair had been captured in what would be their last photo. Dylan was about ten when David's father died. Three years ago.

She missed a few of Dr. Wagner's words about Katherine. "… been admitted to a general medical floor for treatment of a number of cuts and abrasions and general disorientation." He stopped.

Details flew through her mind, catching and releasing like autumn leaves in a breeze – heart attack, oxygen, cuts and abrasions, general disorientation. Her father always provided information for her mother's various medical episodes. She was unprepared for this unfiltered version from a stranger and grabbed at the most curious word.

"You mentioned an incident?"

"I'll let your father fill in the details. What I understand is that your mother became agitated about something related to dinner, broke china and used it to injure both of them. When the EMT's arrived, your father was experiencing breathing difficulty."

The world remained saner because of her father's robust health. Rachel couldn't quite deal with that reality changing. "He's never talked about her being violent." Focusing on her mother was easier. "She's not in serious condition?"

"Neither of them is in serious condition, but the situation is serious. Your mother needs more care than your father can provide. It would be helpful if you could be here tomorrow morning to meet with a social worker."

Rachel recognized fatigue in Wagner's voice from years of listening to David when he called her from surgical rounds at Northwestern Medical Center. She wondered if John Wagner had a wife who worried about whether another woman was at his side during night duty, then closed her eyes to refocus on her parents' situation. Her computer screen saver photo of Dylan and Weezer, his dog, popped up, an incongruous image during this conversation. She turned off the monitor, picked up a pen to take notes.

"You know I live in Chicago? And I've not been involved in Katherine's care." In the next moments decades dissolved. She was once again the oldest sibling, the third parent for her brother and sister. Now the child turned parent for her parents. "Of course I'll be there."

"Good. I'll look for you in the morning during rounds."

"Dr. Wagner, are you suggesting Katherine should be classified a vulnerable adult?"

Sounds of fingers moving across a keyboard preceded his answer. Adding 'vulnerable adult' to the list on her paper, Rachel waited for words that would dictate her parents' future.

"Your mother's cognitive deterioration has been significant since I saw her in early summer. Your father hasn't had any reason to be seen in clinic, so I was unaware of older bruises on his body that the ER guys found. I suspect this isn't your mother's first violent episode."

Suddenly Rachel wondered how their family physician charted odd bruises found on the Kemper kids decades ago and knew he didn't. The memory of crouching over her younger siblings while their mother flailed at them with an extension cord broke her attention. Now it was time to protect her father. He may not have called Katherine's behavior abusive, but Rachel wouldn't look the opposite way.

"Are there bruises on her?"

"Nothing inconsistent with her general medical condition. Your father's given me clearance to be open with you. He'd tell you I am a big advocate for keeping people in their own surroundings so it's highly unusual for me to come to this conclusion. Katherine needs the expertise of a facility experienced in caring for memory-impaired patients for her safety as well as your father's. That makes her a vulnerable adult. As long as she's in their home, some would say your father is also."

"This won't go over easily with my dad. He's very loyal to Katherine and she wants to remain in their home." She slowed down, editing her thoughts into careful words.

Dr. Wagner was quiet. Rachel assumed some hospital detail distracted him and began thinking about how Carrie and Todd would deal with this reality. Her sister would cry, maybe appeal to her husband, Steve, to find a lawyer in his firm to fight this doctor's recommendation. It was harder to predict Todd's reaction beyond a tradition of blazing anger.

"I don't remember your sister calling your mother Katherine."

"Your memory is correct. My mother prefers that I use her Christian name." Rachel held back more information.

"Families are interesting, but you know that better than me." She heard a change in his voice. "Calling you gives me a chance to say I read *Family Games* and have recommended it to patients. You're a wise therapist."

Compliments from healthcare and social work professionals resonated deep. Rachel wondered if Dr. Wagner was amused that a psychologist known for family self-help books was obviously part of a dysfunctional clan. Would he mention to someone else that he sensed hostility between her and her mother? Maybe he'd chalk it up to Katherine's dementia.

"Thank you. You're very kind." Rachel hesitated, not sure where to go next. "Our family doesn't always perform well in these kinds of situations." Hopefully he'd read between the lines.

"A healthcare crisis isn't the easiest time for anybody," was what he said then added a warning about construction near the Wisconsin Dells before saying good-bye. She wondered if his friendliness had to do with her book.

Rachel checked the time, marveled at how life could change in twelve minutes. There were at least two late flights to the Twin Cities

18 CYNTHIA KRAACK

from O'Hare, or she could fly in the morning. All the months of the book tour with unfriendly airports, dirty taxis and tired hotels made leaving their remodeled Chicago brownstone almost painful. She stared out into the hall, not wanting to be away from Dylan, Weezer, and the simple routine of her everyday life. Not while uncertain about the future.

Spontaneously, Rachel considered driving alone to Minnesota, found appeal in taking her new Lexus on the road. At seventy-five miles per hour, the drive would take around six hours. Switching to her cell phone, she called David to share with him the Minnesota news and make plans.

"Hello, there. Done with your paperwork or bored?" His rich tenor flowed over her unsettled emotions. She walked up the stairs to their bedroom, not a room she was able to call hers quite yet, to pack while they spoke.

"Neither. I just had the most amazing phone call from John Wagner, my parents' physician. They're both in the hospital and Carrie and Todd are out of town. Can you imagine how desperate my father had to be to have his doctor call me? I was so surprised I acted like a stuttering idiot just trying to ask if they were all right."

"What happened? By the way, living in Chicago also classifies you as out of town."

She imagined David sitting by the corner windows of their first condo, reviewing case notes in his favorite arm chair and sneaking glances at the lake's night movement. Except for wear and tear of renters, not much had changed with the place. The east exposure of the living room and master bedroom windows made the place worth a fortune. David had furnished it with simple metal and leather furniture that Dylan called an old man's idea of cool.

"There was an incident, as Dr. Wagner described it. Katherine took after Dad with broken china. He may have had a mild heart attack, but the big deal is that their doctor brought social services into the case. He feels Katherine should be placed in a care facility."

He whistled. "The world's turned upside down. Art's not asking you to handle making that happen is he, Rachel? I'd wait for Carrie or Todd to get back."

"This isn't just about Katherine. Dad has older bruising. I think Todd and Carrie are so intent on keeping Katherine happy, they don't stop to think of Dad as vulnerable. That's why I'm willing to get involved. This is about saving him."

"Well, take care of yourself. Dylan and Weezer are comfortable here, so stay as long as you need. Hope you're not thinking of driving there tonight?"

"Actually I am. I can't stand the thought of sitting in another airport. Believe me, I'm wide awake and my iPod is loaded with enough music for a long trip."

Their conversation could have ended, but Rachel found herself sinking back into the loneliness of her afternoon run and pushed to keep David on the phone. "I should have asked if you have weekend plans that Dylan might disturb."

"Rachel, don't go there."

"I didn't know if you were trying to spend time with anyone special."

"Katherine comes on the scene and you begin looking for troubles where none exist." He paused. "Remember, I have Bears season tickets with Matt."

"It's been a tough day," she said in place of the questions she wanted to ask about his plans for moving and if they had a future. He said nothing. "Thanks, David."

"Dylan and I will be fine."

A weariness of sorts sounded in his voice that she first interpreted as irritation that the conversation wasn't ending. Stopping her packing, she asked a question that masked her fear. "How are we going to do this when you're living in Minnesota?"

"Rach, just get through the next few days. There's only so much worrying worth doing in advance. Want to talk to Dylan?"

"I'd love to."

"Hey, Mom, what's up?"

"I got your text about the team winning. You played great while I was watching."

"They weren't that good a team," he replied. "But every game counts for playoffs. Dad and I are kind of watching the Cubs while I do math."

"Well, the reason I called is that Grandpa Kemper's in the hospital… nothing serious… but he asked me to come and help out with a few things. Since you're already staying with Dad, I'm heading out tonight. Need anything from here?"

"Maybe Dad and I can hang out at home. Taking Weezer out from the condo is a pain in the butt. How long are you going to be gone?" Television baseball announcers interrupted Dylan.

"I'll try to be back before Sunday night. Depends on the grandparents." She wanted to give him a hug. "We'll probably have to limit ourselves to calling or texting. Grandpa's house isn't very technology savvy."

"Do you think you can do a supply run on your way back?"

As she listened to Dylan's list of shopping items, Rachel realized he never asked for information on his grandparents. She treated Kemper family relations like her individual chore that shouldn't bother David or Dylan. Suddenly she wished her son knew her Dad and how they both had big hands and bushy eyebrows and loved baseball.

"Hey, I've got to finish packing," she said with those thoughts raising unexpected emotions. "Have a good day at school and a great time with Dad. Kiss Weezer on the nose for me. I love you, Dylan."

"I love you, too, Mom. See ya."

Within fifteen minutes, the lights of Hyde Park disappeared as she accelerated along South Lake Shore Drive then onto the Expressway. Through Illinois she listened to a collection of Chopin nocturnes, but the calming music didn't work any magic. Like a small wind tunnel, her thoughts churned through business demands, personal issues and her parents.

Traffic thinned out on Highway 90 heading into Wisconsin. David labeled the cheese head state a strategic buffer between the Kempers in Minnesota and the Kelseys in Illinois. She kept Chicago as an emotional bunker, turf her mother hated visiting. Katherine thought Chicago unsafe, too crowded, too racially diverse and too dangerous for raising a child.

Crossing into Wisconsin, Rachel risked a ticket to kick up cruise control and settled in for a long, uneventful drive. She turned off the music, picked up her cell phone and left a message for her book publicist and a voice mail on Todd's cell phone. Around Madison, Rachel pulled off for gas and snacks. With a large plastic cup of diet cola and a box of popcorn, she chose 1980s rock music for the next stretch of the trip. Before leaving the gas stop she called Carrie.

* * *

Nothing, nothing in Carrie Kemper's daily life surpassed the sensual pleasure of Manhattan after dark. Sitting thirty floors above Fifth Avenue at a tiny, linen-covered table in the Asian-accented, tall-windowed dining room of Manhattan's trendiest restaurant, Carrie sipped a particularly well-shaken martini and waited for her husband, Steve, to finish a phone call. New York's energy and the buzz of good alcohol made her feel as sexy as the tall, young things in thin-strapped dresses flirting at the bar.

She dug her cell phone out to check for messages from the boys and it rang the '1812 Overture' in tinny tones. Carrie knew only one person in Chicago who might be calling.

"Carrie, how's New York?" Her sister's voice managed to retain its crisp elegance even on a mediocre cell connection. On radio she sounded like a female version of their father.

Carrie looked across the restaurant table at her husband who was now available and rolled her eyes. "Rachel" she mouthed before speaking.

"I never expected the day would come when you would call about our parents' health." With her free hand, she fingered the stem of her blue martini glass. "We're at dinner so I can't really talk. I'll get in the cities around noon and will call you after I get to the hospital. Dr. Wagner is blowing this whole thing out of proportion."

"Stay in New York, Carrie. I'm already on my way to Minnesota."

"That's a bit dramatic isn't it, Rachel?" She turned her face toward the wall and covered her other ear to better hear. "There's no need for you to get involved." Steve touched her arm. Carrie waved him away. "You don't know anything about Mom's care."

"Dr. Wagner called on Dad's request. I do understand what Dad's handling at home."

Carrie turned back to the table and her martini. "He talks to you when he's frustrated, Rachel, and probably exaggerates." She sighed at the buzz kill of her sister's call. "Well, do what you want."

Intending to bring the call to an end, Carrie pulled out one damning comment. "I'm not sure how to put this, Rach. Mom's finding it more difficult to put faces and names together with people she doesn't see very often. I don't want you to have your feelings hurt."

The sound of her sister sucking in air on the other end satisfied Carrie. Two, or maybe it was three, drinks before dinner supplied courage to be honest with Rachel. For at least ten seconds the line was quiet.

"Say hello to Steve and enjoy your dinner, Carrie. We'll talk tomorrow," said Rachel.

Snapping her phone shut, Carrie shrugged her shoulders, enjoying the feel of a new expensive silk blouse sliding over her skin. She turned attention back to Steve who looked right at home among all the affluent Manhattan men with his short hair, tailored suit and stylized eye glasses. Seeing him in this context momentarily unsettled her pleasure in the evening, made her aware of the extra pounds held snug with the help of spandex and how her gold chains might scream Midwest matron. If Rachel had not called, she'd be enjoying herself, glowing like a woman who belonged at this table drinking fifteen-dollar martinis.

"Doesn't that just figure? Not only do my parents ruin our getaway but my big sister thinks she can drive into town and be their advocate." She expected Steve to nod in agreement but he concentrated on a spoon or the base of his water goblet. "I thought she was still touring with that last little self-help book someplace outside of the family orbit."

"If Rachel wanted to help out, why not just say thanks?"

"In the years we've been married, have you ever heard Rachel show any understanding of Mom? If Dad's not able to speak for Mom, somebody's got to be there to do that."

"I don't get why you have to be like that with your sister."

"I'm sorry, Steve. It's not like I asked to be the one who takes care of my parents. For God's sake, what kind of relationship is it where a daughter calls her mother by a first name?" Carrie smoothed her face and lowered her voice. "My sister holds a grudge longer than most normal people."

She settled back in her chair, gave Steve a seductive smile. "You don't have a business meeting until tomorrow afternoon so let's make tonight one to remember." She sucked the olive off its spear, held it between her teeth for a second and winked while dropping the treat back in her mouth. "Please, lighten up, Steve. Look at the city. Isn't it wonderful to be sitting here?"

"It's New York. Lately I've been sitting here more than I've been in Minnesota." He leaned forward, dropped his voice as well. "Did you know that after your father told Rachel about this trip, she got us a reservation for this place through her publicist?" One finger tapped the table. "When I hear you put her down, I hear a lot of self-righteousness. What's with that? I think she's a smart, respected woman. It would be helpful if our boys knew their aunt."

Their water goblets were refilled, dinner plates removed. The table next to them emptied. Steve watched the young couple walk through the entire dining room. Carrie tapped a finger on his starched white shirt cuff, moving it suggestively to his monogrammed cuff link.

"What's 'with that' is exactly what's happening right now. Rachel is a very divisive person in our family. You and I were having a wonderful evening. She called and now you're all over me about not treating her nicer."

He pulled back his arm, shook his sleeve before responding. "Then maybe there's something wrong in the Kemper family. I've asked Rachel or David for more than one business introduction over the years and they have been gracious."

"It's an act, Steve. She's one of the bossiest, most controlling people I know."

"It would be hard to pass your mother in those traits."

Light laughter traveled from a group behind them, the waiter arrived to ask about coffee, dessert or after dinner drinks. She let Steve handle the questions, accepted the small dessert menu offered by the young waiter. Wanted a drink.

"Steve, my mother is in the hospital. Don't talk about her that way." Carrie picked up her martini to cover her emotions, drained it, and put the glass down. "I promise I'll talk nicer with Rachel tomorrow although I wish she'd stay away. We just don't get along and that's all there is to say. Can we order dessert?"

* * *

Rachel remembered the killer maple crème brûlée at the restaurant where Carrie and Steve were dining. Anyone else, she might have called back to recommend ordering it. Carrie's life looked *All American Mom* sweet on the surface, but Rachel suspected a stream of alcohol ran close under her sister's skin. Every therapist was tainted by some family dysfunction, and for the Kempers the dysfunction was spelled '*alcohol.*'

Hoping to relax before what would be stressful days with her family, Rachel turned on cruise control, chose her 'sing along' music list and finished the first half of her trip belting out tunes ranging from rock with the Rolling Stones to the diva days of Annie Lennox. The New Age tone of her iPhone fortunately rang during a break in her songfest.

"Julie, do you ever sleep?" she asked her publicist. "It's after eleven o'clock your time.

"I'm still at my desk. This is what publicists do. I got your message. What do you mean you won't be able to make lunch with the CNN folks? They're hot to talk about including you in a number of segments on family health during October. This is a huge break that could launch you as a media brand. It might take a month before everyone's schedules come together again."

"Give me a break. I'm your easiest going client. For the last six months, you told me to be somewhere and I was there. If the CNN folks want to see me Friday, they should fly into Minneapolis instead of Chicago. Both of my parents are hospitalized."

"They could say you're not serious about this project."

"That doesn't frighten me, Julie. I can be happy with what's already happened with my books." Rachel let Julie push more of the same bullshit and considered hanging up. "In the three years we've known each other, have I ever dropped everything to help my folks?"

Julie grumbled with escalating intensity about making new arrangements. Rachel stopped listening.

"Jules, I'll be honest, I've got cold feet about the exposure a CNN family health month series might generate. Being part of one weekday show on family-based therapy made me feel like I can't walk down the street in a ripped sweatshirt 'cause somebody will recognize me."

"Damn it, Rachel, don't make a hasty decision while you're in crisis. We're close to the really big pay off. Your first book cracked the top twenty; the second book could make the top five. I know I pushed you a lot this year and you're tired. That's part of the deal, lady."

"You're dead right about that tired part. OK, Jules, we can talk next week, but forget what I said about flying CNN to Minneapolis. Tell them I had a family emergency and we'll connect later. I won't be worth shit after a day with the Kempers. Got to go. Don't have a heart attack out there in the Big Apple."

The call disquieted her, reminding her that there might be people at the hospital in the morning looking at her, evaluating what they saw and heard, stealing some part of her identity. On the other hand, Dr. Wagner's professional admiration could help her parents.

Shortly after one in the morning she crossed the St. Croix River from Wisconsin to Minnesota. Suburban hotel chains lined the expressway, but she headed into downtown St. Paul and pulled into the grand old St. Paul Hotel. Handing her key to the valet, she dragged her single suitcase and shoulder bag into the lobby. In thirty minutes she was asleep. Tailored casual pants, a starched shirt and low heels waited for a day maneuvering through healthcare and the Kempers.

Chapter 3

Breakfast arrived too early. Art looked over the assortment of colorless foods on the tray table straddling his hospital bed. From sharing Katherine's many hospital meals, he knew the coffee would be tepid, the orange juice room temperature and the oatmeal totally flavorless.

Rachel was only eight when she taught herself to cook hot breakfasts during Katherine's first time away. At the time, his wife's idea of breakfast consisted of hot coffee and a cigarette for herself and cereal for the kids. Rachel made French toast, scrambled eggs or creamy oatmeal. He never questioned if their daughter was too young to be using a gas range. When Katherine returned, Rachel's cooking meant his wife could avoid coming downstairs in the morning. Things just worked out.

His head throbbed, particularly around the sutures. One nurse had the decency to find him pajama bottoms so he wasn't lying with a bare butt, but there was little else to be appreciated. Outside the sun shone bright, an ordinary day for other people.

Art sat, deep with his own thoughts, a not totally comfortable situation. He remembered really caring about the world, about people, about so many things when he was younger. The bright, demanding, beautiful Katherine changed everything. There was so much about her that he didn't understand. Spending time with her absorbed whatever energy was left after work. That didn't change much as they aged. If not for Katherine, he might have returned to farm his uncle's place, lived a smaller life, maybe a happier life. Art shook his head, shifted on the bed, not sure what the day held for them.

Anticipating Rachel's arrival made him nervous about what to say to her. Katherine long stood between him and open communications with any of their kids, but her stance about their older daughter was quite clear. He tried to reconstruct what steered him away from becoming a more kindly, wise man with children who loved him, to a sad old man in a hospital bed with oxygen tubes plugged in his nose and bad coffee on a tray. All that came to mind was his wife and how, in the end, the peace he earned in their home by being a quiet man, had become more important than taking a stand. He chose a firebrand of a woman and lived as ashes below the blaze of her life.

The stupid pajama bottoms bundled up around his genitals. A monitor on the index finger of his left hand made straightening things near impossible. Art rested his head back against the pillow, closed his eyes.

When Rachel walked in, the first thing he noticed was an expensive-looking leather bag hanging over her shoulder. It might be one of those thousand dollar ones he and Katherine saw on one of the endless lady fashion programs his wife enjoyed. Their daughter lived in a world far from suburban tract houses. Finally her smile registered, offered small comfort.

"Hey, Dad. Am I glad to see you sitting up. You're looking better than I expected."

She leaned over the bed and he wondered if she would try for a kiss or hug. Art leaned back into the pillow when she placed a hand on his shoulder and squeezed gently, as if he had become fragile.

He pushed his breakfast tray aside. "I'm not eating this crap."

Her eyebrows shot up as she backed away. "Can't say that it looks that great but you need to eat something. Maybe if I spread jelly on the toast?" Without waiting for a response, Rachel moved the oatmeal aside and worked on the two pieces of skimpy wheat toast. "Sounds like you had a rough night." She re-arranged the tray with the toast, coffee and juice centered in front of him. "Dr. Wagner's call really caught me off guard. How are you feeling this morning?"

"I've been better. How's your mother?"

"The nurses say she'll be fine. She's disoriented, but there isn't anything much more serious than cuts and bruises." Rachel spoke factually.

"I'd like to see her. She's not comfortable on her own, everything upsets her." He slurped at the coffee. It was awful. "When are the others coming?"

"Carrie could be here by lunch and I never heard back from Todd."

"Par for the course with Todd. Maybe the doc'll send me home."

"I think they want to do some tests, Dad."

There was nothing harsh in the way Rachel spoke, but Art felt tears threaten. He looked down toward his hands, confused by this sense of weakness and emotion.

Nothing in Rachel's behavior suggested that she noticed his shakiness. "I'm not sure I understand what happened. Dr. Wagner said Mom cut both of you with broken china?"

"Yeah, close enough. You know how your mom can get excited over nothing these days." He cleared his throat, relieved tears didn't develop. "She thought the chili had gone bad, and I didn't agree and one thing led to another and she got her dander up."

She extended a newspaper. "I brought you the St. Paul paper. Thought you might like to read the sports. Sounds like the Twins stand a chance in the play offs."

They were on familiar ground, one he could talk about with almost anybody, even this daughter. "At least we have a team worth following. You still like those Cubs?"

"Dad, you always pretend I like the Cubs. You know I still follow the Twins. Now Dylan is another story."

"How's my grandson?"

"He's good. Playing soccer at this time of year. But baseball is what he loves. I wish you could see him play." She slipped the main news section from one of the papers before handing the rest to him. He chose the sports pages.

The printed words blurred in front of him. Reading the same paragraph a second time didn't help. He turned on a morning news show and stared at the television without the slightest comprehension. His thoughts darted back to the mess in their kitchen. He wouldn't be able to handle the cleaning.

"Did you stay at the house?" Art asked Rachel.

She looked up from where she leaned against a wall, reading. "I don't have a key."

"We've had the same locks for years. Did you lose yours?"

"I haven't had a key since I left for college."

"Todd and Carrie have keys. You must have lost yours."

"Dad, I swear Mom didn't give me a key to your house. That's why I ring the doorbell."

Confronted with another odd decision made in the past by Katherine, Art wondered if his wife would have to know if he gave Rachel his key. That made him realize he wasn't sure if he had his keys in his pocket last night.

"Dad, how did a disagreement over dinner get so big?"

"You'll have to talk to your mother." The words rolled out as if Rachel was a questioning teenager. Comfortable words that deflected deep consideration. He unclipped the monitor from his finger, swung his legs to the side of the bed, and stood up slowly.

"Could you get me some hot coffee while I go to the bathroom?" She extended a hand but he moved aside. "Don't worry; they let me get up on my own during the night."

Art closed the bathroom door, listened to the sound of her heels walking away. You goddamn bastard you could have said something about her coming all the way from Chicago, he thought. What if she leaves because you acted like a jerk?

He used the toilet, washed his hands then opened the door to find a nurse straightening the sheets and no Rachel in sight.

Chapter 4

Rachel left the door open to her father's room as she walked out, knowing she needed to get away, worried that he shouldn't be on his own, and aware of the emotional heat that might be coloring her cheeks. A tall, red-haired male nurse with a smile as easy as Dylan's headed her way. Attached to his stethoscope was a Minnesota Twins clip.

"Any chance you're taking care of my father?" She hoped he'd say yes.

"I'm on my way in there right now. My name's Rusty and I'm on for the next ten hours."

"I'm Rachel." She extended a hand, relieved when he did the same. His was large with a comfortable grip. "My Dad insisted on getting to the bathroom on his own but seemed shaky walking."

"It's okay for him to move around. He did take off his monitor clip. Anything else?"

Rachel's first impressions were that Rusty was a guy her Dad might like. "He'll probably ask you for reports on my mother every hour until they see each other." She paused to think. "Beside checking on both of them, I'm here to meet with their doctor during rounds then a social worker."

Rusty answered while listening for her father. "Dr. Wagner usually talks with folks in the small waiting room next to the elevator. If Art's busy when you get back, feel free to take a seat in there."

The toilet flushed and a faucet was turned on behind them.

"I know he needs a cup of good coffee so I'll head to the cafeteria after visiting my mother," she said. "Thanks for taking care of him. We're used to my mother being in the hospital. Never him."

"The first twenty-four hours are often confusing for seniors," Rusty said. "I'm in checking vitals often, the lab is in for blood and he's pretty nervous. He'll be in a better mood this afternoon." Rusty tipped his head a bit and turned toward Dad's door.

God, I'm dying for coffee, Rachel thought while taking the elevator down to her mother's floor. Escaping back to her hotel for a nap this afternoon sounded attractive. She entertained the possibility of driving back to Chicago after her siblings arrived. One long day of Kemper family immersion might be outside her limits for maintaining a civil exterior and internal sanity.

The least he could have done is acknowledged I dropped everything to get here, she thought and regretted her decision about cancelling Julie's carefully arranged lunch with CNN. A row of bright green food service carts formed a bunker of sorts at the door to Katherine's room. Staff pulled trays of breakfast with small brown bowls of oatmeal, cereal or fruit, juice, toast and coffee. Even in a carpeted hallway, the activity created an unpleasant amount of noise. Rachel suspected the staff felt Katherine wouldn't be aware of the disruption.

"Are you Dr. Kelsey, Katherine's daughter?"

She stopped, consciously adopting the polite face she used at book signings or for dealing with nursing staff. Hospital personnel typically assigned psychologists second-class provider status. "Yes. Please call me Rachel."

"Jeri Blanc, nurse shift lead for this unit."

"Good to meet you." Rachel extended a hand, but Jeri offered just a smile. "I've got a few minutes before meeting with Dr. Wagner and was hoping to visit my mother."

"The night shift staff said you were here before she was awake. Nothing's changed with her medical condition. Now isn't a good time for a visit because the staff is trying to help her with breakfast."

"I'll help her." Rachel put a hand on one of the food carts. "By the way, isn't there some other place these could go? Unexpected activity or noise can disorient her."

Jeri moved aside. From a long ago year of hospital rotation, Rachel recognized the subtle straightening of the other woman's shoulders as a signal of nurse authority over the unit, its patients and everything happening in that domain.

"I can have some of the carts moved," Jeri said. "But, if you take a look in her room, I think you'll get a better sense of the kind of care your mother needs this morning."

Anticipating the worst, Rachel stepped next to Jeri and peeked into the quiet room dominated by a hospital bed, its head cranked up for the feeding of a battered, frail old woman restrained by soft ties within its metal sidebars. A giant bruise covered one side of the old woman's face, the kind of marking Rachel had seen on battered women. She looked closer, searching for features that would confirm that this was Katherine Kemper, the proud and beautiful woman who controlled a small universe, and found it in the way the patient spat oatmeal at the scrubs-garbed aide holding a spoon. The disdain, the defiance in the way Katherine threw back her head and stretched her long neck declared that this lowly aide dared to treat the wrong woman like a helpless ninny.

"You probably didn't notice the restraints earlier because of her blankets," Jeri said without a trace of sympathy or gentleness. "She is disoriented and mildly violent. None of that is unusual with memory-impaired patients, which you know. She might not recognize family right now."

On a professional level Rachel knew Jeri told the truth, but as Katherine Kemper's daughter, she saw everything in a visceral, denying reality kind of way.

"I do understand," was what she could say although she wasn't sure what the words meant. "I'll come back later." She then did what each Kemper siblings learned while young, and apologized for her mother's behavior. "I'm sorry if this is disruptive for your staff."

Jeri gave a slight shrug of the shoulders. Rachel sensed the nurse had other issues brewing, other patients' family members to update.

"Why don't you come back after you meet with Dr. Wagner?" She dismissed Rachel like a staff member who should be busy doing other chores.

Rachel stood in the elevator without choosing a floor. On the main level she bought a cup of coffee, found the stairs, walked back to her father's floor. Sitting in the waiting room on a plastic chair that offered no basic human comfort, Rachel closed her eyes. The image of her mother as an angry, old person requiring restraints remained very present. Rachel felt intense relief this wasn't happening to her father. She'd never admit to the next rush of feeling—that after the hell Katherine created in their family, the woman deserved to be at the mercy of strangers.

Sensing another presence, Rachel opened her eyes. Dr. Wagner stood at the door of the small waiting room. He walked in and extended a hand. "Good to see you. I assume you had a safe trip and a short night. Need coffee?"

Short silvery black hair and a scattering of facial wrinkles made John Wagner look like he was about fifty, near her age. His small goatee surprised her. Katherine immensely distrusted men with facial hair.

"No thanks, my father already warned me that the hospital brew is awful." She paused then spoke what was on her mind. "I just saw my mother in restraints."

The doctor briefly established eye contact. Rachel felt his level of concern for her parents and accepted what she read as empathy. He sat down, clasping his hands loosely across his body. "What has anyone told you?"

"Not much. My father says my mother thought the chili was bad and that got her upset. Obviously that's not the story. The unit lead nurse says my mother is disoriented and violent."

"Your mother's dementia is progressing rapidly and her heart is weakening."

Her eyes focused on the doctor but 'violent' stayed in her mind. She had used that word to describe her mother that way to a friend years earlier. She moved attention back to Dr. Wagner's closing words. "We'll do tests today but I suspect she's had a number of small strokes." He slowed down. She waited for worse news. "The past months have been rough for your father. He didn't seek help, but would have been justified in doing that."

"I spent an afternoon with them about six weeks ago. My mother seemed disconnected, uncommunicative." Rachel didn't share that it had been an easier visit because of the silence. "Usually we'd go out for lunch or dinner, but not that day. Dad seemed to think she was a little under the weather."

Sitting forward in his chair, John nodded. "About your father. We're concerned about his blood pressure, which is running high. He knows he's had a mild heart attack and we'll do a catheterization to check for blockages. Usually that would be done today, but we need extra time to pull a plan together for both of them." A page for respiratory therapy interrupted. They were quiet while it repeated. "I think we'll do it tomorrow and if we find a blockage, we'll insert a stent. I'll find a way to keep him overnight for observation."

"I appreciate everything you're doing for them both." She forced a smile. "I don't have a clue why he wants me here today."

"Maybe he thinks you're what he needs. Last night sounded like a serious struggle. The EMTs said someone ripped a telephone from the wall. You've seen their bruises." The doctor stopped talking to drink deeply from the Styrofoam coffee cup. "This stuff is pretty bad."

She sensed he wanted information about her parents that she might not know. The fact that Katherine would attack Dad physically wasn't a surprise. Rachel shifted on the uncomfortable chair, withholding what she knew about her parents' rocky marital history until their doctor shared more of his knowledge.

"Your father's a proud guy and shows great devotion to your mother."

"They've been married a long time," she added.

"He's going to be fine, but his time of caring for her at home is over."

This was why her father had called. He knew Dr. Wagner would force the question about Katherine's care and take the decision out of family hands.

"Beyond the violence, she's incontinent and the family friend who followed them here last night told staff that Katherine sometimes wanders the neighborhood. I think your father found her in this person's garden pulling up flowers."

Information she didn't have. She wondered when all this happened and what words her father used to cover up the incident when they spoke on the phone. "That's probably Jane Gertzen, one of their oldest friends. He has complained about other things, but I didn't know Dad was dealing with any of this." She fought a yawn; the long night of driving and emotional overload of the morning taking a toll. "Living in Chicago, I'm afraid I only know what Dad tells me."

He sat forward, appearing somewhat impatient. Perhaps he was behind on his schedule. She lifted a hand, ready to ask if there was anything else, but he spoke first.

"Do your parents drink much?"

In their fifties and sixties her parents drank excessively, but with a certain élan that covered the occasional spilled drink or awkward social moment. Rachel waited for the doctor to show his cards before she offered hers. "Have you asked them?"

"Your mother had an elevated blood alcohol level when she arrived in the ER and the EMTs reported a number of alcohol bottles on the kitchen counter."

The best answer Rachel formed as a child for the times when Katherine didn't attend events was borrowed from a novel, and had something to do with the stress of raising a family on a woman in delicate health. Later, Rachel learned to suggest it was 'that time of month' that kept her mother incapacitated.

"Yes, my parents drink. My mother has had problems with alcohol since I was a kid. Dad always covered. Since he retired, they usually have their first cocktails around three in the afternoon and put down a couple before dinner. Then they have a nightcap or two. I've talked with him about not mixing alcohol with their medications."

He jotted a note on a folded piece of paper. "I'm recommending she be discharged directly to Evans House, a memory impairment residential care facility. How do you think your father will respond?"

"That would mean giving up the hope she'll get better. My brother and sister think time will be the cure." Rachel stopped and looked down at her hands, long fingers and oval shaped nails so like her mother's.

"Time isn't the answer. I'm surprised Art didn't use the home health professionals that were recommended during your mother's last hospitalization."

"Dad says I should mind my own business when I suggest home health. My siblings won't want me involved in this decision." She paused, then spoke before he could ask more questions. "Communications and decisions in the family always flowed through my mother, so we don't have a lot of history of making decisions together."

Rising from his chair, Dr. Wagner was clearly a doctor mindful of his schedule. "Well, you're the one who is here. Give me ten minutes alone with your father then join us. We can keep Katherine here for a day or two while I push for accelerated admission to Evans House. If your father wants to make alternative arrangements, social services will find her respite care until she can be admitted elsewhere."

"Dad's going to want to visit this place."

"He already did and completed an application about a month ago. She just needs a pre-admission physical."

He had to be able to see her surprise. "That's news to me. Is there anything else I should know?" Her father had played her for the fool, filling telephone conversations with meaningless complaints about doing laundry or cooking meals and blowing off all offers of help. Maybe Carrie and Todd had toured this Evans House as well and she sounded like the ignorant outsider in this conversation.

"Nothing from my standpoint," he said, then left.

In the hallway Rachel saw a middle-aged woman stare into the conference room after the doctor walked out. Irritated by the stranger's insensitivity and her father's insincerity, Rachel pushed the door shut.

Her hands shook as she huddled in a corner of the room and pulled out her cell phone. She remembered no one waited for an update. David had no reason to care; there were no close girlfriends to call. She shoved the phone back into her purse. Breathing deep and slow, she fought hard to calm down. Her parents had pulled her into their crazy-making chaos and she lost all the safety of her own world when she arrived in theirs. But what set her emotions running down dark paths was the fear she might end her days alone, like her mother.

Chapter 5

Languid largess accompanied Carrie's fluttering of a twenty-dollar tip toward the hired driver at LaGuardia. While he placed her luggage curbside, she fingered a new chunky glass necklace purchased from a Soho studio. She checked out how other female travelers were dressed; confirmed she needed to lose twenty, no twenty-five, pounds to be back in the game with those worth watching. It was possible in the three months until the December Silver Ball if she swapped diet soft drinks for vodka-laced juice. But, this morning she needed a Bloody Mary and croissant to get on a plane back to the Twin Cities, the hospital, and facing Rachel. Dieting could wait.

To keep Steve ignorant and happy, she placed her private charge card on the counter for an impulsive first class upgrade. He wouldn't have to know that she wanted the deep seat comfort and flight attendant attention for those three hundred minutes, a small indulgence her sister probably took for granted. Steve mentioned reading that Rachel had signed a multi-book deal worth plenty of zeros. Carrie could remember the heady thrill of selling Healthy Seasons Spice Company almost ten years ago and depositing all that money into all those accounts and investments. She wanted that feeling again. Rachel had a rich husband, even if estranged, so why more money should fall on her was one unfair quirk of life.

A few Bloody Mary's and a short nap later, Carrie watched the Mississippi River lead the plane into the Twin Cities. She fluffed up her flattened hair and decided to head home for an attitude adjustment stop before setting her parents' lives back in order.

Chapter 6

"So, in the bottom of the eighth with two on and two out, Morneau took one of those low swings and doubled. If I hadn't been at the desk, I would have yelled." Rusty handed Art a dampened washcloth. "Take it easy around the hairline on your left side, no scrubbing."

Art followed Rusty's stories about last night's Twins' game to get through a morning wash up with the least embarrassment. Women didn't seem to mind such personal assistance. Katherine usually had a rather royal attitude as a stranger sponged her back or spread lotions on her person.

"Signing that guy to a long-term contract was pure magic," Art said.

"Always need strength in the batting order. Can you roll to your right side? The emergency room crew left some mess on your back. I'm going to untie this gown. Okay?"

Art rolled to his side, conscious of the big nurse's hands. "I'm damn weak," he said. "Couldn't even read the paper this morning. Just saw that picture of Morneau."

"Is this bruise on your left shoulder from last night?"

"When you get old you walk into things. Sometimes Katherine pulls a bit harder than usual to get up from a chair. Part of the territory when you take care of her."

"Lean against my arm and we'll get you back sitting against some pillows here."

"You're good at this," Art said. "Thanks."

"Let's clean your glasses. I hear Dr. Wagner's voice in the hall."

"You're looking good this morning, Art. How you feeling?" Dr. Wagner's face came into view through clear lenses.

"I've been better. Weak and not so steady on my feet. I can get to the bathroom and back, but then I got to sit down. How's my wife?"

"She's sitting in a chair, Art." Dr. Wagner listened to his heart, reviewed the chart. "The weakness you mentioned is normal. Your vitals are improving. We'll keep monitoring them for the next 24 hours."

Who would care for Katherine if I died went through Art's mind as the doctor talked. Somewhere he'd read that caring for a memory-impaired spouse took five years off the caregiver's life. Always healthy, he never worried about her future.

"I wanted you in the cath lab today but it looks like we're on the list tomorrow. Excuse me for a minute." Dr. Wagner checked his phone, a frown formed across his tan face. "If you need a stent, you'll be here two or three days. Do you have any other questions?"

"We'll both be ready to leave after those tests?"

"I'm going to tell it to you straight," Dr. Wagner paused. "It isn't safe for you to take Katherine home. She needs twenty-four hour care. I've talked with Rachel about Evans House."

Never believing this would happen, how could Art say he'd filed the application because Evans House had big windows, a fountain in the dining room and smelled better than the other nursing homes? He couldn't really believe that his wife belonged among the sad cast of residents he saw sitting by the front doors waiting for what? For no one and nothing. At Evans House there seemed to be more activity, fewer lost souls, and sunshine lighting up the lounge areas. Did he know enough to make such a major decision about her future?

As Dr. Wagner beckoned for Rachel to join them bedside, Art turned his head away to hide his brimming eyes. Even whipped dogs get their fight back.

He accepted a tissue from Rusty and dabbed at his nose then his eyes. Something in the way Dr. Wagner touched Rachel's elbow made

Art feel patronized and snapped his self-pity. He wadded the tissue and extended it to his daughter. She took it.

"Art, I told you that Rachel and I talked about Katherine's needs. I told her that you completed the Evans House admissions paperwork. I'll fill in Katherine's physical exam form today."

In the morning sunshine his daughter's face looked angular, like old photos his uncle had from some Minnesota Indian reservations. Maybe the rumors about his mother were true, maybe this was what Katherine disliked about Rachel. He fought to keep his mind in the conversation. They were talking about Katherine's future, and therefore, his own.

"She's probably happy we have to put her mother away." Art could barely push a whisper through an unexpected wave of fatigue and emotion. "Right, Rachel?" He looked her way. She stood quiet, her eyes almost dim, arms crossed over her chest. Art waited for Rachel to respond, but she only swallowed. He wanted to grab her by the arms, make her answer, was shamed by his thoughts.

Dr. Wagner's eyes moved toward the blood pressure monitor. "Rachel voiced no opinion," he said in an even tone. "She thought Carrie and Todd knew more about Katherine's daily needs."

Art snuck a look at the monitor as well, knew he had to calm down.

"Art, I've had a geriatric psychologist assess Katherine and it is both of our opinions that she needs more care than family can provide. And she needs it twenty-four seven." He moved his hand to Art's shoulder. "Are you up to talking about this?"

Art tried easing away before saying, "Don't have a choice."

"Beside their reputation for high quality, Evans House is near your home. They are more than capable of caring for Katherine's needs now and in the future."

"Can't fight city hall, Doctor. If you say Katherine's got to be moved, there's not a lot I can do. You think I can't take care of her myself, and none of the kids want to step in."

"You've done a great job of taking care of your wife, but her needs have changed. Talk about it with your family. A social worker will visit with your family this afternoon." Art accepted the squeeze of his shoulder. "Hang in, Art. You're going to be fine and Katherine will be safe. She'll be in one of the best places for what she needs."

Dr. Wagner made notations in Art's chart. No one spoke. Art watched Rachel, who kept her eyes on the doctor. Art appreciated that the man didn't attempt to lighten the mood.

"Rachel, you're planning to be here for the social worker's visit?"

She nodded once.

"Art, I'm sorry I can't be with you. Rest up, I'll see you tonight and we'll talk again."

"I'm not sure I remembered to thank you for calling last night," Rachel said.

"Not a problem." He was gone. Rusty followed.

Hospital quiet stayed behind in the room. Monitors clicked, the blood pressure cuff hummed, muffled noise from the hallway crept around the partially closed door. Art turned his head to the window, signaling that Rachel could leave as well.

"Dad, we're going to talk about Dr. Wagner's recommendation."

"What difference does it make to you how your mother and I live our lives? It's no skin off your nose. I'm the one who listens to her complain about everything, makes all the meals, cleans her up. I think I should know what's best for us."

Rachel turned her back on him, closed the room's door.

"I didn't ask for anyone to stick their nose into my house and my life."

"Whether you want to believe it, this is the first time I'm hearing about your situation. Dad, you haven't been exactly transparent." He turned his head to look at his blood pressure monitor, turned his head back and tried to avoid eye contact with Rachel during her little protest. "I had no idea that she was violent or wandering the neighborhood. And, why didn't you tell me you were visiting these facilities?"

"Because it's not your business. You're all so damn busy. I've been taking care of her just fine on my own. Am I a doddering old putz who has to be treated like a five-year-old?"

"She wandered across the street to Jane's house across the street."

If his daughter had taken a step toward the bed, Art may have pressed the call button. Her back straightened and all those facial angles flattened into a smooth, emotionless appearance that took him by surprise. After Katherine's first stroke, he'd seen that face on doctors and now understood that Rachel was part of this medical world, an unnerving realization.

"Dad, since I walked in here this morning, you've acted like you've wanted a fight. Why did you call me?" She stopped.

He ignored the question. He thought by staying quiet, she would understand the discussion was over.

But Rachel felt differently. "I could get in my car and leave this mess in Carrie's lap."

He knew she was right. Something about Rachel's stinginess in lending a hand over the past years irked him. There were things he wanted to say to his daughter that never came up during phone calls. "Carrie's been a trooper, but she's got her hands full with the boys. It's time you help take care of us."

"Remember that I have tried. I set up a house cleaner who you fired. I organized grocery delivery that you cancelled. You returned my birthday present for Katherine because I didn't personally deliver it. You're upset about how this is all happening and I'm the one taking the heat."

"If you cared to know more about your mother, you'd spend time with her."

"You're the one I care about, Dad," Rachel said.

Her words sunk into his mind, melting through a block of anxiety and some ache he hadn't known existed. This was why he called Rachel. This was his kid. He didn't have the energy or words to tell her that she was the one he wanted to depend on at this time. The fierceness in her face made him look away. He knew how it felt to be kicked one too many times. He let her carry on, hoping she'd feel better, then pick up responsibility for the situation and give him time to rest.

"So, I was sitting in a hotel room in Philadelphia, after a National Public Radio interview. The two of you left three nasty voicemails about how I didn't come home for her birthday."

"I don't remember making calls on her birthday. Carrie and Steve took us out."

"With drinks before and a few during the meal then one of you hit speed dial. Probably like last night when Mom's blood analysis was beyond the legal limit."

"Don't be such a holy prude, Rachel. You're just like your grand-mother. We are adults sitting in our home, not hurting anybody. There's not much else left in our lives. So we have a few drinks. You try watching television and staring at the four walls when the rest of the world is going its merry way. You don't know what you're talking about. Stick to kid psychology."

Rachel looked away; an angry flush tinted her face.

He regretted his last comment.

"Wrong, Dad. I work with dysfunctional families – some just like ours. Parents and kids. Grandparents and parents and kids. Screwed up kids usually learn some part of their behavior from the adults in their lives."

Down deep Art knew Rachel was like him. But he never got in the way of Katherine's dealing with the kids, and Katherine never dealt well with Rachel. He tapped at his chest, vaguely faking discomfort.

She never raised her voice while digging into his guts. No sweet-ness or shrillness in her voice like Katherine or Carrie, just strong pain. Rachel got angry like a man. "God, my own family acts like I'm the last person to know anything about what has to be done. I do know and it isn't going to be easy."

Art knew she might walk away from a fight, like moving out when David played around. Her chin quivered, the only female he knew with that quirky telltale emotional twitch. She sighed, a womanly sound of exasperation. He tried taking in some air before suggesting they start over.

Reaching out, she touched his arm. "Let's not fight, Dad. I came to help so let's move on. I'm not going to leave unless you want that. We're in for a few rough days."

"Damn right." He heard his voice thinning like the old guys at Knights of Columbus card nights. He cleared his throat, hoping his real voice would appear. "Feels like I can't do anything right." Art tried to remember if he had thanked Rachel for getting here so quickly. He didn't even know if she drove or flew. Silence stretched between them for twenty, thirty seconds. Rachel picked up the conversation, keeping attention on Katherine.

"Well, she's always been a demanding person, Dad. Don't judge what kind of husband you've been by what's happened this last year. You've earned some serious credits with the guy upstairs for everything you've done to care for her."

"How're we going to afford this place?"

"Dad, you don't have to worry about that. You always talked about saving for a rainy day. If this isn't a rainy day, I'd call it at least drizzling. Tell me about Evans House."

"It's a new place with lots of windows. We can mix our things in with their stuff. I can eat with her whenever I want. She'll have activities and people around to take care of her."

Looking at the large wall clock, he was surprised to see the hands at only nine-thirty. "None of those places are really great. They're just holding cells for people waiting to die," he said and looked up. Rachel appeared distracted, maybe not really listening. She was too young to really understand his generation's fear of nursing homes.

Rachel shrugged slightly and picked up his hand, but didn't do any of those female busy actions, just held it. "I can take her through the admission process, Dad. She'll think I bossed you into the move and you can be the good guy."

"Hopefully I'll be out of here in time to get her settled."

"I don't think so, Dad. The move might be the day you're scheduled in the cath lab."

Art thought about his earlier bravado about whipped dogs fighting back, knew he'd fought as hard as he could for the months leading up to this morning. He rested back against the pillows, one hand searching for the call button for help to the bathroom. First he needed to send Rachel on her way.

"Can you check on your mother? No one's told me much about how she's doing." He looked at Rachel and offered an apology. "I'm not quite myself this morning."

"Sure, I'll check on her." Rachel squeezed his blanket-covered foot and left.

* * *

Katherine hated how the plastic reclining chair stuck to her bare legs only slightly less than the seat belt rubbing her tender stomach. She tried to find a buckle, distracted by an annoying skin flap she thought disappeared after the last baby. Giving up, Katherine felt her hair and knew they'd done a horrible job with the comb this morning, maybe even ripping hunks out of her head. She cursed low, spit on the floor, then stretched out a foot to smear the gob. Pain snapped from her toes to her heels like a tripped mousetrap. She screamed, closed her mouth, turned back to the television.

People left her alone since she kicked that awful foreigner who came to put more putrefying cream on her feet. Now some new stranger came in to interrupt her favorite television murder mystery. The woman wore expensive clothes, stupid in a place where people might throw up or bleed on you at any time. She wanted to touch the stranger's pants, wanted to feel good wool between her fingers. Art, never a man of class, dressed her in cheap synthetics.

"Good to see you out of bed." The woman moved to pour a glass of water and offered it to Katherine, bending the straw. "I'll ask if you can have a soft drink. Water gets boring."

Katherine nodded and sucked, watching TV around the visitor's arm.

"This is a first, having both of you in the hospital at the same time. Dad's doing better than I expected."

"I'm hurt worse than him," Katherine spoke so the woman would understand the situation. "Somebody came in here during the night and cut the hell out of my feet. They pull that kind of crap if you don't get into the heart beds."

'You don't remember stepping on broken china at home?"

Katherine heard something familiar in the woman's voice, something irritating.

"Why would I step on my china? I'm here because I couldn't breathe right—but they put Art in my bed in the heart room and stuck me here where people die. They cut up my feet so all my blood would run out. Strapped me to the bed so I couldn't get away."

The visitor looked bored. "What's on television?" she asked.

"Angela Lansbury. I could watch her all day." Katherine broke her television focus to look at the stranger. "I have legs like hers."

Katherine had a moment of clarity and recognized the hair that was too long for a middle-age woman, the voice that sounded like a man and the expensive clothes belonged to Rachel. "Why are you here? Did you leave that man who sleeps with other women?"

Rachel started to speak, but Katherine stopped her. "I peed myself. Right now, I peed myself. If they tie me to this chair like a poodle, they have to expect this." She noticed Rachel's nose wrinkle as her daughter leaned away.

"Stinks, don't it? Someone should take care of me. Did I ask you to be here?"

"I couldn't let you two be on your own right now."

"Huh." Katherine turned back to the television. "Angela Lansbury is such a good actress. She's older than me but looks good. I could look like that if I wasn't sick. Not as heavy, but just as curvy. Your dad likes curvy women."

"Let me press for someone to help change your things. How about if I comb your hair while we wait, Mom?"

"You could check my head for bugs. And, don't call me 'Mom.' I don't want that nonsense." Katherine carefully looked out from nearly closed eyes to watch Rachel's response, nearly laughed at the stupid thing. She settled back in her chair, enjoying the moment.

"Your father hasn't brought my bag so they did my hair with a dirty old brush from the charity box." She shook her head from side to side, and then dug her fingers into her hair feeling for little bumps. Satisfied, she pushed her hair behind her ears. "There's bugs in that bed. I itch everywhere. They all crawl to the crotch, you know."

Rachel took a comb from a big leather bag. Katherine sat perfectly still, enjoying the feel of someone waiting on her needs.

"What you and I could use is more hair," Rachel said while untangling a snarl. Katherine didn't understand why the girl would say such a silly thing. They both had plenty of hair on their heads. Maybe Rachel wore a wig. "I think my hair is the best gift you gave me."

"Why would I give you a gift?" Katherine jerked her head away. She'd closed her eyes, lost track of this person's voice and feared a stranger had walked into her room.

"Who are you? I'm waiting for Art." Katherine leaned against the seat belt and began calling Art's name. He always came when she called. Always. Now she was afraid. He had to come.

"Dad can't hear you."

"You just want him to yourself. He likes girls that look like you."

"I'm Rachel. I'm your daughter."

A tall man in hospital clothes entered the room, gesturing for the stranger to step outside. Katherine continued calling for Art, angry that he'd ignore her.

To earn escape, Katherine allowed the man to undo the belt. She hobbled to the bathroom and followed the directions of a little blond girl who offered clean clothes. They led her to bed and the girl disappeared. For a moment she was vigilant, worried the medical man might push up her gown in one of those ways men had. But he merely threw back the covers and eased her to the side of the bed. She let him talk her into lying down. The soft binders he placed on her wrists assured her. Her television control lay in one hand, her rosary in the other. She'd not fall to the floor or float from the bed when the angels sang.

* * *

Art dozed a few minutes, but woke up anxious about his wife, and worrying about how Katherine would react to Rachel. Problem was, for most of their lives Katherine stood between him and the kids and grandchildren. Until her last stroke, she orchestrated every detail of the family from simple phone calls to holiday gatherings. Most of what he knew about their kids and grandkids was what she told him—Carrie was sensitive, Todd shouldered too much responsibility, Rachel was trouble.

Sitting in a chair, he watched a television sports show while eating lunch. Rachel returned looking tired.

"Had a long morning, Rach? You're dragging."

"Well, you look better and that food is an improvement over breakfast."

"Run down to the cafeteria and get yourself something and a diet cola for me. You can tell me about your mother when you get back." It was important that Rachel come back, that she knew he wanted her to come back. But to say those words was out of his comfort zone.

"There's not much to tell. At first she didn't seem to know who I was and was angry about things that she thought the nurses were doing. For a while, she remembered me. That's about it. Her nurse is going to call if she's ready for visitors this afternoon."

"Carrie'll be here later than we expected. She left a message at the nurses' desk."

"Lunch does sound good. I'll be back in a half-hour with that diet cola."

Art watched Rachel walk out to the hall, talk with his nurse then shake hands with someone he didn't know. For the umpteenth time he wished she'd been a son. David played with fire shacking up with another woman. Art admired his daughter standing her ground for what Katherine called a huge family embarrassment.

He'd read somewhere that Rachel signed a three-book deal worth a lot of money. She never told him that kind of stuff. Hadn't shared much of anything important for years. Cautiously he raised one arm above his head then the other. No pain caught his chest. He folded his arms across his chest and stood to watch replays from last night's baseball games.

"How you feeling, Art?" His nurse came in along with a lab tech carrying a plastic bucket of needles and tubes.

"Tired, but alive. Had to stand for a few minutes. Now I think I'm ready to go back to bed." Sitting, he realized he was more tired than he could describe.

"Vitals." Rusty laid a cool hand on his pulse. How did nurses keep their hands just the right degree of cool? "If you want a nap this is the best time. Social services are scheduled at four." He turned off the television, adjusted the blinds. "I'll close the door."

"Rachel's coming back from the cafeteria. I hate to make her stay in the waiting room."

"She can sit in your chair, put up the footrest and chill while you rest."

"I heard my name?" Rachel came in with the diet cola.

"We were just talking about your father resting and how that recliner might be a good place for you to relax. We'll put Art's name on the pop and bring it in later."

"If I won't hold you up from snoozing, Dad, I could really use a sit down. I didn't sleep well last night."

"Are you staying at the house?"

"I don't have a key." He remembered her saying that earlier, but this time it registered. He assumed all his kids had keys. Katherine must have had a reason.

Art meant to say something, but only watched Rachel as she accepted a pillow and blanket. She had a style that made people feel like they were doing a good job no matter what service they provided. As much as he wanted to talk, his eyes drifted shut.

Rachel was gone when he awoke. Clouds dimmed the afternoon sunshine. He eased off the finger monitor clip and got up to use the toilet. Feeling more independent, he headed for the chair instead of bed. Rusty approved of the choice when he appeared. Clamping the finger monitor back in place, he recorded vitals.

"Dr. Wagner said if your blood pressure settles, you can have dinner with your wife. Sounds like both your daughters will be here this afternoon for the social worker's visit."

Art searched for something easy to say in response without disclosing that his daughters didn't have a close relationship. "Yeah, young people have such busy schedules that it can be hard to pull everyone together even when there's an emergency."

"I told Rachel the cath lab is scheduled for tomorrow afternoon so we'll need to make sure you have enough to eat tonight." Rusty wound his stethoscope around his neck. "Now take it easy. If the Twins stink, you can always watch the Cubs."

Chapter 7

The minivan smelled of boys, athletic equipment and dogs. Carrie counted the days until she could drive something too small for transporting others. She brushed the driver's seat with a lint wand before climbing in wearing her new black pantsuit.

Parked in the hospital lot, the car's air conditioning turned up to its max, Carrie sipped the last of her vodka-enhanced lemonade. She checked her lipstick in the rearview mirror then dug around in her purse for a breath mint. Would her sister look as good in person at the hospital as on the book cover? Abs held tight, she walked with her back straight, hips moving to the internal smoky jazz of an attractive woman she had perfected decades earlier.

Her left ankle rolled outward a tiny bit as she stepped on an uneven surface inside the lobby. Regaining her balance, she almost walked past Rachel who stood by the elevator, talking on a phone. Knowing her voice would be heard by Rachel's caller, Carrie walked up behind her sister and used her most gentle voice to say "Rachel, don't you look good."

"Got to go, Julie," Rachel said. "Talk in the morning."

They hugged. As her arms went around Rachel, Carrie felt no spare flesh on her sister's back. She stepped away first. "What do I need to know about our parents?"

She half-listened to a description of the situation. Rachel's publisher sure chose the right handlers to complete her sister's stylizing making handsome look better than pretty. A historically plain woman, her sister was oblivious to admiring eyes.

Maybe two years ago the men would have been ogling her, not her older sister. The thought was not pleasant. Carrie knew her own prettiness, supported by hair coloring and expensive clothes, had faded while her sister looked not young, but ageless.

Ignorant of normal female behavior like spending time in small talk, Rachel blathered about diagnosis and medications as they walked. Carrie stopped listening, interested in how their parents felt not how the doctors were describing medical conditions. Her sister finally dropped the clinical data as they entered the cardiac unit.

"Dad's in the fourth room," Rachel said. "I think I lost you."

No shit Carrie thought while nodding. "I'm kind of a simple person. Neither of them is dying, so we're in a good place." She moved into their father's room, uncomfortable with the realization that this hospitalization wasn't of the same drill as others when he was in charge.

"Dad, you gave Steve and me a real scare." She bent over for a hug, horrified at the sight of his bruised forehead and tired face. Her arms stayed around him longer than usual. "Rachel tells me that Dr. Wagner says you're going to be fine."

"Yeah, you'll have my legs under your dining room table for a few more years." Their old joke calmed her; let her smile come more from her heart. For the first time he looked old. She took his sturdiness for granted. Mom was the fragile parent.

"Well, you have my full attention." She stepped back from his side, taking a few deep breaths to calm the booze and nerves roiling her stomach. He didn't notice.

"My own robe and slippers would be more comfortable than this stuff. Your mother might like her hospital bag also. You know where I keep it."

From the doorway Rachel spoke quietly. "I checked on her about fifteen minutes ago and she was sound asleep. The nurses said she ate a good lunch and seems more acclimated."

"Did they say if she was comfortable?" Carrie asked over her shoulder, "Is that what they mean by acclimated?"

"She's not fighting with the staff and ate lunch on her own," her sister answered. Carrie turned then, and noticed a small frown line appearing across her sister's forehead. Every therapist had one trait that betrayed a calm façade. Now she knew her sister's.

Setting her purse on the window ledge, Carrie straightened the morning's newspapers and watched Dad sit on the side of his bed, noticing that he held himself carefully. She wondered if that was from the heart attack or if he had bruises beyond his forehead and arms.

"I'd like to move to that chair for a few minutes." He stood and Rachel helped untangle a monitor line. "I don't think Todd will be back in time for that social worker thing this afternoon," Dad said. "I don't want to meet without him."

"Dr. Wagner had to stretch to keep Katherine here one additional day," Rachel responded. "I talked with Todd. He's changed to an earlier flight but will still miss the meeting."

Rachel's calm voice made Carrie feel discounted. Catching their father's eye, Carrie winked to imply exaggerated patience with Rachel's obvious bossiness. He didn't respond. She wanted to be alone with him, to be free to really talk.

"Rach, would you mind getting Dad a can of pop?" She picked up the can on his bed table. "This one feels warm and I recognize the signs of a guy who's gone too long without a cold drink."

Without a word, Rachel left.

"I wanted us to have time to talk. Sounds like you had a tough go with Mom last night. Tell me what happened."

He said nothing.

"Your Dr. Wagner was concerned about alcohol on Mom's breath. I thought you only had one drink on weeknights?"

"I wouldn't talk with Rachel about that—and I'm not going to talk about it with you either, Carrie. Your mother and I enjoy our cocktails at night and we never hurt a fly. There's not a lot of pleasure left in our life."

She'd started the conversation wrong, caught herself frowning.

"You and Todd understand the value of a drink more than your sister does."

"I don't know that I like how that sounds, Dad."

He stayed quiet.

"Is there something I should know before this social worker visit? Is this like the meeting after Mom's stroke about preparing the house and finding a rehab center?"

"Something like that."

If he knew more, Rachel's return gave him reason to change the subject and conversation moved to the weather and air travel and anything but Mom's care until a transport aide came to take Dad to physical therapy. Rachel looked tired, but antsy.

"Want to take a walk, Carrie? It's a beautiful day."

"Sorry, sis, I'm not really dressed for walking. Look at these shoes – newest style from New York. Mom will get a kick out of them." Carrie admired the sleek pointed toes of her expensive shoes while twirling her bracelet around so the latch faced the floor.

"Lucky girl, longer pants legs really do make your legs look like they go on forever." The cattiness of her words made Carrie blush. "I wish I was tall and thin like you," she added.

"I don't know how Steve stays healthy traveling for work." Rachel touched Carrie's hand. "You must take good care of him. He's lucky."

More than Rachel's excessive self-confidence, Carrie disliked feeble attempts at sisterly behavior. She knows nothing about our life, Carrie thought, but kept smiling.

"He takes care of himself. The boys keep me busy, I have my part-time job and then there's Mom and Dad. Sometimes I don't think I could squeeze anything more in my days."

Having Rachel in the rooms felt like standing next to a nosey stranger in an elevator. With Dad out of the room, Carrie hoped her sister might leave. A glass of wine sounded right about now. In New York it would be four o'clock and not too early for a nice red wine. She needed diversion.

Her sister didn't leave. "Why don't we take a stroll," Carrie suggested. "The hospital gift shop has nice things that Mom might like."

"You've always been better at the social niceties," Rachel said. If Todd had said something corny like that, Carrie might have shot back a dig.

"How's Dylan?" Carrie asked as they walked toward the elevators. She listened to Rachel's answer while trying to picture Dylan. No one in Minnesota had seen him for years except for the pictures Dad kept of a dark-haired boy who looked nothing like his fairer cousins.

Rachel's end of the conversation shut down in the elevator. Carrie looked sideways at her sister as they rode in silence. She heard Rachel make a little humming sound that reminded Carrie of lying in her sister's bed during scary nights when they were girls. She felt herself move so slightly toward her sister's shoulder. The elevator door opened. They walked out, side by side, not talking.

Still caught in the comfort of that one memory, Carrie said the first thing that came to her head as they walked to the gift shop.

"It isn't fair that Todd got all the girls. You've got to admit, Rachel that I should have had a girl to fuss over. Remind me to show you pictures of my boys later."

"I'd like that. Todd's girls are beautiful. I'm guilty of carrying a lot of pictures of Dylan on my phone." Rachel extended an arm around Carrie's shoulder. Her sister's touch was gentle. Carrie didn't pull away.

"Did you visit any of these facilities that Dad toured?"

"I'm shocked by that story." Carrie stepped away, her shoes clicking on the floor. "He's devoted to her and knows she'd go straight down hill in a strange place. I'm sure Dad just said he went to those places to keep Wagner off his back." Two young people walking past looked their way. "It's time they change doctors and find someone who can help Mom." Carrie glared at the strangers.

"That decision is out of Dad's hands. She's been classified a vulnerable adult." Without emotion, Rachel could have been reading case notes. "They found older bruises on Dad last night that could classify him as vulnerable with her in the home. They can't live alone."

The information rocked Carrie, her mind unwilling to think of her parents physically fighting. She wondered how a frail woman could leave marks on a big man like their father.

"I think you misunderstood, Rachel. Beyond the bandages, I think Dad's looking decent. You think he's looking for sympathy?" Slowing down the conversation gave Carrie time to process the facts.

"He had a heart attack. That can't be faked. He was still on oxygen this morning."

"The only reason I wasn't here was because you told me to take a later flight." Carrie turned her back to Rachel and headed toward the flower cooler. She poked through the cut flowers and potted plants, resisting the temptation to throw something in her sister's face. Rachel tried opening the second cooler door but Carrie moved so her sister could only stand aside.

She handed a golden mum plant to Rachel. "Dad will like that. He's partial to yellow flower. And Mom likes roses."

Backing out of the cooler, Carrie forced Rachel to step aside again. Without another word, she placed roses in Rachel's other hand then walked out of the gift shop. Through the window, she watched her sister talk with the volunteer and pull a fifty-dollar bill from her pants pocket. Flashy and arrogant, Carrie thought.

They walked back to the elevator in silence. Carrie concentrated on strategies to block the process of separating her parents. She stayed quiet until they exited the elevator. "We need Todd here. He's Mom's biggest advocate. I'd like to talk with Steve and get legal advice from his practice. We'll reschedule this meeting."

"Dr. Wagner and a psychiatrist conducted the assessments. From a medical point of view, she could be discharged in the morning."

"Then you stay with her until Dad gets home. God damn it, Rachel, you can't come in and split up our parents. Mom will die." She thought of her parents sitting at the kitchen table when she brought them fresh bakery. "They love each other. We should leave them alone."

"Social Services became involved before I got here. If Dad wants to fight, that's his decision, Carrie. He's perfectly capable of making decisions about Katherine's care."

"Now it's back to Katherine? Our mother's care. Isn't that what you meant to say? Please don't insult me with that 'Katherine' thing right now." More people looked their way and Carrie lowered her voice. "I'm not questioning Dad's ability to care for Mom. He's just tired. That happens from time to time then Todd or I step in to give him a break. And things go back to normal. We can't talk about this while Dad's in a low mood."

Carrie moved a few steps ahead of Rachel, feeling the last words had been said. Their shoe heels clicked on the terrazzo floor, one long stride and one short.

"You're the Kemper family, right?" A nurse stopped them. "You'll be meeting in this conference room."

Rachel shoved the flowers into Carrie's hands and excused herself for a few minutes.

Carrie entered the room and looked around. She put the flowers on the table, sat down, and eased off her killer heels. The dated taupe walls and geometric upholstered chairs were hideous. She rummaged through her purse, found two Xanax in a small pillbox and swallowed one. God knew her propensity for emotion in the face of authority would not help Mom.

The pill had not brought relief when they sat down together. Their flower purchases implied some kind of pending festivities. Her sister, wearing small wire-framed glasses, looked smarter than the young, pasty-faced social worker. A nurse wheeled in Dad and stayed. Carrie thought about taking another Xanax.

"Jerry McConnell." His hand grabbed, caught hers and pumped with energy. How this almost boy-aged man could be inserted in their lives enraged Carrie.

"I'm sorry this is happening, Mr. Kemper." McConnell reached for her father's hand. "I read Mrs. Kemper's files and it sounds like your family worked hard to keep her at home." McConnell shook Rachel's hand, tipped his head. "But dementia is different for every person so we have to make changes – not only for Mrs. Kemper. I understand you choose Evans House."

Counting to five as she inhaled then four as she exhaled, Carrie concentrated, adjusting her bracelet latch as she struggled to not cry. Miraculously her voice remained steady when she made her play to gain control of the meeting.

"Isn't this the time to discuss available options? Dad, you'll be home soon and Rachel's in town for the next few days. Certainly we can take a breather and look for the right home agency help? If we can afford this 'home' for Mom, we can afford help in our home."

Around the table, Carrie saw three neutral faces. "Listen, I'm at their house four or five times a week. Mom has a few temper tantrums and a few bad days… but if you had ever lived with her you'd know that's just her. She's always been emotional. Right, Dad?"

He pointed to his forehead. "Have you looked, Carrie? I'm covered with bruises. She's a strong woman when she gets upset. Do you want to see some of the marks on my arms or back? Or maybe the ones on my legs where she's kicked me with those orthopedic shoes."

Losing track of her breathing routine, Carrie felt tears, but tried to tap into the anger raised by this whole morning of emotional ambush. "Certainly last night was an awful exception. I've been at home when you're away and she's never laid a hand on me."

"And you're lucky." He turned his head away and began asking the social worker a question.

Control slipped away. Carrie spoke over her father. "Isn't there a place closer to their home that might provide respite care while we bring in other physicians to assess the situation? Did you visit that new place next to the mall?"

The social worker shook his head. "They don't accept dementia care patients."

Carrie turned on the wimpy doughboy. "My husband and I don't appreciate the dementia label being tagged on my mother. She's had a stroke. She isn't herself."

The social worker gave her a look she considered pitying. "Your mother will benefit from the programming at Evans. Visit this afternoon. They'll give you a tour and answer questions."

Carrie dropped her head, rotated her bracelet and searched for another idea. The careful way her father spoke when breaking silence let Carrie know their father's decision was made.

"Katherine gets confused. I found her crying in the front closet last week when I came in from mowing the yard."

Carrie doubted his story. He would have mentioned it to her.

"How is she going to survive the stress of a move?" he continued.

"Exactly, Dad," Carrie said. She brushed at her eyes, but kept her head up. "You need each other. I promise I'll find a way to spend more time with her. Maybe I can sleep over one night a week and Todd could take another so you can have more time to rest."

As Dad held up his hands, she saw the left one shake so slightly, his silver wedding band dull in the room's lighting. The white, somewhat translucent hand he lowered to the table clashed with the mental image of her father's strong, capable hands she carried. She looked at her father as he was this day, at thick hair matted down, slight silver stubble on his weakened chin, dark shadows extending like maps of the years from his eyes to the place where his face used to break in the smile she once called 'Daddy Grins'.

"Dad, please don't do this."

"Carrie, the experts have made a decision that says your mother's not safe. Don't make it harder. Pay attention. It will be you and Rachel taking care of your mother's move." He patted her hand once.

Planning continued. Picking up her purse, Carrie searched around its interior for the second Xanax. Rachel moved closer, extended an arm around the back of Carrie's chair. Carrie sat still as her fingers found the pillbox, worked it open and inched out the familiar oval form. She closed it into her palm then grasped a box of mints, dragged that out and extended it toward the others. They passed. She tucked the mint in her cheek and covertly placed the pill on her tongue.

The social worker talked through what would happen during admissions. Rachel watched Dad, who looked out the window. Carrie began deep, slow breathing again.

Calmer, she pushed one last time to keep the world intact. "Can we talk for a moment about exactly why she can't stay home with the comfort of knowing her surroundings? My parents love each other which seems more important than programming and call buttons."

"Carrie, your father is in the hospital because your mother attacked him." McConnell spoke in the exact tone she would use to ask a clerk for shoes in a different color. "Your mother is in restraints because when she becomes agitated, she can be of danger to herself and others. As her condition progresses, the anger will diminish but other behavior will take its place."

Dad shook a finger at Rachel. "You said nothing about restraints."

"I knew you'd be upset, Dad."

"I'm the one who feeds her, talks to her, gives her a bath each morning. She's the heart of our family. How is this fair?" Dad waved the back of his hand toward the social worker. "He's just a person with a job. He doesn't care about her."

"I should be the one looking at respite care," Carrie volunteered. "Mom trusts me. I know how she likes her chair covers folded and her favorite magazines. I'm around the most."

Her father's red-haired nurse stopped the conversation, fingers on his pulse point. "If we're done, Mr. Kemper needs to rest."

"Dad?" Carrie rose slightly from her chair. "Are you all right?"

He shook his head from side to side before resting his forehead in one hand. Carrie moved from her chair, her legs shaking.

The nurse moved decisively. "Why don't you two get some fresh air and come back in about ninety minutes? Your dad needs a nap and a quiet dinner."

"I'm eating with my wife," he protested.

"First you're going to rest. Then we'll figure out dinner."

They trailed him down the hall. Carrie walked farther and farther behind, now wrapped in the softened world of her own medication, clutching the mum and daisies. She leaned against a wall, watching the nurse lower the foot rests of the wheel chair.

"Do you need help getting into bed, Dad?" Rachel extended a hand.

"I'm not crippled." His reply carried to the door.

"Dad, people can hear you. Rach was just being kind." Carrie squeezed past to put down the mum and pick up a shopping bag. She bent close to her father, whispered she loved him.

As the nurse closed his door, Carrie pushed through a growing sleepiness and insisted they visit their mother. "I got her a new lap blanket in New York. It'll perk up her spirits."

Rachel hesitated before following. "Maybe you should go alone. I need to listen to voice mails. After dinner we can split up and make sure each has somebody in their rooms."

"Skip the voice mails. If anybody really needs you, I'm sure your secretary or agent knows the hospital's telephone number. I'd like Mom to see us together."

"Okay. I just want to be sure Dylan didn't call. Wait." Rachel stopped. Carrie leaned against the wall, closed her eyes.

"Carrie, you fell asleep standing up!"

Disoriented, Carrie forced her eyes open. She wobbled in the process and grabbed for Rachel's arm or bag or anything as her left ankle twisted to the side.

"Shit. Damn heels." She struggled to stand straight on both feet.

Rachel wound an arm through Carrie's. "You took something didn't you," she asked in that neutral way Carrie distrusted.

"I confess. You got to admit this ranks high on the stress meter."

"Why don't you let me take you home? Catch a nap."

"Better idea, let's grab coffee or a cold cola and bring one to Mom. I'll be fine if we're busy. I really want to see her." Shaking off Rachel's arm, Carrie straightened her back and stepped into the flow of hospital visitors. "Coming?"

They walked in silence. Carrie tried to remember if she had laced the lemonade she drank on the way to the hospital and if she took one or two Xanax. Stress could blur her memory these days; turning forty was going to be a bitch.

"Back to that idea of splitting up to keep Mom and Dad company tonight, I just can't figure out who should go where. Mom's more comfortable with Todd or me." She stopped and put an arm around Rachel. "I don't want you to feel bad, but we have our own routines."

At the door to their mother's room Carrie discarded her sister. She straightened her back, shook her hair and walked in first. "Hey, Mom, I'm sorry I wasn't here. Dad looks good so you can stop worrying." She kissed Mom's cheek. "Isn't it nice Rachel could visit?"

Mom leaned into Carrie's embrace. As she stepped back from the chair, Carrie saw Mom's eyes engage with Rachel. Whenever three Kempers gathered, one was always at a disadvantage. Someone always got the ice cream cone while someone else was left at home putting in extra piano practice time. Even as adults.

"Where's Todd?" Mom asked as she looked away. "He's not coming?"

"He should be here after dinner." Carrie hauled a package from her bag. "I brought something from New York for you."

"Where's Steve?" Mom held the package.

"Still in New York." Carrie began helping unwrap the gift.

"Where's David?" Mom looked at the package instead of Rachel.

"David is in Chicago with Dylan."

"I want him to come. I need my own doctor."

"He's not coming," Carrie said while unwrapping her mother's gift. "He's kind of not part of the family anymore. You remember that."

"Pretty." Mom's attention changed to the throw. "Someone will steal it here."

"Mom, no one will take things from you." Carrie smoothed the throw around Mom's lap and legs. "Your old one has holes. It's time for something new."

"Where's Art?"

"He's upstairs," Rachel said. "We'll bring him here when the doctor says he can visit."

"I had another stroke." Mom's eyes lost focus as tears formed. "Your father is eating at Janie's house."

Carrie gave Rachel a warning glance while calming their mother. "Dad is upstairs. I saw him. And your heart is fine. You had an accident in the kitchen."

Their mother slumped back. Carrie soothed her with chitchat about New York and the story about buying her new suit. But small talk didn't work.

"Your father is angry that you don't come home," Mom threw at Rachel. "He says since you lost your husband, you're too ashamed." She sat back in her chair like a crow pecking at road kill. "We don't want people to talk about us. Good thing you've got a different name."

Silence settled in the room. Carrie made an apologetic face toward Rachel, sorry about their mother's rudeness. Mom turned her eyes away.

"Why don't you write about something that would help me? How to make me better? Who wants to read about those disgusting families? I hope you banked money from that book deal so you'll be able to feed Dylan when people don't want that kind of stuff anymore."

"It's probably best we talk about something else," Rachel said with a gentle voice, like their mother was just another patient. Carrie wondered if her sister ever worked in hospital settings. She knew very little about Rachel's life, professional or personal.

"Suit yourself. Your brother will be here soon. He's the one who should be making lots of money. He works hard and that bank never cares. They just keep firing people."

"Todd's doing fine." Carrie felt comfortable moving this conversation to a pleasant level. Steve called her mother's affection for Todd unhealthy. "Rachel, did you hear about his last promotion? I think his title is senior vice president for business development."

"Did I hear my title discussed?" Todd walked in carrying Mom's dinner tray. "Sorry I couldn't be here earlier, Mom. The nurses tell me you're doing well except you won't be dancing on those feet for a few more days. Promise me you won't walk on broken glass again."

Carrie expected Mom's face to light up, but it didn't. He pulled a table toward the recliner chair and placed the tray on it.

"I want to go home. If your father can't take care of me then Carrie or your wife will have to. I can't stay here with nurses tying me up and putting drugs in my water. I want a can of pop."

"How are the two of you doing?" He ruffled Carrie's hair and gave Rachel a one-arm hug. "I heard it meant a lot for Dad to have the Chicago sibling arrive with his breakfast."

"Seems like a long time ago." Rachel stretched her shoulders. "I'm beat."

"Why don't you two get out of here for dinner? Dad's watching news and I brought him Sports Illustrated. I'll sit here with Mom."

"Sounds good to me. I'll drive, Rach. I know a place with nice salads and good wine."

Chapter 8

Todd watched his sisters walk out of the room. Rachel's thick, dark hair had that shiny just-styled look he loved. He wondered how his sister's butt could be so firmly packed unless the seriously non-athletic Rachel now rocked the gym. She carried herself like a person comfortable in the world and he was jealous for that was the walk of his youth, now lost in what felt like the amble of middle age.

Their baby sister's streaked blonde hair, clutter of jewelry and designer handbag looked like many prosperous suburban women—attractive enough, but not worth a second glance. How did Rachel, who was known in the family for baggy sweaters and cheap jeans, pull off this transformation? Even more, Todd wanted to know how it came to be that the pretty sister and handsome son now looked like Rachel's older siblings.

No matter how conscientious he was about sucking in a forty-two-inch waist and pulling his shoulders back, Todd knew returning to a basement full of gym equipment or running each day would do nothing to repair thinning hair which continued to fade from its glory days' gold. A teen-age son was a cruel daily reminder of the good young days.

He'd read once that identical twins were about eighty-five percent the same in their physical and emotional make-up, while siblings shared only about half of any characteristic. Beside long torsos and the inability to play piano, he and Rachel had little more in common than preferring sausage to pepperoni on pizza. He and Carrie were their Mother's children with her tastes for good booze, expensive gifts and impressing others. Like Mom said, Rachel sprang from their orphan father's shadowy family.

Todd turned to watch his formerly elegant mother chow through a dinner of some ground meat entree covered by brown gravy. She ate in a pattern of sorts—two bites of meat, two spoons of peas, a fork of mashed potatoes. Up went the fork twice then she placed it to the left of her plate and picked up the spoon then replaced it to the right and returned to the fork.

Nothing stopped her travel around the food. He watched a chunk of meat break apart between the plate and her mouth; a gravy-soaked bit landing on her already stained gown and staying on the slope of her unbound breasts. Peas fell from the spoon, some back to the tray or down her gown. She picked up dropped peas from the tray with her fingers like a toddler frustrated with the slow work of the fork and spoon. Smacking her lips to capture gravy, she sounded like his dogs at their food bowls. He shook his head to delete the thought.

"What are you staring at?" Her once beautiful womanly voice now sounded coarse and flat. After her first stroke, her altered voice unnerved him and made him wonder how the brain could rob a person of such an integral part of their identity. From the bandages on her feet to the food on her gown, Todd felt anger at Carrie for Mom's descent to this shabby, wild woman.

"The food on your gown. You had something with tomatoes for lunch? Why haven't they changed your things?"

"I don't remember. Why can't they make me better? This is no way for me to have to live." Her voice rose peevishly. "Todd, this isn't right."

"We got dealt a bad hand, Mom. Things could be worse, you know."

"Oh, yeah?" She put down the fork and turned her head toward his.

Her eyes looked hazy, a sign they'd doped her. Goddamn, he had to dig deep to find the bright side of the situation and bring a smile to her tired, battered face. Her oatmeal tone looked bad. Just as Rachel had described, a raised bruise darkened the left side of her face where Mom smacked herself when pulling the phone from the wall. Breaking his focus on her wounds, he really tried to concentrate on his mother, as she would like him to see her. He wasn't sure he could dig deeper to create more upbeat distractions.

"You're sitting there, Mom, eating a decent meal and talking with your favorite kid." He winked at her. "If I had thought to bring a small bottle of airplane brandy, that meal could even be passable." He leaned over and patted her shoulder. "Who combed your hair?"

"Some stranger they let in. She's no good at it."

"You got that right. I could do a better job. In fact, let me try."

They laughed together while Todd drew a comb through her thinning hair. He formed a part near the crown of her head. "Your hair is a bit dingy. I'll have Kris schedule a color appointment for you. No need for people to think you're as old as Dad."

He faked a laugh and waited for her to join him. She nodded her head and looked back toward him, smiling. For a moment he thought he saw something alive in her eyes, those beautiful green eyes. As a boy, he often stared across the kitchen table until she turned her eyes to him for their special smile.

She tilted her head, an old coquettish gesture that touched his heart.

"Do you think I'm pretty?" she asked as if she knew the answer.

"You're my Mom. Every man in the world thinks his mother is pretty."

While Todd combed the left side of her head, she put up a hand and curled hair on the other side around her fingers. When Kris wore her hair long, that womanly gesture blotted everything else from his mind. He finished, a bit uncomfortable with his own thoughts. Clearing this throat, Todd put the comb down.

She reached out a hand with chipped nails. "I should have yellow hair. Men like that."

"Whatever color you want, Mom. That's the mystery of a woman."

"He's gray." He knew the next comment would be off-color, a pattern more common since her last stroke. "Everywhere. You know what I mean," she finished with a wicked smile he didn't want to see.

"More than I need to know, Mom."

There was silence. Busy fingers slowly returned her hair to disarray. He sat on the edge of the bed, searching for another topic to discuss; tired from traveling, discouraged at his parents' state.

"Rachel looks pretty sharp," he finally said, returning to Mom's favorite topic of clothing. "She must have some fashion advisor putting together outfits. God, remember all those old baggy clothes? You used to tell her she looked like a woman who was perpetually preggers."

"She's probably gray, too." She chuckled again then tapped one finger on her tray. "Got fancy too late to keep her doctor husband."

"Let's not go there, Mom. Tell me about your day."

She shrugged. "The television doesn't have anything good. I couldn't find any dog shows. They don't let dogs into hospitals."

"Let me see if I can find your stations."

"Where's your father? He can find my shows."

"Upstairs, Mom. I came straight to see you. Rachel says he's doing fine."

"Take me home. I want to see him."

"He's not home. He's upstairs. Probably eating the same great dinner."

"I'm done." She pushed the dinner tray, sending everything over the table's edge. He jumped back to keep food from splattering onto his suit. Peaches flew faster than his hop.

Like a giant toddler strapped into a stroller, she tried to stand. "I have to go to the bathroom," she yelled for the entire world to hear.

He stepped over her dinner tray, pushed the nurses' station button and began unbuckling the belt restraint on her chair. She strained against his hands.

"Sit down, Mom. I can't get at the buckle."

"I have to go to the bathroom." Her face flushed as she pushed at his shoulders. "Quit holding me down."

"Mom, you're not helping."

Todd struggled with her strength. A nurse walked in, rescuing them both.

"I'll take over," she said. "Katherine, I need you to sit back." She pulled the restraint off with an experienced motion. "Let me help you."

Mom pulled herself up, rising gingerly on her bandaged feet and leaning on the nurse. They moved toward the bathroom. "It's too late," Mom said.

His nose confirmed her statement. He stepped toward the door to escape the odor, fishing in his pocket for tissue to dab at the fruit juices on his pants.

"Well, then we'll clean you up in the bathroom, Katherine." The nurse moved her forward. "Maybe your son would like to visit your husband?"

"I thought I might take her with me." Todd leaned against a wall trying to look calm.

Mom stopped walking and looked at the nurse. "I want to see Art." Each word held the intonations of her old normal voice. Clearly, she could be rehabilitated.

"We need doctor approval for Katherine to leave the floor," the nurse said.

"Don't bother. We'll bring Dad here." He threw away the tissue, knowing the pants needed dry cleaning and he would have to drop them off because Kris was out of town. They needed two incomes, but he wished Kris made more time to take care of this stuff. He walked to the bathroom door. "Could you give my mother a clean gown while you're at it? Looks like she's had to wear breakfast and lunch all day."

Home services would take care of these kinds of emergencies, Todd thought as he walked out of the room. If his father had money to cover a nursing home, then paying for services to keep Mom comfortable at home wouldn't be a problem. On his way to the elevator he grabbed a brochure about the hospital's home health agency and gave it a quick read between floors. By the time he reached his father's hospital unit, Todd had a plan and assignments for his sisters.

Stopping at the nurses' station on his father's unit, he received a positive report. Feeling optimistic, Todd volunteered to carry in a dinner tray. His father sat in a recliner, watching a sports talk show. Experienced from his mother's hospitalizations, Todd noted the monitor next to the chair, the sutures high on his father's forehead, a glimpse of serious bruises and more sutures under a hospital robe sleeve. He remembered Rachel talking about broken china, but wondered how his father cut his forehead.

"Hey, Dad," he said, "Mom's floor must have priority. She's already through with her fine dining." His father held out his hands to take the tray. "Sit back. Let me set this up."

His father held up his hand with its monitor. "Thanks. I'm not totally mobile. How's your mother?"

Todd sorted through his brief visit with her before answering. "She ate well, asked good questions and was able to walk on her own. Except for the bandages, I don't see anything real different than how she was last weekend."

"She went over the edge last night and tried to kill us." His father uncovered the Salisbury steak plate, looked displeased. "She was swinging broken dishes, taking pokes at me. The kitchen's still probably covered with chili and blood." He put the dish lid down, picked up his napkin and silverware, then paused before saying, "The girls can handle cleaning. The doc says I have to take it easy."

"Mom looks like she got the worst of it." Todd didn't necessarily mean physically, but just that his mother was so broken looking.

"I didn't touch her, Todd."

Did his father's voice change? "I would never suggest you would hurt her, Dad."

"She jumped on that broken china like she was crazy then slashed at me enough for about eighteen stitches on my head and arm," he said pulling back his hospital gown sleeve.

"Okay, I see." The stitches made Todd's stomach clench. "Well, maybe her medications need adjustment. She's got a chemical factory going inside with all the pills prescribed."

Dad looked like he wanted to say something, but returned to his dinner, picking at the Salisbury steak and noodles before pushing the tray aside. "I'm not hungry. We need to talk."

"You're right about that, Dad. I did some thinking on the plane about this whole Evans House deal. I think there's a better way that keeps you and Mom together – at home – which is what I know we all want. If Rachel and Carrie spend the morning making phone calls, we could find home health agency people to help with Mom. You wouldn't have to do any work at home, just enjoy being together again."

His father didn't respond. In fact, his face showed little interest or emotion. Todd controlled the conversation, intending to close the sale. "We need to buy the two of you a few weeks to recuperate." Todd gave his father the confident smile clients liked to see. "I remember you promising you wouldn't put her in a home when she signed the power of attorney."

The final sentence didn't quite come out as Todd intended. He played into their traditional pattern of interaction – questioning his father's intentions about everything from picking out a bottle of scotch to deciding Mom's future. Forty-six years old and he still couldn't act like a competent adult when it mattered with this man. His father didn't move. Shifting his view to break connection with his father's displeasure, Todd heard the automated blood pressure cuff engage. Neither of them looked at the monitor's reading.

"That's was a low comment, Todd," his father said. The words were ones Todd generally owned. "We couldn't know that she would get this sick. I took vows with your mother that I'm struggling to keep so I've talked with Father Christopher about all this and I've got his blessing."

"What would he know about what Mom needs? He's never lived with a woman."

"He's a man of God, Todd. I know you might not still believe in the Church, but I do." His ragged breathing sound raised Todd's attention. "Your mother has very few good days. You see her at her best because she tries hard to look alert for you."

"But that just proves that she can be more like her old self if she's motivated. Make the effort and get her out of that frigging chair and back into the world. She'll respond."

"I haven't slept a whole night in months because I don't know when she'll wander. I've found her in the backyard, sitting in the car, running her sewing scissors across electrical cords. I can't live this way. You couldn't either."

"Maybe if you stopped trying to control her and took her out more she'd snap back. Take her on a vacation."

"You're not listening, son. I'm sick of fighting her to put on her shoes or go to the bathroom. I can't walk around apologizing to everyone she insults, like your wife. I know Kris gets hurt when your mother cuts loose with that mouth."

"Mom and Kris never got along." Todd checked his father's monitor patterns, wondered if Dad was too upset. "Sounds to me like you've made up your mind."

"You're a good son for your mother. Give me credit for being a good husband. It's damn tough to admit I can't provide a good home for her. But I can't."

An aide entered the room. They stopped talking while the woman picked up the dinner tray. Todd gathered his thoughts, aware that beyond watching baseball or talking about new cars, he didn't have much of a relationship with his father. He looked at the old man, really looked at him and saw someone who looked remarkably calm while throwing a woman out of the home she had created.

"You son of a bitch," came from Todd's gut. "You've been thinking about this for months and never said a word to Carrie or me. You didn't want us to wreck your plan."

"I'm facing reality." The old man's voice raised, intense in a way Todd didn't know from his father. "You drop in for a visit, then go home to your families. You don't stick around to change her pants or listen to her conversations with people who have been dead for decades. I'd like to remind you that when your mother had her first real serious stroke, Dr. Wagner told us that this day might come. He said vascular dementia doesn't get better."

Dad stood up, removed a monitor on his finger and rubbed his hair. Todd noticed how his father's hands trembled. They stood almost face-to-face. He looked at his father and saw tired, watery eyes. The old man face looking back was familiar, but unknown. His father spoke, his voice sounding as if talking was a hard physical activity.

"It's the timing that surprises me. I wish to hell she and I were sitting in our own home, watching television and none of this happened."

"How about assisted living? You could stay together."

"Todd, I'm not willing to live surrounded by a lot of folks who need help putting on their pants in the morning. Your mother's the one who needs care."

"She's a proud lady, Dad. I think this is going to break her spirit. You may as well dump her on the side of the highway."

"For Christ's sake, that's dramatic crap. You're your mother's boy through and through."

His father stopped talking to cough. The ragged dry sound filled Todd's head. Dad's chest expanded and shook, his shoulders folded inwards. Todd moved closer to help.

"Sit down, Dad."

He shook off Todd's offer, choked down a final cough. "If I don't do something, I take the chance that taking care of her will mean an early death for me—and still leave her to go into a nursing home. What's your choice, son? Are you ready to have us move in with you?"

"Damn it, Dad, don't be such a fucking martyr." Todd dropped his eyes and jammed one hand in his pants pocket. They had reached their normal point of impasse. Todd regretted using foul language. He raised his head, connected visually with his father for a moment and was unsure of what to say or do.

"Guys, we could hear you in the hall," Carrie said as she closed the door behind Rachel and a wheel chair. "It's not good for you to get worked up, Dad." Her smile for their father softened the scold. "You can visit Mom if you promise to stay in a wheelchair. Are you two finished with your disagreement, or are you going to fight in front of Mom?"

"We weren't fighting - just having a difference of opinion on Dad's plan to dump Mom in this Evans House." Todd had other things to say, but was intimidated by sight of Rachel standing with her feet slightly apart and hands curled at her sides, not unlike their mother when displeased. Around the room, they all shut up. He felt his face flush.

"No one's dumping Mom," Rachel said in a voice that wound emotional yellow crime scene tape around further discussion. "You need to hear the facts. Listen to what Dad has to say or talk with Dr. Wagner."

"Lots of people do plenty of stupid things based on so called facts. This is our mother. How would you like your son to put you in some old people warehouse in a few decades?"

Rachel didn't answer, just looked at him with eyes squinted partially shut. Todd was ready to heat up the debate and take on his sister.

"I don't think you meant to say that, son," Dad interjected, deflecting a response from Rachel. "Don't be biting at her. I'm the head of this family with responsibility to make this decision, but I won't discuss it anymore tonight. I want to see your mother."

They were all quiet as Rachel removed the inflatable blood pressure cuff before helping Dad settle into the wheelchair. For the moment, he and Carrie returned to younger sibling status relying on Rachel to know what to do as well as how to do things. Todd felt useless, powerless and pissed. He stepped up to push the chair, but Rachel grabbed the handles and began backing from the room.

"None of that behavior in front of Mom, Todd," Carrie hissed in his direction as they walked side by side behind the others. He shoved his hands in his pants pockets, bit his tongue, but looked Carrie's way with a dropped jaw and slight shake of his head.

"I don't want any of this discussed in her room," Dad said. "I'll tell her about Evans House on my own. Just your mother and me, as husband and wife."

Todd wondered what his father would say and if he'd be gentle when Mom fell apart.

Dad rubbed his hands, no longer trembling, across his hair, carefully avoiding the sutures on his forehead. Todd had to admire his father's gutsy behavior. They separated themselves among other visitors riding in the elevator, then came together to follow behind Rachel to Mom's door.

Unwilling to trust his father's sincerity, Todd watched his old man straighten up in the chair and take control of the wheels. His voice was gentle, but strong, as he maneuvered through the doorway.

"I hear you've been asking for me, Katherine."

"Art, Art, I was afraid you were dead. I was afraid you died and no one wanted me to know." Tears formed in her eyes. She looked like a vulnerable older woman that Todd didn't really know.

"You always have to worry about something," Dad said as he reached for her hand. "I'm not a very good patient. I'm much better at sitting by your side than resting in bed. Don't cry." He reached for a tissue and blotted at her tears. "There. Now let's enjoy all being together."

"I want to go home, Art. This bed is too soft and I can't find my shows on this television. My feet won't get better here 'cause they keep me walking on the floor. If you get dressed, we can go home."

Todd watched his father capture Mom's busy fingers in his hands and noticed how their matching wedding bands seemed too large.

"Now, you know you're always a bit upset in different places. I've got to stay until Doc Wagner finishes his tests. The kids say you're being treated fine. Maybe not as good as having all my attention, huh?" Dad smiled at her in a way that made Todd feel invisible. "I know the Salisbury steak I had for dinner wasn't half as good as making your recipe in the slow cooker."

She looked at the girls. "Why don't they take me home? If you don't want to leave, make Carrie stay with me for a few days."

"Dr. Wagner's got to release you. We're not in a hotel. This is a hospital. We're both here because we've got health problems. You understand that don't you?"

"I'm not stupid, and I wish you'd stop treating me like a child. This isn't a hotel. There's no mini-bar." Todd laughed out loud and was rewarded by Mom's wink.

"I would sure like a drink. Instead of bringing me flowers maybe someone could bring a vodka martini in one of those paper cups from the hamburger place."

Carrie exchanged a look with Rachel. "I told you that we should bring one back after dinner."

They continued bantering until a nurse suggested Dad was needed in his room. Todd and his sisters filed out to give their parents a chance to say good night alone.

"I can't agree with Dr. Wagner, Dad." Todd spoke first in the elevator. "She's a little confused, but she gets what's going on. I wouldn't put it past Mom to play the helpless person to make sure we all pay attention."

"Please, Todd." Rachel interrupted. "That's like saying a baby cries to manipulate adults. It's not like she could act some other way if she wanted to."

"Hey, I know that. I'm not an idiot, but you haven't seen her day by day like Carrie and I do. She's quite capable of carrying on a conversation and taking care of herself."

Joining them, Dad put up a hand and made a slicing motion. "I said I'm not going to talk about this anymore. I told all of you, this is my decision. When we get back to my room, I'd like to visit with Rachel. The two of you go home."

A quiver in the old man's voice told them he was tired. "I do appreciate what the three of you've done today. I know you had to change plans and spend money to be here."

Todd shook his father's hand. Carrie kissed Dad's forehead. Rachel closed the door.

"Doesn't that take the cake," Carrie said as they walked down the hall. "What does she know about our parents?"

"You're wobbling a bit, sis. Did you girls have drinks with dinner or did you carry a few airplane bottles in your purse?"

"Don't go there, Todd. It's been a long day. I've been wearing heels for the past eight hours and I'm beat. I don't need one more sibling jumping down my throat." She hiked her shoulder bag up a notch and straightened her jacket. "What are we going to do about Mom?"

"I'm not sure there's anything we can do. Dad is in charge in every legal sense. I think we have to try to hold her together for a few weeks at this Evans House and keep working on him. We'll be there every day to watch out for her. Are you on board?"

His soft little sister had tears in her eyes as she nodded her head. He thought of offering her a ride home, but wanted to be on his own. They hugged in the parking lot and walked to their cars as the September dusk settled.

Chapter 9

I feel like I've turned into a huge sack of potatoes, Art thought as he pushed himself out of the wheelchair to use the bathroom. Catching sight of the plastic urine collection tray under the toilet rim reminded him that he needed to sit, and he didn't care.

Trusty Rusty, as Art now thought of the nurse, waited outside the bathroom door and offered an arm. Art let himself be supported, wondered how Rusty could look so good after such a long day. "How do you stay so…" He couldn't find the next word.

"Good looking?" Rusty directed a smile toward Rachel who sat in the recliner. "Not what you had in mind, huh, Art? Well, the Twins are up six in the bottom of the first and I'm meeting my wife and friends to watch the game at our favorite sports bar in about twenty minutes."

Art settled himself back in bed and let the commentators chatter fill the room while Rusty took vitals. "Tomorrow's a big day, Art, so you might want to turn in early. I'm going to flag the next shift to continue checking your blood pressure each hour. I'll see you at seven tomorrow morning." The nurse turned off his small computer. "Should I close your blinds?"

"Sure. I don't know what time it is anyway." Art watched Rusty adjust the blinds. Only after the nurse left did he look at his daughter who sat slumped in the recliner.

"Long day, kid? I've been here about twenty-six hours and it feels like months." She opened her eyes, dark circles contrasting with skin turned pale in the room's lousy florescent lighting. "Sorry if I was rough with you this morning. I don't like this whole mess."

"It's okay, Dad. None of this is easy."

"How about we talk about other stuff for a while." Hunger for news about her life and his grandson fed his words. "Tell me what's going on it your life. How's my grandson?"

"Are you sure you want to talk, Dad? You've got to be exhausted."

"I'd rather try to fall asleep thinking about your life than mine." He leaned back against the pillows. "If you meant it, I'll take you up on your offer to help settle your mother at that place. Carrie can fuss with making the room look nice, but I trust you to keep an even head."

"I did mean it, Dad. I'll talk to the social worker in the morning."

Joe Mauer came up to bat. Art watched the kid connect with the first ball for a double. He turned his head back toward Rachel. She shook her head, but smiled like she understood that baseball trumped some discussions.

"Talk about my kid, I got some great pictures of Dylan's Wisconsin camping trip that I thought you'd like—including the infamous big fish he caught. I told you about that." She turned on the bed light before showing him her cell phone. "You look better than this morning."

"I'm dirt tired but not feeling any chest tightness. You look worse for wear."

"Twenty-four hours ago I was eating a sandwich and your doctor called. Haven't slept or been off my feet since six this morning. By the way, if you give me a key, I'll check the house. I can pack some of Mom's stuff and start the kitchen clean up. Business with folks at Children's Hospital just came up so I'll stretch my stay a few days."

"I don't have my keys. Call Jane. She's got a set. Let me write down her number."

Rachel produced a pen and notepad. Nice ones.

"You've made quite a name for yourself, Rachel. Who ever thought one of you kids would be such hot stuff." Maybe being hooked up to a monitor made him feel more open. He yawned, stretched his legs. "Your mother's not sure how to take your success. You know she always thought your brother would be the big shot. She wouldn't watch when you were on TV. I guess she was afraid you'd say the wrong thing, but Jane taped those interviews for me to watch. I'm impressed."

Rachel's face shut down as he realized he was walking back over the grounds he trampled roughly earlier. He searched for a way to sound more positive, move away from Katherine's opinions. Nothing came to mind in time. Rachel stood.

"I should leave, Dad. It has been a long day. Tell Mom not to worry. I use my married name. No one needs to know I'm a Kemper."

"I didn't mean it that way, Rachel."

"I know, Dad. David's name is actually a good protection device for a lot of reasons. Now, you relax. Sleep well. The nurses know how to find me." She kissed his head.

"You were an easy kid although I don't know if your mother ever figured you out." He wanted whatever clouded her eyes to lift. "She understood Carrie's girly stuff easier than your independence and books."

"I'm fine, Dad. It was a long time ago." She picked up her fancy leather bag. "Get some rest." She stopped, dug in the bag. "I remembered that I had one real photo. You can have it."

Art watched her leave and wondered about the sadness he felt. When he replayed the television interviews he saw a damn smart person in control of the world. Sometimes he wondered how it was she succeeded in spite of a topsy-turvy relationship with her mother.

The boy in her photo had never spent a night alone with him and Katherine. Art studied the lanky kid leaning against another boy and slowly recognized his own straight shoulders, dark hair and arched eyebrows. Like an eager reader skipping through a new book, he brought the photo up the light to study his grandson then leaned back to digest the knowledge that familiar large hands held the fishing pole.

Chapter 10

An extraordinary day.

In a moment of clarity, Katherine held on to the big word and mourned all the other words she had lost. She tried to form the word with her lips, but it disappeared like dust blown away on a breeze. All the same, she held tight to the joy that not everyone knew such a difficult word, certainly a college word. Words her children learned attending quality schools. Quality, now there was a word she lived… a life of quality.

The words and thoughts evaporated. She sat in the uncomfortable vinyl chair and looked around, trying to remember what had happened and why her feet were bandaged.

Through the confusion, she remembered Art telling her she was in the hospital and then she remembered the children coming to see her. She straightened her spine, enjoying the power that returned to her soul knowing that she still ruled this family. Laughing as another wave of clarity opened, Katherine savored that her illness drew Rachel from the Chicago stink hole to come here dressed like a wealthy woman. The children all looked well off. They were a family to reckon with. No government money paid for her bed.

Art visiting in a robe with pajamas was a confusing memory. The thought he would not dress when leaving the house made her worry about his sanity. Perhaps he had hired someone to change all the linens and wash all the clothes. That didn't make sense either because Janie was helping him with housework. When she and Janie were young they flipped every mattress in their houses twice a year. No one flipped mattresses anymore. Not beautiful pillow top mattresses.

The hospital could use better mattresses. Her feet and head wouldn't hurt as much if she slept in her own bed. She tried to remember how many weeks it had been since she was home.

Tonight her mind jittered in and out of the present—jumping to her awful situation then planning ways to elude the strangers holding her prisoner then puzzling where her lilac Easter suit might be stored. She called "Art, I want to go to bed" as loud as possible and knew they soundproofed the room so he could not hear her voice. She wanted her red pajamas, a bowl of pretzels and a drink with little ice.

"Time for bed, Katherine. Should we brush your teeth and wash your face?"

She made a dismissive motion toward the tall stranger in blue. "Art will help me."

"Not tonight, Katherine. Let's get started."

"Where is Art?"

"He's in the hospital, Katherine. Remember he came to visit you this evening?"

She didn't remember, but kept quiet. When the lights were out, she closed her eyes and fell asleep, the worlds of dreams and reality merging in the darkness. As the window became bright, she felt rested and let the servants hired by Art help her through going to the bathroom then taking a shower. Finally they brought breakfast. She almost cried, so relieved by the sight of food and coffee.

"Morning, Katherine. I hear you slept well."

Katherine looked beyond breakfast; saw Rachel at the door. She ignored the daughter.

"I brought my own coffee and yogurt so we could eat together."

Rachel wore her hair up like an old woman. Katherine withheld comment because Rachel tended to be offended by suggestions. Breakfast was more important than starting a brouhaha.

"You brought your school work?" she asked as Rachel leaned a thick leather bag against the wall. It was difficult to remember what grade the girl might be in this year.

"No, proofs of my next book. I thought I'd get some work done today if there's time."

The answer made no sense. Rachel pulled up another chair and put a tall coffee cup on the table. They ate in silence. Her daughter wore a wide gold bracelet that Katherine wanted. She watched the bracelet move as Rachel spooned yogurt from a plastic container.

"I'm going home today," she said exactly when Rachel swallowed coffee. "I saw the doctors this morning and they said you could take me home."

"No, Katherine. The desk staff said Dr. Wagner usually does rounds after nine."

Katherine enjoyed the discomfort on Rachel's face when forced to say "Katherine." People probably thought her daughter was a hard-hearted witch—good payback for causing the family so much disrespect.

Cold toast lost its appeal. Katherine didn't like Rachel's tone. "Don't call me a liar." Anger was power in the new order of this world. "Don't call me a liar." She shoved every dish and cup over the table's edge.

Rachel yipped as coffee hit her legs. Katherine pounded her arms on the table, feeling excitement growing with each hit to her bruises. The opportunity to escape arose. She moved quickly over spilled food and dishes toward the door. Rachel jumped as well, grabbing at the hospital gown's strings and calling for help.

"Let me go, you stupid girl." She slapped at Rachel. "I'm leaving for California." The West Coast sun would burn away her confusion and the men knew how to make a woman feel pretty.

The people in blue caught her. "Keep your hands off me you fat bitch," she hissed at the strongest woman. "Why don't you go back to your country? Damn all of you foreign sluts."

Out of the corner of her eye, she saw Rachel leave the room and wailed as her daughter let the strangers take control.

Chapter 11

Hot coffee soaking the insole of her shoe, Rachel left the room and turned her back on staff preparing restraints. She respected their decision intellectually, but not emotionally. If her mother had called for help instead of cursing the nurses, Rachel may have returned.

A young nursing assistant held out a towel. "The ladies' room is three doors to your left."

The simple kindness gave permission for tears. "Thank you," Rachel managed.

Locking the door, Rachel slipped off her shoe, removed her sock, grabbed paper towels and began absorbing the coffee. Finally she focused on dabbing spots from her shirt and pants, ignoring the light pink skin on her lower leg.

She wanted a run with no cell phone, an hour of freedom. John Wagner, wearing gray dress pants, a striped shirt, tie and the same brand of running shoes she preferred, greeted her as she walked back toward her mother's room.

"Tough morning? How hot was that coffee," he asked indicating her stained pants.

"Very. I'm fine. Thanks for asking." She took a deep breath and tried to hold back emotion by talking about anything but Katherine. "I wear that brand of shoes. Yours look new."

He smiled, a genuine personal gesture. "I thought you looked like a runner."

"About four times a week. Usually with a big dog named Weezer."

He moved to the present. "According to the staff, your mother had a pretty good night."

"I've seen dementia up close before. I just didn't expect this." She shrugged.

"Art said you've been traveling so he hasn't shared a lot about your mother's condition."

"There's always some reason why my parents don't tell the whole story. I think he felt I was putting too much pressure on him about the need for help."

"Which brings me to today. Evans House can't take your mother until tomorrow. She's running a slight temperature, which allows me to keep her one more night. I'm increasing her medications to avoid more outbursts. She's going to be more disconnected."

"My Dad will be upset to see her that way."

"It's that or you could take her home for a night."

Carrie might have volunteered for this duty, but Rachel had a sore leg and wet shoes. She fingered her phone while pulling together a response.

"Rachel, I've written orders for one more night. That's what's best for her. You all need to be getting things ready for her move. Have you visited Evans?"

"I stopped last night and spoke with staff. The only time I could schedule with admissions and nursing is during my father's cath test. I bet he liked Evans House because it is new."

"That's what he said. Now, I need time with your mother. I'll be with Art later this hour." He checked his watch, began turning away.

"About my Dad." Rachel found herself unsure of how much to disclose about their family, decided to stay with the one issue impacting her father. "I don't know if my brother will show up for the cath procedure and Carrie will probably be with me. Could the staff call if I am needed?"

"Let's hope your brother or sister can wait with him, but if that doesn't happen we'll call." She read his cool professional voice as an assessment of her family's cohesiveness.

"Thank you."

He tipped his head.

Embarrassed, she realized she needed his attention on a smaller question. "One more favor, could you please get my bag inside the door? I'd rather not go in."

"Not a problem." Released, he finally opened the door and reached in. Katherine's continued wailing for Art rose and then stopped as the door began closing. "She's all right, Rachel. She's safe. Go see Art." This time he spoke with gentleness. "If you'd like to run this evening, I know a few good local routes."

"Thanks. For everything." She extended a hand to grab for her bag but instead squeezed John Wagner's arm, so grateful for any kindness.

To not upset her father, she changed out of her stained shirt and into a sweater. Looking at herself in the room's bathroom mirror, her twisted hair appeared stiff and old. She pulled out the clips, shook it free. There was no way to hide dark circles under her eyes, but she felt better.

Her father looked more like himself—showered and shaved and wearing the pajamas and robe she brought from their house. She relaxed in the quiet of his sun-filled room.

"Good morning, Dad. Did you sleep well?"

"Better than the first night. Your timing is good. I just finished the paper and they suggested I take a walk down to the sun porch. When Doc Wagner does rounds they'll come for me. This room is driving me nuts." He stood and cautiously stretched. "From that frown on your face I'd say something is worrying you more than the spill on your pants. You know you don't have to dress up to sit around here all day."

"I had breakfast with Katherine and ended up covered by my own coffee and yogurt." His lips pressed together, but he said nothing. "This is the second time I've seen her fly into a rage. You should have said something, Dad."

"Sometimes I resent my kids telling me what to do."

It was too early in the day to enter this discussion. "Let's take that walk."

He moved easily, the shuffling steps and hunched shoulders of yesterday gone. She watched him greet another patient by name while tipping his head to the man's spouse with quiet respect. How many times had she told Dylan about his grandfather's comfortable way of dealing with people? Had she ever told her father that she would think about how he might talk with a frightened person when she first worked psyche ward? Probably not.

They settled in chairs near a window wall where they could watch cars enter the hospital's circular drive. A man about Dad's age walked a small dog next to the parking ramp.

"Dylan and I are thinking about getting a second dog," Rachel volunteered. She pushed away that her parents had never met Weezer, not been to Chicago for at least ten years.

"Tell me about your mother. You said something happened this morning?"

She drank deeply before answering, sorting through her mother's rapid disintegration during breakfast. In the end, she decided to tell it straight and gave her Dad a total recount. He relaxed, one large hand balancing on the narrow chair arm without a single wobble.

* * *

Art watched Rachel as she spoke. How she used her voice reminded him of an uncle, a certain steadiness giving each word its own time. When she turned her head toward the window, he realized with some surprise that others might call her a handsome woman. Katherine said Rachel wasn't very feminine. But she was—tall and slightly built, thick hair and graceful.

"Dad?" Rachel broke through his wanderings. "I think I lost you."

"No, I heard all the way to Dr. Wagner's plan for today. So, Dr. Daughter, how do we make this less painful for your mother?"

Her forehead wrinkled. She drew a circle on the table with water droplets. "It's going to be difficult. She's already confused as well as injured. The best we can do is what we discussed last night—have Carrie make the room more familiar with things from home and I'll work with the staff at admission. Until you're home, the three of us will take turns visiting."

"She's going to expect me to be there all the time."

"Dad, I'm not sure how much longer she's going to know if you're there or who we are."

In the weeks leading up to Katherine's first leaving their marriage, Art experienced a growing sense of disquiet between them. He knew she had fled by an aura in the house when he arrived home from work. The morning of the second time, he asked her if she was thinking of leaving as they lay in bed after the alarm clock sounded. This time as she left, there would be no emotional struggle to reclaim her loyalty, if not her love. She was leaving him behind even as her body remained in sight. Around the room he saw men and women sitting together, supporting each other through 'better or worse.' It wouldn't be that way for him. He stood up.

"I think I'd like to go back and wait in my room." They started walking. Art felt more comfortable talking if he didn't have to look right at Rachel. "Todd's not coming today. Carrie should be here soon and if she's gonna cry I'd rather we're in a private place." They slowed down and moved to the side for a gurney to pass. "Maybe she can go ahead to Evans House and you can stay here during my tests."

Rachel sighed and he thought she now understood how it was to accept responsibility for Katherine. Out of the corner of his eye, he watched her lick her lips before responding.

"Your test is smack in the middle of the only time Evans House admissions people had for us. But Dr. Wagner knows how to find me." She hesitated before stepping on her brother's behavior; decided honesty was kindness in this situation. "Todd was plenty rude. I'm sorry you had to have that kind of discussion, Dad."

"He told me how he felt and I told him to stay home. Jack Abram from church volunteered to help move stuff and will come to the house when you girls call. Carrie knows him. His wife passed away last year. Maybe you remember that your mother and I played bridge with Jack and his wife?"

She nodded. He took a breath then continued.

"I've started making plans for my own future. Down the way I'm going to sell the house and move into one of those communities where I can have my own place while I'm healthy then have first dibs on a place like Evans House. Not that I'm anywhere near ready yet."

Rachel hugged his arm. "You better have lots of good years left" was all she answered. Facing the cath scan that afternoon, he hoped she was right.

"Carrie might not be on board with my decision but she'll want her mother to be comfortable." Changing the subject pushed away anxiety he had about the afternoon test. Later, while he and Rachel talked with Dr. Wagner, he felt embarrassed then angry at his younger daughter's failure to show.

"Carrie must have joined Todd's camp," he told them. "Didn't see that coming, but it doesn't change anything. I want to tell Katherine myself. She'll listen, maybe understand."

Dr. Wagner nodded. "Makes sense, Art. There's time between her lunch and your procedure. Let's think about what you'll tell her."

"I know you'll all have a lot of suggestions but I gotta handle this my way." Art didn't say he wanted to hold his wife in his arms and have the feel of her next to him while telling her their life together was over. He couldn't say those words out loud.

Lunch trays were delivered on the floor without an appearance by Carrie. As Rachel pushed his wheel chair to Katherine's room he felt anger that God dealt them such a crap hand. He knew if Katherine cried he might. Wearily his mind went back to times he'd been the bearer of bad news. Those times he knew his arms were steady, his body strong enough to hold her. Now he felt the quiver of his own mortality in his old man's arms. He sent Rachel away.

"Why are you in your pajamas, Art," Katherine asked as he walked into the room. "That's the second time you've driven here in those clothes. You're getting to be a crazy man."

He didn't bother to correct her, just touched his hand against her forehead and felt cool skin. The soft restraints holding her in the chair stole his calm. Rachel had warned him, but the sight made him want to strike out. He pushed away that emotion, accepting that Katherine had moved beyond returning to their little life.

"Dr. Wagner says you're running a low fever."

In one of those cruel turns of her situation, he sensed Katherine being very present as he took his hand away. She reached for him and pulled him closer. "What's happening, Art? Am I not going home?"

The same quiet of anticipating prior separation times returned. Maybe she felt it in how he moved. The immense weight of his failure to keep them together choked him as he tried to speak.

"I can't keep you safe, Katherine. I've tried, and I know you've helped, but it's time for professionals to take care of you."

Tears rolled down her cheeks, and for the first time he noticed her head slightly shaking. Slight tremors moved through her face, her neck and her arms. She dropped his hand. He thought she might be having another stroke and reached for the nurse's call button.

"I don't know what to say, Art. I don't know what to say. Am I so hateful you want me put away? You promised you wouldn't do this." Her green eyes glazed with tears or fever; her hands twisted and turned in her robe. Spittle gathered in one corner of her mouth.

He didn't reach to clean her lips, but knelt next to her chair and tried to draw her into his arms. He raised one hand to brush her hair. If he could hold her close he thought she might feel his sorrow, might know his love would always be hers.

She brought up her arms quickly, smashing his away from her and clocking him in the chin then nose. He lost his balance and went down to his knees. "Get away from me you bastard. You lying, cheating creep. Have your sex somewhere else while I'll be in the cuckoo house. I hate you." Her voice rose in a screech. Two staff entered the room quickly.

One nurse approached him, asked whether he was OK while helping him back into his wheelchair. She slipped fingers over his wrist.

"I'm fine. Take care of my wife. She's had a terrible shock."

"Have his daughter take Mr. Kemper back to his room," she ordered.

"No, Katherine needs me. Let me talk to her."

"She's been upset about everything all morning, Mr. Kemper. Talking won't help. Let us care of her. That would be the most helpful thing you can do, Mr. Kemper. Go on."

Rachel waited for him at the door. He didn't talk and she didn't interrupt his silence as they traveled back to his room. Leaning on her strong shoulder, he moved from the wheel chair to his hospital bed and let a few tears fall. She handed him tissue, perched on the edge of the bed, rubbed his back. His daughter's comfort kept him from sliding into dark despair. Just as when Rachel was a child, she didn't ask questions about what happened with her mother, and he wouldn't volunteer. He would hold the last minutes with Katherine as private as any time spent with his wife behind a closed bedroom door.

Reluctantly he placed the burden of Katherine's resettlement solely on Rachel's shoulders. He asked her to close the blinds against the September sunshine.

"Are you sure you want to sit here in the dark?" she asked.

"I need to rest." He couldn't tell her how guilty he felt about that afternoon just two days ago when the same sunshine stirred desire to escape his life with Katherine. Too much had happened too quickly. He wanted to hold the world at bay for just an hour or two.

"It doesn't feel right to leave you alone," Rachel said as she leaned in to kiss his forehead. She smelled of something clean and simple, like lemons or freshly cut grass.

He patted her hand. "It's nothing new. I'll be okay."

"I know, but I worry." Her hand tightened on his forearm, then she turned and left.

Hospital sounds drifted through his closed door. His thoughts avoided the afternoon's procedure to mull through Rachel's tasks. He wondered what, beyond Katherine, would be missing from their house when he returned.

"Art, the transport folks are on the way."

Opening his eyes, Art startled.

"Take your time." Rusty tapped at monitors. "I'll get your room cleaned while you're out. Any worries about the procedure?"

"I read the materials, watched the video and talked to my doctor." Art wished Rachel was sitting in the chair or waiting in the hall. "Yeah, I'm nervous."

"Rachel and I talked with my supervisor about me walking to the lab with you and assisting the nurses before the procedure. If that's okay with you?"

Embarrassed by the absence of his kids, Art accepted the kindness of another man. "Sounds like a plan. Thanks."

Chapter 12

Walking out of the darkened hospital room, Rachel carried his sadness as company. She tried both of Carrie's telephone numbers and left messages about meeting at their parents' house. Calling Carrie's cell phone—then home phone—then repeating the same routine was acting like their mother, who mastered the telephone as an instrument of psychological torture.

"Carrie, please pick up. Don't disappear. We've only got this afternoon to get Katherine's room ready and you know her best. You're not happy with this move, but we need you. At least return my call." She promised herself this final speed dial would really be the final.

Driving down their parents' street, Rachel hoped to see Carrie's SUV parked on the driveway. If not, she hoped both her siblings were experiencing totally hellish days.

Instead of Carrie's minivan, a contract cleaning service truck was still parked in her parents' driveway. The sight and smells of the mess left by her parents shocked Rachel the night before. Carrie and Todd might be uninterested in the physical damage, but Rachel had pictures on her cell phone.

Not absolutely restored, the kitchen was clean. She would find someone to repaint the wall where the phone hung and repair scratches in the wooden floors. But she felt satisfied that her father could walk into the house with minimal reminders of what must have been a horrific experience. She signed for the work, paid the crew, closed the front door and broke her promise while hitting speed dial one more time. One more time Carrie didn't answer.

With ninety minutes to pack, Rachel wandered rooms where she'd grown up. Todd's green bedroom walls looked unchanged while the space she shared with Carrie had been transformed into a frilly guest room complete with cotton animals dressed in little girl out-fits. Walking past the bathroom door, she remembered the first time Katherine left their family.

Rachel was eight years old, Todd almost four and Carrie not yet born. Her mother's voice was tight, the tone Rachel interpreted as a flag for a slapping. It was a summer morning, and Rachel lingered in bed.

"Rachel, watch your brother take his bath while I go out for milk."

"I gave him a bath last night."

"Don't give me lip." Her mother's hand was quick on Rachel's legs. "You can read that book in the bathroom."

Ducking around another slap, Rachel headed toward Todd's bedroom.

"He's already in the tub. Stop dawdling and get in there. The faster you obey, the faster I can get to the store and you can have breakfast."

Rachel moved fast. Before she could turn around the door slammed.

"I'm going to put this special protection lock on the door so you'll be safe while I'm gone. Ok, Toddy sweet?"

"Ok, Mommy."

"Behave both of you." And she was gone.

Rachel sat on the toilet, thinking about how unfair it was that she had to watch Todd when the girls were going to ride bikes this morn-ing. Only two weeks until school started.

Her brother sent waves of water out of the tub as he turned a toy boat into a paddle.

"Toddy, you need to get out of the tub."

"I'm hungry, Rach. Big hungry."

"Mommy went to get milk. We have to stay here until she gets home."

He stood in the tub, arched his back and let fly a curve of pee.

"Toddy. That's icky." She pulled up the tub drain plug, hating that her hand had to go into his peed water. "You're disgusting."

Laughing like a crazy goofball, her brother climbed from the tub. She dropped a towel around his shoulders. "Dry off."

He threw himself at her, circling into her nightie. She shoved him away. "Use the towel."

He giggled while she looked for his shorts and t-shirt. "Mommy forgot your clothes. Where are your pjs?"

"Mommy has 'em."

She wrapped him in a towel and pulled him next to her then read out loud from her Nancy Drew novel to keep him entertained. The heat became uncomfortable. Todd threw himself against the door, screaming for Mom. She sat with her back against a sliver of wall, knowing their mother had done something awful.

* * *

In the basement, looking for empty boxes, Rachel tried not to think about the sewing area where Katherine made holiday decorations, or the treadmill her mother once used daily to stay a perfect size ten. Upstairs in her parents' room, Rachel filled boxes with basic clothing essentials including light flannel pajamas Katherine insisted on wearing year round, a Halloween sweater her mother loved for its smiling pumpkin, slippers that always sat next to the bed. Rachel used another box for family pictures. In the girls' room, she wrapped two china ballerina figures in towels. On the bottom of the pink dancer "Carrie" was written in ink. She finished one box with her mother's big bead rosary, statues of Jesus and Mary and funeral holy cards that Katherine liked to hold.

Somewhere during the packing she began snuffling and stuffed her pockets with damp tissues. Whatever stood between she and her mother would stay undefined and irreconcilable. Rachel, knowing herself to be damaged by Katherine's rejection, wasted time looking to find some picture or book or thing that would contradict her understanding of their troubled mother-daughter history. But history wouldn't be rewritten. Jack Abram's arrival cut Rachel's brewing depression. Even in his seventies the big man with the big voice, who once could carry two or three kids on his back, stood over six feet and made her feel surrounded as he gave her a hug.

"You're a good kid, taking charge of this when your Dad's down. My kids were champs when their mother was sick. Makes a world of difference." He patted her shoulder

Loading his van with Katherine's things went so quickly. From all the possessions her mother had so carefully gathered in the big four bedroom house, she would spend the rest of her life surrounded by a small pile of things that didn't even fill the back of Jack's van. Rachel wanted to add more, fill the space.

"We've got enough here, Rachel. She won't really need much," Jack said so gently that she had to fight the urge to throw herself in his arms and cry like the child he had known.

Carrie had not called as they left for Evans House. Rachel followed Jack's van and walked in with him at her side, a comfort she hadn't expected. Unloading Jack's van took fifteen minutes. He set Katherine's recliner in a corner, ran cable for her television and tried to distract Rachel with funny stories about her parents. She sent him off with one more hug.

Before she could prepare her mother's room, Rachel met with the admissions counselor to complete the last paperwork and then introduced herself to staff her mother would come to know. Bright lights and a steady hum of background noises reminded her of doing hospital rounds.

Bland vinyl-covered walls showed small holes where other residents had hung pictures. Institutional carpeting kept the floor warm but not comforting. A low-tech hospital bed with a high bumper-edged mattress stood pushed against one wall. Thin sheets covered the mattress, sheets that could be easily changed by staff and laundered in an industrial washer.

She started personalizing the room there, placing a soft blanket and thick quilt, both washable, over the bed's sheets. In the middle of the pillows she set a teddy bear, then hung ruffled valances on the room's single window. Rachel covered a small table with a doily before setting a lamp on it and family pictures. She loaded the small in-room refrigerator with soft drinks and bottled water. To camouflage the industrial cleaner odor of Evans House, she hid Katherine's favorite sachet behind the dresser and under the recliner.

Moving into the hallway to view the room, Rachel smelled early dinner preparations. She imagined the diminished faces of elderly women who would sit in appointed seats for this meal, and the next one, and the next, until they could no longer be moved to the dining room. The thought pushed her back into the room. She pulled the door closed, not surprised that it did not latch, and turned on the small television. With an afternoon talk show playing in the background, Rachel folded her mother's clothes into drawers and onto hangers in the closet.

"Looks nice." A staff member stood in the room when Rachel turned around.

"Thanks. I can only hope this will make her feel comfortable. My sister's the decorator. My name's Rachel Kelsey." She extended a hand. The woman smiled and extended hers.

"I'm Greta. Don't worry. Lots of the ladies don't bring a thing from home. The recliner is perfect. Care for coffee? Some of the staff chill in the lounge while our ladies rest after lunch."

"I admire all of you for working with these folks." Rachel's eyes brimmed.

"What's not to like? I worked in hospitals for years and prefer our residents."

"Will you be here when I bring my mother tomorrow?" 'Mother' fell from her lips easily.

"She's one of my charges. Tell me about her."

Rachel didn't know what to say. "I live out of town. Carrie and Todd know her better."

"You live in Chicago. We all recognize you from the morning shows and your books. Specially *Family Games*."

"That's who I am." Rachel felt awkward, wanting to just be one of the Kempers. She drew back, wary of Greta's expectations. "This is the real life. Writing a book is a lot easier."

"It's going to be fine, Rachel. Listen, if you're not up for coffee, I should let you finish."

"Thanks for the invite. I wish I had the time, but I need to get cleaned up and back to the hospital because my Dad is alone and having tests. I'll look for you tomorrow?"

"I'll be at Katherine's side for the first few days." Greta smiled. "Good to meet."

By three thirty Rachel returned to the hospital, going straight to the cath lab where her father waited in observation after receiving one stent. She fed him ice chips and wiped his forehead while he lay immobile.

"You must be his daughter," said a lab tech dragging in her plastic carrier of tubes and swaps. "You have the same eyes and nose." She drew vials of blood, slapped labels on each one and left.

"I'd like to sleep." The weakness under his wispy words alarmed Rachel. "Why don't you go visit with your mother?"

"He's doing well," the nurse recording his vitals offered. "A little nap would be helpful."

Rachel headed to Katherine's room, expecting to find Carrie. But her mother was alone, sedated, and waiting for a long dead cousin to arrive and play cards.

"Esther, I thought you were coming for lunch. They served hours ago. Are you wearing dungarees?"

"Sorry, I didn't have time to change," Rachel said. "What would you like to play?"

She let Katherine use any female name that came to mind as they played Hearts and Crazy Eights. Katherine created her own rules, acting coy about forgetting how to use trump.

"If Art insists on any more children, I'll name the next one after you. If there has to be a next." Katherine sighed deeply. It would be interesting to play along as Esther. Would Katherine declare all of her children to be Art's idea? But Katherine's head drooped and she began snoring. Rachel stayed in the room, lost in thought about the next morning.

Carrie showed up shortly before five as Katherine still slept, propped against pillows, a drool droplet forming at the corner of her lips. She leaned over to kiss their mother. Rachel noticed a coffee stain on her sister's incorrectly buttoned blouse. A lipstick fell from Carrie's open purse. Rachel picked it up.

"I don't know if you got my messages this morning," Rachel asked in a whisper as she leaned close to Carrie for a sniff check while returning the tube. One whiff confirmed Carrie's nonchalance was fueled by booze.

"Yesterday tuckered me out. I unplugged the phone at home and never turned on my cell. I was afraid Steve's sister would expect me to pick up the boys if she knew I was back. Anything important happen?"

"Didn't you remember we had to get the room ready at Evans House? And Dad went to the cath lab alone." Rachel gave in to the day's frustrations letting her voice grow beyond the whisper. "You smell like you've been drinking."

Carrie snorted and threw her shoulders back. "Rach, you're so self-righteous. My mother's about to be incarcerated as a loony. My big sister arrives and I'm yesterday's news. I'm tired. So I poured myself one long drink and had a soak in the bathtub before coming here. Just one drink that might have given me a little buzz on an empty stomach. Don't worry Ms. 'Holier Than Thou,' I'm not drunk."

"Growing up in this family, I think I know drunk."

Rachel recognized Carrie's helpless look and hated the whine under her sister's voice.

"I can't tell you how awful I felt when you called this morning. Let's face it, Rachel; I'm here all the time, doing what I can to manage their house as well as my own. Then you fly into town and my opinion's no good. It's a bitch to be discounted."

"When I leave you'll be right back in charge, Carrie, and I'll be the jerk for putting Mom into Evans House. Don't you think that's a good deal?"

"I don't really have to stand here and be lectured." Carrie turned to walk out of the room.

Rachel wasn't sure if her sister actually wobbled, or if fatigue and hunger just made her imagine Carrie was unsteady. She pulled her out of the room in case their mother was listening. "But the bigger question is, why drink over this stuff?"

"If I had spent the afternoon overeating, would you be upset if I showed up smelling like taco chips? Do you think it's your sisterly duty to protect me whenever you choose?"

Rachel opened her mouth, but Carrie flipped up a hand and continued. "When Steve travels, I like to take a hot bath before bed and a drink helps me relax. I guess I didn't know how the alcohol would affect me in the middle of the day. Honest. So chill."

"Dad and I win on having a hellish day. You didn't see their kitchen. You and Todd left him alone in the cath lab facing a stent insertion. Alone."

"You can handle it, Rach. You're cool. I'm the one who's always wound tight. Let me go down to the cafeteria, get some food and coffee before I see Dad." Again, Carrie wobbled then corrected her balance. "He doesn't need to know about any of this unless you need to tell?"

It was a classic line her siblings used as children. "He can't have a second visitor until he returns to his room in about four hours," Rachel said thinking Carrie would pick up on their father's condition.

Carrie winked and gave her a bit of hug. "Look at the good side, big sis. You'll leave, but I'm stuck here the rest of my life." She walked away with quick small steps that implied she was needed somewhere else. Her jeans were tight, her blouse baggy—an aged suburban kid.

Staff started rolling dinner carts into the halls and Rachel realized she'd not eaten since the spilled yogurt that morning. Her family never changed. Her father wanted sympathy and someone to take care of chores. Her brother wrapped himself in self-righteousness. Carrie took a hot bath, got drunk and avoided everything. She found a small waiting room empty, shoved the door shut with her foot and sat down, put her head on her arms and stretched her tired back. A few minutes later she pressed David's speed dial number.

"How tough is it?" His voice took the edge off her loneliness.

"Well, I spent the day preparing a room for Katherine that included a hospital bed with institutional sheets. My brother refused to help, my sister got sloshed, and Dad went into the cath lab and came out with one stent." Her voice pitched upward and she sucked in air to keep from crying. "I'm moving Katherine tomorrow morning."

"I can be on a plane and in Minneapolis tonight if you want. Dylan, too."

She thought about accepting his offer for a moment, felt the comfort of David's kindness. "You knew exactly what I needed to hear. That's worth gold, but it's better that I finish this up on my own."

"How's Art? I sent flowers."

She slunk down in the chair and leaned her head back. "Beyond the one stent I think he's doing pretty well. The plant is beautiful and surprised him."

She didn't say that Art was confused about her relationship with David because she wasn't sure she understood their future either. She didn't have energy to open that subject.

"When are you coming back?"

"I'm hoping Tuesday."

"Let's plan on spending next weekend as a family. Dylan and I can do the shopping and cooking." In the background, his desk phone buzzed.

Two days of normal life glimmered like a mirage in the middle of the Kemper emotional desert. "Thanks, you've given me something to look forward to."

"Remember my offer, Rach. I can be in Minnesota in three hours. By the way, my Mom says I should tell you, you're a good daughter."

"Your mom's a great lady, David. People in my family might disagree with her opinion."

"Screw 'em, Rach. Come back to Chicago. Your boy misses you. His insane dog misses you. And I miss you."

"Thanks, David. I miss you," she almost stopped but added one more word, "all."

Hanging up, Rachel made her way to the hospital cafeteria. She brought a salad back to her father's side and ate while telling him about the house being cleaned and Katherine's room and plans for the next morning. All the time they talked, she knew he was waiting for Carrie.

Chapter 13

Life never moves as fast as a video game, Rachel frequently told Dylan when reminding him real people need time to think and to feel before making major decisions. The rush of events since John Wagner's call two days earlier left little time for emotional processing. She awoke at four in the morning. Not due at the hospital for many hours, she wrestled with thoughts about her parents, her relationship with David, her siblings.

One image continued to stall all her thoughts—the small pile of her mother's possessions in Jack's van. All that remained of a lifetime of building the perfect outfit, dining room, and holiday decorations stayed behind. Over and over Rachel remembered items she chose for the Evans House room, wondered if she knew what her mother valued in all those rooms of stuff. When she got out of bed at five, Rachel knew that she would trade all the bits and pieces stuffed into their Chicago home for the support of good friends and family if she ever faced a similar day.

Carrying in her father's morning newspaper, Rachel saw his sadness in tired eyes, unshaven white stubble-covered face and overall quiet. They sat in silence, each supposedly reading about the outside world. She looked over the edge of the national news section, thinking she should talk with him about his homecoming. His eyes moved down the sports page columns in a way that told her he wasn't truly reading. At half past eight, Rachel folded the paper and stood.

"Time to go?" he asked. "Will she do okay, do you think?"

"She'll do fine. I'm actually more concerned about you."

He forced a small smile. "She's going to cry, you know."

"Anyone would, Dad. I'll be back to pick you up after she's settled. Count on a quiet evening."

He nodded and she left before either of them questioned today's plan.

Her mother sat in the vinyl chair, dressed in street clothes, and eating toast. She looked up with a look that was indecipherable.

"How's your breakfast, Katherine?"

"Your father makes better toast. He slices bananas."

Rachel wondered where to go with the discussion.

"Don't make me go there," Katherine whispered. "Don't take me away from Art."

"The doctors say you need special care." She used her parents' phrase from tough times, "We'll all have to do our best to make this work."

Katherine stopped speaking. Assuming Carrie and Todd would not help, Rachel made arrangements with Evans House for a staff member to accompany them on the drive. At ten o'clock, Rachel dragged a cart with Katherine's bag and flower while the hired stranger pushed her mother's wheel chair to the hospital's front door.

They settled Katherine in the back seat of the Lexus and sat the facility's staff person next to her. She remained quiet as they left the hospital parking lot. Rachel relaxed her hands on the steering wheel, concentrating on the road and avoiding the sight in her rearview mirror.

At the first stoplight, a soft moaning began in the back seat. "Don't do this. Let me die. What have I done? Don't do this."

"Mom, we don't have a choice. You'll be fine."

"Call me Katherine you bitch-dog."

The back of Rachel's neck tightened. Her mother moaned and muttered in the back seat. The Evans House employee murmured comforts until Katherine slapped the woman's arm. Each block felt like the last miles of an emotional marathon.

Like a large mute child, she moved through the short admissions process not acknowledging greetings or answering questions. At the door to her mother's room, Rachel felt satisfied with the way sunshine brightened familiar belongings.

"Here we are, Katherine." Rachel used her softest tones. "This room gets morning sun, your favorite. I brought some of your African violets and put them on the window ledge. The watering can is under the television so Dad will be able to keep them healthy."

She eased Katherine from the wheel chair and settled her into the flowered recliner. "Do you want the green or burgundy throw?" Katherine extended a hand toward the burgundy and Rachel helped pull the soft cover over her mother's legs. "You have your own re-frigerator here so you and Dad can have a can of soda whenever you want. Would you like one now?" She opened a can, poured it into a large flowered plastic tumbler from home and set it on the table.

Katherine's hands trembled in her lap. Rachel put her own hands over Katherine's and looked up into her mother's eyes and saw the kind of vulnerability of a kindergartner dropped off at the schoolyard without a friend in sight.

"You don't need to be afraid of anybody here. They understand what you need. When you're ready, you'll meet other people. Dad will be around as soon as he can. We all want you to be safe." She tried to embrace Katherine but her mother ducked away into her chair.

"Where's Art?" The words were whispery. "Tell the nurse I need Art."

"Mom," Rachel's voice lowered with the word as if her mouth was forming the gentle whispery kiss dropped on a newborn's fragile fore-head. "He's still at the hospital. I hope I can get him here tomorrow."

"When will Rachel and Carrie be here?"

She ignored her mother's slip. "Tomorrow. They'll be here tomorrow."

Rachel turned on the television, patted Katherine's shoulder light-ly and watched her mother sink into the familiar sounds of an old drama. When Katherine's concentration was completely involved, Rachel left to visit one more time with the intake coordinator. She needed to know they wouldn't leave her mother alone. On the way, Rachel found a restroom and ran cold water over her wrists, then splashed her face.

"She'll do fine."

Rachel blinked water out of her eyes. One of the Evans House staff members stood at the restroom door.

"This is a good time for you to get away. Greta will call this afternoon with an update."

"I'll look in once more. She just seems very vulnerable."

"She is vulnerable. Stop if you must, but don't interfere."

From the hall Rachel peeked inside the doorway to see Greta standing at the door to Katherine's bathroom. Rachel listened as Greta attempted to talk Katherine out of the bathroom.

Feeling conflicted about her own need to be away, and Katherine's obvious confusion, Rachel left Evans House. She sat in her car, watching the traffic. A young mother with a large dog at her side pushed two infants in a double stroller past the van. Rachel followed them visually, her hands wrapped tight around her sides. In a pocket, her cell phone sounded.

Reading "Private Call" in the phone's screen, she answered "Rachel Kelsey."

"Dr. Kelsey here."

"David. I didn't expect to hear from you. Is everything all right?"

"I had a lull in schedule here and was calling to ask you that question. I take it you've settled Katherine or you wouldn't be answering calls."

"She's already bedeviling the Evans House staff." Rachel searched for any humorous stories to share with David. Nothing came to mind.

"Don't do that, Rachel."

"Don't do what?"

"Don't sit there and stew. Where are you?"

"In Evans House parking lot." She rubbed her forehead. "This was rough. It's such an ending. I was thinking how she used to wear that one string of pearls even with jeans."

"Not the kind of thing a man notices about his mother-in-law, but it sounds right. Hey, I didn't call to talk about Katherine. I wanted to be sure you were holding together."

Her mind went to a very bad day in her life, another day when her mother stood on the opposite side of the bathroom door.

"David, did I ever tell you about the first time Katherine left us?" Even as she asked the question, Rachel knew she'd never told anyone that story, not her husband or a best friend or even a therapist. Now she needed someone to hear.

Blinking as tears came to the surface, Rachel looked down the bare sidewalk where the young mother had walked and told David what she remembered about that August day.

"Rachel, I wish…"

"What kind of woman locks her kids in the bathroom and drives off to California with another man?"

"A woman like Katherine. Get your crying done then move on. Don't pick at the scabs."

Rachel used a sock stuffed in her running shoes to dry tears. She saw part of her image in the car's rear view mirror, the same face she remembered after discovering David's infidelity.

"I've got to go, David. Dad's being discharged soon." There was silence on the other side. "David?" Miscellaneous muffled hospital sounds filled her ear. She repeated his name.

"Sorry, Rachel. I've got to go. See you in a few days. Don't let the Kemper-gators get you. Move on, babe."

Chapter 14

Waiting for Rachel, Art's thoughts wandered far beyond the patient escort's small talk. He stepped from the wheelchair and into the Lexus passenger seat, then sat with the door open while Rachel loaded plants and his bag into the cargo area. The escort closed the car door. Art knew he should thank the young man, but he couldn't find his normal behaviors.

"I'll make us a lunch of scrambled eggs and toasted muffins," Rachel said. She looked tired. "I didn't have time to do real grocery shopping, but will do that when I pick up your prescriptions."

"Maybe Carrie took care of things." He pulled at the hospital bracelet. "I talked to her this morning. She apologized." He scolded her and she promised to make it up to her mother, but said nothing about Rachel. "Maybe we could stop on our way home and see your mother." Rachel's hands were slender against the steering wheel. "I'd like to see how you fixed her room."

"No." She turned on a directional for the exit ramp. "Doctor's orders are that you rest for three days. Carrie can take you to Evans House on Wednesday."

The SUV swayed slightly as she turned. He closed his eyes; found the swaying motion upset his stomach. "Did you find the paint for the kitchen wall," he asked before she could say anything more about doctors and orders. "Jack said he'd be over this afternoon if you found it."

"The can is on your work bench."

She pulled into the garage. He swung his legs out, pleased his feet felt stable. Rachel opened the door into the kitchen. He hesitated, then stepped in.

The first thing he noticed was a clean smell, like chemicals mixed with furniture polish and all smoothed with a fresh breeze through an open window. The kitchen looked wonderful, cleaner than he could remember. Rachel snuck behind him to place one of the plants from his hospital room on the breakfast bar, another one on the table.

"Welcome home, Dad. Want me to cut off that identification tag?"

Not one word came from his mouth as he held out his arm.

"Jack moved a wing back chair from one of the upstairs bedrooms into the family room." She snipped through the plastic bracelet. "I'll take your bag upstairs. Go in and sit down."

The family room with its mismatched furniture still felt like home. Art cautiously stretched to open blinds. He turned his back on the wing chair and picked up the morning paper before settling in his own recliner.

After lunch, he returned to the family room and dozed during a baseball game. Over dinner of chicken breasts and salad, they talked about Dylan, about the Lexus, about anything but the Kemper family and David. Tired by nine o'clock, he delayed leaving the family room for the empty master bedroom.

She had turned on a table lamp, folded back the spread, and turned down the blankets to show fresh sheets. Clean pajamas waited on the dresser where Katherine's rosary collection used to be. He dragged himself through getting ready for bed. Once under the blankets, the sounds of his daughter moving around the kitchen and family room helped him to sleep.

When he awoke around midnight, the house was silent. The circle now closed that began decades ago when he drove Rachel to college. As each of his children left, Art felt them snatch a little part of his waning youth. In the dark, aware of each breath, he thought about the possibility of having a heart attack in this room and knew he would most likely die alone.

Days later, when Rachel left for Chicago, Art couldn't sleep in the quiet house. Empty bedrooms reminded him that he had lived his best years, his most useful years. As tired as he made his body during the day, Katherine's empty dresser drawers and vacant pillow lit up his mind in the dark.

This time there was no pretending she might return. She'd been a kicked kitten returning the first time that Christmas Eve, a shiner closing one lovely green eye and bruises around her slender neck. He took her in, filled with sadness and so much anger. She carried a suitcase he didn't recognize, wore a coat he had not bought. He had no idea what to tell the children in the morning. But, somehow it all got figured out. They made it work for thirty-five more years. Until now, when all that he loved of Katherine existed only in his memories.

These were thoughts he couldn't tell Rachel when she called each day in the following weeks, always on her own unpredictable schedule. He wondered what kind of life she lived that she couldn't set one time for them to talk.

"You sound winded, Dad."

"Never know when you're going to call." He took the handset to a chair in the family room. "I was downstairs putting together my own exercise place so I don't have to go out just to work up a sweat. Your mother's sewing room is perfect – it's got cable, a telephone line and that little window."

"Can you fit the treadmill in there?"

"Jack's coming over this afternoon to help me do just that." The kids might be sensitive to dismantling the old sewing room so he added, "I gotta move on, Rachel."

"I understand, Dad. You're thinking about what you need. If you said you're putting that stuff into the living room I'd question your logic."

He liked Rachel's approval and let go of a chuckle. "I've been following Doc Wagner's advice and walking every day. The snow last week pushed me to think about winter. If you visit this weekend we could lift weights together. Did you ever think you'd hear your Dad say that?" Again he found himself chuckling, this time Rachel joined him.

"I'm sorry I have to pass. Let's hold the father-daughter weight lifting until Thanksgiving. Tell me how things are going with Katherine."

Talking about this new era of Katherine no longer slowed Art's thoughts. "Yesterday morning she gave me a complete grocery list for Thanksgiving dinner and it looked like the real thing. Today she was planning your Aunt Martha's wedding and the woman's been dead for six years. Got feisty when I reminded her a few years had passed. Nothing much has changed."

"Sounds okay, Dad." Her cell phone rang in the background, but she didn't rush away. "Back to the exercise room—maybe you could have Todd or Carrie pump iron with you. Since Carrie's visiting every day, you could develop a new hobby together."

He looked at his watch and saw he only had an hour to fix lunch before Jack arrived. The guy was always early. "I haven't told her about what I'm doing downstairs and your brother hasn't been here since September. Listen, I got to get going. Still have some junk to move around before Jack gets here. You know how old men don't like to be kept waiting."

"Sure, Dad. Take care."

"Say hello to my grandson and David. Are you sure they won't come for Thanksgiving?"

"I'm positive it'll just be me. They already have their airline tickets for Philly. I'll call tomorrow."

He hung up, went back to the basement and moved the last boxes to the backroom. Katherine would crap if she ever saw her old sewing room. The front door opened as he walked up the stairs.

"Hi, Dad, it's me." Carrie's voice carried through the hall, cheery and light, almost girlish. This kid still showed a lousy sense of timing.

He stepped into the kitchen, "Hello."

"Just visited Mom and thought I'd drop off a few treats on my way home."

Carrie didn't take off her coat, a good sign. He watched her unpack low-fat frozen yogurt, dry-roasted nuts, heart-healthy cookies and baked sweet potato chips. When Katherine lived at home, Carrie brought real baked treats.

"What happened to the carrot cake and cookies? I've lost twelve pounds since I came home from the hospital. Exactly what the doctor told me to do. I could splurge a little."

"I did notice your pants are getting baggy in the rear. Maybe I should take you shopping for new clothes?"

"At my age black pants are black pants until a belt doesn't hold 'em up or there's holes in the knees. I've got time to shop if I need anything."

"It doesn't look like you've taken time to shower." She reached up and cleared cobweb from his hair. "Busy with something?"

"Just straightening things in the back basement." He held back sharing more information. She'd start crying and he'd really miss lunch before Jack rang the doorbell.

"Why didn't you give me a call? You don't need to do heavy lifting by yourself."

"When did I become an invalid? Doc Wagner told me to get off my ass and move around. That's what I'm doing."

"You could use Mom's treadmill."

"That's my plan."

"Let's go downstairs and see if there's a better place for it than in the furnace room. Maybe out in the rec room area where you could watch television."

She shrugged out of her coat and moved toward the basement steps. Art followed, knowing he was about to be caught. He thought about a gentle way to defend his new use for the sewing room, but his mind changed gears as his eyes took in the breadth of Carrie's rump in sweatpants. Not only was there more butt than he expected, but her buns jiggled as she walked. She chatted about Steve's call last night and the weather in San Francisco. He bit his tongue, but heard Katherine's words about women letting themselves go.

His daughter stopped at the sewing room's open door. Art admired the new blue paint. He kept his eyes focused on the now bare window while Carrie looked over the room.

"Dad, I can't believe you did this to Mom's personal space. She's still alive."

"That's right, Carrie, but she's never going to sit at a sewing machine."

"What about that beautiful Christmas table runner she had on the cutting board? Did you throw it away?"

"Carrie, that runner had three years of dust on it, but I didn't throw it away. Everything is in boxes and labeled. If you take up sewing you're welcome to all the stuff. I didn't throw anything away."

Her tone changed, resonating with childlike sadness that demanded he listen. "You painted over the stencil she and I painted. It took us a whole day. What were you thinking?"

She hit a nerve. He couldn't find the simple words to tell how sad he felt while covering the leafy trellis stencils. His daughter wouldn't believe that he bought the paint at Wal-Mart after midnight when he couldn't sleep and started working on the room when he got home. With two kids and a husband, she couldn't know the loneliness of almost three thousand square feet of furnished house.

"I wanted the exercise stuff in a room with a door to keep the grandkids out. "

Carrie turned abruptly and walked back upstairs. Again her rump moved ahead of his eyes. He knew Katherine would say something. She and Carrie took pride in their looks.

"Your Mother used the treadmill to keep in shape. She wore a size ten until the second stroke. I've got a rowing machine coming this afternoon and a set of weights in the garage. Come over and use the stuff with me. Winter can be a tough time to keep weight down."

She made it to the top step before turning to glare his way. "What are you trying to say, Dad?" Katherine's eyes looked at him. If he squinted he could almost remember Katherine at Carrie's age, a much slimmer Katherine.

"You've gained a few pounds."

"I don't have much time to do anything about that. When I'm not working, I spend most of my days driving the boys places, visiting Mom, coming here to check on you."

"Take the time you'd stop here for yourself. Unless you want to exercise?"

"If I want advice I'll go to my doctor. No wonder she starved herself to stay thin."

"Your mother wasn't thin, but she had nice muscle tone. You're too young a woman to let your looks go, Carrie."

"Are you through? Mom is a far better judge of what looks good. I've got to go."

She walked out, wrapping her unbuttoned coat around herself. He watched from the door as she recklessly backed the minivan out into the street and nearly crunched Jack Abrams' van in the process.

"What's with Carrie?" Jack said walking toward the front door. "She seemed in a hurry."

"Yeah. Listen, I haven't had time for lunch. Want to go to the burger place before we move that treadmill? My treat for helping out."

Chapter 15

Carrie drove too fast for their quiet suburban neighborhood roads. Her minivan swung from one side to the other through tight curves. Her mind moved with less control to phone calls that she needed to make before the school day ended.

In an hour Brian, her friend and boss, needed to know if she would renew her contract and work part-time for another year on the foundation's development staff. Her husband thought it best she lessen the stress in their lives if she backed off from working. Carrie Kemper, who once had her name on a profitable company, knew agreeing to that would relegate her to doormat for the family.

She lifted her foot from the gas pedal to touch the brakes. If unresolved about how to manage Brian's call, the second call would be worse. With no refills left for the meds she needed to sleep, to stay awake, to function; she agreed to Steve's request that she re-connect with her psychiatrist. She thought Rachel planted that suggestion with Steve.

At home she put the dogs out, opened a can of cola, and poured it over ice then stared out the kitchen windows. Dad was right about the weight. She added 'diet cola' to the grocery list. She lunged for the phone when it rang, grateful to have a reason to stop thinking.

"Hey, Sis, it's me."

Caller ID told her Todd was calling from his cell phone—probably with another string of complaints about their father.

"I just got home from the folks' place and let the dogs in from the yard. I'm thinking dogs have a pretty nice life," she said, keeping her voice light, but rushed.

"Did you talk with Dad about bringing Mom home for Thanksgiving weekend?"

"We got sidetracked by his decision to get rid of Mom's sewing room so he could have a nicer place for the treadmill and some new rowing thing."

"Mom could use an exercise program. That damn Halloween sweater is so tight it looks horrible." Todd slurped at something, smacked his lips, and annoyed her with his rudeness. "Carrie, if we don't get her back home soon she'll die a fat, babbling idiot."

"That's a bit extreme, Todd."

"You know what I mean. This daily visiting Mom is eating into my marriage. Kris is ready to throw me out if I miss another family event. You're lucky to have time during the day." Something interrupted his voice. "Oops. Got to pay attention to the road."

"I do work, Todd, just not full-time." She considered asking his opinion about quitting her job and knew he'd say it was nice to have such problems. "In fact I'm running late for a business call. I didn't take care of the Thanksgiving deal." She tapped her finger against the phone. "I'm better at house stuff than dealing with Dad about touchy subjects."

"You're soft, Carrie. I'll call Dad tonight and lay out our plan. A big old family Thanksgiving complete with big sister Rachel." His voice became clipped. "I'm pulling into my parking spot. Have a good afternoon."

His number disappeared. She scrounged through the cupboards for food, purposefully staying away from all her normal booze storage places. She had to get through the calls, shower and dress before picking up the boys for music lessons. With a sack of pretzels, a can of nuts, and her cola, Carrie headed upstairs to her office.

Aside from legal papers and a box of pictures, the antique table she used as a desk was her only remnant of Carrie's Spices, the company she sold when their younger son was born. Her company had wonderful offices above warehouse space in an industrial area along the Mississippi River. On the sly, she bought two wonderful condo units in the old building before developers took over the area, dreaming that some day she and Steve would escape suburbia..

Today, she fantasized about turning her old desk back to a dining room table and hosting small dinner parties of the kind of people she met through her fund-raising development activities—clever, powerful folks with interesting events on their calendars. City people with addresses near the lakes and kids in private schools. She reached over her head to touch her fingertips to 'The Prez' brass nameplate on her chair back as she answered the phone.

"Carrie, is this a good time?" The museum's executive director, a Bostonian blue blood, had a wonderful voice Carrie enjoyed. He wore his hair a bit too long, his clothes a bit too snug and his sexual preference like a badge. She liked him for all those reasons. More, she liked him because he respected her for her real talents.

"Perfect. I'm sitting at my desk and organizing Silver Banquet papers."

"I like the sound of that. I'm willing to be as flexible as possible to convince you to increase your time commitment. Work more hours at home or find another intern to carry some of the putzy work. We need your expertise and connections. And I need your sense of humor or I'll get as dried out as a pile of dinosaur bones."

Steve didn't like Brian. He called her boss a classic fop, as if anyone other than a rather conservative old-line lawyer would use the word 'fop.'

Odd how these opposites each wanted more of her, each asking her to 'increase her time commitment' to their unique causes. Brian wanted more of what she was ten years ago to woo the big buck players. Steve wanted clean underwear, well-behaved children and a stocked refrigerator while he cemented his senior role in the firm. She wanted a drink.

"You're a sweetie, Brian, and that's why I love you. You put up with all my complaining, but the facts are my parents are a huge time commitment right now and this is a critical stage in Steve's career."

An alternative proposal developed in her long-dormant executive brain and steadied her voice. "Is there any possibility of taking an unpaid leave of absence—maybe six months—to settle my parents?"

She pulled six months out of the air. Two months to make it through the holidays. Two more months to quit drinking and lose weight. Two months of cushion just in case her mother crashed or Steve demanded additional support.

"I don't know, Carrie. Work might be the best thing you do for yourself. The foundation really needs extra attention. If we hire out the entire capital fund campaign, I might not be able to keep the board supporting an internal development staff."

"Let me take that chance. If you can't do the leave of absence, I have to resign." She covered a small sob with a cough then stabbed a Carrie's Spices letter opener into her thigh.

"When do you want to start this leave?"

"Now, Brian. This week." She heard weariness in her voice. "I'll work with the Silver banquet committee pro bono to keep it on schedule. But I can't do more."

"What's happening? How about meeting me for a drink or is Steve at home?"

"He's in San Francisco. There's just a lot going on and I'm not feeling very well. Remember your depression story? I may have caught the same bug." The joke sounded weak, was weak. She needed to make Brian hang up. "My family needs time. I need time."

Definitely a new age kind of guy, Brian doled out caring and she let his voice sooth her nerves. "I'll see what I can put together. You get yourself to the good shrink and I'll staff the Silver committee this week."

Barely holding herself together, Carrie thanked Brian and hung up. She rested her head on the desk until she remembered there was vodka in her office supply closet. The phone rang again as she poured her first drink of the day into a cup with yesterday's coffee residue. Steve's caller ID came up. She let the phone ring as she gulped vodka like warm juice. "The Prez" has fallen a long way since accepting a handsome buy-out check for her 'little' company. She'd never admit to her husband the fear that there was so much further to fall before she hit bottom.

Chapter 16

Blueberry pancakes started Katherine's day on a high note that dampened when she was denied seconds. She walked back to her room, hoping to find pretzels or cookies still hidden somewhere. The magazine basket yielded a tissue and a small unicorn she'd forgotten. Behind the bed, cellophane glistened. She sat on her bed and tried reaching for it, but got a bit woozy bent over so long.

"Something wrong, Katherine?"

God, she hated people walking in without knocking. Katherine looked at the aide, wished some of these foreigners would take names like 'Betty' or 'Jean.' She moved her eyes away from the corn chips package, not wanting to attract attention to her small stash.

"I'm hungry. I want more pancakes."

"How about yogurt or applesauce? We can grab some on the way to exercise."

"I hate yogurt. Tastes like sour cream. I'd like something salty."

"There'll be chips with grilled cheese sandwiches at lunch."

"I feel wobbly. I don't think I should do all that exercise today."

"Come sit out here and I'll get you some juice and crackers. You can watch activities."

The young woman put a hand under Katherine's arm. Once standing, Katherine stepped quickly to the left, planting her left foot on the aide's right toes.

"Careful, Katherine. I need both my feet."

Katherine ignored the comment and kept moving away from her hidden snacks. She agreed to sit in the parlor and was rewarded with a carton of juice and small pile of crackers. She thought this place served too much starch for ladies who should be watching their weight.

She wasn't allowed back in her room until after a lunch of soggy grilled cheese sandwiches. Dimly she remembered there were peanuts or candy bars hidden somewhere in her room, but couldn't recall where to look. Sitting on the edge of her bed, she looked at the lock on her refrigerator. She thought they might as well post a sign that said people thought her too stupid to know when she was hungry or thirsty. The memory of sitting on her bed one afternoon and opening all the cans in the refrigerator to find just one beer, made her snicker out loud. No one here seemed to understand that sugar could never replace the taste of good hops.

Drinking, drinking anything, broke the boredom. She blamed Rachel, the only one in their family able to afford this kind of prison. Art didn't have enough money to pay all these guards.

Moving from the bed to her recliner, Katherine noticed the arms were worn. She'd have to ask Art for a new chair, especially if she was to have holiday visitors. She sat down, pulled up the footrest and settled back, focusing her eyes across the room to the wall calendar.

"Today is Tuesday," she said out loud. "Anyone care that we have a lot of days left in this stupid week?"

No one answered. The staff all paid attention to really crazy old codgers up and down the hall. I'd don't want no one to touch me again today," she said to the empty room. As she turned on the television, she realized this was a clear thinking day, not necessarily a good thing. It could be the kind of day when her neighbor's coughing brought daydreams of hitting the old skinny bird with a table lamp.

Worse, she might remember how life used to be while waiting for the fog that typically held her mind in a trap. In the moments of clarity, Katherine missed Art and talking with him about the children and planning dinner. For just a few minutes, Katherine thought about their home and took pleasure in remembering the lovely silk rose flower arrangement on the living room coffee table. She wanted to cry, wanted this to be a normal day when she could barely remember the past five minutes.

"I'd like to take a shower," she told the aide who came to suggest another crafts session.

"Katherine, this isn't your shower day. We're making clothespin Pilgrims this afternoon."

Katherine refused to waste clear thinking on gluing yarn to wooden clothespins. She saw samples of the ridiculous Pilgrims and thought the project looked tacky. She wanted a shower.

"Art's coming later today and I don't feel very clean." She wrinkled her nose. "You're a woman. You know how a man is turned off by a lady who smells like yesterday's underwear." Katherine kept her eyes opened wide with her head tilted slightly toward the bathroom.

"You can stay in your room, but no shower. The staff is busy."

"I'm going to write a list of things I need Art to bring from our home. We have a very nice home not very far from here."

"Your paper and pencil are in the chair pocket. Do you need help?"

"Help with what?" Katherine dug for the paper and pencil. "Just leave me alone."

She wrote her list: magazines, pix of dog, anjel lite, red hels, silver bowl trofy, gud paint brus, kalyfornya beeds. Looking at the list, she couldn't remember if they ever had a dog.

By the end of watching a murder mystery show, she believed Art would skip visiting to spend the day in bed with that tramp down the block. The one he had roast beef with last Sunday. She climbed out of her recliner, grabbed his framed photo and crashed it against the dresser edge, wanting him to be scarred like her. As she raised one foot to grind her heel on his face, an aide rushed into the room.

"Katherine, let me pick that up for you."

"Thanks. I lost my balance and dropped that picture. Good you were close. I almost stepped on all that glass. I'm here, because I stepped on glass." She peeked to see if the girl believed the story. "You're the Indian girl aren't you? Your kind thinks white people are stupid."

"I was born in Cleveland, Katherine. My parents are from Pakistan. We've talked about this before." The Indian tossed the glass and tissue in a wastebasket then removed the plastic liner bag. "Why don't you wait for Art in the living room?"

"What time is it? My clock is always wrong. My daughter bought a cheap one. That's my daughter who's a doctor. You know she married an Indian, the other kind of Indian, the kind who gets drunk."

"Your clock is right; it's a bit after two. Art is expected here before tea. So you've got time to join the news discussion group or listen to music with the ladies." The young woman held out a hand to guide Katherine from the room.

"I'll be out in a little bit. I have to tinkle." Katherine pushed the aide's hand aside and turned toward her own small bathroom. "You can leave."

"You might need some help with your undergarment."

Katherine felt herself for the bulkiness of a diaper. "Shit. Why don't people let me have regular underpants? Everyone's too lazy to do laundry, that's why. I'm taking these things off."

The embarrassment of being treated like an old drooling, pooping in your own pants fool infuriated her. "Get out of here. Don't try putting your hands down my pants. I don't keep my money or jewelry down there." She felt the power surge that helped when fools underestimated Katherine Kemper. She swept the young woman against a wall with one sure, strong push.

"Leave me alone. Leave me alone." Katherine raised her voice as loud as possible to let everyone know she was able to take care of herself. Then, conscious of listening ears, she lowered her voice to hiss, "I want my own underpants."

Other staff filled her room. The power surge fueled Katherine through one mighty move toward her bed to grab a lamp, anything to clear them out.

"I'll call authorities if you don't leave the room. These are my things."

Katherine snatched up a book from the nightstand and swung at people as they approached her. Confusion clouded the last of her clear thinking and she moved toward her bed, sitting down too quickly. Her heart started moving in the way that made her dizzy.

"Katherine, I have something that'll make you feel better." She recognized the tall woman who could speak German in the same harsh tones as Katherine's own Mother.

"I'm fine." Katherine heard how weak she sounded. She took a breath for strength. "They're hiding Art. Maybe he doesn't want to see me because I'm in diaper pants."

"Art will be here soon."

Katherine tucked her hands between her knees and thought about not causing a scene, about acting quiet so people would leave the room. If she closed her eyes she could do it, she could make them disappear.

"Come on, Katherine, take this. It could be a long afternoon if you're unhappy."

"Not unhappy," Katherine replied. "Pissed off. Call it what it is. Go away."

Cool hands freed one of her arms. Fingers rested on her wrist. She turned deep inside, ignoring anything that happened around the room. Someone removed her shoes; a blanket was laid over her body. She slept, knowing how Mother would scold for wasting the daylight.

When she awoke, she got off the bed, pulled off her slacks, took off the disposable underwear then used the toilet. With the door still open, she walked back to her closet to look for a fresh dress. Outdoor work clothes hung from the hangers, all her ironed house dresses missing. She remembered leaving all her beautiful full-skirted, flowered dresses with Jeffrey but the other dresses, her Minnesota things, should be here where these saggy-kneed dark pants hung.

Katherine pulled on a different pair of slacks over her naked butt, giggling as she felt fabric ride over her skin. She found her purse on the bookshelf, put on her shoes then wandered out to wait for Art. They were going out for drinks and pretzels, the little square ones with salt.

Rain fell in the free world. Katherine sat, counting from one to thirty-nine, assuming Art would show before she ended. A crazy old coot from the men's wing wandered by, smiling at her as he rubbed his crotch. "You're not getting into these pants so you might as well jerk off somewhere else, you bastard," she said as he stood in a corner. She stood up, shook her purse at him. He scuttled away. Katherine spoke to his back, "My husband's on his way and we've got plans."

She had to start counting over. This time the numbers lost their order and she gave up. She worried the rain would keep Art from coming and she'd be alone in this place forever.

Their friends must all know by this time that she was in this place for rehab. Hopefully, Art let them know she would be home for the holiday party season. Carrie would need to put together a few good outfits for Art's company holiday dinner and the Knights of Columbus dance and the Silver Ball.

* * *

"Stop feeling sorry for yourself, Katherine."

"Mother, I didn't know you were visiting today."

"That's why you're wearing those awful rags. I don't know what that man sees in you."

"He likes to dance with me."

"I never saw him as the dancing type,"

"You would have liked California, Mother. You should have come to see Jeffrey's house and pool and cars. We went to a party where Cary Grant said I was pretty."

"He should have taken a belt to you, Katherine."

"He did, Mother. He did."

"Not your sinning man, Katherine, your husband. Your husband wasn't enough man to keep you home or to punish you when you came home."

"Pooh-pooh, Mother. Kiss my…"

* * *

The room was quiet. Katherine heard only her own rapid breathing. No one sat in the other chairs. She was alone, waiting for someone in a strange place. Her stomach churned slightly, her palms were damp. She swallowed and closed her eyes. Time passed, taking away Mother and Jeffrey and more of her memories.

"Katherine, we've been looking for you. How'd you find your way into the staff lounge?" It was Art who put an arm around her shoulders, an old man but looking snazzy in navy pants and a wine-colored sweater.

"Where's your coat," she asked. "It's snowing out."

"Not snowing, Katherine. It's raining."

"I want to go to that steak place for fish and a Manhattan. Maybe we could take my mother. She says it's not safe to eat here and I saw that Filipino spit in Jake's ice tea. I refused to eat the lima beans last night. Those beans give me the runs."

"We went out Sunday, remember?"

"I remember you were going to take me shopping to get ready for our turkey meal and buy me a Christmas dress."

"I don't remember saying that, Katherine." Art took her arm.

There were many things she could say to this man, but not one came clearly to mind. She let him lead her back to her room. Maybe he'd like a snack.

Chapter 17

Rachel relaxed as David navigated lane changes in the mad rush to O'Hare on the day before Thanksgiving. She slid her right hand into the car door's map pocket, felt her sunglasses still in place, and was comforted.

Dylan dozed in the back seat. Rachel's thoughts flew fueled by high-octane emotions. Past, present and future forced to merge into one lane where everything slowed.

If she had control over their lives on this day, they'd still be sleeping, starting an extended holiday weekend with a few extra hours of rest. If David hadn't been sleeping in someone else's bed a year ago, they wouldn't be heading toward this first major holiday apart. As her mind threw accusations at David, she felt impatience with her own failure to understand what she wanted of their relationship.

A small car cut off a commercial van. David eased off the brake and swore. She smiled, knowing he only swore while driving.

"Traffic could be worse," he said. "It's going to be wicked cold in Minnesota."

Tears congested behind her eyes and in her sinuses like an unwelcome head cold. She wanted him to acknowledge that this heading toward separate holidays was painful, to say he wished this day was different, to ask once more if they shouldn't reconsider putting their marriage back together. On the other hand, she wondered if it was time to find a new relationship, one without all their baggage.

"Do you really think you can spend four whole days in the same house with your parents?" was what he said. "Any emergency escape plans?"

How could she tell him she had a Friday breakfast with the chairman of the board of the nonprofit whose job offer was in her carry-on bag? Late-departing geese moved across the distant looking like they were flying north, not south. She was aware of losing her own sense of direction, wasn't sure whether she was flying north away from David or exploring the way to follow him to a life she could barely visualize.

"I might do some Christmas shopping. Maybe Carrie might be interested in a few hours of deal hunting." Rachel looked sideways at David, uneasy with the ease of her dishonesty.

His eyes stayed on the road as he responded. "If someone else said that about their sister, I'd accept it, but I can't see you with Carrie at the stores. Name one you'd have in common."

"You're right. I guess I'll have to rely on my running gear to give me an excuse to get out." Two September runs around the neighborhood where she grew up had made her feel old.

"I'd suggest you use that indoor track at the hospital. Cold air is rough on your asthma."

"I know you think this whole plan is wrong, but it is what it is. It's too late to change things."

"It's not too late, Rachel. For Thanksgiving, yes, but I'm thinking of the bigger picture. I'd like us to spend Christmas together and make plans for New Years. I've got a few ideas." His voice was intimately low, not meant to carry to the backseat and Dylan. "I can't say I understand exactly what you're doing, Rach, but I want to talk. We've only got a few months before I move."

There it was—part of what she wanted to hear him say, just not enough. How she wanted to respond was "It doesn't seem like it was only a year ago today that I woke up early to bring warm pumpkin bread to you at the hospital and that embarrassed ward clerk had to tell me you weren't on duty." Rachel glanced again at the back seat and stayed in character of her son's mother, not her husband's betrayed wife as she said, "I'd like to spend Christmas together. Are you on duty this year?"

"It'll be the same as last year. Do you remember when I was on?"

She remembered quite vividly pretending everything was fine for Dylan's sake through two painful days last Christmas. "Yes. You were off on Christmas Eve and had call duty Christmas night."

When he was paged that night she decided she didn't want to live with constant doubt that he was really going to the hospital. Now it was time to give David credit for a year of working on their relationship. Rebuilding trust felt so risky. She didn't want to repeat her father's marital life.

David queued into O'Hare's giant parking garages and pulled into valet parking. Rachel worked on controlling her emotions. Taking comfort in the familiar, she opened the back seat door, shook Dylan's shoulder and smiled as his eyes opened.

They walked through the moving crowds of holiday travelers, shoulder to shoulder in their post-affair family formation with Dylan holding the middle ground. She felt David look her way over Dylan's head and raised her eyes. He gave her a slow wink.

"Mom, why don't you come with us? You and Grandma Kelsey always have a blast together. We could chill." Dylan looked ahead, his words sent toward the carpet.

"Grandma Kelsey did offer to share her bedroom with me when I spoke with her last night." Rachel knew how Jeri's concern for all their happiness was genuine. "But I promised Grandpa Kemper I'd be in Minnesota."

"This all sucks. Putting Weezer in a kennel, being here in this stupid airport with a million people, not having Thanksgiving together." He hitched his backpack up higher on his shoulders, a motion she recognized as defensive.

"Drop it, Dylan." David sounded like a surgeon faced with a doubting team. "Your grandpa needs support. Don't try to guilt Mom."

"That's not why she's really going to Minnesota. I'm not stupid, Dad. I've got friends who split their time over the holidays. This is just a practice run."

There was no opportunity to stop in the forward motion of holiday travelers. They were three bodies among thousands, yet Rachel could no more keep walking forward than she could absorb the pain in Dylan's comment. So stop she did, holding onto Dylan as her feet planted on O'Hare's soiled carpeting. David stopped as well and they stood like three small boulders in the flow of men and women and children and baggage.

Dylan's face, still smooth-cheeked, was no longer childlike. She recognized that the hand she extended didn't comfort him, so much as hold him back. His eyes did not ask for motherly assurances. Rachel straightened her shoulders, felt his anger.

"I'm sorry, Dylan," was what she said, biting back the terms of endearment that she wanted to use in place of his name. "We talked about all this and you said you were cool."

"That's what you wanted to hear, Mom. It's not like Dad and I are just doing some father-son thing. Next year who's going to be taking me to the airport to visit who? You know I think about this. It's my life, too."

"Let's not make this into something we can't handle here, son," David said. "Your Mom has a family obligation, and, fortunately, you and I have my wild Mom looking forward to seeing us. It's not the first time we weren't together for a holiday."

"That was before you messed everything up and Mom became semi-famous. I've heard you talk about that new job in Minnesota and leaving us behind. Not that you've told me anything about moving."

"We'll talk this weekend," David said. Rachel looked his way, saw his sadness. "We're keeping the Chicago Avenue place and I plan on flying home to do the stuff we always do."

"But when Mom goes to New York and you're in Minnesota, what's going to happen to me?"

"Dad's right, Dylan. This isn't the time for us to talk. I don't have travel planned for months."

"No one ever asked me if I like having a mother who's on television. It's weird when people look at us. Like those old ladies over there."

David and Rachel both surveyed the scene. She saw the middle-age women. David turned a half-circle to shield Dylan, moving closer to her left side, the place he used to stand.

"I promise we'll talk later. Let's get Mom to her gate."

"Warn me before you start the big father-son talk. I've got questions."

They began moving forward. Rachel dropped into step with them, their old family formation back in place with David on her left and Dylan on her right. For the moment, Rachel allowed herself the comfort of being flanked by her guys.

They sat together at her gate. She organized her carry-on stuff. "I think I left my scarf in the car. That'll give me one excuse to leave the house. I'll have to go out and buy another one." She smiled to indicate it was a joke, that she could live without a scarf for a few days.

"Take mine," David said and removed his then gently wrapped it around her neck. "It'll remind you of me." He kissed her lips quickly.

The counter clerk called first class boarding.

"Have a good trip, Rach." David stood, helping her gather her things. "Don't let the Kempers get you down. We'll think of you when we eat Jeri's cranberry dressing."

Rachel stowed her bag into the overhead compartment and sank into her seat. She turned her head toward the window, away from eyes of those who seemed curious about who paid so much for these seats for a seventy-five minute flight from Chicago to Minneapolis. She brought David's scarf to her nose and sniffed for his scent.

"Good looking guys you left at the gate."

She blinked at the solid grandmotherly woman who now sat in the aisle seat. "My son and his father. They have another plane to catch."

"You're Rachel Kelsey. Your voice is so soothing."

Turning back to the window while the stranger took a breath and dipped toward a cloth bag stored under the seat, Rachel scanned O'Hare's blank windows. The plane pushed back from the gate. She tried to relax, to rest while hanging between Kelsey land and Kemper territory.

* * *

In her rental car, Rachel made a snap decision and turned toward Minneapolis instead of St. Paul's suburbs to find her way to the Lake of the Isles area. She drove through a neighborhood of old stucco homes fantasizing about life here. Her cell phone surprised her, playing the 1812 Overture.

"We're sitting on our plane and thought you were almost at your folks." She slipped into David's voice, pulled it around her like a familiar wrap.

"Actually, I'm wandering Minneapolis. Stay on for just a minute, David."

"Something wrong, Rach?"

She pulled over to the curb and focused intently on a house across the street to control her delicate emotions. "I didn't want to say anything this morning and upset Dylan. The Minneapolis foundation offered me their executive position. They delivered the offer yesterday."

"That's great, Rach. Well, it makes for an interesting situation."

"Do you think you might have time for drinks and a talk next week?"

"I'm off Wednesday. Name the place." He broke away to say something to Dylan about a newspaper, then he returned. "Don't fret, Rach. You know you'll obsess if you start thinking too much and push for answers before questions even get asked. Dylan and I miss having you with us."

"Ditto." She heard his need for her to confirm the feeling was mutual. "I better get back to the St. Paul side of the river or they'll be all over me about why I didn't come directly. Have a good flight."

No one answered her parents' doorbell so Rachel used her key and entered the quiet house. On one side the dining room table stood covered with china and crystal, all upside down. To the rear of the house she could see grocery bags and mixing bowls crowding kitchen counters. Her phone played again.

"Smooth trip, Rachel?" John Wagner's voice surprised her.

"I just stepped in the door."

"Sorry, I thought your plane landed about an hour ago. I have a break between patients and wanted to see if you could grab a cup of coffee this afternoon."

Just a simple question, not requiring any commitment or deliberation, yet Rachel let her emotions jump beyond the coffee shop. Everything had been so informal between them up to now. She decided to not tell him about the job offer or David's move.

"That sounds wonderful but I have hands full with my family."

"I know this awkward, but I would like to get to know you better." He sounded sincere. Carrying her luggage up the stairs while they spoke, she considered an answer. She moved in her old room, closed the door without answering.

"Just a cup of coffee. A chance to make a new friend. I think we have a lot in common."

David was right; she rushed to answer questions that weren't being asked. "I hesitated because I'm multi-tasking and couldn't talk very clearly while carrying luggage upstairs. Coffee sounds wonderful, but maybe Friday?"

"I'm on call third shift Friday. How about Saturday?"

Even as she answered, his response put the entire possibility of a relationship with John Wagner in doubt. She knew how it was to be with a doctor. She confirmed a time and address while wanting to feel excitement. David's scarf on the bed whispered something else.

Todd's bag and briefcase lay on the bed in his room across the hall. Rachel plunked her luggage in a room where nothing remained of girlhood treasures except twin beds. She unzipped her suitcase and took out a few things to hang in the closet, changed from her traveling clothes into jeans and a sweater and headed downstairs to face the Kempers.

Chapter 18

Noise in the kitchen stopped Rachel. Waiting on the stairs, she tilted her head to watch Carrie. The thin weave of her sister's holiday sweater stretched unattractively, outlining back flab and bra straps. On her way between grocery store bags and the refrigerator, Carrie stopped to pick up a glass and drink. It would have been natural to grab her sister, to hold her close and whisper comforting words. But too many years and too many conversations had passed since they touched in the casual intimacy of sisters.

Rachel walked down the steps, entered the kitchen, extended a hand for a partial hug.

"Damn," Carrie said, crushing a bag, unaware of Rachel's presence. "Damn, damn, damn."

"Carrie, can I help?"

"How long have you been sneaking around? I saw your rental car." Her sister's face was perfectly made up although lipstick color clashed with ruddy cheeks and a reddening nose. Substantial diamond stud earrings sparkled in her ears. "I've made two trips to the grocery store, but can't finish the damn shopping." She tipped the glass upside down into the dishwasher. "I forgot the sausage for the dressing."

Her sister's distress layered confusion over the room's chaos. "You look festive. So like you to get dressed up for the holiday. Let me give you a hug then I'll help." Rachel extended her arms.

Carrie turned away. "You don't want to get too close. I didn't have time to shower this morning and have been cleaning in between grocery trips."

There wasn't anything to do but step back, or be stepped on, by her sister. Rachel moved and assessed how drunk Carrie might be before eleven in the morning.

"I'm curious about why you agreed to be here this Thanksgiving." Carrie threw the question out like a floor supervisor displeased with staff behavior. "You've not been here since you had a baby to show off about a dozen years ago." Her sister's hands pushed into pockets already stretched over the widest part of her hips.

"If you've decided to divorce David, this isn't the best time to come here and share the news. Having an upbeat holiday is all that is really important to us." She made a small sniffling sound. "God knows if we'll have another Thanksgiving with Mom."

Some part of Rachel noticed how Carrie was able to deliver the first body blow of the weekend with far less emotion than the missing sausage evoked. Katherine's wickedness still existed in this kitchen where pain had been doled out with the same calm as vegetable soup. The woman she called Katherine set these dynamics in place. Without her in the middle, the spokes of their family wheel were little more than decorative.

Her sister pulled paper towel from the counter and blew her nose. She looked at Rachel over the paper, wadded it up then turned to throw it away as she spoke. "You took yourself out of the Kemper family a long time ago. Do us a favor this weekend and try acting like a visitor. Use your nice television personality. Dad wants you here for support, not pushiness."

Old demons slithered through Rachel's struggle to remain calm. Totally a peaceful person, she thought it would feel much better to slap Carrie than reason through the alcohol and hatred.

"Before you try to sound like Katherine, you have to understand she never needed booze to say that kind of stuff, Carrie." Her sister's insolent look didn't change. "Are you this mean to your children, too?"

"You think I'm being mean?" Carrie rotated her shoulders back, fidgeted at her wedding band with one thumb. "I call this honesty. Maybe people aren't honest with small-time celebrities."

They stood ten feet apart in the place where once Rachel nurtured this baby sister. She had loved Carrie with the pure intensity of a child.

"I don't know what you want to fight about, Carrie, but I'm not going to respond to your delightful welcome." Rachel stepped aside to approach the kitchen sink. "Are your boys home today?"

"No, were you hoping to spend some quality auntie time with them?"

"I just didn't want you to go home full of booze and vent your unhappiness on them." Carefully, she didn't touch her sister's sleeve as she reached for the faucet. "I'll take over here. Go sleep off your breakfast."

Carrie stared out the kitchen window for at least thirty seconds before responding. Rachel knew there would sparks if Carrie insisted on staying.

"There's still a lot to do here," Carrie finally said. "Dad and Todd want everything to be perfect. If this weekend goes well, there's a chance Dad will bring her home."

"What happened to her can't be undone, Carrie. Dad can't take care of her."

"Well, don't say I didn't warn you." Carrie headed for her shoes and coat. "I'll get out of here. The recipes are all on the counter." Her coat stretched over the stuffed sweater. "Steve's a bit demanding these days and I have things to do at home.

"By the way, Kris wasn't very happy about Todd's decision to stay here for Thanksgiving. She doesn't understand our family holidays are numbered." Carrie rubbed the end of her nose, a stress habit from childhood that cut through Rachel's frustration.

"Carrie, let me…"

Her sister moved quickly, grabbed her purse and left. The door closed with a whoosh.

Rachel walked around the messy kitchen, replaying their exchange. She ground cranberries with more energy than required. Putting away clean dishes, she found a second glass of clear liquid tucked in with the measuring cups. Warm vodka splashed her tongue when she tasted the fuel of her sister's courage.

The room looked tidy by the time of Katherine's majestic entrance through the back door. Todd escorted Katherine, holding her arm and the door at the same time. He wore gray flannel pants, a starched open-neck shirt and navy blazer. Behind them, Rachel could see her father loaded with bags. Katherine stopped, looked around, and focused on Rachel briefly before shifting her eyes toward the refrigerator and the liquor cabinet.

"It's after noon so I'll have a drink," Katherine said. Her voice had a rusty quality, a scratchiness suggesting fatigue.

"Mom, we should really get your coat off and get you settled before beginning the party," Todd said. He moved Katherine out of their father's way then helped ease her arms out of the coat with the gentleness of a father undressing a young, beloved child.

"How about a trip to the bathroom? I can help," Rachel offered.

"I've not lost my last pecan. I know when I have to go to the bathroom." Katherine turned away to walk toward the family room. Rachel knew her mother would head where the flowered recliner once stood.

"Christ almighty! What the hell's wrong with this chair? Who took my chair? Art, Art, Art! It's that bitch from across the street. Go get my chair from your playmate. Right now."

Rachel snuck into the powder room, not quite ready to be in her family's drama. She knew that if the morning's activity already triggered Katherine's anger, someone was bound to get hurt as the weekend developed. At least Dylan was safe with David's family.

There was a rap on the door.

"You can come out now," Todd said. "Or do I have to run all the way up the stairs to pee?"

She opened the door for her brother. "Sorry, guess I got lost in thought."

"Like how to avoid Mom or something more interesting?"

Carrie's warnings came to mind. She wondered if Todd also felt she had no right to be here. She didn't feel comfortable directly asking why he was here so she backed into the question. "I can't believe you're staying here with a whole big empty house just ten minutes away."

"This was my idea. Mom feels best if her favorite son is around." He winked." And where's Mom's favorite daughter? Did Steven need something?" He pushed her out of the bathroom. "We can talk later. I've got more important things on my mind." The door closed.

Rachel returned to the kitchen, washed her hands then looked into the family room where Katherine sat in the remaining recliner, covered by one of her throws and slurping down something with ice. Glancing at the kitchen clock, Rachel noted it was twelve ten as the drinking began. She turned away from what she couldn't control and started preparing lunch.

Chapter 19

The mid-day sun seemed to disappear behind gathering clouds, so Art turned on the family room's lights. He could hear the kids talking in the kitchen and felt content. He could also hear Katherine drinking her watered-down vodka with great, greedy swallows.

She crooked her head to look at him. Her fair skin had a pink glow from the brief walk into the house. Her eyes were bright, and he thought she looked like a bird ready to swoop on an unsuspecting bug. A slight smell of urine surrounded her, but he chose to ignore that while enjoying the sight of her in her proper place.

"Why is that person here? I thought this was just going to be our family and you brought a guard from that prison into our home. She's listening to everything we say. I won't eat food she makes."

As Katherine started whining, Art's emotions raced like a rabbit caught between escape and a large dog. He kept his back to the kitchen and Rachel who stood watching.

"Katherine, that's Rachel. She's come from Chicago so we can all be together for Thanksgiving. Just relax." His hand rested on the warmth of her head.

Art lowered his hand to rub Katherine's shoulder before bending down to place a small kiss on her cheek. Her skin smelled like one of his grandchildren instead of a woman's face cream and make-up. The stylist curled her hair a bit too tight but she definitely looked presentable in the new outfit he'd bought for the weekend. He paid to keep her nails trimmed and she took pride in her hands, rubbing them with cream so many times a day that he bought the cheapest big jug of lotion at the drugstore. Of course, this was just another phase, and chances were she'd soon be obsessed with brushing her teeth or changing her socks over and over. But today he enjoyed the feel of her soft hands.

Not even glancing at Rachel, Art guessed she'd have a cautious look on her face; her shoulders held tight as a racehorse in harness. The same quiet way of standing just outside open doors she started when he and Katherine fought decades ago. When he did turn, he saw Rachel moving into the kitchen. He followed.

"Where's Carrie? I thought we were all going to have lunch."

"She had things to do before Steve gets home today. Soup and bread are ready."

"Your mother knows who you are. She just needs time to adjust to being home."

"Don't worry about it, Dad."

"Well, I just want you to know she appreciates you coming home so we can all be together this holiday. It would be good to have you here at Christmas. Dylan, too."

"I'm here because of you. Don't pretend she wants me here. And please don't talk about Christmas."

He didn't listen to Rachel's caution. Suddenly he needed assurance that there would be other events to anticipate. He let his loneliness push for a commitment. "With you and Todd here, I thought we'd keep her home until Monday so we could bring up the Christmas tree and start decorating the house."

"I'm scheduled to fly out Saturday."

His first drink was helping him relax, stoking a sense of holiday anticipation. The kids' presence made the house feel right, the smells of baking made him happy. Rachel baked a better pie than Katherine, and he hoped they'd have one for dinner tonight.

"Come on, Rachel. Sundays were always our family days. It would feel like a million bucks to have some brunch, put the tree up and watch football together."

"I can't stay, Dad.'" She pushed her hair behind an ear with the back of her hand then walked away.

Chapter 20

Changing into jeans before lunch, Todd looked around his boyhood room and thought everyone needed someplace like this – a constant haven. He patted his stomach, a few pounds lighter since September, and slipped on the edgy new eyeglasses Kris disliked. Todd Kemper taking back his game.

His weekend game plan was easing Mom back into the house. "You're acting like someone who was left starving in the desert," he said as she pulled him across the kitchen floor for lunch. "Don't they feed you at that place?"

Mom pulled to a stop, like a dog wanting to smell some spot on a tree. "Is she crabby?" she said pointing an unsteady finger at Rachel. "Maybe she should eat in her room?"

"Mom, what are you talking about? Rachel flew in this morning, made us lunch and is baking wonderful stuff for tomorrow. She will be responsible for me regaining all the weight I've worked so hard to lose." He pulled out Katherine's chair and helped her settle. "Be nice to her." His father watched then moved to his own chair. The old man had really developed that trick of letting others care for Mom.

Rachel carried bowls of soup to the table. "This is for her, but needs to cool down. I'll bring yours next."

He moved the bowl closer to the center of the table as his mother grabbed for it. "Let me butter and cut up a piece of bread for you, Mom."

"I want my soup and I butter my own bread."

Mom sounded like an outraged child and he struggled to not snap back as a parent. His father watched, but didn't offer a hand. Rachel carried in the remaining bowls of hot soup and walked around the opposite side of the table, away from Mom.

"Let's do it my way so you don't burn your mouth." He moved her bread across the table. She grabbed one piece, ate it quickly, and watched as he buttered more.

Rachel sat down, a small smile tight across her lips. His sister's eyes smoldered and he wished she could pipe down her emotions. Maybe Dad had put the squeeze on her about bringing her kid home for Christmas.

One of his strengths was staying low during emotional gunfire— here, in his own home, at work. He knew how to keep a smile on his face while chatting about mundane topics like football scores or a neighbor's new car when tensions rose. Carrie nicknamed him 'sniper' in their teens when he frequently teamed his observations of others with a wicked sense of cynicism to make Mom smile. His older sister's serious view of the world fed many inside jokes.

"So, Rachel, we haven't talked since your last book trip. How's the big time?" He ignored his mother's demand for more butter on her next chunk of bread.

"Along with a few hundred other folks, I just got an invite to a holiday party at the mayor's home." Rachel's smile looked more genuine. She put down her spoon and moved the butter dish out of Mom's reach. "In Chicago, that's big. Not so big here."

Sibling jealousy pressed against his newfound game. Rachel might not be their parents' favorite, but she had the corner on family brains and successes. First-born and first in almost everything, maybe the first divorce. "How's David taking your success?"

She raised her eyes from her soup bowl. "He's very supportive." She put her spoon into the bowl, her eyes darkened. He knew he'd been caught trying to push her buttons. She rose from her chair. "Anyone need anything else? I'm going for a quick run. Just pile dishes in the sink."

"Isn't there dessert? On Wednesdays we have cake at the prison."

His mother's continued whining made Todd wonder if Carrie might be right about the need for home health help if Mom left Evans House.

Rachel turned back to the table. Her kind voice surprised Todd. "I did see ice cream in the freezer. Would you like a scoop?"

He watched Mom lick her lips and recognize Rachel.

"If you have chocolate syrup I'd like two scoops. My husband always puts chocolate sauce on our ice cream. Do you know my husband?"

Mom's game was out of line. He tried to give his sister an escape. "Let me get it, Rach. I know my way around an ice cream scoop. You're the amazing woman—a millionaire who makes soup and does dishes."

"And you're an important man, Todd." Mom's voice was steady. She reached over to pat his hand. It was the kind of comment Kris mocked along with his mother's whole belief structure that his salary and bonus supported a big house, nice cars, kids in private school and major vacations. Of course, he didn't go out of his way to tell his parents that Kris pulled down significantly more income. Money was always a worry, but his in-laws would make sure the kids didn't suffer financially if there was a divorce. He'd be the one without a safety net.

"I'd like that ice cream now."

Todd entertained Mom for two hours, growing more irritated with Rachel's time in the kitchen and his younger sister's absence. He called Carrie around three only to be annoyed when she blew off his suggestion that her family come for cocktails.

"Let Rachel take care of the parents for a while." Carrie could have been paying a pizza delivery guy for all the warmth in her voice. "She doesn't spend much time pulling the load."

"Carrie, you're kinder when you're sloshed."

"Shut up, Todd. I'm tired of the drinking comments. People in glass houses shouldn't throw stones."

"Speaking of glass, maybe I'll start cocktail hour early. Dad's pretty much been glued to football and Mom could use a nap but won't lie down. She's like a super-sized three-year-old when she's tired."

"Tell Rachel to figure it out. She's the expert on dealing with all things psychological."

"I'm not my sisters' keeper, either of them. She's upstairs on a phone call."

"Probably billing some patient who can't get along with their family." Carrie chuckled.

"Yeah, well have a pleasant afternoon with your family."

"Get lost, Todd. You weren't there this morning dragging in groceries and making that soup you ate for lunch. I'll be there tomorrow morning." She hung up.

Rachel walked into the family room.

"Why is that cook walking around our house? She should stay in the kitchen."

"Katherine, both Todd and I've told you that's Rachel, not a cook. You better behave yourself or I'll drive you back before dinner." Like old times, their father stood up for Rachel.

Silence followed—the uncomfortable silence Todd remembered from childhood when their parents fought. He could use silence to make Kris uneasy whenever they disagreed. Often she would cave. Checking his watch, he knew she and the kids should have arrived at her parents' home. He texted her. She sent him a two-word response.

The sound of ice cubes rattling in an empty glass made him jump. One of Mom's amusing habits, rattling ice cubes to call anyone's attention to her need for a refill. It reminded him of his kids' high chair years when they banged spoons for attention.

Todd waited for their father to respond. The silence grew until she extended her glass one more time to rattle the ice cubes.

"You guzzled that like water. How about some soda?" Dad took the glass from her hand.

"I know what I want and I want you all to stop acting like I'm an idiot. Maybe I should go to my parent's for the night."

"Katherine, your parents passed away twenty years ago. Maybe a nap before dinner would be a good idea?" Dad placed a hand under Mom's arm. "Come on. It's been a big day."

Rachel moved to her other side, helped stabilize Mom's attempt to stand. It looked like Mom curved her fingers into his sister's flesh as they walked. He turned away, grabbed the television remote.

"Dicey isn't it?" Todd said when Rachel returned. Down the hall, the bedroom door closed. "She changes like lightning."

"Vodka doesn't help."

"Don't get preachy, big sister."

"If you think you'll anesthetize her with mixed drinks, you're wrong. You guys want to play with fire, you will deal with the consequences." She picked up Mom's glass. Todd turned to a football game.

Chapter 21

Katherine sat quietly while Art removed her shoes. He led her around as if she didn't know the bedroom where she slept for forty years. She used the bathroom; let him tuck her under their covers. The room was cool, the way he liked it. He shook her favorite quilt over the other covers. She picked up a corner and curled on her side with the quilt tucked under her chin.

Listening as hard as she could, she wasn't able to make out what they were saying in the other room. Art's voice seemed louder than the others. Her parents would be surprised. They thought he was such a quiet man. A boring man. That's why she had to leave again.

The quilt near her nose held a faint smell of old perfume, not her mother's, but something familiar. She rested her free hand on her stomach, on top of the baby that grew inside. Art's idea, not hers. Sex wasn't all that thrilling with him, but better than nothing. This would be the price. She could do without children. It would hurt. Her mother had been quite clear that childbirth was an awful, painful punishment for that crazy moment of forgetting God put you on earth to remain true to Him. Women bore the pain for luring Adam away from God's purity.

Her sister's voice answered Art. Katherine was confused. Time was confusing, this drifting from the comfort zone in her parents' home to the place where she and Art lived. She wasn't aware of time shifting, but hated being caught unaware when called to the present. There was no baby. Her parents were dead. She was alone.

Rolling on her back she stared at the ceiling until the light fixture seemed wavy, perhaps ready to fall on the bed. She closed her eyes so that wouldn't happen. She'd have dinner, watch television and go to bed. She'd sleep in this bed, alone. Art would have to find his own place to sleep. His smell bothered her, his noises disgusted her.

He'd brought her here to have sex. That realization made her sit up then get out of bed and make her way to the door where she pressed the lock. Then she put on her shoes and crawled back into bed. Art hated these shoes. He'd understand she wasn't interested in him if he made it through the lock and saw her shoes. Flat, old lady shoes, not the spiky heels she wore when she was beautiful. Old, fat-lady clothes and ugly, short-cut hair should send a message to any man. I'm done with you, with all of you. Then she relaxed, turned to her side, and let sleep happen.

She seldom remembered her dreams. Life and dreaming blended someplace in her life. They said she wandered the halls at night talking to the staff and telling crude jokes, but they lied. When she did remember dreams, they were about her holiday dresses and trying them on for some unseen person. The black velvet fit like a glove. She dreamt she swirled in front of the sewing room mirror, enjoying the sound of the velvet. The long black skirt and taffeta jacket were a bit snug but regal. She couldn't zip up the satin pants and matching top. With every outfit she removed, her body became more aged, heavier, shapeless. Finally she stood in her white underwear in front of a mirror. She pulled out a huge elastic waist pair of slacks just to cover her ugliness—to stop the laughing she heard in the other room.

The dream was too lifelike as she awoke and her hands felt the synthetic fabric of her clothes and her feet in old lady shoes. She needed escape, for the nightmare to end. No one heard her calling.

Chapter 22

While Katherine rested, Art relaxed in the rich smells of Rachel's baking pies and rising bread dough. Reluctantly, he pushed up from the table and carried his mug to the sink. "I better get my errands done while your mother snoozes," he said. "Think you'll be okay if I'm gone?"

"Enjoy the sunshine, Dad. I'm going to be busy here and Todd is listening for any sound from the bedroom."

His favorite wool jacket hung a bit looser these days. For the first time he wore a new hat he bought at Macy's. As the garage door went up, he thanked God once again for providing the opportunity to make a good living for his family and added a prayer for His presence through these next days.

An all-Christmas radio station made him feel like the clock had turned back a handful of years. He was once more a husband looking forward to surprising his wife with unexpected flowers. Opening the florist's front door, his eyes were overloaded in the most pleasant manner.

"I'm here to pick up the Kemper flowers. I think they're under Katherine Kemper's name," he said to the young clerk. "K-e-m-p-e-r."

"Yes, sir. I'll have to look in the cooler. I'll be back in a minute."

Art walked around the greenhouse, a place of mystery to him. Mums and poinsettias crowded every surface, reminding him of Katherine's clustering flowering plants in the living room and dining room. Once he retired, she expected him to water the damn things, and he put on a good show grumbling about doing woman's work while not really minding. The memory made him hungry for more than cut flowers in the center of the dining room table, so he carried a half dozen white mums and an equal number of poinsettia plants to the counter. He squinted at the bunch, wondering if he had enough to recreate Katherine's plant clusters.

"Would you like cards for any of these," the young clerk asked.

"Do any of them have special instructions besides watering?"

"No, I meant gift cards." He saw her look sideways at the center-piece order form to place his name. "Mr. Kemper," she added. She looked up with a tired face. "If these are gifts, your wife will want cards.'

"No cards. We're having a crowd for Thanksgiving and my wife likes to make a fuss."

"Lots of ladies like to have bows attached to keep their plants looking nice until Christmas."

For a moment, the façade almost cracked as Art thought about how Katherine no longer fit into 'lots of ladies.' "My wife likes the plaid ones. Add one or two of red."

The bill for almost three hundred dollars surprised him. He made a mental note to leave the watering can out as a reminder to protect his investment. The clerk offered two gift cards along with his signed receipt. Art shoved all the paper in his jacket pocket.

It was that time of day when inside lights and undraped house window gave viewers a picture into the life of the neighborhood. The evening sky deepened into an almost purple before true darkness. Driving down his street, he saw Janie in her dining room.

Impulse made him stop in front of her house, take one of the little gift cards from his pocket and write 'Thanks, The Kempers' across it with a pen he always carried. He pulled a plant from the backseat then headed up Janie's walk.

Was it ten years ago, or even twenty, when he held an umbrella over Katherine's head as she carried pies up this same sidewalk to trade for Janie's famous bread? The men started Thanksgiving with a brandy and a sample of their wives' baked treats. None of them could picture a time when only Art and Janie would be left at the front doors of these big family houses. Never once did they talk about this stage of life. He rang her doorbell.

"Art, what a surprise!" Janie had lost some weight and a familiar holiday sweater hung loose on her shoulders. Her eyes widened as she gazed at the tall wrapped package.

She pulled at his arm. "Come in. My kids aren't due for another hour."

"Ours came today. Katherine's taking a nap so I went to the florist." He felt damn awkward. "The car's running. I wanted to give you something for all the times you've helped us out. Katherine would say you deserve more." In Katherine's state, they both knew this was a lie. He held out the package. "I hope you've got a place for this."

"You must come in, at least until I unwrap it. Katherine and I usually bought holiday plants at the grocery. Florist plants are so beautiful, but so pricey." She put a hand under his elbow and led him into the foyer. "Set it on that table. I'll get a scissors."

He wanted to back out the door. Looking out Janie's dining room window, he saw blank windows in his own house and was thankful to be unseen.

Janie made quick work of cutting paper away to display a beautiful large white mum plant. "It's gorgeous, Art. Simply gorgeous. I'm going to put it on my buffet table." She gathered up the wrapping paper. "How's things going at your place? Katherine happy to be home?"

"It seems so." He shrugged. "We'll see how the next days go." Art backed toward the door. "Have a nice Thanksgiving with your family."

"Thanks again. You have a good time, too. You deserve it." She patted him on the arm, then to his discomfort stood in the lit doorway as he walked to his car. He put the car in reverse and pulled across the street into his own driveway and garage.

Carrying the centerpiece and all of the flowers into the house was a small production. Rachel helped him unwrap plants and fussed over the ribbons. Her cheeks were flushed from working in the kitchen and she looked like his sister, his only sibling.

"Am I cheap or are these worth three hundred bucks? I tell you, I wasn't prepared for the high cost of flowers." A terrible rattling sounded from the bedroom. "Katherine?"

"Help me! Somebody help me! I can't get out of here. The water's coming."

Art slammed a plant down and ran as best as he could for the bedroom door. The knob wouldn't budge.

"Turn the lock button, Katherine. Listen to me, turn the handle." Her hysteria grew and he knew she couldn't understand. "Rachel, feel the tops of the doors for the wire key. She's locked the door. No, just go get a screwdriver from the kitchen tool drawer."

The wailing continued as he felt the tops of each doorframe. A rhythmic dull pounding sounded from near the door's bottom. He stripped the screwdriver from Rachel's hand and wedged it into the top hinge pin. It popped and he repeated the same process with the second hinge. The door slid forward. He moved it aside not noticing its weight or bulk.

Katherine sat on the floor; a nail file embedded in the palm of one hand, her forehead red and rising into a bruise. He heard water flowing in the bathroom. Without needing direction, Rachel stepped around Katherine to investigate.

Kneeling, Art put his arms around Katherine's shoulders, bringing her head to his chest while lifting her wounded hand.

"You're OK, Katherine. You're OK." He murmured meaningless words over and over as he rocked her tensed body.

Rachel was at their sides with a damp washcloth and towel. Her wet stockings and feet left prints across the bedroom's plush mauve carpet. "Let me help, Dad. A few minutes won't make that much difference in the bathroom."

The hand Rachel extended to Katherine was rock steady, giving Art the luxury of taking a deep breath while leaning back against the doorframe. Rachel assessed the wound. All she said was "Do you want me to pull out the file?"

He nodded, giving over control of the crisis. Katherine struggled slightly in his arms, reminding him that her care demanded more strength than his body held. Rachel quickly extracted the file then brought the washcloth over the wound. Katherine screeched like a Halloween witch, the sound bouncing throughout the hall. They struggled, Katherine reeling in his arms, Rachel moving aside.

"Let me help, Dad. We don't want you hurt. I'll stay here, you look for Todd." Katherine was beyond knowing who handled her. He unwrapped his arms, pushed himself up from the floor, thankful to give his place to Rachel.

Opening the basement door, Art heard the rec room television volume cranked sky high. As he hurried down the steps, he felt an increasing pressure in his own chest. He put a hand out to the wall at the bottom of the stairs before moving further into the basement. In spite of the television, Art heard his own breath.

Todd stood, rummaging in the old refrigerator under the steps. He turned with a smile and a bottle of wine. "Dad, I thought we might go Italian tonight with Carrie's lasagna."

"What the hell are you doing? You said I could count on you to help out this weekend. I don't need a God damn wine steward. Your mother's flooded the bathroom and hurt herself."

"I'll take care of the bathroom." Todd closed the refrigerator and headed for tools. "I thought she was asleep."

"No one stays asleep forever. Turn the water off. The red handle next to the water heater. Turn it left." Without waiting for response, Art turned off the television then cautiously walked up the stairs. His heart beat rapidly, a light sweat cooled on his face.

"We're in here, Dad," Rachel called from the family room. Katherine lay on the sofa. Her hand was bandaged and elevated on a small pillow; her face cleaned. A light blanket covered her. The lights were dimmed, placing Katherine's face in shadows.

"We could use some ice for her forehead." Rachel stood up. "I'll get it if you stay with her. She doesn't want to left be alone."

"You stay. I'll get the ice pack." In the kitchen, Art first found his nitroglycerin tablets and put one under his tongue. He wrapped the small ice pack in a towel as the tablet melted. The discomfort in his chest was not his heart, but most likely caused by the returning fear of what Katherine might do next. He weighed the ice bag in his hands as if testing the burden of caring for his wife.

"This should help that bump." He settled the pack on her forehead gently. "Let me see your hand. What were you thinking?" The question came from kindness but he heard how fear roughened his voice. "Maybe we should give you a pill to help you calm down. I'll sit with you while Rachel finds the bottle."

Katherine was quiet even after Rachel returned with her pill and water.

"You both take it easy," Rachel said. "Todd's got the toilet fixed and is working on cleaning up the bathroom. A hand towel got wedged in the pipe." She took the water glass back from Katherine. "I'll rescue dinner."

Art settled on the ottoman next to Katherine and let himself be calmed by sounds of the kids' activities. From where he sat, he could see potted flowers in the living room. All of sixty minutes ago he had impulsively bought artificial holiday cheer, just trying to bring back some part of what used to be normal. He realized Katherine wore old, mismatched clothes. She kept her eyes closed, but he knew she was faking sleep.

"Katherine, do you want to go back tonight? Sleep in your own bed? I'll come for Thanksgiving dinner. You need to be happy."

She opened one eye then the other, an ungodly habit he always hated. "I want to stay here. I just had a bad spell. Just a bad spell. I'll be okay now."

"That cut on your hand's pretty bad. Maybe we should take you to the emergency room?" He picked up her hand and turned it over in his. "Rachel did a nice job of wrapping it. Looks like the bleeding stopped. How much does it hurt?"

"I've had worse."

He thought her voice sounded normal, odd after such an emotional episode. She left her hand in his, as relaxed as if they were sitting on the couch watching television. Her eyes closed and he closed his own, savoring the presence of his Katherine, the sounds of the kids and a moment of peace.

"I was trying to kill myself." Katherine spoke softly. "I woke up all alone and didn't know where I was or who I was and then I remembered everything and I don't want to go on. But I screwed up." She pulled her hand back from his. He followed it, wanting to keep feeling what was left of his Katherine. "Right now I'm having a good minute. Mostly life is a b-i-t-c-h. Help me, Art, help me."

"What do you want me to do?"

She held out the bandaged hand. "Put me back to bed with my pills. Loosen the lids and I'll do the rest. Just help me."

If this was the last lucid moment they shared in her life, he wanted to talk about their time together or say a prayer for strength. "Don't talk nonsense. You had a bad dream."

He rubbed her arm with his palm then gently ran the back of his hand down the side of her soft face. He spoke slowly, looking for words to take them back to safe grounds.

"We'll have dinner and watch old holiday videos and you'll forget this. You can't ask me to help you do that, Katherine."

Her arm tensed next to his. She laid her head against the pillow then turned her face toward the sofa back. Tears leaked from her eyes, hung up on the ends of her glasses, then smeared down her cheeks, but she stayed silent. He rummaged in her pants pockets for tissues and wiped her face dry.

Minutes passed. His back ached from sitting on the ottoman, but he held her hand and felt an important opportunity pass. Damn if he knew what was expected, or right. He swabbed at Katherine's tears again, wished he'd not listened to Todd about this whole Thanksgiving plan.

"Is she sleeping?" Rachel's voice broke the quiet. "Dinner's ready."

"I don't think so." Art rubbed his wife's arm. "Katherine, Rachel has dinner on the table." She laid still, tear tracks drying and her lips beginning to separate as she breathed. "Katherine." She was asleep, an immobilized vacant creature.

"Maybe you could bring me a plate and I'll eat in here. Best she not wake up alone."

He let Rachel put a hand under his elbow and help him up from the uncomfortable ottoman. She squeezed his shoulder then left him to watch Katherine.

Chapter 23

A crisis junkie, the emotional stew under his parents' roof rejuvenated Todd.

In the hall he strained, without success, to hear his parent's conversation. Giving up, he looked for his sister in the kitchen where overcooked lasagna cooled on the stove, dinner plates and silverware waited on the counter, the bottle of wine remained unopened, a bloodied towel lay on the floor near the laundry area. He dried his hands, opened the wine and poured himself a glass.

Rachel didn't speak when she entered the kitchen.

"Carrie would be upset to see her masterpiece burned," he said. Rachel looked up, but remained remote. "Do you think Mom had another stroke?"

"If Dad had any inkling this was a stroke, he'd have called 911. I think she'll be okay."

"What were they talking about in there? I would swear I heard normal conversation taking place in the family room."

"Really? I was putting away the first aid stuff. Katherine just asked Dad to help her with something." Rachel gathered things from the refrigerator then chose a placemat from a drawer.

He watched her set up a dinner tray, surprised at how she made the overcooked lasagna, a bowl of salad, and a plate of fresh bread look so pleasant. She folded two napkins into little crowns and set a candle in a juice glass. Domesticity was Carrie's bailiwick, but here was Rachel pouring coffee into Dad's favorite mug along with just the right splash of cream.

Remembering the years Rachel fed their family, he found himself wanting his big sister to make his evening warm and comfortable. He wanted a napkin folded like a crown and fresh bread on his plate. "The table isn't set. What do you have in mind for our dinner, Rachel?"

"If you want to set places for us, go ahead, or we can eat at the counter. There's plenty of lasagna that's still good to eat. If you're starving, help yourself."

She left with the tray. He finished his wine and poured more then poked around the lasagna with a fork.

"Here, let me cut you a piece. Don't be a baby just because the cheese got dark on top." Rachel took the fork from his hand, placed lasagna on a plate, spooned sauce over the slab and offered it to him. "See, taste this. Carrie did a great job. That sauce is homemade."

Todd opened his mouth, but Rachel handed him a fork. She raised an eyebrow and grinned. He settled himself at the counter with his dinner. She made up a plate for herself, poured a glass of water and sat next to him.

They ate in silence, quiet broken only by forks scraping on plates and the crunching noise of salad vegetables. Todd emptied his second glass of wine, conscious of the sound of his own swallowing. He wanted more, but loathed breaking the quiet by pushing his stool back to grab the bottle.

Rachel stood up. "Want anything?"

He pointed to the wine. She handed it to him and refilled her glass with water.

"How about some big sister advice?" The question came out before he had thought through its implications. In this kitchen with the sister who was always there when things were scary to a little kid, he desperately wanted to talk about his own family. Rachel never snitched.

"Anything to do with why Kris and the kids are away for Thanksgiving? You two always start the Christmas season with a brunch Thanksgiving weekend."

"We couldn't agree on a plan. Her father's retirement was important to her and Thanksgiving with Mom is important to me." How quickly their mother came into the picture when he started talking about his priorities. "I thought I negotiated an agreement to fly out Thanksgiving night. I was wrong."

He watched Rachel's face to see if she detected his semi-truth. He couldn't tell her that Kris made the arrangements then told him she was taking the kids to Philadelphia on her own. Twenty years of marriage didn't outweigh all he owed Mom. She always held that Dad wasn't a particularly caring guy, yet what he saw tonight was the kind of relationship he craved.

When he put down his wine glass, Rachel was watching him. "Guess I got lost in a thought," he said. "I wish we were together for the holiday, but this is where I need to be."

Rachel looked toward the family room before responding. "This certainly isn't the first time we've been commanded to appear at a Kemper holiday gathering by the possibility that it could be the last. I'm here because Dad needs some support."

"I want to be here, Rachel. I'm a simple guy who likes to be with his family. No one has to 'order' me. It would have been nice for you to show up more often." Rachel looked irritated, but he stayed on point. "We're all she's got."

"All they've got," she corrected., "and Dad's got good years ahead. He needs encouragement to get reconnected with his old golf buddies and the poker playing crew or the church gang."

"He spends time at Evans Home. They're always looking for volunteers."

"That place makes him feel old. He should be spending time with healthy seniors and planning for a future when Katherine will not need him."

"If you think Evans House makes Dad feel old, what do you think it's doing for Mom?"

"Todd, she's far from reality. Remember lunch today and the 'that woman' routine." Rachel made a face and shook her head.

"Everyone makes mistakes, Rach. Why hold a grudge?"

"This isn't a grudge. My relationship with our mother is exactly what she demanded. We had a serious blow out when I married

David because he wasn't Catholic. When we had Dylan baptized in the Presbyterian Church, she blew a fuse. She called me an embarrassment to the family and said she'd prefer if I forget she was my mother."

Pointing her fork toward him, Rachel finished her little lecture. "Our mother even had a lawyer contact my publisher to claim defamation because the biography in my first book connected my name to the Kemper family."

Todd squirmed on his stool, vaguely remembering Mom telling her version of these stories. Mom wanted comfort which he willingly gave thinking Rachel had made it big enough in the world and could find her comfort somewhere else.

"I still called regularly," Rachel continued. "She would never come to the phone. Then she started writing wicked letters."

"Kris received some of those letters. You girls should have taken some of what Mom said with a grain of salt. You remember how she used to blow up about something small then forget the whole thing? You're too sensitive."

"Did she call Kris a disrespectful bitch or imply that you weren't the father of her children? Did she cut up birthday presents and send them back to you wrapped in garbage?"

"How come you didn't call us and ask us to talk with her?" Todd kept the onus on his sister and remembered how uncomfortable his discussions with their mother had been about similar treatment of Kris.

Rachel shook her head. "Why would I have called you or Carrie?" Her face changed, all emotion slipped behind neutrality. "That's history. What about you? You asked for advice. I'd like to be helpful."

"As big sister or shrink?"

"As Rachel." She patted his hand then moved away. "Think about that while I check on the parents. She may be ready to eat and we've got a kitchen that's a disaster. If you're thinking you'll weasel out of helping to clean this place, you've got me confused with Carrie."

He picked up plates as she filled a coffee carafe and left.

Dad's voice carried into the kitchen. "I fed her some of my food. That was a big slab of lasagna and enough salad and bread for two. Coffee would be great, right, Katherine? You two figuring out the world's problems in there?"

"We talked about past holidays," was what Todd heard his sister respond. He waited in the kitchen. She handed him a tray of dirty dishes. "I meant what I said about the offer to listen and about helping with kitchen duties."

He recognized a teasing tone under her words and remembered how Rachel would kid around when he was scared as a boy. "Bossy older sister. Must be a genetic trait limited to first offspring. I never had any pull over Carrie."

"Our little sister was born a pleaser. That's why she slept around in high school."

"But you weren't living here then. How did you know?"

"There were telephones. While our mother may have slept around, she didn't want to know her baby girl was doing the same thing."

"I was right here." The news that Carrie confided in Rachel felt like a betrayal of a special brother-sister relationship.

"And you talked to Katherine. About everything. You'd find a way of letting Katherine know any dirt." She shoulder bumped him good-naturedly. "Now take out the garbage like a good man."

Chapter 24

The soft, dry fragility of her mother's skin stayed with Rachel while rubbing lotion in her own hands. Bandaging that nasty wound, Rachel felt the physical reality of her parents' aging; saw where she might be in twenty years.

When Katherine asked for someone to help in putting on pajamas, Rachel escaped upstairs and let the guys deal with the situation. Clearing a pile of dainty pillows from a chair in the guest room, she rested for the first time since leaving Chicago.

"Rach, are you sleeping?" Todd's voice accompanied a small knock on the door.

The words reminded her of little boy Todd coming to her door at night after their mother disappeared. Without words she'd lift up the covers, help him settle his stuffed animals and favorite blanket in her narrow single bed.

"No, just resting. Come on in." She straightened up, couldn't believe her cell phone's digital display of seven thirty.

He stepped into the room dressed as a true Midwest suburbanite in khakis, a crisp cotton shirt and dark sweater vest. "How about we get out of here for a while? Talk."

The chair felt good. The thought of putting on pajamas almost trumped curiosity about her brother's life. "Give me ten. I'll meet you downstairs."

Escaping the tropical heat of the Kemper house, Rachel filled her lungs with cold air then tilted her head back to look for stars in the clear November sky. She followed Todd to his car.

"This Acura is a beauty," she said. "I thought you'd drive a big SUV to cart kids."

"Kris does." He started the engine by the time Rachel slid into the passenger seat.

"Remember going to the auto show each year with Dad? I took him to the Chicago show about ten years ago and we sat in every luxury car on the floor." She adjusted her seat.

"He still talks about that. What do you drive these days?"

"I was driving an old Volvo that we're saving for Dylan when he starts driving. In August I indulged myself with a Lexus RX including a nice accessory package. Silver."

Rachel chuckled when Todd whistled. Car ownership was competitive in their family and she just took first place. They stopped at an upscale steak house not far from their parents' house. Todd led her to a tall leatherette booth in the bar. He ordered scotch and water for himself, chardonnay for her and chatted with the waitperson.

Watching them talk, Rachel examined Todd as a stranger might and saw a once-handsome man entering his middle years – hair thinning at the crown and fading from golden blonde to a lesser shade, unremarkable green eyes receding above a strong nose where tiny broken blood vessels marred pale skin. His chin, once the anchor of an athlete's face, was now rounding flesh. She would be older than her parents were now when Dylan turned forty. Would she see age in his face or be surprised one day that her son had become middle-aged?

Todd raised his glass with a grin before drinking. Rachel sipped her wine in silence. Sitting and waiting for others to speak came easy to her in her clinical practice. The skill of easy banter with book reviewers, interviewers, audiences, even people close to her, had been difficult to master.

The way Todd shifted his weight, ever so slightly forward on his seat, signaled his readiness to talk. Rachel held still and looked directly his way, allowing him to look into her eyes if he wanted. He focused closer to her throat.

"I often have to remind Kris how much we owe Mom," he finally shared. "Mom helped finance graduate school, made sure Kris and I could afford a decent house when we were expecting Mellie. Mom's always been there for me and I hate how Kris disrespects that past."

"David worships the chair where his mother sits." Rachel could picture David and Dylan playing Scrabble with Jeri about now. "I wish you knew Jeri – she's a great mother-in-law." She stretched her legs under the table. "Kris never stood a chance with our mother."

"Well, my wife sure picked a hell of a time to lay down ultimatums. I'm six months into this new job, Mom's dissolving, the holidays are right here."

Under a simmering tone of irritation, Rachel heard loneliness in her brother's voice and knew he was frightened about life without Katherine. She felt sympathy for Kris who loved a man who primarily loved his mother.

"What kind of ultimatums?"

"It's not important." Todd raised a hand for the waiter, pointed at his almost empty glass. "I don't want to pick through the minutiae."

The hours since leaving Chicago seemed much longer when filled with Kempers. Rachel dropped a pointed personal question. "Do you know how you feel about Kris?"

"Pissed." A fresh drink in his hand, Todd relaxed. "I've been busting my hump to keep all the balls in the air. Clay's having school problems, Mellie's looking at colleges, Evans House is out of my way. I leave the house at seven each morning and don't get home until after seven." He drank, began to put the glass down, but took a second swallow instead. "Sometimes seven thirty."

"You visit her every day?"

"I certainly do. I bring her treats, tell her a few jokes, make her smile."

"You don't need to do that, Todd. You've got to accept that she really doesn't know if you're there every day or once a week."

"Rach, you don't want to see what's going on. Mom could have a better life."

"She's dying, Todd. Bit by bit, month by month. You've got to deal with it."

"And you don't know what you're talking about. You just wish she was dead."

"Katherine's been a big influence in your relationship with Kris. I remember struggles between those two all the way back to where the wedding should be held."

"That's history. I don't want to sit here and rifle through all the bad stories. If you want to do remembering, then remember that you weren't at our wedding either."

The cruelty of his comment planted a chink in the emotional shield she carried within the family. Angered by the direction she thought Todd might take their discussion, she also found herself curious about how far he might go. Whether this time he would justify her placing him with Katherine in the despicable category.

"You got married on the day we buried our daughter," was all she said. This faded mama's boy couldn't understand what it felt like to at the graveside of your first child—no mother or father or sister or brother by her side. David's parents offered them comforting arms.

"Still the one for dramatics, Rach? I'm not saying it's not tough to have a baby die right away, but you could have made a big difference in how my marriage started. You could have helped your living sibling."

For perhaps fifteen seconds Rachel wanted to salvage a relationship with Todd. Then she remembered David turning back the flannel blanket wrapped around their still daughter, his strong surgeon's hands useless, and how he kissed the baby's forehead.

"Screw you, Todd. You're just as narcissistic as our mother. You want my advice? Your wife is sick of living with a mother's boy who can't face the reality that the one person on this earth who still thinks he's perfect is dying. You're a jerk, a real jerk. How dare you even talk about our loss that way? What would you know? She was your niece. The first Kemper grandchild."

Dragging her jacket from the booth, Rachel stood. She felt unstable; as if she'd run a marathon and her legs could no longer be counted on for support.

"We're done talking. Let's go," was what she could say without screaming obscenities that were clustered with tears on the edge of her self-control. She walked away, suppressing public display of emotion with well-learned Kemper discipline.

They didn't speak as Todd drove. Traffic lights, street lights, house lights streamed past Rachel's eyes like a ribbon of blurry whites, greens, reds. She looked down at her jeans and noticed tiny blood spots from Katherine's wound, and found herself thinking of her father sitting in the family room cradling her mother's bandaged hand. She wanted the man who cradled their daughter to hold her close.

"Rach, I think I had too much to drink. I was stupid."

She sat in her quiet and let his words become part of the darkness – just another meaningless ribbon beyond the window. "You got that right," she said.

Katherine stood looking out the front window as they pulled into the drive. Rachel had a fleeting memory of her brother running off the bus to be the first in the door with school news. She'd be helping Carrie cross the street while Todd entertained their mother. The blank-face woman standing in the half-dark room didn't care to hear his stories anymore. One day soon she might not even know her son who still moved to walk in first and give her a kiss.

Rachel hoped her brother felt only pain of that day.

Chapter 25

Art felt for his glasses to read the clock when he awoke on Thanksgiving morning. Fifteen minutes remained before he was due downstairs to relieve Todd from the second shift of keeping watch outside Katherine's bedroom door.

Rolling to his back, Art said his morning prayers, adding thanks for the presence of his children and a petition for extra strength through the day ahead. He considered if he should talk with the kids about their spat and trusted that Rachel wouldn't let a disagreement ruin dinner.

By the time, he pushed himself out of the old twin bed, Art felt holiday anticipation begin. He straightened his back, rolled his shoulders a few turns then stretched his neck before pulling on the clothes he'd worn Wednesday. Holding on to the banister, he moved down the stairs, thinking about turning up the furnace before waking Todd. The smell of fresh brewing coffee sidetracked Art to the kitchen where he poured himself a mug. Coffee in one hand, he stood in front of the thermostat, but couldn't adjust the temperature without turning on lights.

"You found the coffee," said Rachel from the dark hall.

"Good God, girl," Art's mug twitched. "You scared the tar out of me. Where's Todd?"

"He slept through the night. You can turn on lights."

While flipping the switch, Art experienced both disappointment and embarrassment about Todd. In the bright hall light, Rachel looked a bit worse for spending the night sleeping in a chair. He blinked, surprised to see his daughter as a middle-age woman, one who might have her own early morning weaknesses and aches.

"Once the oldest sister, always the responsible one," he said thinking of his only sibling, Louise. "I'll have a word with Todd. He promised he would help make this work."

Rachel looked at him in a way he didn't appreciate. "Dad, Todd was drunk." She waited for him to respond, but he couldn't. "If you don't mind taking over, I'll shower."

Without waiting for agreement, she walked. He settled into the chair outside his own bedroom door. Rachel sang softly as she moved into the kitchen then up the stairs. The comfort of a woman's voice, fresh coffee and a warming house replaced thoughts about his son. Until Katherine coughed, he drank his coffee in peace. When he opened the door, he saw her curled on her side in bed, looking at her bandaged hand.

"What happened? Did someone hurt me?" She looked up at him with childlike innocence. In the dimness of their room, her face was almost anonymous – all soft folds and ashen skin, lashless eyes offset by coarse whiskers on her old-woman chin.

"You don't remember?" She shook her head as she rolled over. "You had an accident last night. We shouldn't have left you alone."

"Can we eat?"

"Some things don't change. Not a good morning kiss, just your stomach to be satisfied." She held out her bandaged hand to him and he took it very gently. The wrapping looked fine. Turning it over he placed a kiss on her fingers wishing he could say "all okay" and make everything wrong disappear. He didn't dare ask about their conversation before dinner last night.

With effort he got her out of bed, cleaned and dressed. She did what she could and waited patiently for him to hook her bra and tie her shoes. He combed her hair, trying to fluff up the side flattened by the pillow.

With all the wonderful smells from Rachel's baking, Katherine's insistence on eating cereal seemed disappointing. "We've got this good pumpkin bread because today is a special day." Like a patient father he held a small piece toward her. "Do you know what day today is?"

"My anniversary?" She raised a hairless eyebrow, a shadow of his young Katherine.

"No, it's not our anniversary. Just lookin' for a gift, woman? It's Thanksgiving. All the kids will be here and we're going to have a feast. Rachel's making dinner rolls from scratch."

"She makes good bread. Rachel should have been a baker. Did she make this bread?"

"In fact, she did."

Katherine bent to his hand and nibbled on the bread. She repeated herself while chewing. "Rachel should have been a baker."

"She's done far better, Katherine."

Katherine looked beyond him, her eyes not really focusing. She wasn't to be rushed that morning, and he didn't mind. He stood at her side as she took her medications, swallowing each pill individually then drinking a little water and making little 'hucccking' sounds. Life felt normal.

"Need help?" Carrie, wrapped in a holiday apron, stepped in to rub Katherine's shoulders. "Pesky medicine, huh, Mom?"

For the second time that morning, one of his daughters appeared when Art wasn't ready. The unpredictable state of all his adult kids in the house surprised him. "When did you get here?"

"Just took off my coat. Call me Stealth." She laughed. "Come on, Mom, how about a little laugh at my feeble joke."

Katherine quirked her head and smiled. "Pretty hair," she said.

"I did it just for you. I'll do yours later so you look great for dinner. Want to sit in the family room?"

"I thought your Mom and I might spend some time downstairs looking at her pictures. We'll stay out of your way." Art began helping Katherine to her feet.

"I want to work in the kitchen," Katherine said, pulling against his hand.

"No, the girls are doing the cooking this year." He guided her to stand.

"But my mother will want to know I made the dressing. Carrie doesn't know how to mix the sausage and eggs with the spinach. I need an apron."

"Katherine, its better we're out of their way. See, they're chopping things now and you can't use a knife with that bandaged hand." He could see her interest in the topic shift.

"I want to see the dining room table."

He let her lead him to the dining room where the table looked like a million bucks with their best china set on a deep gold tablecloth. He waited, but she didn't notice the centerpiece.

"I sit here," she said touching the end chair. "Father will sit next to me on one side with Mother on the other side. You're across from me. Carrie, Todd, Steve, Janie, Ruth, Angie." She frowned. "There are not enough chairs."

He patted her hand, but did not correct her. "You always need something to worry about. Let's get out of the way. I've found your favorite pictures."

He walked ahead on the stairs, with her hand on his shoulder and her other hand grabbing the railing. Katherine settled into position behind him, relying on his stability. He put a hand over hers; holding on for what might be the last time they'd take this trip together. In all the months since that September day, he'd not really come to grips with what now settled in his heart. Katherine was never coming back home to live.

With patience and sadness, he helped her down the last two steps then gave her a hug. She stepped back, confused. Gently he turned her toward the photo gallery he assembled. The somber faces of her parents on their wedding day stood where she would look first. She picked up the framed photo of her oldest brother from World War II as she sat down, upstairs activity forgotten.

"Henry, Aggie, George, Lucille, Jim, Mary, Bob, Ruth, Katherine. I got to wear a long dress and gloves." She picked up another photo. "Look." She pointed to herself and smiled.

Time passed as Katherine spoke with ghosts raised by the pictures, but Art didn't mind. She held a photo of herself and their children taken on Rachel's confirmation day. Their daughter was at that gawky early teen stage, almost as tall as Katherine, and thin as a dowel.

"I miss Rachel," Katherine said. She rubbed her thumb over the photo. "Why doesn't she come visit me?"

"You just saw her upstairs. She made the pumpkin bread."

"That's your sister upstairs. Louise. She doesn't like me."

"Katherine, Louise died five years ago. You went to the funeral."

"I told Rachel to go to hell. That's where she is."

Not correcting Katherine gave Art some discomfort, a feeling of complicity in making this house inhospitable for the daughter who he now valued at his side. Katherine kissed the picture, and then wiped it on her shirt. Art rubbed her knee, his silence one more betrayal.

Before he could think of just the right thing to say about their daughter, Todd opened the basement door and yelled, "How about joining us for some great looking hors d oeuvres? I'll help Mom up the stairs."

"Ready to join the family, Katherine?" Art steadied her as she used his arms to pull herself up from the chair. She reached back to take the family picture. "Let me carry that and you hold onto the rail."

"I should put this in the sewing room," she said. "I like it on the window shelf."

"Why don't you let me do that?" Art took the picture. "You go upstairs with Todd." She turned to their son and extended her hand for assistance. Todd reached for her and Art saw the damage of last night's booze on his son's face.

For the next hour, he watched Katherine hold herself together during a light lunch. Carrie's boys, Jake and Rob, stayed slightly apart from the adults. Carrie snapped pictures that he knew he would throw away, preferring to hold on to memories of Thanksgivings when Katherine was queen of the house, the one orchestrating each detail.

Todd sat next to Katherine, keeping her plate and glass filled. Art released Katherine's care to her favorite child. He didn't ask questions. Eventually her head dropped to her chest, her mouth opened slightly and a tiny snore sounded. The boys laughed when Katherine's second snore broke loose. Todd reached to shake her shoulder.

"Son, leave her alone. We'll have a more pleasant dinner if she has her twenty minutes of shut eye now."

"OK, you're the boss," Todd said. "I'll get myself another one of these. Anyone else need a fresh drink?"

Art extended his own glass to Todd then leaned back, finally able to relax while Katherine slept.

"How the Bears playing?" he asked Steve then called the boys to join the men for Thanksgiving football television watching.

Chapter 26

"Mom, wake up."

Katherine opened her eyes, saw a room of strangers and wondered what they wanted. She pushed her glasses into place, wiped her nose on the gauze covering her hand. As she truly awoke, the faces became familiar. She looked at Carrie, didn't know what should be said.

"Is it time to go home?" she asked just because those words came first.

"No, Mom, you are home. I thought you'd like to get dressed up for dinner. I brought my curling iron so we could be beautiful when Steve takes pictures of us at the table."

Katherine let Carrie talk her into leaving her chair. She enjoyed listening to Carrie chatter. All the fuss with that hot 'curling' thing frightened her and she closed her eyes.

"Now pucker up. We're going to put color on those lips. Your favorite shade." Katherine obeyed then snuck a peak in the bedroom mirror. She looked younger than most of the women back at that place and laughed out loud.

"You like it, Mom?"

"You're a good girl." Katherine patted her daughter's hand. "You keep my jewelry safe when your father takes me back to prison. You look nice with gold."

"Don't call Evans House that, Mom. It upsets the boys."

She felt her daughter's distress or something deeper, something like the lost sense of the people around her at that place. "You should lose weight. You'll be happier," she said and patted Carrie's arm. "Momma knows what's right."

Katherine walked on her own into the living room, claimed the chair nearest the door; her favorite place as a hostess, and was surprised to have that memory. While her family talked, she put faces and names on each person present and ignored Louise who stood in the doorway.

They raised a glass to celebrate Thanksgiving. She smiled at Todd; grateful he'd made her whiskey sour strong. She drank it in three long swallows then held her glass out for Todd or Art to take the hint. Todd responded although Art tried to hold him back.

"This will have to last until dinner or Dad will be all over me. Agree, Mom?"

She smiled and nodded at her handsome boy. The party was much better than any at the prison. There were real drinks instead of fruit punch. And she liked being with young people and hearing them talk. The conversation was impossible for her to follow but it moved with brightness around the room. When she finished her second drink she felt brighter as well.

Her senses reeled when they walked into the dining room. They sat her at the foot of the table with Carrie on one side and Todd on the other. The boys sat in the middle chairs with Steve on one side of Art and Rachel, or maybe Louise, on his other side.

The youngest child said grace, a tradition she thought she started. Or maybe her father started it. Around the table hands were folded and heads bowed. She swallowed her wine, and then bowed her own head. Staring between her folded hands, she decided it was Rachel at Art's side. The thought of a ghost at the table was crazy.

She had to rely on Carrie to spoon foods onto her plate and Todd to cut up turkey and butter the rolls. Todd kept her wineglass filled. His wink told her this was a secret. Louise (no, Rachel) would be snippy if anyone got piss-faced. Damn Lutheran.

"How's the Rachel Kelsey Empire growing?" Carrie's husband asked the Rachel/Louise woman. Katherine didn't understand the question, certain her daughter had not married a king.

"Pretty good, Steve. We're almost through with the next book."

Katherine thought their talk was boring. She tickled Todd's hand and winked at him. "Stupid," she said slowly, trying to whisper toward him.

"Mom," Carrie said. "Steve's just being polite."

"Actually I'm interested in what Rachel's up to. Folks at the office ask about my famous sister-in-law and I don't have lots of opportunity to really talk with her."

"If you like her so much, why don't you move in with her?" Katherine quirked her head toward Steve. Everyone looked her way. She smiled, pleased to have their attention.

"Katherine, I don't think that came out quite right," Art said in his hurried voice.

She looked his way, saw his frown. "Oops. That's just what my friends at the prison say. Sorry, he wouldn't leave you… you're prettier," she said patting Carrie's hand. "My pretty girl."

Carrie turned away to talk to the boys. "Rob and Jake, you can go watch television until dessert. Take your plates into the kitchen. I'll get coffee."

Katherine watched as they walked away. She would have liked more wine but the bottles were removed. She moved her wine glass closer to Todd and nudged his arm.

"Too late, Mom. Dad's giving me that look."

She overheard Carrie's husband talking again with Rachel and the word 'sex' floated down the table. She was offended that they would talk about such a thing at her table.

"You two." She waved a hand across the table, struggled for a moment to pull her entire thought together and was pleased to find words so easily. "We haven't used that word at this table," she thumbed her palm against the gold cloth and was momentarily distracted by the fact that someone used the Christmas linens at Thanksgiving, "since Art found my Uncle Nick showing Todd pictures of naked women in the attic."

Carrie, who was pouring coffee into Art's cup, lifted the carafe. Todd inhaled. She noticed both and continued, reaching over to hold Todd's arm. "You remember how Uncle Nick got you drunk on sloe gin?" She sighed, the weight of maternal responsibility heavy on her shoulders. "I was horrified when you asked me questions about ladies' nipples. You must remember?" She looked from Todd to Art then back to Todd.

Art spoke first. "Katherine, that was a long time ago and I'm sure neither of us really remembers everything exactly."

"But I do remember. Isn't that odd that such a thing should come into my mind. I can't even remember the name of the place where I live." She felt alive, in control of her mind and mouth. "Sit down, Carrie. Let your husband pour his own coffee."

"I don't remember any of this stuff," Todd pulled his arm away but she followed his motion. "I think you've got a television movie mixed up with real life."

"The doctor said you'd blank it out. Selective memory." Katherine laughed with her power. "I've got no memory or no good memories. Entirely different things." She laughed again. "It was all so frightening to a little boy, that we were worried you'd turn out queer." She purposefully took aim at the woman she now recognized as Rachel. "Instead, Rachel's a lesbian. It's a gay life, isn't it?"

Listening to Rachel take a deep breath was satisfying. Missy prissy pants head didn't let a minute pass before protesting. "I've been married twenty years to a very real man."

"I saw the way those nurses at the hospital looked at you. Some of them were drooling. That's why I don't want you here. You are an unwelcome distraction."

Katherine paused, struggling to figure out the next amazing thing to say to stay in control of the dinner table. She focused on Rachel, but felt fuzziness as words dissolved. She was tired of this game. She pushed her plates to the side and laid her head on the table, dismissing the family.

Chapter 27

Rachel rose from her chair. Katherine's arm swept a water glass toward lit candles.

"Son of a bitch," Todd exclaimed as he dove for the glass and was doused.

"Let's get her to bed." Her father stood. "She's likely to be dead weight." He placed his napkin on the table. "Come on, son. She's said far worse. Her mind goes to smut when she drinks." He put hands under one arm. "You're paying the price for all that wine you were pouring."

Hefting Katherine from the table took the best of both of them. Rachel sat back down and watched as they cajoled Katherine into moving.

Carrie didn't offer to help. Instead she appeared to be studying Rachel.

"Don't worry, I'm not a lesbian, Carrie. And, even if I was, I wouldn't be interested in my own sister." Under the table, Rachel's hands came together in a tense grip. "For God's sake, just be relieved she didn't have a chance to take out after you before falling into her plate."

"There wouldn't be much for her to talk about." Carrie gathered plates on her side of the table, stacking them for a trip to the kitchen.

"That's true. You were always the sweet baby of the family," Rachel said quietly and enjoyed the shocked face of her sister. Carrie clearly feared that more than one deep secret they shared might be opened.

Steve took the plates from Carrie. "Rach, no need to dig into Carrie. Let's rescue what's left of the day."

They left her alone in the dining room. She examined the table while everyone else picked up the leftovers of the meal. Moments like this, when she pulled at someone's emotional string then regretted the damage, haunted Rachel. She should be better than her mother who cut through the family fabric like well-used shears with little worry about ragged edges and holes left in the wake. In the silent room, Rachel felt her own shame for acting like her mother's daughter.

She carried serving dishes to the kitchen where everyone gathered, each person mixing or pouring an after-dinner drink. Rachel estimated their father could handle about one more stiff mix. Carrie might start crying while finishing the one in hand. Todd was already on edge and might turn cynical or mean. Steve switched to coffee, the designated referee. She returned to the table empty handed.

Her brother-in-law stared out a dark window. Carrie rubbed Todd's hand. Rachel bent her head when she saw the simple gesture, remembering all the times their little sister would offer that sweet comfort when living in this house turned ugly. No more anger remained in her gut just a need to stand up, end the discussion and bring another holiday to its end.

Todd had questions. "Uncle Nick had a great old house with a huge attic. We set up a bowling set there and he always had the time to play when I visited. You didn't tell me if Mom was right."

Their father drained his glass. "I don't know what happened. For a whole summer you were constantly at his place. Then suddenly your mother wanted nothing to do with Nick. It was just like that. She wouldn't talk about why and I didn't push. Raising you kids was her world. I didn't question a lot of things." He raised his glass. "Anyone else need a refresher?"

"You can't just drop it there."

Rachel found it difficult to look at her brother as he spoke. "If anyone hurt one of our kids, Kris and I would stand shoulder to shoulder. Some guy might have been showing me dirty pictures and you didn't punch out his lights?"

"Times were different. How would your life be different if I slugged your uncle?" He shrugged. "Maybe I'll have coffee." Dad left the room.

"You were never there for me." The words were sent like a spear toward Dad's back.

"That's a bit expansive," Rachel said. "It sounds like the folks had an understanding about how to raise us. Dad was hardly absent."

"Rachel, wouldn't you tell David if someone in our family messed with Dylan?"

She tried to not hurt her brother, but she wanted to save her father from more sorrow this day. Looking at Todd's slack, drunken face, she remembered last night and opened up her box of family secrets.

"Todd, do you remember a few years ago when Kris asked me to pick up Mellie from that soccer camp near Milwaukee?"

He nodded. Crossed his arms over his chest.

"Mellie was harassed by one of the counselors, a college guy. One night he waited in the mailroom for her to pick up a package. He was waiting there naked."

Todd's face blanched before a red flush covered his cheeks and bridged across his nose.

"Kris called me because I could get there in an hour. Mellie stayed at our house the rest of the week. She begged Kris to not tell you the full story." She kept her eyes on him alone.

"This is the only thing I'm going to say as a professional. Sometimes a kid can only stand one adult at a time. Sometimes parents make decisions about holding information from each other. Our mother might not have told Dad about Uncle Nick. Or, maybe, it never happened."

"Anything else my wife trusts with you? She got your phone number on speed dial?"

"I was the one who could get to Mellie. Family members help out."

"If you're so good at this family stuff, then why did yours break apart?"

She saw cruelty in his eyes as he controlled the emotional pin.

"You're out of bounds, brother."

Todd partially stood up, stopped as Carrie raised a hand. Her eyes had that wavy look that predicted tears, or maybe too many drinks. God, the place was awash in booze and pain.

"Sit down, Todd. We've got pies to cut," Carrie said with classic Kemper avoidance. "The kids will be disappointed if they don't have dessert."

"Don't you think we've got more important things to do than feed your kids pie?" Todd's tenacity took Rachel by surprise.

"There isn't anything more to talk about." Carrie took command. "We know Rachel's not a lesbian and that Mom protected you from Uncle Nick. So let's try to get Thanksgiving back on track."

Feeling guilty about her own role in tonight's war, Rachel followed Carrie to gather pies and whipping cream. They scattered to corners of the family room with dessert, Carrie sitting with her boys, Todd nursing another drink, Dad turning on the television. Steve settled next to her. She searched for small talk, safe talk.

"Still traveling, Steve?"

"I feel like I know Boston better than Minnesota these days. Might have to become a Patriots fan."

"I'm not sure I understand what keeps you there?"

"Probably one of the biggest product liability cases in the biotech industry. I'm sure you've read about it."

She hadn't associated the case with Steve. "That's not expected to go to court until spring?"

"Right. Carrie's getting tired of a weekend husband."

There was a lull. Rachel looked at her sister who stared without the slightest interest at the television. She wondered where Steve wanted their conversation to go, what he wanted to say about Carrie.

"Do you mind if I ask how David's doing?"

"He's fine. And don't worry about asking. We spend a lot of time together."

"Did I read that he is the finalist for a position with that new University of Minnesota heart clinic?"

"You probably did."

"That's quite an achievement." Steve crushed his paper napkin. "If you're done with your pie, I'd like to see those family pictures downstairs."

She knew Steve didn't care about the pictures, but followed him. With a lawyer's directness he spoke as they reached the bottom steps.

"I'm worried about Carrie and could use some help. She's drinking. If I don't call by the time the kids go to bed, I get the sense she's almost in the bag. The boys tell me things."

Rachel listened to Steve, aware of his litigator prowess, protective of what was left of her sister's trust. She liked him, but he wasn't blood.

"She's my sister, Steve. If you think she drinks too much, you're probably right. All my family drinks too much. Talk with her."

"I hoped you might call her, maybe make as assessment?"

"I don't practice on family, but I can find her the best therapist in the Twin Cities."

"She's already been through a couple. I don't know if that helps."

"Maybe it's time for treatment?"

He shrugged. "Might be the right thing to do, but there's kids to consider."

"Talk with her this weekend." She knew Carrie would deny any problem, probably cry. "Take your family home. Carrie's had it for the day." Walking up the steps, Rachel decided to catch an early flight back to Chicago after her business lunch the next day.

Chapter 28

In the dark bedroom Art nursed the last of a scotch and watched Katherine sleep. Under disappointment about tonight's dinner brewed an old sense of powerlessness. His buddies joked about their wives ruling the family roost in the good-natured way of men. There was give and take in those relationships, something he'd never had in this marriage or in this bedroom. Katherine ruled this roost or walked over anyone who challenged her.

What was left in his glass tasted bitter. He knew by Rachel's announcement that she was leaving early that there was no hope for a Christmas gathering.

He spoke to Katherine in a quiet voice like the nurses recommended when she had surgery, loud enough to sink through Katherine's consciousness, just in case she could hear.

"I love that girl, Katherine. She might be the brightest of our kids. I like the way she thinks, the way she stands up to her problems. I'm sad I let you drive her away." His fingers tightened around the glass. "I thought she was tough enough to make it without my interference and I was right. She's doing mighty fine for herself, but I miss her."

In the dim lamplight, his wife's complexion looked unnatural. Her head lolled to one side. He wished he had been stronger as a man, more involved with defining their family values.

"But your Todd's in a mess. What you did to him tonight was unforgivable. We agreed to leave that Nick stuff buried. You pissed me off tonight, Katherine. We all went down in flames and you led the way." Even if she lived for many years, this would never happen again, he promised himself.

Chapter 29

Carrie scrunched her eyes shut against the weak November morning sun, moved her left foot toward Steve's side of the bed, and found cold sheets. After Thanksgiving's awful family experience she expected him to be busy diverting the boys' attention with wholesome activities.

"I'm taking the boys for breakfast then skating. Sleep in." He kissed the air near her head.

For the moment, Carrie felt the simple security of Steve's love without the poisons of his constant travel or her drinking. They would skate and go to movies and make family meals for the few days he was home. The boys would relax.

She accepted that her drinking contributed to the tension at her parents' house since Rachel arrived. After a shower and coffee, Carrie cleaned out all her hidden booze – scotch from her file cabinet, airline bottles in a shoebox and purses, more in her coat pockets. She decided to vaccinate her home against the Kemper family disease for the holiday season, hoped the cure would hold throughout winter.

Those good intentions followed Steve out the door Sunday night. She substituted a little pink sleeping pill for a stiff drink as she soaked in the tub before bed. Her mind quieted, her limbs became calm. Feeling bleary, she dried herself, pulled on a nightshirt and climbed into bed. Her sleep was heavy and dreamless.

Some days the sleeping pills slowed her morning. With the museum's Silver event barely two weeks away, she pushed herself to work full days.

Nothing was incomplete when she arrived ahead of Brian at a trendy downtown Minneapolis lunch place. From their favorite table, Carrie watched as fashionable, svelte women walked through the restaurant. She knew how they felt, how each pair of eyes directed their way confirmed those feelings. Holding her shoulders tall and wondering why her stomach wouldn't flatten on command, Carrie felt like last year's stretched-out sweater.

Brian entered the restaurant with the kind of self-assurance she wanted back. "Your ex-wife predicted you'd age well," she said as he kissed her cheek. Other women, even a few men, watched him settle in his chair. She let herself enjoy his hand on hers, his intimate smile. "You're in a good mood. Someone new in your life?"

"Yes there is. He was in the employment practice group at Steve's firm. Jeff Gordon."

"I know Jeff. He contributed $10,000 to the Museum in memory of his niece."

"That is exactly why I need you back, Carrie. You can walk up to any contributor and make them feel their gift was special." His eyes took in everything about her. "That sweater is a good color on you. But you can't camouflage shadows like those under your eyes." Brian never lied to her. "I thought you'd look more rested after a few weeks away. Lots going on in the family?"

"The usual. My mother's slipping. Steve's still in Boston and the boys are deep in hockey. But I earned these shadows by putting in a lot of hours on the Silver Banquet."

He ignored her final words. "Planning anything for Christmas?"

Looking for distraction, she picked up a menu. "Not much. A quiet year."

"Bring your boys to my place. Steve and Jeff can talk business. You and I will hang out in the kitchen. We're doing a big Christmas buffet mid-afternoon. My sister and her kids are coming. A completely family-friendly holiday."

"You're sweet, but I'm hosting my brother and his family for brunch and Steve always makes a fuss if we have to leave the house on Christmas."

"How's Art?"

"Pretty unhappy. Thanksgiving wasn't a success." She ducked down to take papers from her tote bag. "Maybe we should start going through the banquet plans?"

"There's no hurry. I know you've got everything ready and we can go over that top donor list in five minutes. I told you about Jeff, now I want to know about you. Not your parents or charming husband or little jock kids."

"You don't need to worry about me, Brian. As long as we've known each other, you know the holidays can be my Waterloo." She tried a smile.

"Are you seeing the shrink or are hockey games claiming priority?"

"That's not fair, Brian. Being with the boys is good distraction."

He fiddled with a spoon, tapped it against the back of the menu. She watched his hands. "As a friend, not your boss, I'm going to ask the big question. Are you drinking?"

"Only water and too much diet cola." She pulled out her beautiful woman smile and slipped into a flirty voice. "Why do you ask? Are my hands twitching?"

"We go way back, girl, so I'll be honest. You're face is puffy and there's an ugly spot on your cashmere. I think it was hard to pull your-self together for lunch."

"Back down. I've been pulling all-nighters to catch up on the fund-raiser. I've not had a drink since Thanksgiving." Her eye twitched. "That's all I'll say."

"OK, let's switch subjects and talk about the big event." Brian painted his words with over-inflated pleasure. "I'm wearing the Armani tux with a glorious silver cummerbund made by that quilter in Stillwater. What do you have planned?"

"Going shopping right after we finish."

"Then let's get to work so you can hit the stores." He waved for the waiter and put on his reader glasses. "I'd suggest midnight blue. It always compliments your hair."

* * *

The carefully chosen silver and deep blue gown Carrie bought that afternoon hung untouched in its bag the morning after the Silver Banquet. Its shadowy outline puzzled her when a ringing telephone awoke her.

"So how was the dinner? I hope my flowers reminded you that I wanted to be there."

Steve's cheerful voice pissed her off.

"They're in the refrigerator. I didn't open the box."

"Come on, Carrie. I couldn't do anything about the judge's decision to hold a pretrial meeting yesterday."

"I didn't go, Steve. Jake got into a fight at hockey that meant the ER for stitches. His coach called just as I got out of the shower. When we got back to the house, I heard Rob throwing up in the downstairs bathroom. He was burning with fever."

"What about the babysitter?"

"There wasn't a babysitter. Jake was going to spend the night with the Greggs. Robbie was supposed to be at a sleepover."

"Why didn't you try your dad or Kris?"

"It's done, Steve." She caught sight of herself and the bottle of Johnny Walker in a mirror. She looked bad, smelled booze on the sheets and had to pee. "You woke me and I'm not really up for talking. Why don't you call later and talk to the boys?"

Three weeks and two days wiped out by one night with Johnny. A hangover, two needy kids and her frustration spelled a day from hell. That feeling stretched through ten days of shopping, baking and whatever else was needed to deliver a wonderful Christmas. Each morning she fortified herself with cold vodka-laced orange juice and an antidepressant or two before waking the boys. Steve stayed additional days in Boston, arriving home on the twenty-third ready to party.

Christmas morning, sipping orange juice, Carrie surveyed the house and felt relief that the presents were right, the decorations festive and all the foods turned out well. When the doorbell rang, she and Steve walked to the foyer holding hands. Holiday spirit trumped fatigue.

"Hello, Sis." Todd gave her a listless smooch. She extended her arms. He stepped away.

Cat, his youngest child, took the hug. "Merry Christmas, Aunt Carrie. We visited Grandma."

"Sorry, we're a little late." Kris said as she followed the kids. "Merry Christmas, Carrie."

They hugged. Her sister-in-law's shoulders told a story anything but merry. "Merry Christmas, Kris." She held on a bit longer. "Everything is ready and we have plenty of time before you have to leave." Carrie stepped back, spoke just to Kris. "You've lost some weight."

Kris shrugged and did a brave smile. Carrie understood the look.

"Thanks for adjusting your plans for us, Carrie. We have to leave around one thirty." Kris rambled. "Christmas dinner will be crazy at my brother's. Then all the grandkids are going to bunk down in their family room. By this time tomorrow I'll have three very crabby kids."

"I don't understand why Todd's not going along? He loves your family celebrations."

Kris might not have heard the question as she turned away to grab tissue from her purse. Carrie smiled at Steve who was mixing a mimosa for Todd. Her husband wore his silly red cardigan sweater and a Christmas tie loosened at the neck.

He brought a glass to her. "Carrie's doing virgin this morning. She tells me her antihistamines are playing havoc with alcohol."

She kept her smile in place feeling like the fat kid offered carrots instead of chocolate. "The boys wouldn't be very happy if I was dozing off while we play family games this afternoon. It's hard enough for me to have any credibility with a controller unit."

Kris turned her head and lowered her voice. "I hate when Todd's feeling rotten and drinks. He's getting more like your mother." The kids laughed in the other room as Mellie demonstrated some crazy dance step. "Are you giving up drinking?"

"Don't ask that, Kris, not on Christmas." Carrie felt the fake grin might fall off her face.

"Let's have a toast," Todd said walking into the kitchen. Now he gave her a small hug. "Merry Christmas, to those who mean the most to me in the world." He raised his glass. "My beautiful wife, my children, my lovely sister and her family."

"So, bro, why aren't you going to Chicago?"

"It was a rather spontaneous decision and we couldn't arrange dog boarding."

"Go. We'll take the dogs for a few days. Make Kris happy." She expected Kris to say something and saw the truth in her sister-in-law's blank face.

"Aunt Carrie, did you make peanut butter fudge?" Todd's youngest daughter asked in the sweetest way as the group ate brunch. Evergreen boughs twined with plaid ribbon and gold string decorated the table. Candlelight added to the brightness of the winter morning.

"I have a box of peanut butter fudge on the counter with your name on it, Cat, along with a few caramels and some devil's food candy." The child was stunningly beautiful with a tomboyish personality not unlike Rachel. Ironic now that the child's nature had developed that Todd named his youngest a version of their mother's name. Cat's personality made her a favorite of everyone, except her father and her grandmother.

"You're going to get fat, Ms. Cat," Mellie taunted. "You'll have to wear elastic waist pants like Grandma Katherine."

Cat giggled. "I'm too young to worry about that stuff. And you sound like Grandma."

"Stop it. I don't want to hear another mean word out of you about your grandmother." Todd shook the child's shoulder. "No disrespect for Grandma in front of me. Shame on you."

Carrie saw Steve's shoulders tighten as the scolding continued. Kris looked annoyed, but stayed quiet. The kids were uncomfortable. Cat's lips trembled.

Mellie interrupted. "We didn't mean anything, Dad. I'm the one who started the joke."

"Don't worry, honey." Kris reached across to pat Mellie's hand, did not touch Cat. She turned the conversation back to the kids, asking them about plans for their school break.

Cat stayed quiet, Todd's arm draped around the back of her chair. Carrie sensed the child's wariness. Steve teased the boys about playing video games all day and night so they'd go back to school with their eyes popping out of their heads. Cat, the most aggressive video game player of the cousins, seemed reluctant to join the laughter.

Todd poured more champagne. He offered Cat a sip. She shook her head. "Come on, Cat, don't stew. It's Christmas." He waved the glass in front of the child. "Last night you were begging for a little taste."

"Don't let him talk you into it, sweetie," Carrie said. "Champagne's a hard habit to break. You'll have to find a rich husband to keep you supplied." She tried for the right joke to stop this replay of scenes from their own childhood.

"My sister, the one who hid a glass of vodka in our parents' china hutch, should know."

"That's enough, Todd." Steve put his napkin on the table. "As master of this suburban castle, I say Cat and Jake will help clear the table. Everyone else downstairs to sort presents."

Kris watched Todd trot down the stairs. "Would you mind giving him a ride home later? I'd feel better driving to the airport."

"No problem. Do you mind if I keep this one here?" Carrie swooped down on Cat, gently tickled her arm. "How about spending an overnight with us this vacation? Jake would like that, right?" Her son yelled his approval. "Would that be all right with you, Ms. Cat?"

Her sister-in-law's eyes were too sad for Christmas. "Maybe I should tickle your mom, too?" Carrie dragged Cat in one arm to Kris' side and extended an arm. "I'm so envious of all the fun you'll have with your Chicago cousins. I have half a mind to hide in your luggage."

"Please come, Aunt Carrie. I'll share my fudge."

"There is one big guy and two young guys who would be upset." She twirled Cat away, but kept an arm around Kris and spoke quietly. "Things are worse than I thought, huh?"

"Like you said earlier. Not on Christmas."

"Call if you'd like. You're important to us." Cat came back for another twirl. "Forget the table. Let's get to the presents."

She watched her brother and came to conclude that he was a dick head. He bullied his son into getting another beer, made caustic comments when Steve suggested switching to soft drinks.

"Better be nice to Steve. He's giving you a ride home later," Kris announced. All eyes lifted from shredded wrapping paper and boxes.

"It's Christmas and I want to drive my own family to the airport." Todd looked for support. "I don't need a sober cab." His wife ignored him as she gathered their kids.

Carrie piled the kids' gifts on a bench in the hallway as his family put on coats. "You can leave your gifts here. I'll make sure Uncle Steve doesn't play with anything."

"Kris, can we talk?" He held his voice steady. "Come on, just a moment." He took her limp hand to lead her a few steps away. Carrie heard every word. "I just realized I was a complete horse's ass this morning. Change your reservations to tomorrow. I really want to talk, make it up to all of you."

"Todd, you're drunk." Kris stepped back, all calm and withdrawn. "Apologize to Carrie and Steve. Now I'm taking the kids where the big holiday uncertainty is deciding between roast beef or ham or both—not who's going to have their guts cut open at the table."

In the hall Cat stood holding her box of candy. Around her the other kids talked about video football. Todd's daughter waited, all childish beauty as well as painful stillness.

"I'm sorry, Kris." He turned his wife to look at Cat's image in a mirror above the fireplace. "I don't want her to grow up looking that sad. Please."

"How could you sit there pushing champagne on a child who's scared to death of adults drinking? Don't tell me you don't want her to look sad. Katherine may have trained you to take crap and show a happy face, but our kids are growing up with more honesty."

He stood too close. The kids could hear everything. "You'll be back in two days. Maybe the kids can stay with Carrie and we'll spend a night somewhere?"

"Can your mother live without you for a couple of days?"

"I'll put in a few extra visits while you're gone so she'll be tired of seeing me."

Everyone heard Kris inhale quickly. Carrie couldn't think of a distraction to stop the scene.

"I didn't want to say this today," Kris almost whispered, "but if your new place is ready, it might be better if you've moved."

"Come on, Kris. It's Christmas." Her brother's bravado evaporated. "Everything looks hopeful on Christmas."

He stepped aside to let her gather his children. Mellie offered him her arms and a kiss. Their son agreed to a quick hug. He held onto Cat longer than she expected. Bending over he whispered, "Love you, Ms. Cat. You're very important to me."

"Sorry, Dad. Your breath's kind of stinky." She pulled away. "Watch the Christmas movies tonight. Promise, Dad. You can manage the microwave popcorn on your own." The child's distress infected Carrie. "Don't forget to feed my hamster. Please?"

"I promise." He crossed his heart like drunks everywhere do when scared.

They left with a chorus of "We Wish You a Merry Christmas".

"Coffee?" Steve clapped him on the shoulder. "There's a fresh pot brewing."

"I'll have coffee and read the paper. You can take me home whenever you want."

"You're welcome to join us when we visit Katherine or we can drop you off on the way," Carrie said and offered cookies. There was no nice way to ask him to take his drinking home.

He grabbed two decorated angels. "How do you think Dad's doing, Carrie?"

"Not great. We invited him over this evening for dinner, but he's going to the neighbors. Something about a bunch of folks getting together to play cards. Sounds odd for a holiday, but whatever. Steve thinks it's healthy for Dad to get out socially. Right, hon?"

Steve's mouth hung open just slightly, his head tilted back into the chair's cushion—a guy sitting in his own living room with the sports section open on his lap, a few crumbs of some snack on his chest, just giving in to the quiet.

Todd steered her away from enjoying her family's peace. "Notice how things keep disappearing from Mom's room? The family pictures, those silly little china statues, her goofy glass angel are all gone. The place is beginning to look like a pilfered ghetto studio."

"I've got a lot of the stuff downstairs." She saw the fact challenged what he wanted to believe. "After she threw a few things on the floor and cut herself, the staff cleared her room."

"Are they keeping her on her meds?"

"I ran into Dr. Wagner recently. He said she's continuing to have mini-strokes. Some day the big one will strike." Odd how she could talk about this so unemotionally on this messy holiday.

"He wants to make Dad feel better about Evans House."

"I've come to agree with them. You'd be happier if you pulled away from this fight." Steve would never respond to a suggestion by rolling his eyes or blowing air through his nose as her brother did on Christmas in her home.

"I'm not sticking my nose into anything, Todd, but I do hope you and Kris can get through this rough spot. Just a sisterly suggestion that you watch the facial signs of your displeasure. The small things make a huge difference. Whatever Steve and I can do, please call."

"People feel they can say all kinds of things on holidays, sis. I'm sure Kris will tell you whatever you want to know. But I prefer to keep my relations with my wife private."

He got up and stretched. "I'm going to bother my nephews. Let me know when you're ready to leave. As usual, great food, sister."

Chapter 30

Todd waved farewell to Carrie's family. On the shittiest Christmas day of his life, his sister offered food and disapproval. Carrie without booze was about as much fun as Rachel.

His damn pockets produced no keys and Todd remembered leaving his on the kitchen desk. He turned from the front walk to activate the garage door opener. As it went up, he faced a darkened cavern. In spite of Kris' badgering, he had not replaced burnt out light bulbs.

"Damn it." He stumbled over kids' clutter. Thankfully someone had forgotten to lock the inside door. The smells of sleeping dogs and yesterday's dinner welcomed him home.

Without the sounds of his family, their house felt crazy big. The liquor cabinet held enough Scotch to fight his loneliness. He grabbed a tumbler, dropped in some ice and poured. Dogs circled him for food or attention as he drank a first installment of attitude adjustment.

Here and there he flipped on lights, stopping in the living room where the Christmas tree glowed in the early evening darkness thanks to Kris and her habit of setting timers. He'd found her crying there a few days ago and kept walking.

While draping his coat over the newel post, a card addressed "Dad" caught his eye. Putting his glass down, he ripped apart a Santa sticker.

"Daddy, We'll be thinking about you. Promise. Don't be lonely. Kiss the dogs good night. We left a treat in your room! Love, Mellie and Cat. XXXOOOO"

He carried the card to the wet bar to top off his drink before letting in the dogs. They carried in cold air and high spirits. For a full minute, Todd stood with the door wide open, remembering when the kids were little and he'd wait here for Kris to arrive home from daycare. The dogs would run back and forth. Small faces looked out the car windows and this house waited to be put in play. A handful of years ago. Years he wanted back.

In one hand he held his scotch. His other hand began to crush the girls' card as anger at Kris grew. She would not deny him his fatherhood. He closed the front door, straightened the card then started up the stairs to the guest room, which his kids now called Dad's Room.

His legs moved like a child's, eager to find a treat, even while his heart accepted that his daughters were caring for him. That acceptance diminished him in the house where he had once been king. He slurped at the scotch and moved; now holding to the stair railing for the last steps.

The girls left a timer on the small dress lamp. Its glow made the guest room look inviting. They had made up his bed, blankets smoothed and pillows plumped. A small pile of wrapped packages stood on the coverlet protected by Cat's favorite stuffed animals. He pushed the dogs out of the room, shut the door. Booze and fatigue blurred everything as he sat on the bed's edge.

He unwrapped the first package, a box of chocolate covered raisins, the kind he insisted they buy at the movies. Cat covered the outside with an assortment of stamped images of stars, dragons and Christmas trees. A bag of his favorite popcorn mix filled the largest box. The stupid Christmas video he rented each year was the flat package. His girls had no idea watching the video alone would be punishment. A picture of three kids in their pajamas eating popcorn and hamming it up for the camera stole his breath when he opened the last gift.

"See, you can't get away from us!" proclaimed a note in Mellie's extra round writing. He brought the paper to his face to sniff for scented ink. Just the slightest smell of bubble gum slapped his nose. He came unglued, slid to the floor, held his head between his hands.

His mother would challenge him to remember who got the better deal at the altar. There were always winners and losers, those who were in power and those who carried the garbage in his mother's book of life. Mom would call him a loser if she saw him now. What he didn't know at this moment was what Mom would tell him to do to change his life.

The clock radio turned on playing Christmas music. Six o'clock. Somewhere he heard the faint tones of his cell phone and dashed like a crazy man down the stairs. "One call missed," the message pad said. He worked through to locate the number originating the call. Kris's cell phone. Not caring who answered, he dialed. When her message came on, he mumbled "Missing the kids" and disconnected.

A dish of his favorite beef stew with reheating directions surprised him in the frig. Next to the stew was a small piece of expensive aged cheddar with a half bottle of a good cabernet sauvignon decorated with a green ribbon. The love he read in the meal left by Kris bolstered his spirits, indicated she was still in the game with him, implied there would be better Christmases to come. He decided to shower, put on fresh clothes, visit his mother then have a late dinner.

Evans House lobby Christmas tree looked inviting, even with the small white fence that surrounded the Nativity set and other holiday figures. For the first time Todd considered that the fence was there to protect the decorations. He heard singing from the music room and saw his mother sitting near the door, her hands keeping time.

"Hey, Mom, you're wearing a new Christmas sweater." He gave her a kiss on the cheek. She turned a blank face his way.

"I don't welcome strange men kissing me." She crooked her head to one side. "I should know you. You're part of my family?"

When Mom pulled the bad memory act with Rachel, it was amusing. Squatting down next to her chair, he felt hurt. "It's Todd, Mom. Remember your favorite kid?"

Mom rested back against the chair and seemed to chew her tongue as she looked at his face. "My son's a young man off visiting some girl that he wants to marry. Name like Santa."

"Kris. My girl is Kris." His knees tired. "Want to take a walk and look at the tree?"

"I don't want to miss cookies. We're leaving cookies and tomato juice for Santa."

"Not tonight, Mom. Remember Kris and I brought the kids this morning to open gifts?"

"I'm really tired. No naps, no crafts, no story time, just visitors, visitors, visitors. But Art says I have to stay here. My chair is here." Her voice sunk lower and lower. "I have to stay here 'cause the chair is here. I can't go home. No place to sit there." She rubbed her chin.

"You seem happy here, Mom. People to sing with, better cooking than Dad's, staff that have to come when you call." Todd wanted a logical response.

"I like it when I remember the words. Piano makes me remember the words. I can sing everything." She began warbling "Away in a Manger" but stopped when confusion took over. "I need the piano."

"I'll sing with you, Mom." He took her hand. "Away in a manger, no crib for his bed."

She shook her head from side to side and tapped a beat with her toes. He continued to sing, waiting for her to join in. On the second verse he stumbled around, unsure of the words.

"My son sang that song in the third grade church program. He was a shepherd. I used an old sheet to make the costume and he was so happy. A good little shepherd boy." Again her eyes were distant. Her lips stopped, partially opened. He helped her walk back to her room.

It was as if a greedy monster reached into Todd's chest and twisted his heart into a mass of pulp. The day had really been too much. He wanted his mother to offer advice, his wife to stay in their marriage until he could sort all this out. He handed Mom over to an aide, walked away. On impulse he turned on his Blackberry and searched airline websites for Chicago flights. In the parking lot he called Carrie. "I'm grabbing the 8:15 to O'Hare. Will you take care of the dogs?"

"Hello to you, Todd. Does Kris know you're coming?"

"Merry Christmas, Carrie. I'll be home tomorrow night." Todd
hung up.

Chapter 31

"It's cool that we had a normal Christmas," Dylan said after David left. White lights twinkled in evergreen boughs lining the mantle. "It was great to be really together. What will we do next year? Will you and I have to go to the Kempers?"

"We won't spend it with my family." She made a goofy face. "Let's put off talking about all this stuff until tomorrow. No serious topics during what's left of Christmas. Right now I have to call Grandma Kemper. Do you want to talk to her?" They both knew she was joking.

"I want to bake a frozen pizza and watch a movie. If you want to watch with me that would be good." Dylan and dog sprinted to the kitchen.

"Wait until I'm done with this call then we'll talk about the pizza." She moved to her office, waited for Evans House to connect.

"Happy holidays. Evans House."

"This is Rachel Kelsey, I'm calling to speak with my mother, Katherine Kemper."

"You just missed her, Dr. Kelsey. Lot of our residents went to bed early. Is this an emergency?"

Rachel wondered what might constitute an emergency conversation with any of Evans House's residents. "No, I just wanted to say Merry Christmas. Did she have visitors today?"

"I saw your brother leave this evening, your sister and her family were here and your father spend most of the afternoon. She had a busy day."

"Thanks for remembering all that. I hope you had time to enjoy your holiday as well," Rachel said, always polite to these special caretakers.

"I had a nice day with the family, Dr. Kelsey. You're kind to ask."

Hanging up, Rachel held onto the well-being of the last thirty-six hours. She checked for voice mails and listened to well wishes from David's mother and a long rambling message from Carrie about Kris taking Todd's children to Chicago. Their father seemed oblivious to Todd's situation during a phone call that morning. She erased the messages.

"Is it OK if I make a pizza?" Dylan and Weezer stood in the doorway of her office.

"You put in a good pizza then let's take Weezer for a twenty minute walk. He's been cooped up today." Her son scowled. "Come on, humor me. It's Christmas."

Chicago's damp cold air promised new snow. They headed out ten minutes then turned back. She wondered if the Twin Cities could feel as free as Chicago with her family in the same radar circle. With effort, she shelved the whole Kemper crew to enjoy her son and dog and the quiet of Christmas night.

They squabbled about who ran faster while they kicked off shoes and hung up coats. She loved the bright pink of his still young thirteen-year-old face, thinking how little time remained before he started shaving. He pushed her slippers out from under his shoes and handed her the old hoodie sweatshirt she frequently wore around their drafty old house.

"Mom, are we going to buy another house like this or a loft like Dad's?"

"Living right downtown isn't my thing. You'll help pick out our next place. I'm thinking Minneapolis is the better choice, maybe near one of the lakes. I saw a few houses with yards."

He slapped paper plates on the counter. She replaced them with stoneware. "It's Christmas. We'll eat on the real thing." Dylan dug in the fridge for drinks, held one up for her approval. She nodded. "Instead of a movie, how about I pull out the old videos and we look at how cute you were and how funny Dad and I looked?"

Before he could answer, her cell phone played its tones in the front hall.

"I'll be right back, it might be Grandpa." She rushed to answer. "Hello, this is Rachel."

"Todd's in Chicago." Kris' rage squashed Rachel's calm. "He drove here from the airport, but I made him leave. He kept saying all these crazy things about wanting me to leave my family. He's been drinking. I'm afraid he might be on his way to your place."

The entire state of Wisconsin failed to buffer Rachel's world from Kemper hysteria. She took a deep breath, wondering if she really was willing to deal with Kris.

"Are the kids all right?" was what she chose to ask.

"They're all in the basement watching a movie and didn't see him."

"Then go back to your family. I don't know if Todd will be able to find me, but if he does I'll deal with him. If he comes back to your brother's, call the police."

"On Christmas?" Her sister-in-law whined. "I don't think I could do that to Todd."

The doorbell sounded. Weezer ran through the hall to the front door followed by Dylan holding out the house phone.

"It's Dad. Uncle Todd is at his place."

"The doorbell's ringing, Kris, and David's on the other line. I'll call you back in a few minutes." Rachel hung up the phone. "Tell your Dad to hold on a minute." The doorbell rang again. Now that she knew it wasn't Todd at the step, she found the sound ominous. She looked out the small door window at a suburban police officer.

"Tell Dad to definitely stay on the line," she said over her shoulder while opening the door. "Merry Christmas, officer. Can I help you?"

"Sorry if I frightened you. Are you Dr. Rachel Kelsey?"

"I am, Officer. Is there a problem?"

He stepped aside and pointed to his squad car. "We have a little girl in the back who says she's your niece."

Rachel stepped out and saw Cat's white face in the squad window.

"It's Cat. My niece, Catherine Kemper. We call her Cat. Tell me where you found her?"

"She found us. Wandered into the precinct and said she was being held in the area by a non-custodial parent. Wouldn't give us any information except your name and general address. Anything you know would be helpful."

"Let me get my shoes on. Can I bring her in?"

"How about telling us what's going on then we'll make that determination."

"You'd have to understand my family. Holidays are never good. Her parents, who live in Minnesota, are separating. It's been very civil from what I know. My sister-in-law is in the Chicago area spending a few days with a brother's family. I don't know his first name and his last name is Smith and they live in a northern suburb. I know that's not that helpful."

Rachel took a deep breath. "My sister-in-law just called to tell me my brother flew in uninvited from the Twin Cities. Cat might have overheard her parents disagreeing."

Clinical training helped Rachel regain her emotional center. She took another breath and stood perfectly still as the officer looked her over. Dylan stayed close behind, the dog whimpered behind the living room doors.

"I'm a psychologist, Officer. I specialize in working with families. Cat's my brother's youngest child. She'll be safe with us. Dylan, come here?" Rachel reached out to put her arm around her son's waist and drew him toward the door. His face looked pale.

"If it's possible, I think it would help both the kids if we could bring Cat inside?"

The officer shifted his weight before answering. Rachel sensed softening in the big guy. "I'll need some kind of ID. Usually we'd call in Family Services, but it's Christmas and I recognized your name. My wife's a big fan."

Her purse hung on a coat tree behind the door. Knowing police were always concerned about weapons, she told him what she was doing with each step and offered the officer her purse. "My driver's license is in the small blue wallet."

"I'm appreciative. My partner just waved from the car that he got a positive ID on your car plates. What can you tell me about that little girl to make sure she's your relative?"

Rachel realized how little she knew about her nieces and nephews as she searched for a few facts. "Her birthday is in May. She has a sister named Melanie. Her parents are Kris and Todd Kemper. They live in Lake Elmo, Minnesota. She has green eyes like my son and a birth mark on her lower arm like mine." Rachel pulled up her sweater sleeve to show the officer.

"Will you sign to accept responsibility for your niece?" He extended a notebook and she read through the form. It seemed clear cut.

"Of course."

"We'll need one of her parents to call us within twenty-four hours and come down to the precinct to confirm that the child has been returned to a custodial parent. If they fail to do so, we could issue a warrant to place that young lady in a foster home until matters are resolved. Here's my card."

"Thank you." She stepped into slippers and opened the storm door. "Let me come with you. She must be frightened out of her mind."

"She was quite calm at the precinct, but things got a bit out of her control. I take it she's not used to big cities?"

"No, Lake Elmo is a very quiet St. Paul suburb."

They walked down the stairs. Rachel absorbed the crying energy of her niece as the child propelled out of the squad. Above Cat's head, Rachel smiled at the officers.

"Officer Rameriz, you've been very helpful."

He spoke to Cat before leaving. "Young lady, the first thing you do is call your mother. I'll expect a phone call from her, or your aunt will be in hot water. The next thing I say you must listen to very carefully. Running away can land you in very big trouble. You could be put in jail or worse. Make a plan with your aunt, she's a smart lady, and do not do this again."

"I won't," Cat whispered then started crying again. "I'm sorry."

"Merry Christmas," Officer Rameriz put his hand on her head and extended his other hand to Rachel, "to all of you. I hope everything works out. We'll need to hear from the young lady's parents." He walked away.

Rachel began dicing apart 'everything' as she closed the door with Cat clinging tight. Dylan extended the phone, the dog managed to push his way out of the living room.

"Tell your Dad I'll call back." She moved toward the living room, skirting the dog and sliding Cat at her side. "Let's take off your coat then we have to call your mom and tell her you're safe. She must be worried out of her mind."

"She doesn't know I'm gone. I got the little bedroom by myself. The big kids all are sleeping down in the basement but they wouldn't let me be there 'cause they wanted to watch a PG-13 movie." Cat took a shallow breath. "I wish we were at home."

"Your Mom only has an hour to call the precinct so can you tell me quickly what's going on?" Rachel eased off the child's coat, noted her festive Christmas pajamas. She kept her arms around Cat, feeling the child slightly shaking. "New jammies?"

"Mom always gets us new Christmas jamas. She wouldn't let us wear them last night so we didn't get to take a jama picture with Daddy." Cat wiped her eyes then nose on one sleeve. "He was crying on the front porch and she just yelled at him."

Dylan came back in with the phone. "Dad's still holding."

"Cat, can you go with Dylan and get some tissue for your nose? You can have a slice of pizza. I need to talk with Dylan's father."

The child shook her head quickly, moved closer. Rachel rubbed her back softly then gave a tiny push toward Dylan. "Would you like to stay here tonight?"

The child nodded quickly. Dylan put his arm around Cat's shoulders as they walked to the kitchen, a display of empathy that pleased Rachel. They should have had more children. Dylan didn't deserve to be an only.

Taking a breath, she brought the phone to her face. "Did Dylan bring you up to speed on the last ten minutes?"

"It's taken almost two decades, but your family's craziness found its way to Chicago. Todd might be at your front door in about ten minutes. He remembered visiting us at this address ten years ago. Fortunately I wasn't at the hospital."

"I'm not sure if I can multi-process the needs of our kid, who is acting like a wonderful grown up guy by the way, an upset little girl who witnessed something nasty between her parents AND my drunk brother." She took a breath. "First time a police officer came to the front door. Hell of an ending to a very nice Christmas."

"Could rank right up there in the Kemper family holiday best." They laughed together. "Let me tell you about Todd. He came here after Kris sent him away. I didn't smell any booze, but it was obvious he had been drinking. What he said was that he was looking for a place to spend Christmas night." David paused. I offered him the sleeper sofa, but that didn't seem to be what he wanted. I gave him your cell number. Then as he left, he pulled a piece of paper from his pocket with your address."

She listened to David, thinking of last Christmas when the two of them were barely able to be together under the same roof. Next year they'd be in a different city, maybe apart.

"Want me to come over, Rach?" David's voice brought her back to the present. "I'm only off site on call. Maybe I could distract the kids. And if your brother shows up, I don't want you to deal with him. I know you're the psych, but I'm a man and I know a bit about what he's feeling."

"You're nothing like my brother." She sighed, thinking of the long night ahead. "If Todd shows up I'll call. If he doesn't show up, I'll call you to help track him down. Hopefully Kris will let us care for Cat tonight."

"Who'll take care of you?"

She smiled as emotional cookies crumbled. This townhouse was supposed to be her fortress against the Kempers, a safe zone to raise Dylan. "I love you, David. Got to pay attention to the kids now."

"Remember the rules of a good clinician. Don't get in the middle of a domestic."

The same thought ran through her head along with a sinking sense that she was already involved with vulnerable kids at her side. She really didn't think Todd would turn violent, but had to assume he was working on a thin emotional thread to hop a plane on Christmas night.

"I promise to keep an even head. And I'll call if anything changes. Merry end of Christmas."

The kids were doing well. Cat sat snug against Dylan as they watched an animated video about a fish looking for its mother. Weezer lay next to the little girl and she ruffled his fur with one hand in an absent-minded comforting motion.

"Sorry to interrupt. Put the movie on hold, Dylan, and you two can pick it up later. I've got to call your mother, Cat, and she'll want to talk to you."

Cat straightened up. "I don't know where my uncle lives."

"I have her cell number."

The child seemed reluctant, almost whimpered.

Pushing Weezer from the couch, Rachel wrapped a throw around Cat and sat down on the sofa.

"You know you're always welcome to call me and we'll always have a place for you to come if you've got a problem, Cat. That's what family does. But I can't do something that's going to make your parents suffer. So, think hard about that as I dial."

The house was almost quiet. Rachel moved to her home office and picked up the phone.

Cat was right. No one had missed her. The adults were concerned about dealing with Todd and assumed Cat was sleeping. Rachel accepted her sister-in-law's rising hysteria, trying to sort out what Kris wanted to have happen. They agreed Cat would stay in the city.

Rachel remembered David's late night visits after he moved out of the house. He'd talk and talk about all the reasons for her to forgive his affair until she asked him to leave. It had been a hell of a time to learn how deep Katherine's seeds of insecurity were planted. David had proven himself to be a bad guy and Katherine taught her offspring to destroy any enemy.

She called Todd and left a message.

"Todd, it's Rachel around eleven Christmas night. We're all concerned about you. Please give me a call. Here's my cell phone number and my house number. Call at any time. I know you have my address and you're welcome to come here."

Then she dialed David and gave him a blow by blow.

"Todd's got your mother's gift for the dramatic." A Christmas jazz song played low in the background. "Always wondered if Todd or Carrie would become more like her."

"I better get the kids tucked in and brew some strong coffee. Can't face waking from a deep sleep to deal with Todd."

Dylan and Cat went upstairs for bed without protest. She washed Cat's face, brushed her hair and resurrected one of Dylan's old stuffed animals before tucking the child into the guest room bed. The familiar routine brought gentleness to the evening. She pulled the bedroom door part way shut before checking in on Dylan. A bedside light showed an empty room.

Her son waited in the living room in comfortable old athletic clothes, standing long and lean like his father. "I'm waiting with you, Mom," he said. "If Cat's Dad shows here and is messed up, I don't want you to be alone."

Rachel produced a smile, kept her empty arms quiet. "Dylan, you're a great guy."

Maybe he noticed she used 'guy' not 'boy' in her response, or maybe he crossed some maturity border while she spent time with Cat. She noticed his shoulders stay strong as he picked up a book, his iPod and blanket.

"I'll just hang out here. What are you going to do?"

"Make coffee then finish holiday cards for Julie. Agents are worse than mothers about hounding you to get things done." Turning toward the kitchen, she asked if he wanted anything.

"Maybe a Mountain Dew so I don't fall asleep. Not that I'm tired."

The first hour of their watch went quickly. She tried Todd's phone again around one in the morning. She jumped when her cell phone trilled.

"It's Kris. Have you heard from Todd?"

"No. All is quiet here."

"How's Cat? Did she tell you that Todd kind of took her apart at Carrie's brunch? He's hard on her, Rachel, and she adores him."

"We didn't talk much. She spent most of the evening with Dylan and went to bed about midnight. No problems."

Holidays gone wrong, family in a mess, emotional overload had chipped the calm Kris into the brittle and frantic woman calling her sister-in-law for false assurance. "I'm worried about him, Rach. We weren't very hospitable when he showed up here. I know he might have been drunk, but he was crying." Kris choked up. "We were drinking too, and I wanted him to feel as lonely as I feel all those nights and weekends he spends with your mother. I wouldn't even let him see the kids. What kind of jerk slams the door in the face of her kids' father on Christmas night?"

Rachel thought Kris' self-assessment accurate. "It sounds like you've had a long, rough day. Why don't you take a warm shower, a cup of tea, and go to bed. Cat is safe." She focused conversation on her niece. "Cat can stay here as long as that works. Dylan and I would love to have her."

She listened to Kris ramble before ending the call by suggesting they keep the phone free. At three in the morning, she sent Dylan upstairs. At four she went to bed where she tossed and turned in sleep disturbed by memories of Christmas past.

At seven thirty, Rachel sat in the kitchen, watching the coffee pot fill, thinking about her father dealing with two young children and a baby the second Christmas Katherine attempted to spend in California. Carrie was about eighteen months old, Todd about seven. Tapping sound on the back door broke her reverie. David unlocked the door.

"No news," she said. "He hasn't answered any calls."

He opened his arms; she moved into his strength and placed her head in that place where his shoulder and neck came together.

"We had such a great day together, I didn't really want to come back here last night," Rachel said. "Maybe I had a premonition that my family was on the move in our zone."

"Back to the part about 'I didn't want to come back here.' You two could have stayed with me downtown."

She patted his back, the last small pat turning into a stroke, then softly moved away. "I don't want to confuse Dylan." Protecting their son always took top priority. "You would have been proud of him last night. He stayed up with me until about three. His idea."

"Good for him. And you did the right thing by letting him feel like he was protecting you." He smiled at her, his eyes looking into hers, nothing else claiming his attention. "Since there are children upstairs, we should probably sit down and share a cup of coffee."

"David, why didn't we have more children? We could have adopted."

"There's really no answer to that, Rach. We had two of our own and were blessed that one was healthy."

It was a conversation that had no satisfying end, but she loved that David didn't push it aside. As she started to tell him that, the ring of her phone filled the tiled kitchen.

"It's me, Rach." Raspiness made Todd's voice sound like their father.

"I'm glad to hear from you, Todd. Mighty tough night. Where are you?"

"Guess it was pretty crazy to take that flight to Chicago. It was just so damn empty here at home that I couldn't stand it. I thought Kris would see I was serious about being with her."

"Did you say you're at home?"

"Second stupid move of the night. I drove home. Saw David in case he doesn't tell you."

"You drove eight hours at that time of night?"

"Yeah. I thought a lot, sang Christmas tunes with some Southern radio station, drank bad coffee and ate junk food I found at two truck stops. I feel like hell this morning."

When all was over, Todd and Carrie could always be counted on to look for sympathy about how life treated them. Rachel looked across the counter at David and rolled her eyes.

"Do you remember the Christmas our mother disappeared," she asked with a sense of responsibility to the little girl sleeping in the guest room. "Do you remember how you were afraid that Dad would also go away?"

"Jeez, Rach, do we have to drag out the sad stories now?"

"Yeah, we do. I've heard plenty from Kris and you about all the adult stuff going on. You probably don't know that your little Cat tried to find you last night and was brought here by the police. She heard everything that went on when you and Kris were having your disagreement."

"Go back. I don't know what you're talking about."

They were all sleep-deprived as well as holiday-dazed. She spoke as she felt, protective of Todd's daughter upstairs and the other two kids sleeping across town.

"Cat heard everything and because she loves you, she put on her coat and boots and went looking for you. She found a police station."

Like their mother, Todd could put on the sober face and come out swinging when faced with proof of bad behavior. "Fuck, Kris was giving it as well as me. It was all just a bad deal. Just a bad deal. Let me talk to my girl."

"I'm not getting in the middle of you and Kris unless the kids are threatened."

"I want to talk with Cat."

"She's sleeping and could benefit with time away from her parents' stress."

She looked for David after saying those words. He sat in the living room, in his favorite chair near the fireplace, far out of hearing this conversation.

"Thanks, Rach. I really appreciate your self-righteousness. Kris and I are having a rough stretch and that's our business. So are our kids." His words slurred together. "Kris is the one who sent me away. She can kiss my ass."

"Okay, we're through talking. You're home safe. Cat's here safe. You know what I think. I'm going to make myself breakfast. You might do the same. It's your choice, but I suggest something to eat, not drink over ice."

Chapter 32

Steve's corny family calendar swung back and forth as Carrie opened and closed the refrigerator door. The man chose to celebrate her daily sobriety report with rows of red stars and periodic tallies.

She could honestly count on both hands the days she remained totally sober—Tuesdays and Fridays, the days she had appointments with her shrink. Each Monday Steve flew to Boston before she drove the kids to school. Her breakfast included something mixed with orange juice.

"Get your things in the car, boys," she yelled toward the staircase. "It's Tuesday and I have an appointment. Come on." She grabbed her purse, no kids in sight. "Is it too much to get you two out of here just five minutes early?"

"You don't need to yell, Mom. We're right here." Rob stood at the door. His pre-teen voice quivered. "You're not wearing shoes. Give us a break."

What mattered in her life was now defined by driving kids, running errands, watching hockey or participating in Steve's business entertainment. Sex generally fell into post-Saturday evening activities. At school the boys hopped out of the van and she waved good-bye to their backs. As she pulled back into traffic, Carrie realized she and Steve had not made love his last two weekends home, but beyond that, their marriage was sound.

"Come on in." Dr. Jansen smiled and held his office door open. Light washed over the cherry desk and sparkled on glass surfaces.

"I'll pull a few blinds or we'll both be squinting," he apologized. She sat in her usual chair, draping the coat over her knees like a security blanket.

"You know you just broke our routine." Tilting her head with a teasing smile, Carrie took control. "I usually sit in the reception area thinking about how to start. I suppose we'll dive head first into work." As soon as she shot her mouth, he turned serious brown eyes her way.

"Let me take your coat."

"No thanks." Carrie slipped out of her boots, tucked her feet up in the chair, and pulled her coat closer. She felt a hook open at her waistband. She looked at Jansen and forced a smile. "It was a good weekend."

"Tell me about it."

"The boys' hockey teams both did well. Steve was in great spirits and we did some fun things. January can be difficult, but I think I've managed this one."

"What kind of fun things did you and Steve do?"

"If you mean did we have sex, no. We can have fun without having sex." Carrie straightened her legs, confused over her running mouth. "I don't want to talk about that."

"What did you plan on talking about?"

Forty-five minutes later she left, emotionally hung over, hungry and thirsty. She stopped at the grocery then popped into the liquor store for a few essentials. By eleven she sat at her kitchen table with a plate of deli chicken wings and a Twins tumbler filled with ice, orange juice and vodka.

For the umpteenth time she wanted to call Rachel for the real truth behind Todd's Chicago trip. She considered cleaning the mess on her desktop but walked past her office to plop onto an unmade bed. The comforter felt good on her shoulders until the phone rang.

"Did I wake you up?" Her father's voice sounded accusing.

"Hi, Dad. No, the alarm did that six hours ago. Remember I've got kids to get to school."

"Your Mother is having a good day. Thought you'd be there after dropping the boys off."

"I had an appointment, Dad. I might visit later this afternoon. The boys are carpooling to hockey. What's up with you? I drove past your house yesterday, but you were out."

"I was probably in the family room. I haven't seen you since New Year's. Just kind of wondering if you were still alive."

"Dad, I see Mom every day and I talk with you all the time. Between the kids and the weather, it isn't exactly easy to get out much more."

He was silent, most likely disapproving."

"Well, I wondered if you would mind doing something around my birthday. Maybe we could meet at Bakers Square for pie. They've got good coffee."

"Dad, I should have thought of your birthday. How can it almost be February?" Carrie sat up fueled by a gigantic rush of guilt. "What do you mean Bakers Square? Why not here?"

"I wasn't trying to be pushy."

She knew he was most certainly trying to be pushy with that old people attitude of expecting the world to plan every activity far in advance.

"I will call Todd and Kris then get back to you with a date. Do you have anything on the calendar we need to work around?"

"Knights of Columbus have their meeting the Thursday before and that's it."

They settled on a Friday for a small celebration. Steve suggested inviting Art for dinner and Carrie complied, buying steaks to grill and a variety of deli dishes. She put out a mini bar for the evening, serving herself just one small vodka and sour while setting the dining table.

The doorbell rang. Carrie put on her happy face. "Happy birthday, Dad." She gave him an air kiss. "Thanks to Steve, we're doing steaks on the grill even though it is freezing cold. Hope you're hungry."

"I've been looking forward to your good cooking all week."

By the time Todd, then Kris with the kids, appeared, Carrie wanted to be in bed. Steve held the door open each time with the same line about the weatherman forgetting that the coldest days of winter were supposed to be over. Subzero cold invaded the foyer. She bit back the urge to yell at him. Her strategy for the evening became moving things along as quickly as possible.

Adults sat in the living room and talked of generic topics. Carrie watched her family, feeling like an outsider to the small talk. She visited Katherine every day, seldom watched television after three o'clock and could care less about car tires.

Kris offered to clear plates. They carried plates back to the kitchen side-by-side in silence. "You have plans for tomorrow night?" Kris asked. "Todd has the kids."

Carrie stopped running water. "What did you do to get a night off?"

"Surely someone told you that Todd's living with your Dad? That's not great for Todd, but they manage." Kris stopped. "My God, no one told you. This family is so screwed up."

Carrie tried for a noncommittal response. "Maybe Dad said something."

"You're kind of in your own world these days, Carrie." Kris placed a hand on Carrie's arm. "Are you all right?"

"I have been distracted. Mom's condition really gets me down."

"She was never keen about me as a daughter-in-law." Kris stated a true fact.

Carrie closed the dishwasher. "In-law relationships are tricky. Steve's family is big on email, but don't talk much. They'd be better off talking now and then. You know how emails can be misread." She saw Kris' forehead wrinkle. "Steve and I don't do a lot of email, but we talk every night when he's away. He's my best friend."

"I think I might have been Todd's only real friend at one time." Kris made a snorty sound. "Maybe we can change the subject. What do you think of Rachel's move? My kids are wild about her and Dylan settling in Minneapolis. Too bad she doesn't like suburbs." Kris stopped talking as Carrie dropped a cup. "What is wrong, Carrie?"

"Nothing. Nothing's wrong. The cup slipped." Carrie turned to the sink, flipped the faucet on and squirted soap into her palm. "Is that move thing all finalized now? You know Rachel's schedule is unpredictable so we just don't seem to connect."

"She'll be here in February, live with your Dad until renovations are done in the house she bought near Lake Calhoun. You must have known some of this? My kids have been emailing with Dylan for weeks. You know Mel and Cat think the world of Rachel."

"I haven't spoken with Rachel since the holidays. I know she called a few times but …" Carrie let her voice drop. She took a deep breath. "Won't this be disruptive for Dylan? Moving during the school year, not to say anything of leaving his father?"

"David's already here. I thought Steve helped him hook up with some sharp real estate agent in Minneapolis who handled those great new river area lofts?"

"You're right. Steve did send me an email with David's new address for our files. I'm not sure if I should send a welcome gift." Carrie thought of the two lofts she owned in that area, a secret from the rest of the family. "We never got to know David very well."

"So I won't get Christmas cards or graduation announcements if Todd and I divorce?"

The tone of Kris' question implied a joke, but Carrie moved forward with caution. "You're more like a second sister to me and you're Jake's godmother. We've been backups for each other as long as I remember. Why I even know where you keep things in your cupboards!"

Her feeble joke earned a quick hug from Kris. "You're a funny thing, Carrie. So quiet, but protective. Why couldn't your brother be more like you?"

Carrie didn't answer that Todd was like her, only his protective instincts centered on their mother. Katherine let her girls find their way in the world assuming they'd settle under the wing of a protective male, but she personally sheltered her only son. "Tell me what you know about Rachel's new place. I bet she found an old house to renovate."

"You know your sister. With all that money she could have bought an old dump and demolished it to build new. Todd says it's a nice bungalow with a big addition. She found an old classmate to handle remodeling the inside. I guess Dylan's going to attend Breck. Wonder how she managed to get him in so quickly?"

"My sister's a hot property on the self-help shelf. I suppose that brings some privilege."

"Let's take a drive into the city tomorrow and look at the place. We could have lunch in Uptown? Just the two of us."

When the evening wrapped up shortly, Carrie watched her brother kiss his kids as they climbed into the family minivan before he slid into Dad's car. Steve closed the front door.

"Don't know why it always seems so cold when we have your Dad's birthday thing. By the way, dinner was great. He really enjoyed his steak." He locked the door and turned off the front lights. "Good job, honey." She leaned against his chest, feeling his warmth while her feet chilled with the last of the outdoor air.

"Should we have invited David?"

"Didn't cross my mind. Who brought that up?"

"Kris mentioned him. Once Rachel moves, we'll have to figure it out."

"This is the first time you've mentioned Rachel. Art says they're coming in about a week and will be staying with him and Todd. Apparently Dylan is an ace baseball player so Breck's coach is drooling to get him on board."

Carrie thought of the baseball photo button of Dylan from a few Christmases ago. The concept of Rachel driving a boy to practices and sitting through Little League games, doing the same things she did for her boys, didn't fit.

Steve stepped back but kept his hands on her waist. "Let's celebrate your birthday this year. Have a big party. That would help blow out your doldrums. No family, just our friends."

"That's so much work, Steve. I'd rather just go out to dinner with you and the kids. Or maybe you and I go downtown for the night."

"I'll ask the Janz girl to help. She can come up with the theme and organize things."

The boys ran into the living room. Steve picked up Jake and held him straightjacket style. He no longer giggled like a little boy but struggled good-naturedly against his father, testing his strength when held in a man's strong arms. "We're going to celebrate Mom's birthday big time this year. Suggestions?"

"Anything would be more interesting than Grandpa parties." Rob won his release. "All Mel wants to talk about is indoor soccer or boys and Cat's such a little kid. It's boring for us guys to have sit downstairs with them while you talk, talk, talk up here," he grumbled. "Maybe Mom could do a spa thing then we could each take a friend to the movies?"

Steve looked at her over their sons' heads. She could see him invite her to laugh at Rob. And she could have laughed, or at least smiled. Instead she ruffled Rob's hair then turned to go upstairs. "We've got weeks to talk about this. Right now, I'm going to bed. I'm beat."

She walked past the hallway light switch, preferring the dark and moved through their bedroom by instinct. Still in the dark she changed, brushed her teeth, washed her face and used the toilet. Once under the covers Carrie remembered how her mother used to keep the lights off when trying to draw Dad into the bedroom to finish an argument. Far from thinking of her mother's current disintegration as spiritual or natural, she couldn't escape the image of the snake that lived under her neighbor's garage shedding its skin as it disappeared. As the Evans House months continued, Carrie feared one layer or other of her mother's shed skin maybe slipping around her shoulders. Her mother's daughter, once a compliment to taste and appearances, now suggested similarities of certain dark traits.

Tuesday Carrie sat in Dr. Jansen's office. She crossed her ankles, kept her hands quiet in her lap and knew why she sat this way to impress the therapist with her genteel background. She waited for his last words of small talk then cut to the snakeskin sensation.

"Lately if I notice myself saying or doing something like my mother, I get panicky. I drink like her. I've got her damn depression. Will I continue developing my mother's personality traits?"

"Think about her in totality, Carrie. Do you manipulate your kids, shame your husband, and tell malicious stories about other family members?"

"I said I know it's irrational." She turned quiet, letting the shrink earn his money.

"You have good traits from your mother as well?"

"None that come to mind." Setting a pretty table or arranging flowers hardly counted as critical in today's world.

"Are you drinking?"

No shit Sherlock, Carrie thought. "You want me to be honest? Some. Some socially, some alone. Not like before Christmas." She tossed her hair back. "I'm on too many meds to be careless. Nothing to excess."

"It's not like you to take risks. Let's review the danger of any drinking with Lexapro and Xanax in your system."

"Don't. I don't need a lecture. I'm not in a therapeutic mood. I'm sorry."

"Carrie, you don't have to apologize for being honest. I'll give you a break on the lecture but in exchange, I'd like you to take a step back and talk about this mood. What's up?"

"Nothing. My brother's separated, my sister's moved to the Twin Cities. They're both living with my father. And I found out by accident. If I don't ask, no one calls. They act like I'm nothing in the family. Nothing. I'm in my own little world where there's gray skies and slush."

She loved his brown eyes behind funky metal frame glasses. Usually just sitting in his office brought respite. This day she tried bringing her eyes up from entwined fingers and thought she saw boredom lurking where she expected support. She stopped speaking.

"That would be enough for today," she said.

"We've got time, Carrie. Something just happened. We were talking about a sense of separation from your family. Where did you go from there?"

Carrie wanted to go anywhere else. All the hours of talking and emoting in this room felt like time misspent by a spoiled suburban housewife with nothing better to fill two hours a week.

"I really need to leave. I know what I should be doing. Maybe I'm just too lazy to get out of the house or pick up the phone. Todd and Rachel are justified in not sharing their lives with me. They don't need approval. I'm the only one looking for a friend." Facts were facts. "Odd, I was popular. I helped Todd get dates. Maybe I should have stayed in the work world."

The sun shone like ice cubes in clear vodka. Carrie turned her eyes from the window to her therapist. He was the one who took her side or helped her see that others weren't really taking sides. "Maybe we should change our meeting time. I'm almost forty and not as clear headed as I need to be in the early mornings. I have obligations."

"Because of your mother?"

"Because of what goes in my morning juice, my mid-morning diet cola, my lunch coffee. I'm still drinking. Remember, we just had that conversation."

Dr. Jansen tried to stop her, but she wanted out of the leather furnished suite. She held up her hand. "My dime and I need to leave."

"I think you should stay. I want to know what your plans are for the rest of the day."

She lied, saying the first things in her head. "I'm going to the spa for a massage and pedicure, then lunch with my old boss."

"I'm glad to hear you're being kind to yourself as well. I'll see you in a few days."

There should have been a question in his voice, Carrie thought. She didn't correct him. He was the gatekeeper to her meds. She nodded her head as she gathered her coat and purse.

"Fuck off," she thought as the door closed.

Chapter 33

A shopping list crinkled in Art's pocket including items like toaster waffles, yogurt and dog treats. With Todd, Rachel, Dylan and Weezer living at the house, grocery shopping was a regular job.

For Dylan, Art would grocery shop every day. From the afternoon three weeks earlier when they arrived and the kid looked him in the eyes then extended a hand to shake, Art loved this grandson and his big dog. They talked that night about baseball. Now they were into deeper subjects and listening to Dylan's insights, Art recognized the old soul in his grandson.

Tulips were on special and he bought yellow ones for home and pink ones to bring to Katherine. He slammed the trunk lid, pushed the cart away and smiled. For the first time he was truly being a grandparent and doing a decent job. He played with the thought of taking all the grandchildren to an April baseball game, the boys and the girls.

Putting everything away tired him out, but he got back into the car for the trip to Evans House. Standing at the open door of Katherine's room he watched her fidget in the now beat up recliner. He stepped into the room aware of his own vitality.

"Feels like spring's just around the corner, Katherine. I brought you tulips." She didn't respond so he directed her, turning her stooped shoulder toward the pink flowers. He tipped her chin upwards, the softness of her skin reminding him of sweeter times.

"How much those flowers cost?"

"Your voice sounds kind of rough today. Did you have a difficult night?"

"How much those flowers cost?" He tried not to look at her restless hands clutching the recliner's fabric like crow's claws on road kill.

"Don't you worry about the cost of flowers. They were on sale at the grocery this morning. Having Todd at home and now Rachel and her boy means a lot more grocery trips. But you know about feeding a family. Rachel pays their share. Seems like we go through paper products the most. I might stop at that big wholesale place and buy a case of toilet paper and one of paper towel."

"Put those puddings where I can see good." She pointed to the tulips.

He picked up the vase and put it on the bed table next to a battered doll. "Better?"

She stared straight ahead, maybe at the tulips, maybe at the wall.

"Rachel's boy made dinner for Todd and me last night. Thirteen years old and able to cook up a spaghetti meal. Sliced apples for salad. Rachel must have taught him that."

Last night's meal would stay in Art's memories forever. Three generations of the men from his family sitting around the table, all easy with each other. They ate every last strand of spaghetti and never once talked about anyone else in the family. Dylan had a great sense of humor and kept Todd laughing. He didn't tell Katherine any of this.

"Todd says Dylan's a real strong athlete. Taking after our side of the family. Remember watching Todd pitch when he was a kid. I'll go to some of Dylan's games."

She cleared her throat. Art stopped talking for a moment, hoping she might connect with something he'd said. Her hands picked over the surface of the chair with less intensity.

"Rachel's into fixing up that old house she bought in Minneapolis. Todd tried to get her to buy a place in Stillwater. Bought in a fancy neighborhood by Lake Calhoun so I guess I'll have to get used to driving in the city again. She'll be close to her office and Dylan's school. He's going to Breck. Our girl is very well off. "

"I thought Rachel was dead."

"Now Katherine. She brought you a new sweater on Sunday."

He smelled her dirty pants, that awful fresh crap smell. The damn chair wasn't coming home when she didn't need it anymore. It had to smell like a dirty dog bed. An attendant came to clean Katherine. His original plan had been to stay through lunch, but his heart and mind weren't cooperating. She wouldn't miss him if he left.

"Art, those are beautiful tulips. How was Katherine this morning?" Britta, the house manager, appeared. "Would you like me to put them someplace out of danger?"

"Every time I go into her basement storage area I feel like she lived some kind of secret life. She'd buy us store brand canned vegetables to save a few pennies then horde glass flower vases."

"I'd like to visit with you and the family soon about Katherine's care."

"She's slipping. You're not going to kick her out?"

"No, Art, except for acute hospital care Katherine won't have to ever leave Evans House. But she needs more care than we can deliver on this side of the facility."

"Tell me what you're thinking." He moved away from Katherine's door, not wanting to chance that she'd hear this conversation.

"If this is a good time?"

"Britta, I've been having a good morning. I drove my grandson to school, filled the cupboards with food for my family, bought my wife tulips. That may be all the 'good time' I get today. Want to sit here or do we need to go to your office?"

They sat down at a table in the craft area. "I had our physician test Katherine yesterday, and while it may be a bit premature, we want to take advantage of having a bed available in our nursing unit."

It wasn't a rational connection but Art's thoughts moved back to a time when the school principal called them to school to talk about Rachel. He and Katherine sat in the teachers' lounge, the two of them across a table from Sister Agatha. The nun's first words of 'we've tested Rachel and have some recommendations about making a change in her assignment next year' came to mind as Britta shared results of the doctor's assessment.

He looked attentive but found it easier to stay with the memory of Sister Agatha's pronouncement. "The Lord requires we all make the most of our gifts and Rachel has a bountiful intellect. She's wasting time in second grade and we think she'd do better going straight to fourth grade."

He and Katherine walked home. His mind was busy with assessing what was best for Rachel while Katherine worried out loud about the child developing a big head and the cost of tutoring to make it work. Bringing himself back to Evans House and Britta, he thought about the countless times he and Katherine made big decisions together about their kids, finances, futures. Sadness moved through him easier now and he found himself comfortable making decisions alone.

"Let's do it. When will you move her? Is there anything we need to do to prepare her?"

"We need to freshen the new room and do a bit of staff shuffling. Let's say we'll make the move in two weeks. Katherine won't understand if we tell her anything in advance so I'd suggest you and I talk about this again as the day gets closer."

"There's not much of her stuff to move. Feels like we've taken everything home but her chair, stuffed things and clothes."

"We can move it all." Britta lowered her voice. "You should spend time visiting the late stage unit. You'll notice less movement of residents, more of an institutional setting."

He concentrated on one drooping tulip while clearing his throat. "I'll make a visit and tell the kids this week." She nodded. "Now I've got to get some things done before my grandson gets home from school. Thanks, Britta."

The sun warmed his face as he walked to his car. The air held that tease of better days to come. He stood by the side of his car and stretched. There had to be a way to reclaim what was left of his healthy years.

Heading out of the parking lot, the wild idea of buying a cell phone answered that need. Dylan's asking him for a cell number challenged Art to join the digital life. Being able to talk with his grandson or answer an emergency, even if away from home, added purpose to getting up each day. And that whole texting craze could connect him with Todd whose thumb flew over a phone's keyboard all the time.

Thirty minutes later he walked out of a big box store with a smart phone in his jacket pocket, feeling like a man with purpose. He sat in the parking lot to dial Dylan's number. The boy was in school yet Art wanted his first call to be to his grandson.

"Dylan, this is your grandfather leaving a message. I took your advice and bought myself a mighty neat phone. A smart phone. The guy at the counter helped me program your number and your mother's and a few others so I'm up and running. Hope your day's going well." He stalled, not used to calling people without a purpose. "I'll give you my number before I hang up. You make sure to call if you ever need a ride. Or want to talk. I'm ready to be mobile." He chuckled at his use of the vernacular then chuckled more, enjoyed the expansiveness of sitting in the car and talking on his phone.

Katherine would never know this phone number. He registered the phone in his own name and walked out of the store with his own voice mail message ready to greet anyone who might call. For a half century they'd been partnered, Art and Katherine or Katherine and Art.

He put his key in the ignition, but before he turned it decided to make a second major purchase. Back in the store he headed toward computers, ready to replace the ancient model in the basement. He'd set it up in the family room corner where Katherine's chair used to sit so he could email friends, manage his finances, look up interesting things and watch television all at the same time.

The phone rang in his pocket as he unloaded his computer at home and for a moment he was frozen, unsure how to answer it. Finally he stopped fumbling. "Art, here," he said.

"Hey, Grandpa, this is so great. What model did you get? I'll show you how to text."

"It's an Apple." Art laughed low. "Let me get used to talking. Do you need a ride?"

"Mom's supposed to be here any minute. But thanks, Grandpa."

"I got busy this afternoon and spent a lot of money."

"Did you buy a big screen TV?"

Art laughed out loud. "No, that would be your Dad's thing. I bought a laptop computer and printer and a desk. We'll set it up when you get home. Then you can show me how to search the web and what's up with that YouTube place. I really liked those barking dog videos."

He enjoyed the early evening as they worked on his computer. Finally Dylan went upstairs to do homework, Rachel reviewed work and he sat down to read the phone's instruction manual. Todd came home around eight in a rotten mood.

"I don't know why we leave Mom in that place. She just sits in that chair and scratches at the arms. I swear she'd crapped herself while I was visiting." He dug through the refrigerator.

"There's a plate in the oven for you." Art joined Todd in the kitchen.

"Dad, I want Mom out of that place." Todd placed a beer down on the counter.

"You're kind of like a stuck record, Todd."

"Maybe I should talk to an attorney. I don't agree with how you're taking care of her."

"Son, I've never once put my nose into your problems with your wife. I haven't picked Kris apart, made suggestions about your financ-es." Art stood at the counter where the last fight with Katherine began. "You've told me how to manage your mother's care, told me to sell this place and criticized every decision I've made about car repairs, even my choice of vermouth. Do you know you can be a real critical bastard?"

Todd started to walk away, but Art wanted to finish what was on his mind.

"It's time we pull together. We've got a chance to stay a family even without your mother. She'll move to a nursing unit as soon as a bed is available. Even though she's still living on this earth, she's trapped in an awful, goddamn hell. No one can help her."

Art kept his voice low enough to not draw Dylan into this adult sorting out of issues. "And she can't help you, son, but I'm here.

Maybe it's time you take advantage of that. You'll all be on your own in a few enough years."

"You'll live to be ninety." Todd spat the last words out, an implication that the wrong parent was blessed with longevity.

"I understand that you'd rather it was me sitting at Evans House. Just be smart enough to not say it to my face." Torrents of words flowed from his mind, few that Art could say at this point. "What I expect from you is to be a gentleman. We've got a boy upstairs who doesn't need to experience the worst of this family."

"I've been waiting for you to get in a few licks," Todd said. "It must be killing you to sit here at night and talk about the basketball and road construction when you really want to tell me what a fuck up I am. Just didn't have the courage until it was only the two of us here."

"This conversation just took a wrong turn," Rachel interrupted. "Dad said nothing about how you're handling your life. But Dad, can we talk about Katherine. What happened?"

"Would you stop with the 'Katherine' deal? She's our mother, not some old lady from the down the street. Call her 'Mother' when we talk. Can you do that, Rachel? Be respectful."

"I am acting out of respect for what she wants. Do you think it's been easy?"

Art heard the pain. "That's enough, Todd. Rachel's not the one making you unhappy."

Taking control fed Art's growing sense that it wasn't too late to bend this family into something better. He gave Todd's arm a quick grasp. "We're going to be alive after she passes so we owe it to each other to make amends." Through his son's sweater, he thrilled at the feel of his son's strong arm.

"I didn't always like how your mother ruled this family, but I let her do it. That made my life easier. Maybe it's not too late for me to step up and do my part?"

"Sounds like Grandpa's been reading Mom's books." Dylan walked in the kitchen, two pencils in one hand. "I was looking for a pencil sharpener. Sorry."

Rachel reached out and pulled her son into a quick release kind of hug. "There's one in the far left kitchen drawer."

"I think you should give Grandpa space," Dylan said.

Art was struck that Rachel's instincts of staying geographically and emotionally distant from the family gave Dylan room to grow up unscathed.

"Yeah, I guess that's what I'm asking." Art blundered with the unfamiliar expression. "But Dylan, doesn't that mean to leave me alone? I've had enough of that."

"I meant cutting you some slack if you want to try new stuff."

"That's good." Art nodded his head up and down. "I'm trying new stuff. And, yeah, I did read your mother's books. Kind of long in the tooth, but I managed my way through."

Todd took his dinner plate to the sink and cleared what was left into the garbage disposal. He rinsed it, placed it in the dishwasher. "Got to love teenagers for cutting through the junk."

Art's temper rose again at the caustic comment, but he saw Dylan shoulder bump Todd and take a harder bump back, all with grins. The kitchen expanded as his family roughhoused. He put his own shoulder into their bumps and smiled when they held back. "Good to know you respect an old man."

Chapter 34

Todd watched his nephew take the steps two at a time and wished he was in his own kitchen surrounded by his own kids. "I've got a few calls to make," he told his father and Rachel then followed Dylan. By the time he closed his bedroom door, he had dialed his house. Kris answered, a hint of laughter in her voice.

"It's me. Wish I was there to hear what's making you laugh." He held his breath. "I really mean that. I miss that great chuckle."

"We've got a dog with a baseball hat tied to his head. Cat thinks it's hysterical. I'm not sure if I'm laughing at the dog or her." Her voice changed. "What's up?"

"I miss you all. I know it's not a visitation night but I wondered if I could stop in and just hang out with you guys? Watch television or help with homework."

"I'm in my sweats and not going anywhere. You okay?"

"Yeah, I'm fine. Now that the new job isn't all that new I'm getting the hang of cutting out earlier. You'd like that, having me be more or less on time for dinner?"

"It isn't just that, Todd. I can handle late dinner."

"Let me hang out tonight. We don't have to talk about anything more serious than Easter basket candy. If you don't mind including me in planning something for Easter?"

"I haven't had the time or energy to think that far ahead."

"I'll be there in fifteen minutes if you don't mind. Please stay around."

She sounded hesitant as she asked a second time if he had something he wanted to talk about. Her joy was gone although he could hear Cat's crazy laugh in the background.

"Nothing at all. I can sit here and watch television with my Dad, but I'd rather sit with you all and hear about your day and hug a kid or two and relax. Nothing more."

"Maggie is coming the day after tomorrow because I'm going to San Francisco for that conference so I'm trying to tie up household stuff. You do remember I'll be gone that night and you were going to take the kids out for dinner?"

"You don't have to have Maggie stay with them. I've cleared my calendar."

"We'll talk when you get here."

He stopped in to tell his father he was going 'home' for a few hours. He drove carefully thinking of Dylan racing up the stairs and the look on his sister's face as her eyes followed her son that said 'he's all I have in this world'.

Chapter 35

"I want my flowers. Katherine spoke out loud in the darkness. At least she thought she said the words out loud. "I want my flowers." She rocked from side to side in the bed. "My flowers. Bring me the pretty flowers. The flowers the man brought. The pretty man flowers."

No one answered.

She heard a mouse under the bed and hoped the cat would catch it. Mice in the drawers scared her. She had to be brave about the mice during the night. Mother couldn't leave the bedroom in the dark to take care of a big girl afraid of such small things. She settled into her bed, tugged her covers over her head and felt the mice moving up her legs.

She screamed and screamed and screamed as she pulled at her clothes and tossed everything off the bed. Mother didn't come. Only strangers, who knew her name, but had strong hands.

Chapter 36

Dylan held a stuffed bunny for Katherine as they drove to Evans House Easter morning. Each time Rachel glanced across the front seat, she wondered when his hands had become so large. He was an unwilling companion, eager to move on to an afternoon with his father.

"Grandpa surprised you with that Easter basket this morning." His head turned away from the window. "I wonder who suggested the gift certificate for downloading music?"

"Grandpa had a lot of fun planning all those clues and stuff."

"You know I still have your first Easter bunny." How could she tell him there was almost nothing in the world as precious as a small boy clutching a floppy bunny in one arm with a thumb in his mouth? "It's in a box in the basement with a bunch of other weird things."

"Think about all of the junk that Grandpa's clearing out of his basement. I saw a box of Halloween costumes with a date that was thirty years ago." He turned back to the window. "We've got tons more boxes to unpack than Dad moved. Probably boxes with junk like that stuffed bunny."

"Some of the stuff we moved is Dad's." She drove past the church. "I'm unpacking the dining room today, then the kitchen. I want us in our own place soon."

"Does Grandpa know?"

"He's helping me hang pictures upstairs on Tuesday." She saw the way he tipped his head. "It'll be a couple of weeks before everything is done."

"I feel kind of guilty not doing Easter with him. Should we be going to church?"

"Grandpa needs time for Todd and Carrie and their families."

"Dad and I go to church to listen to the music. We tried out a new church on Palm Sunday. Dad said there were a couple of thousand people at the service."

She turned into Evans House parking lot. David going to church was a surprise.

"Why didn't our family go to church? Cause you and Dad are different religions?"

"We just fell out of the habit." She disconnected her shoulder harness. Dylan sat still.

"Mom, I hate going in there. Rob and Mellie tell me stories about when stuff was better, but I never even met her when she was normal. This whole pretending to visit her sucks."

"My mother had a difficult personality, Dylan. Dad and I thought it was better…"

"Dad used to call her KTB, you know, Katherine The B…"

"I know what it means." She turned to him. "I need company doing this today. Okay?"

"Sure." Lack of enthusiasm gave the word a heavy sound. They walked in silence.

Bandages wrapped two of Katherine's fingertips and her thinning hair looked freshly washed. Dylan moved straight to Katherine with the bunny.

"Happy Easter, Grandma. You're the lucky one this year who gets the stuffed bunny. It plays music if you press the paw."

Katherine's eyes watched Dylan. He led her hand to the music button. "Try it Grandma."

She turned her head to him. "Pretty boy," Katherine said. "Art baby?" She nodded her head up and down. "Yes, Art baby." She craned her neck to look at Dylan. "Ta, ta, ta, ta," she said slowly then squashed the bunny's paw. "Art baby like music?"

Rachel extended a hand to Dylan's shoulder. "He does look like Dad, doesn't he?"

"Goes the cotton nail." Her mother began singing, spindly notes without tone. "Up and down, up and down, up and down…"

"We know that one. Sing with us, honey. 'Here comes Mr. Cottontail up and down the bunny trail. Hippitty-hop-hop…'"

They sang through what Rachel remembered of 'Easter Parade' then 'Jesus Christ is Risen Again' before Katherine's head drooped. Rachel tucked the bunny back into her mother's arm and drew up the covers. They left silently.

"That was weird," Dylan said as they walked out.

She let him see her sadness. So many years of anger had numbed her while watching her nemesis decline. This morning reminded her that Katherine was far beyond such descriptors. She walked slower, torn between running back to hug her mother and moving with the day.

Dylan bumped into her shoulder purposefully. "She's kind of like a really old baby."

"That's a good way to think of her."

"Then how come Uncle Todd acts like she understands everything?"

"Every once in a while she has had a very lucid moment and connects with something or someone. Then people hope again."

Rachel noticed the top of Dylan's head came close to her ear as they split paths to climb into her car. She listened to his plans for the afternoon, but turned on the radio before exiting the parking lot.

Chapter 37

Carrie, absorbed in a small spot on her cream pants, didn't notice Rachel's Lexus or Dylan waving as Steve drove into Evans House's parking lot. Steve appeared distant, well dressed, like a man with a purpose. Carrie knew her eyes were puffy, she had been crying before putting on her make-up.

"Just focus on this visit, honey," Steve whispered near her ear then took her hand.

Watching the boys search for their Easter treats this morning, a sense of time rushing away stole her calm. She followed them from room to room, aware of the ghosts of two little boys in footie jammies chasing behind these strong, athletic kids.

"Why are we here? Grandma won't know us anyway." Rob's question made sense.

"Because it's Easter. We don't want any of our family to be alone on a holiday." She could have tried for something more insightful, but knew it didn't matter.

"Aunt Rachel and Dylan just pulled out." Rob squirmed as she prodded him forward. "Maybe she's tired of visitors?"

"It's important to Mom and me that we visit Grandma as a family. We'll only stay a few minutes because we need to get to eleven o'clock Mass." Steve put one hand on Rob's shoulder.

"Easters were more fun when we were little kids and we'd have a really big hunt with Mel and Clay and Cat at Grandma and Grandpa's house. There'd be all kinds of cool stuff."

Carrie turned her face away while Rob spoke. Perhaps the emotions of the day heightened the smells as they moved past the front desk and toward her mother's room. She sniffed, then held back from another deep breath until they stood at the door.

"Happy Easter, Mom," Carrie said. Her mother startled like a child awakened from a nap. "Looks like you're having an Easter parade of family this morning." She leaned to kiss her mother's cheek then moved aside, gesturing the boys to come to her side. Both stayed near the door. "You two can sit on the bed." Neither moved.

"We were just talking about all the fun the grandkids had at your Easter parties." Carrie prattled on about meaningless Easter outfits and hams and whether the tulips were in bloom each year. Her stomach churned, she felt dizzy and the facility cleaning products smell intensified.

Five minutes turned into ten. Her mother stared at the boys. Steve stood in the doorway. Fifteen minutes into the Easter monologue, Carrie felt her heart race off in a very abnormal manner. The dizziness she had been experiencing earlier turned into a visual merry-go-round and her breathing accelerated.

"Carrie, are you all right?" He moved closer. She held up a hand, saw it wobble in the air. "Put your head down. Guys, stay with your Mom."

She bent over on the uncomfortable chair, struggled to breathe. Everyone's eyes were on the back of her head. Steve brought a nurse. The boys moved to the hall. Shamed by the whole spectacle, tears filled Carrie's eyes. Steve squatted at her side, one hand rubbing a circle on her back. She kept her head down, one mascara-tinted blob ruined her linen slacks.

"Urgent care is open at the clinic." The nurse held Carrie's wrist in a cool hand. "Your pulse is fast. Did you have breakfast?"

"We had a huge breakfast," Steve said. "Maybe too much coffee?"

"I didn't really eat." Carrie heard her voice sounding like an older woman. She used to sound like a girl when she was weak. "I'm feeling better." She willed her heart to slow while cold sweat trickled down her back. "This is rather difficult," was all she offered in explanation.

"You mean your mother's move?" Carrie heard kindness in the nurse's voice. "It's more difficult for you. Katherine doesn't understand."

Carrie struggled to regain her dignity. Her hands still shook. "We have to go. I should change these pants." She gestured at the mascara dots.

"As a nurse, I suggest urgent care or at the least taking it easy for the next few hours. Get some protein in your system." She rested a hand on Carrie's. "Church isn't a good idea."

"You heard what the nurse ordered," Steve said. "If you don't want to stop at the clinic, we're going home and you're sacking out for a few hours."

Weak misty tears continued as Steve rounded up the boys. They walked out in silence with Steve holding her elbow as if she had become a fragile creature. She let the boys worry.

"So urgent care or home? I can drop the boys at church and call your Dad to give them a ride."

"No, don't bother anyone." She sneezed. "Let's go home."

Chapter 38

Todd honked at his sister's car as Steve pulled out of Evans House. Steve waved and drove ahead. "Looks like they're in a hurry," he said to his father via phone. "Hold seats for Kris, myself and the kids. I'm just stopping now. You can have Mom all to yourself later."

He found her sleeping. Her aide popped in. "Your sister got sick while visiting and that agitated Katherine. We just settled her. I can open the card with her later."

"How's my sister?"

"I think she hadn't eaten breakfast and got woozy."

"Too much Easter candy. She's got a sweet tooth," Todd joked. "I guess I'll be early for church." He handed over the card. "You have a good Easter."

Carrie occupied his thoughts as he drove away. She was more their mother's daughter than Rachel. In fact, Carrie kind of replaced their mother in a weird way. His kids loved her house, his father depended on Carrie, and he knew her table always had an extra place set. He thought of her as Mom without the critical edge.

Crawling across his father into the pew, he dropped daisies into the girls' laps, earning himself a small kiss from Kris. They looked like a million bucks—the girls in new spring outfits and Clay in pressed chinos with an oxford shirt. A thinner Kris stood out from the rest of the suburbanites in a sophisticated, geometric print dress. She was the woman he wanted.

No one would call Todd religious. Mass on holidays with the excitement of a packed church and loud music kept his interest. Lifting his head, Todd surveyed the church to find people he knew, listened in on the readings for a while, then daydreamed through the sermon.

From teen years on, he thought about sex while the priest offered insights on Christianity. Sometimes a pretty girl a few pews away shed her clothes in his thoughts. There were the years he replayed his Saturday night dates. As an adult, his mind went back to making love to his wife. Easter was no different. He wondered if Kris might let him into bed if the day went well. He shifted around on the pew, trying to get comfortable. The thought of make-up sex was hot. He tripped over words as the congregation recited prayers. Mass progressed.

Shame flooded over Todd when he noticed his father fingering a rosary, his lips moving along with the beads. Dad's faith was straightforward—you paid attention to the priest in church and prayed on your own time. The rosary brought Mom into their pew. Todd bowed his head, rubbed away moisture from his eyes.

They exited church into a bright, warm April day. "Happy Easter, pretty lady," Todd said on the side to his wife. He'd learned to keep Kris and the kids as separate topics in their marital counseling. "Can't believe you convinced Clay to wear that oxford shirt. He looks good."

"Happy Easter and thanks for the flowers. You didn't stay long with Katherine."

"Long enough. Carrie got sick when they were visiting. Maybe you can call her later?"

Kris frowned just a bit, a gesture that reminded him how she preferred he manage his family's relationships. "I'll give them a call on the way home," he corrected himself.

The return of her smile signaled that she noticed his effort. "I should have invited them," Kris said. She looked at him from under her eyelashes. He liked her vibes.

They stood by Kris' minivan. "Any of you want to ride with me?" he asked the kids. "Or with Grandpa? We guys get lonely." Cat jumped his way and Todd pushed Clay toward Dad.

"The flowers were a good idea. You're really trying, Dad."

"We both are, Cat. Which reminds me to call my sister." They sat in the church parking lot as cars jostled to exit. Todd dialed and Steve answered.

"Hey big guy, I hear my sister got out of Mass by fainting?"

"She didn't really faint, just had some wooziness. Probably a bug."

Chapter 39

The boys rode bikes in the soft April warmth, delighted to escape church. Carrie watched from the living room. She wanted a drink, something cold and distracting, nothing herbal. Parked on the sofa with Steve reading the paper across the room, her hidden stashes were out of reach. Xanax swallowed while changing would have to do.

Her mother kept many secrets although none probably as big as Carrie who carried the secret history on this twentieth anniversary of the termination of her first pregnancy. A secret she didn't share with anyone, even her therapist. Before accepting Steve's proposal, she told him what he could accept with a story of suffering a miscarriage before dating him. While they were sexually intimate, her half-truth almost ended their relationship. Sex was okay. Getting caught a sin.

That baby would have been in college now. Only lately did she imagine that she lost a girl—now a young woman she saw as a dark-haired, tall stranger. Big sister Rachel garnered public sympathy when she lost her first baby. Carrie dragged shame alone.

"You look like you could use a nap," Steve said. "I'll keep the boys busy. Kind of worried about you."

"Don't be. Sorry I'm screwing up Easter." As he lowered a blanket over her she struggled to stay quiet, to not cry or confess. "I love you," she said when the blanket covered her shoulders and he kissed her head.

"I know. Don't cry, Carrie. There will be other Easters."

Chapter 40

Todd called Carrie's house again in the early evening as he drove back to his parent's place. It had been a damn nice day. Kris sent off ready for sex signals during dinner, a long walk, an open mouth kiss in the laundry room, but then let him drive away. He squirmed in his car seat.

"Hello." Steve's deep voice ended as he thought about Kris.

"How's she feeling?" Todd asked. "Back on her feet?"

"She went up to bed about ten minutes ago. Maybe a migraine. How was your Easter?"

"Good. Spent it with Kris and the kids. We had a nice day."

"Glad to hear that, Todd. Can't talk. I'm flying out to Amsterdam tomorrow."

"The travel must get old. My sister's a trooper."

"She's amazingly self-sufficient." Steve cleared his throat. "Want her to call?"

Todd recognized Steve's words as a brush-off. "Does she ever ask you to stay home?"

"When I'm around for more than a few days the boys' routine comes unglued. Not that I don't wish that I could be home more." Steve muffled the phone to talk to a boy.

"I'll let you go. Tell her I called and this is what she gets for eating too many chocolate Easter eggs."

His father stood at the stove when Todd walked in the back door. "Whatcha doing, Dad? I thought you had enough to eat at our place this afternoon?"

"Believe it or not, I'm waiting for this water to boil. Thought I'd make some Jell-O for tomorrow's dinner."

"I talked with Steve. Sounds like Carrie spent most of the day sleeping. Steve's off to Amsterdam tomorrow." Todd filled a glass with water. "Do you wonder if Carrie is happy?"

"I think married men and women should be at home with each other a lot more than folks do today. Their marriage is good, but that doesn't mean Carrie is as happy as she could be."

His father stirred rather intensely. Neither of them spoke while the metal spoon clinked over and over against the clear glass bowl sides.

"You know, Dad, I kind of think of Carrie as Mom's clone. They kind of look alike. Carrie fusses about things like flowers and always has extra food in the house to be the perfect hostess. And she drinks more than she should."

His father inhaled rather deeply. "That's a big statement. Be careful how you use it."

Chapter 41

The call came in the midst of Carrie's thirty-eighth birthday party when she was in the garage looking for more bottles of Chablis. One of the boys brought her the phone.

Her father wasted no time. "Your mother fell and the nurses think she had a serious stroke. They're waiting for a hospital transport. Her leg might be broken. I got ahold of Todd. We'll meet you there."

He sounded like a tired drill sergeant pulling the troops together for another run up another hill. She was drunk and knew it. No one got to be critical of the birthday girl.

"We have a house full of guests, Dad. It's my birthday. What else do you know?"

"I told you what I know. The aide checked your mother about an hour after they put her to bed. She was on the floor and unconscious. They called the hospital because her leg was at an odd angle."

"You said she had a stroke."

"Dr. Wagner said it was coming."

"I'll be there as soon as I can, but that might be some time. Can you have Todd or Rachel call me?"

"I thought you might give me a ride. I hate these emergency night drives."

"Sorry, Dad, I can't leave. Isn't Todd around?

"I'll drive myself." He hung up. No 'oops, I guess I forgot your birthday' or 'take your time'. The quick disconnect told her she had disappointed him.

She carried three bottles and a six-pack of ale into the kitchen with the phone receiver stuck under her chin. It clanked to the floor. "Shit," she said to herself then giggled, "I didn't drop anything that matters." A friend chuckled with her and rescued the wine. "The bar has to close soon or we'll have to hire every cab from downtown St. Paul to drive your sorry butts home." They laughed together.

Steve came looking for her. She thought he looked rakishly handsome, still built and carried his wineglass like a man, whatever that meant. He bent close to her and she assumed he wanted to kiss her cheek. Instead he asked why one of the boys ran the phone to her.

If she told Steve about her father's call they'd have to deal with making plans, sending people home, ending the party. Her mother's heart had a knack for putting a damper on life events. She wanted this night to herself with the just-right balance of wine and friends and antidepressants. Always balancing the scales.

Steve waited. A sigh like a delicate wind escaped her lips. "I don't suppose I could get away with saying the kids ordered an outrageous number of pizzas and Dominos was checking delivery time?"

He pressed the caller identification button. "Your dad?"

"Right. Mom was breathing odd and the residence called for a hospital transport. Dad was asking if I'd swing by and pick him up. He thinks she's had another stroke."

"I can give you both a ride. You shouldn't be driving."

"It's his view that she had a stroke. I was going to dial Todd and ask him to give me a call from the hospital. I told him we had a house full of people and I'd do my best to get there if that was necessary. I also told him people were here because it is my birthday. Only saintly sister Rachel called today. I ring everyone and give them stupid cake parties and no one reciprocates."

She smiled as a friend wandered in looking for a clean glass and white wine. Steve disappeared with the phone while she opened a new bottle and chatted. Somewhere in the crowd were two hired college students who were supposed to keep the kitchen tidy and the bar stocked. She went in search of her helpers and reminded them that although the guests were fascinating, they needed to stay on top of kitchen and serving responsibilities.

"Carrie." Steve motioned to her from the den. She followed him with reluctance. "Rachel spoke with the attending physician and they've confirmed a stroke. Your mom is in a coma. Todd is on his way to pick up your father and suggests we take our time. It sounds like your Dad's come unglued. What do you want to do?"

The wine tasted sour in her mouth and her stomach did that awful clenching that sometimes preceded an attack. She assumed the anxiety attacks would disappear after Easter, but no luck. Xanax wasn't a possibility this evening. She tossed back her remaining wine.

"I don't want to go. She'll be in the hospital for weeks. I'll be all bummed out, but nothing changes. Nothing. Maybe it's time I change and act more like Rachel. She didn't coming flying home every time Mom had a cold."

"It's not a cold, Carrie." Steve closed in on her, enfolding her in his long arms and leaning her against his chest. Suffocating her into submission. "You know you'd feel like shit if anything happened and you stayed away. We'll have another party next year." His hands rubbed her spine. She let her hands fall to her sides then moved one near his crotch. She wanted real comfort. He stepped aside just an inch or so, treating her touch more as if it were accidental. "It's almost midnight. People are leaving already, at least everyone with babysitters."

Habit won out. The dutiful daughter couldn't stage a revolution even with good wine running through her veins. She moved from Steve's reach and slipped out of her strappy shoes.

"I could ask someone to give me a ride to the hospital. You can stay here and wrap up the party," she offered. "Or I could drive myself and be very careful. I'll stay off the freeways." She managed to drive the kids home from baseball or soccer on serious amounts of prescription drugs with a small vodka sour wash. Of course, Steve and the kids didn't need to know about that success.

"No way are you driving. Let me ask Chuck and Lea to take over. I don't think many people are planning on staying a lot longer. I'll drive you to the hospital."

"I'll get my purse and change my shoes." She carried extra medication in her purse. Running shoes looked funky with her off-the-shoulder cashmere sweater and short black skirt. They rode in silence. Carrie obsessed about what to expect at this hospital. She anticipated conversations that would take place, who would take what role, how long she might have to stay.

"I assume you'll be there the rest of the night," Steve said. He had that ability to weird her out by saying out loud what she was just beginning to think.

"I'll ask Todd or Rachel for a ride home."

"Carrie, would you ever consider living in the cities?"

The question was so unlike Steve that Carrie had no response except relief he didn't know about her warehouse condos.

"You don't have to answer." She recognized the dream under his voice. "Something about Rachel renovating that bungalow near Lake Calhoun set me thinking. The boys are missing something by not living in a more diverse neighborhood."

"We should talk. You might be surprised."

But once his secret wish was out in the open, Steve couldn't stop talking. Staying awake was difficult with his voice coming to her out of the dark. She leaned her head against the window and let her eyes close. Vertigo hit quickly. Putting one hand against the door handle and the other on the console, she opened her eyes. They were at the hospital. She focused on Steve's wedding ring instead to keep the world from swirling again.

"I'll stay until we find Todd or Rachel. You're looking a bit green. Sick?"

"Everyone looks worse in these lights. We're both tired."

Todd sat alone in the cardiac lounge area reading an early edition of the Sunday newspaper. "You didn't have to dress up for Mom." His voice held a touch of exasperation, like someone pulled from a more pleasurable activity to sit in a hospital on a Saturday night.

"We had a house full of people. It's Carrie's birthday."

"Sorry, Sis." Carrie thought the apology sounded authentic. Her judgment wasn't rock solid at the moment. "You know how bad I am about dates. I'll take you out for breakfast."

"How's your mother? Was it another stroke?"

"Probably. Dad is with her and the doctors. Apparently he's got a do not resuscitate order on file, but the leg injury made it necessary to bring her here. I'm blown away."

"Of course there is a DNR in place." Carrie said and sat down, clumsy in her descent. "Why would we want her to suffer if there is a natural end?"

Todd watched her moves, but she ignored him and turned toward Steve. "I'll call you as soon as we know anything unless it can wait 'til morning." Steve waved, then entered the elevator before Carrie slouched back against the sofa cushions. Her brother ruffled through the newspaper, giving her a few moments to settle into their normal hospital patterns. He extended a section of the paper. Her purse tumbled to the floor and they both bent to grab it.

"Carrie, you smell like you're wearing Mom's favorite perfume. Something expensive over ice."

"I was drinking wine. I didn't expect to leave my home so I had more than usual."

"And what's usual these days?"

"Keep your opinions to yourself." She turned her head to keep a belch from drifting his way. Wine gone sour churned through her stomach.

"We're a family that likes drinking, little sis. It's a party just if there's a bottle in the house." He reached over to rub her shoulder. "Just watch out, kiddo. Steve's a smart guy."

Angry words threatened to come with the next burp, the emotional drunken stage. Carrie changed the subject. "Where is our esteemed big sister?"

"Dylan had some friends sleeping over so she couldn't bail. I told her I'd call if anything happened here."

"So typical." Carrie hated Rachel perching slightly above the family's messes. "She'll waltz in, all calm, and the doctors will fawn on her."

"Cold, Carrie. You sound like Mom."

"Shut up." Her hands trembled. "I need a bathroom."

"Need help? Why didn't you stay home if you couldn't walk a straight line?"

"Be a good brother and get me a coffee. Even one from the vending machine."

"I have an extra." Todd held out a cup. "It's the real stuff. Go to the bathroom. When you come back you can have the coffee or curl up with my jacket and sleep."

She hightailed it to the bathroom. Kneeling next to the toilet she choked as everything from the party burned its way from her stomach and through her mouth.

Chapter 42

Light and people sounds floated through some unknown quiet that pressed heavily on her, like lying just under the surface of the water at their old lake place. Katherine thought she was able to move her foot, then her leg. Something held her leg in place. A shadow hung near the edge of her mind speaking in a language she vaguely remembered.

Her mother would be calling for dinner soon. "Katherine Mary… Katherine Mary." She flew across the Beudior's field and crossed the road, genuflecting to the garden shrine. "Immaculate Mary, your praises we sing. You reign now… dancing in the rain, we're dancing in the rain. What a wonderful feeling…" No feeling in the fading light.

Chapter 43

Since the Lord wouldn't release her, Art faithfully visited Katherine each day. He tried without success to pressure the kids to do the same until Katherine could return to Evans House's hospice unit. Todd heard first about his frustration about the girls' resistance as they shared time in Katherine's room.

"Pick your battle, Dad. Mom probably doesn't know if she has visitors."

"But, if she should pass, I don't want her to be alone."

"We can't sit here all day. The nurses will call. By the way, I'm going home for dinner."

"What's going on with you and Kris? Shouldn't you be moving on with your lives?" Art noticed his son's spine straighten. The boy had a weak chin, not a Kemper trait.

"The stuff that brought on the separation didn't develop in a few months."

Those were words from Rachel's *Family Games* book, but Art spoke from personal experience. "Thirty years from now, if this was Kris laying in a coma, you'd forget all the small stuff. In the scope of fifty years together, a few months apart aren't much."

Looking out the window, he stretched his hands, feeling the arthritic ache triggered by playing computer card games. "Your mother spent almost a year in California with her cousins when you were just a little kid. I didn't know if she'd come back when she walked out with two suitcases and I didn't ask questions when she returned on Christmas Eve. Insisted on cooking Christmas breakfast and dinner the next day. Lousiest Christmas I've ever had, including that one in the service. But, when you celebrate your fiftieth no one remembers those times."

"I don't remember Mom being gone that long."

"My sister Louise took care of you and Rachel and ran the house. Rachel remembers."

"Rachel's told me about the second time Mom went away."

"She was old enough to understand. Rachel doesn't say much about a lot of things. Not everything deserves to be dug up." Art stretched. "I gotta get going. I'm meeting someone for dinner myself."

"Some of the guys from church?"

"No. A lady. She lost her husband to Alzheimer's about a year ago. I ran into her at Janie's Super Bowl shindig. We talk now and then."

"You're dating while Mom's dying?

"Hold on to your pants. Glenna's been around for a long time. She and her husband are quite a bit older than us. She wouldn't consider 'dating' me as you put it. We just have a meal somewhere and talk." Art turned away. "Say hello to Kris and the kids."

Changing his mind, Art returned to Katherine. Taking one of her hands in his own, he rubbed a thumb across her knuckles then turned it over and ran a finger over the palm. There was slight movement and he smiled before setting her hand back at her side.

Chapter 44

His father was wearing clothes that were unfamiliar tickled Todd's thoughts as he drove home. He rolled his own wedding band with his thumb until traffic grew heavy and demanded full attention. Staying true to new commitments, he drove into the garage exactly on time.

The kids no longer treated his coming as a big deal. Clay continued watching television. Standing at the sink Mel held her cheek his way for a kiss, a gesture just like her mother.

"I see two of my kids. Where's Cat?"

"Biking home from Molly's," Mel responded. "She was supposed to be home now."

He could smell the meat and spices, realized how he took such simple things for granted as part of his home. "Your Mom makes a wicked pork roast."

"I made it, Dad. I do a lot of the cooking." Mel checked her phone. "Mom's in the den working on stuff for some client who is a big deal. She's totally stressed. If I could drive, I would have picked up Cat.."

He wasn't comfortable with Mel's approaching sixteenth birthday and impending drivers' license. "You've got plenty of practice left before we talk about scheduling a driving test."

The phone rang and he let Kris grab it. Her hysterical yell from the den stunned Todd and Mel. "Cat's been hit by a car."

"Mom, is she all right? Mom?" Mel's high young voice bounced off hallway walls as she ran. Todd moved faster.

"Who was that?" he asked first, wanting more information.

"Molly's mother. She's with Cat." Kris kept one ear to the phone. "A teenage boy turned the corner, came across the entire street and caught her rear tire. Cat was wearing her helmet, but one of her legs is broken. EMTs are a block away."

He stood with Mel glued to his side, waiting for the sign that they could leave to be by Cat's side. Molly's mother held her phone to Cat's ear letting Kris murmur all sorts of things. Her tone changed as an EMT asked questions then directed them to meet the ambulance at Regions Hospital.

Hearing hospital, Todd moved into action "You two stay here. If we need you at the hospital, we'll call Grandpa to pick you up."

"Clay." The boy sat staring at the television. "Are you deaf?" Todd yelled as he strode toward his son. "Did you hear anything? There's something going on in this house."

"Chill, Dad. This is just a really good story about steroids in base-ball. What?"

Todd put a hand on Clay's shoulder and gave him a rough shake. "God damn it, your sister's been hit by a car and you're drooling over a piss stupid baseball television show about hopped-up athletes? Join the living."

"What did I do?" Clay tried to brush off Todd's hand. "You're hurting me, Dad."

Mel stepped in, turned off the television and bumped Clay out of Todd's hold. "Dad, get in the car with Mom. I'll take care of Clay. Go." Mel pushed him toward the garage. "Call us."

Todd drove Kris' minivan, substituting speed for fear. They both jumped out at the emergency unit entrance, Todd staying to give keys to the valet while Kris ran ahead. Kept in the lobby area until Cat was placed in a room, they held hands. Neither spoke.

Their daughter was so small on an adult-size gurney. Her eyes stayed closed as she struggled to breathe. He reached out to touch her soft, fine hair spread wild across the pillow.

The injured left leg with its peculiar angle and blood oozing from a nasty scrape on her shoulder seemed secondary to the ragged gasping noise of her breathing. The sound reminded him of his mother. He wondered how they could both break legs in odd accidents before he started praying, almost commanding God to pay attention. His eyes remained on Cat's face.

"Hey girl, we're here. We love you." Kris murmured. Cat opened her eyes, the pupils constricted by shock. "You're going to be okay." Her eyes moved to Kris then him. He squeezed her hand very gently and swore to himself that he wouldn't leave the hospital without his child.

A nurse walked in. "The chest X-ray was fine which is good. We're having problems with Cat's asthma."

He drew his thumb across Cat's knuckles. Kris' voice cracked as she asked questions and provided information about their daughter's medical history. While his heart remained in crisis alert, he was comforted by Cat's presence and the relative calm of the emergency staff. He focused on the asthma as their main threat, ignoring wounds and blood.

"Isn't there something you can do to help her?"

"I'm Dr. Smith." A young doctor brushed past Todd. "Let's elevate your head while Nurse Rebecca sets up a nebulizer tent." Cat's shoulders and head moved up slowly. "If the two of you could step out here, I'd like to show you X-rays."

"What have you given her for pain?" Todd wanted to know everything. Katherine's hospitalizations taught him a thing or two about advocating for a patient.

The doctor named two unfamiliar meds. "May I call you..."

"Todd." He extended his hand. "And my wife, Kris." The words came natural. My wife. "Could we talk in her room? We'd rather not leave Cat alone."

"Just two minutes. You'll be able to see her X-rays better on the hall screen." Dr. Smith moved them both toward the door. "And, we'll be out of Rebecca's way." As they stepped into the hall, the doctor gave directions about Cat's wounds to a second nurse.

"She's going to be here overnight?" Todd fought the urge to bolt back.

"The leg's fractured in more than one place with a serious amount of tissue and muscle injury. I've got a pediatric orthopedic surgeon on his way to look at these X-rays and examine Cat. She'll need surgery. Good news is that while the injury is messy, it's not unusual. After surgery, there'll be physical therapy. Summer can be boring for a kid in a cast."

Kris leaned against the wall, color washing from her face. Todd moved to her side and took one hand. "What about her asthma?" he asked.

"This attack's bad but we're on top of it." Dr. Smith flipped off the X-ray screen. "With the treatment she's getting, she'll be breathing easier in the next few minutes. Attacks from shock are more challenging."

The doctor smiled as he faced them. "That is one self-possessed kid. She told us everything she knew and didn't cry though she's in a huge hurting way. We know you have United insurance and her doctor is Steven Rice. Then she told us she had asthma and was allergic to sulfur and aspirin." He ushered them back toward Cat's room. "Also gave us her date of birth, the hospital she was born at and that you had a C-section." Kris startled. "Quite a storehouse of information."

"I don't feel good," Cat said as they entered the room. The nurse wiped her face with a washcloth. "I think I'm going to throw up." In less than thirty seconds, she did and tears rolled down her face as she gagged into a plastic bin.

"Could be the medicine I just gave you to help you breathe. Rough trade off. You breathe, but you barf. Feel better or should I keep this here?" The nurse brushed Cat's hair.

She mewed a quiet response that she was okay.

"Mom and Dad are probably relieved to hear the room is quiet?" The nurse handed Kris a clean cloth. "Here, Mom, finish wiping Cat's face. I'm going to give her scrapes a little clean up while we wait for the orthopedic doctor. Could sting here and there."

Kris took the washcloth. "What about this gouge on her neck? Will she need stitches?" Todd envied Kris' purpose. He moved to Cat's feet and watched.

"Dr. Smith will be putting a butterfly bandage on it, or maybe two. Gravel abrasions usually heal without scarring. We'll have a plastic surgeon take a look later this evening."

"Kris, I'm going to call my dad. Have him check in on the kids. I'll call them also." He stepped out and tried his father's cell phone number. His father sounded relaxed as he answered.

"Dad, sorry to interrupt your dinner. Kris and I are with Cat at Regions. A car hit her bike and she's got some nasty injuries. Nothing life threatening, but we could be here for several hours, maybe through the night. Could you check in on the kids?"

"Cat's going to be okay?"

"She has a broken leg that needs surgery, but everything else checks out. We're lucky."

"I'll get over to your place and make sure the kids are okay. Don't worry about them. I'll sack out on the couch if you want."

"Thanks, Dad. We'll keep you updated."

"Mr. Kemper, the police want to talk with you and your wife."

Todd hung up and saw Kris standing with an officer in the hall.

"Mr. Kemper. Your wife's updated us on Cat. The young man who was driving was under the influence of marijuana at the time of the accident. He knows your older daughter and wanted to tease Cat when he swerved toward her. I suspect his parents will be calling you."

"It was Billy Backer, Todd. The boy who took Mel to homecoming."

Todd looked at his wife then the officer. His hands clenched and he felt his spine lengthen. "That shit. What's Mel doing hanging out with a kid who smokes weed?" He looked at Kris, then away. "What charges will this Backer kid face? Our daughter could be in cast all summer."

"We'll keep you informed, Mr. Kemper." The officer tipped his head and walked away.

"I want the books thrown at that kid. Next time he could kill someone. I don't want him driving around our neighborhood."

"Todd, lower your voice." Kris tugged at his arm but he shrugged her off. "Calm down."

"How could you let Mel go out with a scum bag?" He lowered his voice, but stared down Kris. She stepped away, breaking the intimacy they shared since arriving at the hospital. His anger grew with knowing Billy Backer's name.

Her arms crossed her chest as she drew back. "You were pleased she was asked to the dance by one of the soccer team stars. Maybe Mel didn't go out with him a second time because he was a jerk. None of that is important right now. This isn't Mellie's fault."

"You heard the cop. That kid knew Cat was Mel's little sister."

"That doesn't make Mel responsible for this accident." Kris began turning away. "Todd, please settle down or take a walk. I want to concentrate on our child."

He took a deep breath, jammed his hands in his pants pockets and walked. Kris never looked his way before entering Cat's room. From Clay's blank television stare to this one-time boyfriend of Mel, he saw threats to the family's security. Kris had to see that his absence made the kids vulnerable. He slammed one palm into a tiled wall to calm himself before heading back to Kris and Cat.

"Sorry, a dad has a right to get angry when some young punk hurts his daughters." He tried putting an arm around Kris' shoulder. She didn't bend. His tension remained, his palm stinging in a bad way. "I got worked up, but I'm okay now."

He was still okay when they drove home around two in the morning. There was no discussion about whether he would stay the night. They fell asleep side-by-side, tired to the bone and frightened to the soul by their daughter's tortured breathing when her asthma kicked in three more times. Surgery would be in two days and now they knew the asthma might be a problem.

Kris was on the phone in the morning when Todd awoke. "Hospital" she mouthed. He sat next to her on the bed. "She slept through the night and woke up on her own this morning. Thank you. That's great news. We'll be there as soon as we get the other kids off to school."

"One of us can go right now and one stay here," Todd suggested.

"It's not that easy. I'm supposed to be in Minneapolis for a presentation at nine. Absolutely the most crucial presentation on this account."

"So you go. I'll give the kids an update and go to the hospital. Cat will understand. I can make changes in my schedule for the next few days. You've done it often. We got to pace ourselves."

Her anguish perplexed him. He accepted similar offers many times through the years. "New client's really stressing you?" She nodded, her face tired. "Talk later. Now, go stand in the shower for a long time, then do magic with makeup."

"Don't say anything mean to Mel."

"I've got to say something. Kids will talk at school."

"Don't blame her, Todd."

"I was emotional last night. Have a little confidence in me."

He found a decent shirt and pair of dress slacks in their closet, dressed and headed downstairs. Mel sat at the kitchen table, red-eyed with a pile of used tissues.

"Daddy, I heard Billy Backer was the one who hit Cat. He's such a stoner. About a dozen kids texted last night. I hope he's not in school today cause I couldn't stand seeing his face."

"Did he light up during homecoming?"

"I didn't see him do that, but we didn't spend that much of the dance together. Probably not, 'cause he could lose his eligibility if he was caught."

"Did you know he was a 'stoner' before you went out with him?"

"I heard stuff but the team was heading for a great record so I didn't think any of them would be stupid enough to risk it." She sat up and shook her hair back, her face open in the early morning sunshine. "Dad, I don't hang with stoners. I hate being around kids who are messed up."

"We'll talk later. Get your brother. I've got to get to the hospital." He needed a notebook to record all the things to be talked about later.

Driving to the hospital, Todd replayed Kris' stress. Painfully he remembered describing such scenes to his mother without much compassion for his wife. Without Mom's steadying his rose colored glasses, he saw he might have been a bastard. His hands were in claws on the steering wheel. He needed to share his revelation with Kris. Later. He wasn't good at later.

"Good morning, son." His father stood outside the elevator doors on Cat's floor.

"Dad, why are you here so early?"

"I have a breakfast meeting here with John Raymun about the church development campaign. Thought I'd see if Cat was awake."

"Is she awake?"

"Very much so. Made me promise to look for a banana nut muffin and some odd flavor of fruit juice. Thought I might look for a stuffed something in the gift shop." His father's voice slowed. "Cat's going to be here a while isn't she?"

"At least a week. Surgery could be tomorrow then there will be days in traction before we move her home." Todd felt awkward. "Thanks for putting your plans aside last night."

"This is where you belonged. Sick kids clear the deck of a lot of unimportant junk. Kris on her way?"

Todd covered for Kris, realizing he didn't know how his father would react. For the last five months they'd talked about basketball, baseball, work, technology, the weather but generally avoided much personal discussion. "Yeah. We both have work things to clear off our calendars. She's making a few phone calls now and I'll do the same later."

Art tapped his pants pocket. "Figured how to put it on vibrating so I don't have to worry about my phone ringing in the wrong place. Amazing technology." He held out his hand. "Good you kids can manage work while being where you're needed. Call if I can help."

"Thanks, Dad. Have a good breakfast."

"I almost forgot. I'm picking up Dylan after school today so he can visit Cat. If your kids are interested, I'll take them out for pizza before I drive Dylan home."

"That's great, Dad." Todd couldn't remember his kids having a meal out with his father. "You know, Dylan doesn't have to miss baseball practice. He can visit on the weekend."

"Heard from David. He'd like to help in any way he can. He's a decent guy, too bad he rubbed your sister wrong. Now I gotta skiddoo."

His father took off toward the elevator. Todd watched his father walk away with a distinct loose hip movement and recognized Rachel's stride. Looking at his watch, he wondered what else could happen before eight.

Chapter 45

"Sorry to hear you've got two family members hospitalized," Art's breakfast pal said. "Any changes in Katherine's condition? And, what about your granddaughter?"

"Katherine's the same." It was easier to not talk about his wife. All the small twists and switchbacks of her trail were merely time fillers. That Katherine's care was now hospice remained family confidential. Visiting her that morning, Art thought she might be irritated that one of the grandchildren was claiming attention. "Cat's fractured leg needs surgery. She'll be here for at least a week."

"It's a sad story about the Baker boy. His grandparents are parish members." They sipped their coffee. "Family and church keep you busy, Art. Seems to agree with you."

"Todd and Rachel and Rachel's boy are all staying with me. My family has given me a new lease on life, John. For the first time I feel connected to my kids." He was babbling to this guy who he knew mostly from church volunteer work. "I'm trying to help the grandkids and get out into the world so I can be relevant in their lives."

John smiled, a younger man's smile still ignorant of ailing spouses and dying friends. "You seem energized at committee meetings. Good for you. I can't imagine what it's like to go through what you and Katherine have experienced."

Art watched John bow his head briefly before tackling a huge breakfast. Katherine dragged the family through stages of praying before meals. Out of respect, he bent his own head and found a few words of prayer silently lift from his heart. "Let this be the day you take Katherine home, dear Lord. For this I pray. Amen."

Chapter 46

Carrie sat propped up in bed, the phone trapped between her shoulder and ear, talking with Steve. She closed her eyes trying to remember when these nighttime calls made her feel connected to her husband in a sexy way. Tender breasts stretched her t-shirt and she shifted for comfort. Steve hadn't commented on these mounded mammeries, but it had been another two-day home visit with no time for intimacy. They had to talk this weekend.

She blamed first trimester hormones for unexpected tears and considered breaking their code of conduct around phone calls, serious discussions were held for face time.

"Steve, I'm not going to call the doctor. It's just a viral thing. I'm certainly not going to die in the next 24 hours." She didn't say she'd seen the doctor earlier in the week to confirm the pregnancy. "I feel awful that we haven't been able to visit Cat."

She heard the clinking of plates delivered by room service to his Chicago hotel. He rambled on while eating, telling her stories about the day in an almost girlish way that annoyed her tonight. He stopped in mid-sentence. "I get the sense you aren't with me. It is late."

"You're right. I should try to sleep."

"Maybe you should try a brandy and honey mix. You sound husky."

"I've taken so much medicine I don't think I should risk brandy."

"Go to sleep. I'll be home Thursday night and take the boys to see Cat. Did you send flowers?

It was the kind of question that made her consider screaming. "Tulips."

Steve gave an approving sound on the other end. "Good thinking. Take care of yourself."

"I'll send pictures so you remember what I look like." She regretted her catty comment, regretted much about the recent weeks. "Good night, Steve." After hanging up, she turned off the bed lamp. When she closed her eyes, brown pill bottles with red warning stickers stood with neon-like brightness behind her eyelids. She wanted a daughter, a baby to name Katie who would be as perfect as the boys. The amniocentesis in the next six weeks couldn't tell if drinking or drugs had impacted the baby.

After midnight she gave up trying to sleep and went downstairs to make a cup of tea and read. Nothing held her attention. Between the refrigerator and alcohol cabinet, Carrie sat down on the kitchen floor. If the kids wandered into the kitchen they'd be frightened, but she didn't care. It was time for everyone to face the real world.

In spite of self-adjusting her medications since the positive home pregnancy test, she had to tell Steve all the facts. He would be stoic and Catholic, protecting the unborn then damning her if Katie was born with problems. She wanted someone to focus on the seventy percent possibility that a healthy baby could be born. The immensity of that thirty percent on her boys and their future paralyzed her thinking.

Most of her prescription drugs were hidden until she made a critical decision. Suicide felt like a better action than facing her sins on earth. The Catholic Church was quite clear about eternal damnation. There could be no funeral service, no burial in consecrated grounds. "I'm damned," she whispered in the empty room, hearing her own whimper. "Damned."

The dogs approached. Rain sheeted the kitchen windows. Her nightshirt hung damp, crumbs and fuzz stuck on clammy skin. Carrie rolled to her hands and knees then stood, feeling like a homeless person in her own kitchen.

Upstairs she swallowed a Xanax then stood under a warm shower, guzzling a tumbler of iced vodka. Hair still wet, she turned off all the lights, snapped on a small book lamp and settled back against the bed pillows.

"Mom." Jake's voice came from the other side of the bedroom door. "Are you all right?"

Carrie turned on her bed lamp before moving from under the covers. "Yes, honey." She opened the door. "My fever's gone and I took a shower. Did I wake you?"

Her youngest son's sleepy eyes raked across the bedroom. Nothing was out of place.

"I thought I heard you crying."

"Jake, I'm so lucky to have you guys here to take care of me when Dad's gone." She smoothed his bed-tousled hair. "I felt bad for myself about being so sick. You should get back to sleep. Want me to tuck you in?"

He shook his head 'no' and turned. She would love to hug his strong, lean body but he'd hate that. "Good night, Mom. Hope you feel better."

"Love you, Jake." Carrie listened for his door to close. Maybe he was being sweet, maybe he was keeping watch for Steve. She closed her door, turned off the bed lamp and watched the digital clock numbers change. In the dark Carrie wanted her mother, the one person who kept her focused on running a good home. She needed the calming force of her mother's observant personality.

Sleep wouldn't come. The desire to take control over her personal mess didn't shut down. She went to her office and on a pad of paper drew a line down the center, with a plus sign above one side and a minus sign above the other. Rapidly she captured the reasons for rebuilding her marriage including Steve's affection, the boys, their lifestyle, the baby, her husband's kindness, their sex life, the way he smiled when she did anything special for him.

Four words landed in the negative column – loneliness, uselessness, damaged baby. Mom would call her self-centered; tell her to make a few friends. But Mom wasn't a part of the world any more. In fact, Carrie wished they could all stop watching Mom die. When her time came Carrie would spare her family the drama.

Fragile gray light outside brought the end to another night. While tired, she acted on the urge to write Steve a note and mail it to his hotel. Words flowed. She loved him, but was so lonely. There were better days to come and she was determined to become a happier person. She wrote his name on the envelope, found his hotel address and set the two on her desk. Down the hall, the boys' alarm clocks began to buzz.

Getting the boys out the door took more effort that morning. Fog and rain turned the roads into crawling parking lots. Like most of the kids streaming from cars, neither of her boys turned to wave. Carrie watched out the window until their backpacks disappeared then zipped into the drive-through of the local Java shop for an espresso to drink for the ride home.

Slurping the hot brew, Carrie pulled back into traffic. Brake lights flashed ahead. She avoided slowing for a yellow light by pulling into the right turn lane and accelerated around the corner. Holding her espresso and steering with the same hand, she tried to pull on her shoulder harness with the other. Her minivan swerved. She over-corrected and tapped the brakes.

The driver of a huge Ford Navigator made the same decision to avoid the intersection's red light while turning left, not anticipating Carrie's swerving. She gave up on the seat belt as she saw the behemoth vehicle race toward her door.

Upon the first impact, the hot espresso fell from her hand. The liquid burned through her cotton knit pants. She cried out loud while wildly grabbing for the steering wheel. No seatbelt in place, the impact threw her across the car then forward toward the dashboard. Her foot slipped from the brake and her vehicle went forward to be hit by another car on the right.

It was all so quick, so long. She no longer tried to grab for anything in the minivan as a pressure in the center of her chest exploded. Her body crumbled, or maybe become part of the vehicle. It made no difference.

Chapter 47

Riding with Rachel, Art thought they might be the next Kempers placed in hospital beds. But he said nothing as she wove her way on wet congested roads into downtown St. Paul, swerving into any opening. His thoughts toggled between prayers, imagining the extent of Carrie's injuries, and questioning what God expected him to shoulder.

"Where's a squad car when you need it?" Rachel said out loud, tapping on the steering wheel as they came to a stop a mile before their expressway exit. Her phone rang. He was unnerved she would answer while driving in these conditions.

"God, I'm so glad it's you. Carrie's been in a bad car accident and we're on our way to Regions. Traffic is awful."

Rachel nodded and wound her way into a different traffic lane. Art closed his eyes, prayed for his other daughter.

"You're at Regions finishing a consult? Can you meet us at the ER? With traffic, we're about ten minutes away. I'll call you when we get closer."

She hung up and concentrated on driving. His hands clutched his pants legs as they exited the expressway.

"We're here." Rachel's face remained tight as she called David. "Watch for us." She hung up and rubbed a hand across her face. "I hope you don't mind David meeting us?"

"It will be a blessing."

Somehow they entered the building. Art watched David hold Rachel in a long embrace, speak quietly into her ear. Rachel's shoulders stiffened, her head bowed forward.

"This is going to be tough." He extended a hand to Art. "Come back this way."

Opening a door, David stood aside for them to enter. At the last moment Art felt his legs tremble and hung back. Rachel tugged gently. "Dad, Carrie needs us."

"I know," he mumbled and accepted the strong arm of his son-in-law as they stepped forward. The opening of these doors meant decisions, sacrifices, fear. He envied Katherine who knew nothing of what was happening.

A doctor, his scrubs splattered with blood, waited. Art didn't want to think this was Carrie's blood.

"I'm Dr. Tom Blake. Let's step in here before you see Carrie." They filed into a nondescript small room. "It's touch and go. She was not wearing a seat belt at the time her vehicle was hit and suffered extensive internal injuries as well as serious head trauma." He paused. "Also important, your loved one suffered a heart attack. We assume she was on medications?" Art sensed Blake was going to say something further but changed words. "If she survives, the brain injuries will cause permanent damage. Do any of you know what medications Carrie might be taking?"

"I know she's taking antidepressants and Xanax," Rachel volunteered.

The doctor's eyebrow went up. He opened the door. "You can see her for a second. She's unconscious and there are people working on her. Where's her husband?"

"Chicago. I called him," Rachel answered. "Corporate jet should land at Holman Field in a little over ninety minutes."

Confronted by the bright lights and heat of the treatment room, Art breathed in deeply before recoiling from the stew of scents. And then he saw Carrie, a deep red mark on her bare right leg and horrific bruises disfiguring her pretty face. Staff surrounded her, bloody used paraphernalia piled on the floor.

Instinct carried him toward her side, his arms extending to gather her close. "God, not our child," he begged in his heart. His hands extended, needing to be assured her heart still beat.

"Steady, Art. Touch her here." Art heard David's voice as if swimming below water and hearing conversation taking place above. He struggled to quiet his hand before laying his fingers on Carrie's leg, relieved to feel the warmth of her skin. Standing there, feeling her alive, he looked beyond the medical staff, back to her face. Her eyes were closed above an intubation tube, her nose squashed with lacerations carved into her forehead and cheeks.

He didn't listen as David described Carrie's condition, just concentrated on transferring strength through his fingers to her leg while begging their Heavenly Father to understand an earthbound father's terror. The most difficult prayer entered his mind, and he bowed his head with its burden. "If it is her time, let her go in peace, without pain." Art knew emptiness. He saw the mask of Katherine's face and swore he'd not let it settle on Carrie.

When he spoke out loud, Art's voice was lost in the busy room. "We need to find a priest." David said a lay minister had been in with blessed oils.

A nurse directed them from the room as monitors squawked and Carrie's body twitched. Rachel took Art's hand. One of their hands shook. Her face was white and he heard her swallow, but he had no comfort to offer.

"I don't want her to die," he said then bit his lip. They stood together in the hall. Once or twice Art tried to talk, but the assurance that everything would work out could not be offered.

David brought a chair and Art sat down, accepting the deference for his age. The hall clock moved slowly through five minutes, then ten. Art stood. "Could you find out how she's doing, David?" he asked. "I don't hear the machines."

"Sure, Art. Do either of you need anything else?"

"I need my daughter to be all right." Art heard his voice shake. He felt like a very old man, knowing that one of his children dying before he and his wife was against every law of nature. God's worst punishment. "Go check. Please."

"Sit down, Dad." His daughter offered her strong arms and he accepted her help as he lowered himself to the chair. Rachel slid her back down the wall to wait on the floor beside him. She leaned her head back, eyes closed. He watched David move into Carrie's room. Glancing away, Art realized another ten minutes had passed. Time felt like a promise. He thought of bartering with God, knew he had nothing to offer.

Reaching into his pocket for a tissue, Art felt a twinge around his own heart, a mild grip then release. He hesitated and held his breath, waiting for some change. He released his breath and drew in deeply. Nothing happened. Opening his now runny eyes, Art watched David walk towards them, extend a hand to Rachel to help her from the floor and shake his head slightly.

"She went into defib." He stopped talking; gathered Rachel to his shoulder then squeezed Art's shoulder with his other hand.

Like that his baby, his pretty little girl, was gone. Art looked beyond his living daughter, blind to whatever was happening in the hallway, not sure if his God was punishing or merciful. Whatever was the truth, he could not find the words to pray for Carrie's journey home.

Chapter 48

The hospital's call had caught them before her father had showered. His hair looked thin and flattened. In the harsh institutional light, Rachel saw a fine silvery shadow covering his face. He wore a baggy green polo shirt and black pants with his everyday shoes. "I need to speak with your mother," he said, his voice as low as a dying man's whisper. "I need to talk with her." Then he began sobbing and she placed her arms around him, her own tears wetting his shirt.

Accepting his frailty, she felt responsibility for the family settle on her shoulders. Straightening her back, she curved in closer to her father, hoping his heart could take the shock.

"Dad, Mom's not going to understand and I don't want to leave Carrie yet." Rachel cradled her father the best she could, surprised at strong muscles across his shoulders.

"Your mother has a right to know what's happened."

"Let's stay here for a little while then I'll take you home so you can shower, or we'll go straight to Mom. Just a few minutes, then we'll do whatever you want."

"Who's going to call Father Kevin?"

What she knew about the rituals of death came from her profession or sitting through memorials and funerals. During services where women so often filled more pews than men, she thought how caring for the dead, like caring for the newly born, fell more naturally along gender lines. She had much to learn about death's protocols and rhythms. "I'll do whatever needs to be done, but you'll need to help me figure it out."

"It's not that difficult–you call Father Kevin, then Todd, then go pick up the boys and then…" Art's voice quivered. "It's not that difficult. Carrie would know what to do. She has everyone's telephone numbers." He pulled away from Rachel. "She's a chip off her mother. Knows what to do whenever anything happens."

They made their way back to Carrie's side. Hospital staff moved around the small room, sliding equipment out, picking up larger medical refuse from the floor. Two quietly removed tubes, cleaned her body. One stepped aside and extended a hand to Art.

"I'm sorry for your loss, sir," she said. "We'll leave you alone so you can be with your family. There's a chair and a stool here."

One part of Rachel's mind was aware of the nurse dragging a chair next to Carrie's side and helping Dad settle. The rest of her mind refused to accept what was happening. Her emotions were both raw and numb.

"My God, she's hurt everywhere the eye can see," her father said while slowly surveying Carrie as if inventorying each abrasion, bruise, cut. "Whoever hit her should have to come in here and see what they did. Did they tell us if the other driver was hurt?"

"Cuts and abrasions. He was driving a bigger vehicle. Another car was involved and the driver was taken elsewhere with non-life-threatening, but serious, injuries," David volunteered.

"One of us needs to stay with Carrie." Dad said. He looked at her sister's face, raised a hand and touched one of the unblemished areas. A man in shock, he repeated. "I need to see Katherine."

She was grateful that David suggested a plan because she couldn't.

"I'll stay here with Carrie and wait for Steve while you see Katherine. Okay, Rachel?"

Her voice came out soft, as if Carrie slept between them. "We'll see Mom and go to Regions, then home to give you a chance to change your clothes, Dad. Then I want to come back here." She walked around to help him up and the weight of his arm in her hand alarmed her. "Are you all right?"

Art hesitated. David suggested they step away to visit the men's room together. Sorrow slowed his walk to a shuffle. Rachel was alone with Carrie. She whispered prayers, hoping there was a God. The big sister, the one who so often comforted young Carrie, bowed her head.

David met her alone as he walked back. He put an arm around her waist. "Cat came through surgery fine. I called Todd and he will pick up the boys and meet Steve back here. He's talking with your Dad right now. Keep an eye on Art. He's shaken."

She was in the Twin Cities to be near this man. The kindness in his eyes, full lips that almost never pursed in disapproval, were the bedrock of life, what was missing in the plain living of her current days. Her eyes clouded again.

"You know I still love you, David? If it had been you in this accident, I would be devastated." She extended her hands upright. "You are the kindest, most dependable person in my life. Why have I been so stubborn?"

Close, he took her hands. "I love you too, but I hurt you. Nothing to figure out. Keep the positive feelings, Rach. After we get through the next few days, we can talk about us. Now you're going to have more than enough to handle." After a long squeeze, he let go.

She took a deep breath before she could speak. "Carrie would have loved fussing over my new house. I really thought once school was out, we'd get the boys together and do something. Why did we have to keep such distance?"

"Decades of dysfunction. If we were living in Chicago it might have been hours before anyone called to tell you about Carrie's accident." He kissed her hair. "Don't be hard on yourself. You've already done a lot of good for the Kempers."

"We should go." Art's voice sounded choked back in his throat as he rejoined them and Rachel knew he had been crying while talking to Todd. "We'll come back, and in the meantime David will take care of her."

She tucked her hand through his arm. The next words she said came naturally as soon as she understood she needed to be with family as they walked this trail of sorrow. "Maybe Dylan and I can stay at your place tonight?

Chapter 49

He let Rachel lead him through the lobby; his hand tucked into the corner of her arm. Walking through the hospital doors, Art pulled back as the most intense need to return to Carrie rushed through his heart. His girl couldn't be left alone.

"They'll move her into some forgotten corner," he said. "Rachel, do you think she's still here, watching us leave her?"

Rachel stopped walking and looked back at the hospital. "I've been wondering the same thing. David is with her and will make sure she's cleaned up for Steve and the boys. She wouldn't want them to see her this way."

They stood silent, neither in nor out of the hospital. "I have to see your mother," he said.

He sat in Rachel's car, watching the hospital as they pulled away. He folded down in the seat to watch it get smaller and smaller in the side view mirror as they moved away from Carrie.

Six months ago she was filling the family kitchen with the fuss of Thanksgiving dinner preparation, making the process look uncomplicated. Carrie was always there to fill the refrigerator with future meals, make sure seasonal projects were completed, keep the house feeling like the home Art liked.

Tulips and lilacs in blossom reminded Art of his spontaneous purchase of flowers at Thanksgiving and how Rachel helped him put together arrangements. A glass of booze tucked in the poinsettias let him know Carrie finished their clumsy efforts. He never told anyone.

"Your mother and I thought we did good raising you kids," he said. "You all graduated from college, found good spouses, had nice kids. You're all well-adjusted."

"We have done well, Dad. You worked hard." His daughter continued looking ahead.

Art wanted to talk about Carrie, needed to talk about her. "She had the easiest life of the three of you. After selling that company, all she had to do was take care of the kids." Art looked back out the side window then straight ahead. "So how is it that she's in an accident wearing torn pajama bottoms and that tee shirt? She always looked good, her hair curled, and nice clothes."

"Maybe she was running late, Dad. Maybe she wasn't feeling well and that was the best she could do. Lots of women wear sleep pants and tee shirts that don't match."

"You know it wasn't easy for your mother. Parenting wasn't her cup of tea. You girls were a real challenge for her. She was jealous of you two. She hated that you worked and she felt Carrie was wrong staying home. I never understood her attitude about you girls."

"Carrie was in a car accident. It had nothing to do with how you parented."

"Well, when I see Steve, I'm going to tell him that what would have really helped her is if he had stayed home more. My girl was lonely." He bit his lip and held his thighs tight with both hands.

Rachel patted his arm. "We don't really know if that would have made Carrie happier."

He had his belief and said nothing as Rachel stopped in front of the hospice center. He moved from the car alone then halted fifteen or twenty feet away, sensing Rachel scurrying behind him. She didn't scold or say a thing, just tucked her hand in his arm again. They moved quickly, her long steps setting the pace. She stopped and he stumbled a bit. "You want to be alone?"

"I think so. I'll be better after I see her." He took a deep breath. "I won't stay long."

Rachel gave him a small hug. "I'll be waiting." The feeling of her arms stayed with him all the way to Katherine's room even though his thoughts stayed with Carrie.

A nurse greeted him with a smile. "We have good news. Katherine's been awake off and on this morning and responding to simple questions." Art listened, his head down. "Is everything all right, Art?"

"No," he started then felt his knees begin to shake. "Could I sit down?" The nurse pulled a chair toward him. Deep, unspeakable grief pushed his body down. He had to say the words out loud, to share the news even though he couldn't accept Carrie's death.

"A car accident took our daughter, Carrie, this morning." 'Died' began forming but wouldn't move across his lips. "We've been at Regions with her." He put one hand to his forehead. "I'm not sure what to tell Katherine."

"I'm so sorry, Art. We thought it was odd Carrie hadn't called yet. I know morning sickness was taking its toll."

His head snapped upright. "Jesus Christ, she didn't say anything to me about a baby. She told you she was pregnant?"

"I'm sorry. I assumed you knew. She told Katherine."

Sympathy crossed the nurse's face and she reached out to pat his hand. Art forced himself to absorb this new information, this second loss of a grandchild he'd never meet. "I don't know what to tell my wife."

"Art, she won't understand or remember if you tell her."

"I don't think I want her to know," Art said. "Maybe she'll never need to know."

The nurse agreed. "We'll be thinking of you. You do what you need to do with your family. Katherine is cared for here."

"She's tough, isn't she?" he said to the nurse. "How is this fair?"

She shook her head. "I don't know, Art." She came to his side. "How did you get here? Is there someone waiting for you?"

"Rachel is in the lounge. I wanted to see my wife alone." He tipped his head to acknowledge her concern then walked to Katherine's room, conscious that his feet shuffled along the floors. Nothing remained in his soul to mimic the walk of a younger man.

His wife lay in the semi-dark, head turned toward the door, a small line of drool moving from her mouth down her face and onto a washcloth. They'd combed her hair. He walked toward the bed to the woman who stared vacantly past him.

"Katherine," Art said standing at his wife's side, but not touching her. "Katherine, why did you leave me again?" He bowed his head, teary eyes blurring the room's outline until he saw Carrie's bare leg again. His tears flowed, peacefully released in the presence of the woman who had been Carrie's mother. "Don't take this wrong, my beauty, but I would give anything if things were different." He straightened and placed his hand on Katherine's thin hair, felt her scalp through fine strands. "I might not be here tomorrow. You be good to the nurses. Rachel's waiting. We got to get back to Carrie."

A nurse insisted on walking him to where Rachel waited. They exchanged a few words and it was as if he saw his daughter shouldering responsibility for the family. Maybe later he'd step back up; maybe he'd take the affection this daughter offered.

"Dad, I brought these." She held up small packets of tissues. "Take one. The day's not going to get easier." He let her tuck one into his pants pocket. "Do you want to go home to shower or could we go back to Regions?"

Grief seemed to propel the first thing that came to his mind out his mouth. "What will those boys do now that Carrie's gone?" He thought his voice sounded feeble as he stumbled over not saying *dead*. Katherine was supposed to be dead. He could put the word comfortably with her name. Carrie was the one he'd planned to call first with the news when Katherine passed. "Did you know Carrie was pregnant?"

Rachel shook her head.

"I didn't either. The nursing staff knew. She had morning sickness they say."

She continued to hold his arm as they walked in silence. He started to open the car door, its weight anchoring him for a moment. Rachel took over and held it open. His body felt light against the car seat as if the shoulder harness kept him from lifting to the roof bringing his mind again to Carrie and the horror of crashing about inside of her minivan.

The morning's rain and fog were gone. Art closed his eyes against the May sunshine as Rachel drove from Katherine's place and back to Carrie. He rested his head and let his mind go blank.

Chapter 50

Todd pulled up to the hospital with Carrie's boys as Rachel walked her father to the entrance. She watched her father extend an arm to each boy stepping from the car. Jake, who looked like her sister, moved quickly to his grandfather's side, but Rob stood apart.

"Grandpa, I know this is real bad. Uncle Todd wouldn't say anything." Rob's tone was defiant.

Rachel knew he wanted assurance that he had jumped to the wrong conclusion. Before she could answer he began running, away from the hospital, away from them.

"Rob, stop." Her voice amplified against the hospital's concrete surfaces. She stretched her stride, leaving her father to deal with Jake. Reaching her nephew's side, Rachel put her arms around his shoulders. He resisted.

"You're her big sister and some kind of big shot doctor. Why didn't you help my Mom?"

"She was in a car accident, Rob. Another car hit her. Rob. It wasn't her fault."

He sobbed, tears flowing, arms still at his sides. "I was mean to her this morning. I wouldn't say good-bye at school."

"She didn't think you were being mean. Moms know that kids love them even if they don't say anything. Let's take you and Jake to your parents." From her pocket she drew out a tissue packet. "Put these in your pocket."

She delivered her father and the boys to Steve. Rachel waited for Todd. Five minutes passed then ten. From a corner chair in the waiting room, she stared at a space on the wall, her mind a waterfall of thoughts, holding on to nothing.

"Rachel?" Todd stood in front of her, the maturity of grief stealing the last of his young man carefree looks. "Were you with her?"

"Yes, Dad and David and I were here. She wasn't alone, Todd." The feel of her brother's arms was unfamiliar and they fumbled, coming close. He stood taller, bowed to her shoulder to accept comfort and offered nothing in return. Rachel supported his weight and grief.

"I hated her when she was a baby," Todd said. "She was all pretty and cute and Mom loved her so much." He whispered near her ear. "Was she drinking?"

"No one said anything about that," Rachel answered honestly. "The nurses at Mom's place told Dad that Carrie was pregnant."

Todd sucked down air nosily. "Fuck. I wonder how Steve felt about that."

"I let her down big time," Rachel said, already burdened by the truth.

"Beside parents and me what did you have in common? Does Mom know?"

She shook her head. "They told Dad it was better to not tell her." Rachel began gathering her things. "We'd better join the others. We're all called to some hospital every few months for all these little bumps in Katherine's life and so quietly we lose Carrie."

He looked at the floor, fished in his pants pocket for something, and finally looked up. "I wasn't ready to lose my sister today," he said, "but it will be just as hard to lose our mother."

Later Rachel wouldn't be able to remember how their hands came together during the walk to a quiet room in the back of the emergency department. The future looked grim, but the wail of Carrie's youngest son on the other side of the closed door marked this day as almost the worst the Kempers could survive.

Chapter 51

Todd kept a sports channel turned on in the bedroom as he polished shoes for Carrie's funeral. He couldn't remember what the announcers said ninety seconds earlier. His sister's death overshadowed everything including Cat's recovery and his return home. Boxes of clothes and shoes stood in the corner of their bedroom, untouched. On the dresser, roses he brought for Kris drooped in a few inches of murky, foul-smelling water.

He dropped his head, closed his eyes against the dull ache of pre-dawn whisky drunk alone in the kitchen. Kris talked about the day ahead, but he didn't listen while rubbing one dull spot on his left shoe.

"It's awful we're not able to help Steve," Kris said as she clipped a simple necklace over her sweater. "I was closest to Carrie, but with Cat in the hospital, I've been useless."

He heard her ask for confirmation that they weren't somehow responsible for Carrie's accident and didn't know how to answer. As the time to leave approached, fear blotted every other emotion. If Kris really turned his way, he'd tell her how he felt.

She opened the blinds, appearing pale and fragile in the morning sunshine. "Steve has been so overwhelmed." His wife paused. Everything paused. He exhaled, sickened by the roses.

Kris continued. "Imagine losing his wife and the baby. Talking with Steve's mother, they don't know where more booze or pills might be found once life gets back to normal."

"It isn't going to return to normal, Kris. Not for any of us." It was too late to tell her about his rising panic.

"Thank God, Rachel's been at Steve's side to plan everything." If he acknowledged his wife's comments in any way, they would both be lost in tears and emotion. "Did you speak with him last night? You were outside so long."

He ignored a hidden question beneath Kris' observation and turned the television off.

"How does Rachel know what to do?" He finished his question without saying *funeral*.

"I don't know." Kris turned to him. "I don't know how the four of us would make it through today without you here. Whatever you need from me, I'm here for you."

She squeezed his arm. He nodded, hoped she could interpret his answer. Noise from the kids seeped into the bedroom as she opened then closed the door. Stepping into their bathroom, Todd ran a comb through his hair and brushed his teeth for the third time that day, welcoming the sharp mint taste in his dry mouth, wanting a drink.

"Dad, Mom's ready to go." Tyler's voice came through the door. "Are you okay?"

Tyler meant the question quite innocently. Todd knew the sound of a kid worried that a drunken parent was throwing up behind the closed door. "I'm fine, just brushing my teeth." Todd checked his appearance once more in the vanity mirror then opened the door.

"Aunt Carrie gave me this shirt for Christmas. Is it okay to wear it today?"

"You look good," he said to Tyler and thought how young his son looked in his gray dress pants, dark shirt and tie. Enormous black leather shoes replaced Tyler's typical untied sneakers. "It's the right thing to do," Todd put his arm around Tyler.

"What's this gonna be like, Dad?"

"I don't really know, son."

They walked downstairs together. Mellie stood alone in the hallway, tall, thin and achingly beautiful. As she turned, Todd saw tears in her eyes, knew he should open his arms to offer comfort or at least touch her shoulder. But he couldn't.

"Where's your mother," is what came to his lips. "I'm not up to driving."

Chapter 52

Dad's hand rested heavy on her arm. In the short time since they left home, his newly tailored dark suit and starched white shirt changed to the baggy look of an old man's outfit. She placed her free hand over his and moved faster, trying to break the shuffle of his steps, bring him back to the minute.

"I hope things are the way Carrie would have liked," he said, clearing his throat repeatedly after the words left his mouth.

'What would Carrie like' was now a string of questions without answers. Rachel wondered if her sister had consciously faded into the caricature of a pleasant middle-age woman, or if the family merely assigned Carrie many of Katherine's more comforting traits. Beyond flowers and foods and colors, no one knew very much about what Carrie liked.

She patted her father's hand. "Don't worry," she said. "I think the arrangements cover everything."

"Your mother always had the right touch, knew what people expected."

They stood at the chapel door. She had worked hard to make sure everything was perfect.

He hesitated. "I need to sit a minute."

Rachel beckoned to Dylan who stepped up and led his grandfather to a chair. Flowers surrounded Carrie's coffin with banners proclaiming her roles: Mother, Wife, Daughter, Sister.

She approached her sister, reaching out to touch Carrie's shoulder like when they were girls sharing a bedroom and all the fears of the night. Not for the first time, the sight of waxy, overly-made-up skin split Rachel's fragile calm like a finger pressed into a healing wound. Her hand jerked over her sister's body as if searching for a button to close, a curl to straighten, a cut to staunch.

"Carrie, my beautiful little sister," went through Rachel's mind along with a memory of the day before Thanksgiving when Carrie walked past an attempted half hug. Pulling her hand back, Rachel knelt and racked her brain for the simple words of faith to ask God to welcome her sister into His kingdom. She knew the words, but couldn't recapture the spirituality that gave all those rote phrases meaning. What she grieved was throwing away the luxury of a sister in the effort to become a person apart from their mother.

She heard the criticism of her distance under the voices of visitors during the visitation, saw how others comforted Todd and their father without stopping to say a word to her. Like their mother, she faced their rebuff with a stiff back.

Rachel raised her head, looked at her sister's damaged face and whispered, "I loved you so much when you were born and Mom gave you to me. We grew apart, but I always thought we'd find our way back to enjoying each other's company. I'll take care of your boys. They won't forget what a good woman you were. I promise you that, Carrie." She pushed herself up from the kneeler, gazed around the room at her brother and his family, her sister's family walking in and the three men who mattered most in her life–Dylan, David and her father.

"I wanted Carrie to have your mother's best rosary," her father said as he approached. "Your sister has your mother's beautiful hands."

Todd entered the chapel holding his wife's arm like a cautious child led to danger.

He stepped in front of Rachel without acknowledgement and stood at the coffin side. How often had people called Todd and Carrie two peas from Katherine's family pod with their blonde hair and green eyes. Her siblings had been beautiful children, but failed to develop into the strongest adults. So close, she caught the slightest whiff of whiskey and backed away from offering comfort. Dad moved to Todd's side. They bowed their heads.

Chapter 53

The second summer Katherine disappeared, Rachel assumed responsibility for Todd and Carrie as well as managing the house. Barely into her teens, Rachel understood there was no one else who would step in to help the family. Their mother screamed as she left that caring for three kids would kill her. Another miscalculation on her mother's part. The morning after Carrie's funeral as she showered, Rachel wondered how her siblings' lives might have been if their mother had not been in a perpetual search for some form of escape.

"How're you holding up?" David stood outside the shower with a cup of coffee.

Opening the shower door, she took the coffee. He grabbed a towel and wrapped it around her shoulders, rubbed her back dry.

"Not well." She sipped at the coffee when he patted the towel in place. "I'm glad Steve's parents are able to stay for a few weeks. Carrie started planning the boys' summer, but finding someone to be a live-in housekeeper isn't going to be easy. Steve's got to be back in Boston in two weeks." She set the coffee mug down. "We're lucky Greta is willing to come from Chicago to be with Dylan one last summer." While Carrie's boys weren't exactly her worry, the matriarch mantle lay over her shoulders.

"What I should do is go for a run." She twisted from side to side, small crunching sounds coming from her neck and back. "I feel middle-age. Actually, I feel much older."

"Do you want me to stay tonight? I've got rounds and office until seven."

"I'm worried about how Dylan is reading us sleeping together," she said feeling embarrassed that she craved so much of his comfort.

"We talked. It's good for him to have us both in the same place."

Leaning into his chest she allowed herself a rest against the steady rhythm of his heart. "I'd like you to stay." Words she should have said a year ago.

She dressed and drove to her sister's house, to the lost young boys with their frightened eyes, and the angry husband with carefully-controlled face, and his confused parents. From the driveway, she saw Rob and Jake on the deck with their dog. She got out of the car and joined them. First she rubbed Rob's shoulder then gave Jake a hug and let him lean into her shoulder as long as he wanted. "How's the morning going?" she asked.

"Grandma made us pancakes and sausage for breakfast then said we needed fresh air." Rob kicked at the deck surface. "She didn't use the right syrup or remember orange juice."

Behind the words, Rachel heard 'she didn't do anything like our mom'. "It's going to be tough for some time. Maybe we should start a list of the little things your Mom did to keep the good traditions going."

"Dad's really mad at that guy driving the Navigator," Rob volunteered. "I'm afraid he's going to kill him. Then where would we go?"

"He is angry, but won't do anything like that. You mean the world to him. Lots of people love you and will care for you. You have three grandparents, Uncle Todd, me and your dad's brothers."

There was silence. The boys said nothing. As the time stretched out, she thought about what she might say to Steve.

"My Mom was really unhappy," Jake blurted. "I saw her sitting on the kitchen floor the night before... before the accident. She was crying." He looked beyond her shoulder. "I should've called Dad, but I didn't want them to fight."

"You know she wrote your dad a letter that night and said she loved you and was looking forward to the summer. When you saw her, she could have been making some good decisions. Sometimes it's hard to think through stuff." Rachel knew about a lot about facing demons at midnight. "I'm sure she wouldn't have wanted you to remember that."

"Grandma told you about the booze in my closet, didn't she? Is that why we have to have a babysitter this summer?" Jake's voice trembled.

"Your Dad has to go back to work and you two guys are too young to alone here so that's why we have to find a housekeeper. And, yes, we'll keep talking about things like drugs and booze and being responsible. That's our job." Rachel thought the adults were jumping to conclusions about the stash and believed her nephew's story about hiding the bottles from his mother to keep her safe.

"Can't we live with Grandpa or you?"

"We've got to figure out how to keep you three guys living here in your family's home."

He shrugged. "As long as we don't get a babysitter."

"Young man, you might be beyond the babysitter stage, but think of Rob."

With another shrug he turned away from her to race to the house. She watched his funny short step run and saw Carrie running to home plate at some long ago softball game with the same strange movement.

Chapter 54

For weeks following Carrie's funeral, Art looked to morning Mass for strength. In the comforting quiet of a nearly empty church, he could put a hand over his eyes and let memories flow. He waited with bowed head and outstretched hands to ask Communion, standing on the exact same spot where Carrie's coffin had rested. For a treasured few minutes, as the host melted on his tongue, Art found peace in prayer.

Weekends he returned home after church and slept through the morning in his recliner. On weekdays, he stopped at Katherine's hospice facility, then the bakery before driving to Carrie's house for breakfast with her boys. Art liked that Debra, the nondescript woman Steve hired as a housekeeper, looked like middle-age wives he saw at the grocery store, and nothing like Carrie.

"Good morning, Debra. Today I brought donuts. There's plenty for all of us."

"Good morning, Mr. Kemper. Jake just came downstairs. He's in the family room." She took the donuts from him. "I'll have one here in the kitchen. Would you like a cup of coffee?"

He accepted coffee in a bright poppy ceramic mug Katherine once gave Carrie filled with Valentine candy. No one remembered that except him. The house seemed to wait for Carrie's return, not one item moved by those who passed through its space. From what the boys said, Debra spent the majority of her days cleaning. She made weak coffee.

"Hey, Jake." Art put a hand on his grandson's bed-tousled hair, enjoying the coarse strands under his fingers. "I brought chocolate donuts."

"Not yet, Grandpa. I just got up."

Art longed to inhale the lingering sleeping smells of a healthy kid and forget Katherine's room. Instead he sat next to Jake on the couch and waited for Rob. Even after Rob joined them, after the donuts and milk and weak coffee were gone; even then they often sat until mid-day waiting for something to happen. Only when Debra asked if he was staying for lunch, would Art acknowledge to himself that Carrie wasn't coming downstairs. Then he would leave.

At home he made himself a sandwich and waited for Rachel to call from work. Most days, she invited him to her home for dinner and company. With Weezer by his side and Dylan talking about the Twins or yard work, Art could feel like normal life continued. He sat in a big chair on Rachel's screened porch, watching her neighbor fuss with rose bushes. The guy had no clue how to prune, and Art had no desire to help.

"Watching you watch that guy gives me permission to say your yard needs a little attention, Dad." She stood behind him, a glass of lemonade in each hand.

"Don't sneak up on me that way, Rachel."

"Why don't you take the boys to your house and put them to work?" He noticed how they always spoke of the two as *the boys*, never *Carrie's boys*. "Keep them busy a few mornings."

"I'm not helping them, am I? That housekeeper must think I'm an idiot."

"She knows about the family's situation, Dad."

"I know buying donuts isn't helping any of us, Rachel, but damned if I know what else to do. Do you think working on the yard would help? What else we can do for our guys?"

"Doing something physical would help all of you. Take on their yard. You know Carrie would have planted tubs for the front steps and some annuals around the trees."

"I'll have to ask Steve," he said, but his mind was slowly thinking about where he saw plants advertised and what chores he let slide last fall after his heart attack.

* * *

Her father's silver hair moved slightly as the ceiling fan circulated air. With the dropping sun, she saw his profile more than the true features of his face. All the years when she was living at home he wore dark suits for work or church or special events. Now khaki slacks and open-neck shirts fit the softer man he had become.

"Since you asked, I do have a plan in mind. We need your help to make it work," she said as he seemed to slide into thought. Not for the first time, she wished she could keep him here instead of returning to his big old house. A future topic to talk over with David.

"Shoot."

"Rob and Jake need family this summer, Dylan's on the loose because of the move, and he tells me Cat will be spending time alone. So I proposed to Steve that we get the kids together afternoons this summer. Greta will be here for a majority of the days, but she doesn't know the Twin Cities so I thought David, you and I might each take an afternoon and spend time with the kids. Golf, go to parks, that kind of outing."

She waited to see if he could think beyond his current melancholy to remember the good days of spring when he discovered the fun of sitting on the sidelines of a grandchild's sporting event or taking the group out for pizza.

"I don't know what I'd do with the guys every week and Cat's on crutches."

"Dylan says you promised to teach them how to golf."

Her father sat back and blew out through his mouth. "Do you think I'm up to that? I don't know anything about little girls."

"You raised two."

He cleared his throat. "You can't say I was very good at it."

A neighbor child's shrill, indignant cry carried in the summer air. Fragile silence stretched between them like a spider web formed of memories easily tattered by an errant rough touch. She knew it was a time for forgiveness.

"You worked hard, supported us and were physically there at the end of each day. When Mom disappeared, you were my entire adult family. That's what I remember."

She stopped, knowing he would catch any insincerity, but trying to say words that would lead him to the future. "Look how you've stepped into the kids' lives this spring. Everyone on Dylan's baseball team knows you by name."

A small smile formed and he almost chuckled. "Cat reminds me of you. Unfortunately, I've heard your brother speak to her like your mother used to speak to you. I gave him some advice, but you know how he is."

"That's why Cat needs to be included, Dad. The boys will help with getting her in and out of places. It'll be good for Dylan to be responsible for someone else. Weezer's a poor substitute for a sibling."

"You're trying to build some kind of safety net around these kids?"

"That's right, Dad. We adults are going to watch a lot of kid baseball and soccer and hear a lot of bad jokes and put miles on our cars and I hope we can make a difference." She laughed out loud. "And we adults are going to get to know each other—you and David and Steve and I." She gestured toward her remodeled kitchen. "I'm ready for a bunch of kids in this house."

"If it doesn't get in the way of your mother's care, I'm in." Rachel tried not to frown. "What about Todd or Kris joining in?"

"They seemed relieved when I asked about Cat. But, Dad, they're not in jobs that give much freedom." The way he sat in the chair made a hug nearly impossible, but Rachel managed to wiggle an arm around his back and squeeze gently. "Thanks."

Chapter 55

"Katherine, you should see the calendar on our broom closet door. I got soccer games two nights a week, baseball games on Wednesday. Tuesdays I pick up Carrie's boys and Cat then Dylan for golfing lessons or lunch and 'chilling' together. You'd hate it."

He sat by Katherine's side, patting her cool hand. "I never had so much fun although the car's putting on some miles. That drive to Minneapolis can be nerve-wracking. On the other hand, Rachel always puts on a good dinner."

Katherine moaned, a sound like a cow lowing. Sometimes she would move her head and work her lips. He no longer blamed her for the poisons she'd nourished in their family.

"Cat's almost off crutches. Probably walking without them by end of July. She can't swing a club, but she rides in the cart with me and the boys have learned to be real gentlemen around her. You'd like that. There's not one of them that forgets to use Mr. or Mrs. when they talk to adults. They might be full of the dickens but they're learning. Good kids, Katherine, good kids."

Chapter 56

Weezer moved quickly, oblivious to the beauty of geraniums and roses balancing on generous greenery. Rachel tugged back on his leash. "I can't believe these flowers. I didn't expect to enjoy the neighborhood's yards. Just look at those blossoms, Dylan."

"It's not Chicago," he said.

"I know you've made some friends at school, but you probably miss the Chicago group. Do you mind hanging out with your cousins? I know this is an unusual summer."

"It's cool, Mom. Just chill."

"You're being a good sport, going from an only kid to this mess of my family."

"Next summer will be better, but this year family's good." He snorted, a boyish sound letting her know he was going to throw a zinger her way. "Anyway, I think the mess in your family stopped in your generation. We agree we're all pretty normal."

They walked in through the back door into a sunroom that served as base camp for the first four weeks of the summer plan. A neat freak, Rachel mastered the ability to accept projects left partially completed, video games on the floor, books laying on the sofa or chairs. "Do we have any lemonade or did you guys polish it off yesterday?"

Dylan shrugged. "Don't know. Jake's the big lemonade guy. Rob and I drink water. We're athletes in training, remember?"

"I remember when we had groceries in the cupboards and milk in the fridge." Rachel searched the kitchen for anything cold to drink more exciting than tap water. "You know I took care of Todd and Carrie when they were little. There was one summer when your grandmother was gone that the three of us made a fort in the family room and just kind of lived there. Grandpa even let us sleep there at night. I like having your cousins and Grandpa around."

"So why don't we live closer, like where we could all bike to each other's house?" He brushed her away from the refrigerator. "I miss getting around on my own like in Chicago."

"You never got around Chicago by yourself." She couldn't say that as long as Katherine lived, it was important to keep distance. "Your father and I are city people—our jobs are in the city, your school is here. I think you'd hate the suburbs."

The doorbell rang once. "It's Dad." Dylan and Weezer moved before she could set her glass on the kitchen counter. She gave them time to exchange greetings before following.

David leaned above Weezer's back for a kiss. "See if you have that CD in your room," he said to Dylan who took off running up the stairs.

Rachel watched Dylan's long, thin legs disappear around the stair landing. "What brings you here in the middle of the morning?"

"We need to talk. Our son left this at my place over the weekend." He held out a bag with the label of a music store. "Take a look inside."

Rachel opened it, hoping she'd see a stupid adult comic book but found what she'd dreaded, two doobies in a white envelope. "Crap, crap, crap." She stamped one foot.

He spoke as they walked back to the messy sunroom. "I looked at the name on the envelope. It doesn't ring any bells and it has a St. Paul address. What would he be doing there?"

She sat in a wicker chair, then pulled out the envelope and read the name. "It's the girl Steve found to be with the kids on Sunday nights, the college student daughter of a neighbor. I gave her a ride to her dorm once."

"Don't look so forlorn," David lifted the envelope from her fingers. "We've trusted Dylan through a lot of situations. This isn't the end of the world."

Dylan moved into the room, big athletic shoes making a silent entrance impossible. "Sorry, Dad, I couldn't find it. Something wrong?"

Rachel watched Dylan's face as David set the yellow record store bag on a table. She expected defiance. The insecurity and confusion moving through his eyes surprised her.

"Before you say anything, I know what's in that bag. Jake found it in their kitchen and brought it here a few days ago. We didn't know what to do with the stuff. I thought if you found it, Mom, you'd go ballistic. So I brought the bag to Dad's. I was going to trash it at the Twins game and I forgot."

"Why didn't you just tell me?" She swatted the dog's nose from the bag.

"I don't remember, Mom. Rob thought the babysitter might get upset that her stuff was missing and quit. I wanted to talk with Dad."

"Why not with me?" Rachel found her maternal pride smacked up one side. "We just spent forty-five minutes walking and running the dog. There was plenty of opportunity."

David smiled, aggravating her instead of calming the waters. "It doesn't matter."

"Hey, I swear none of us touch that stuff." Dylan's voice squeaked. "You believe me?"

"Of course," Rachel responded. How easily drugs threatened the protection plan. "Steve should know," she said, speaking over Dylan's quick protest. "The boys can spend a few Sunday nights here or with Grandpa instead of keeping this girl."

"Mom, don't squeal."

"We have to talk with Steve."

"They like that sitter," Dylan insisted. "Rob says she's a looker and lets him borrow new music."

"We have to talk with Steve."

"I know, but Rob's going to be so pissed off if their Dad fires Janel."

"It's out of your hands, son." David stood, shook out his pants legs and tightened his tie. "What time do you need me tonight to help with prep for tomorrow's party?"

"Why don't you come for dinner and stay over, Dad?"

"Dylan." Rachel scolded lightly.

"You've got enough stuff here to wear, Dad. I saw your jeans in the clothes hamper."

"Dylan," she tried to end the conversation.

"Why don't you just move in with us?"

"Why don't you let Mom and I figure that one out. Guys don't get in the middle of other guys' love lives. Remember? Take the dog out and give us a minute."

She followed David to the front door, feeling loose-jointed.

"I have late call so it's better if I go home tonight," he said, dampening her arousal. "Rachel, I'd like to bring someone tomorrow if that's all right with you."

Her bones returned to their normal rigid form, her shoulders moving up. "Who?"

"A new surgeon who's joining the group in September. He's young and moving here without any friends or family. Think it would be a problem?"

Her smile happened naturally. "No problem. We don't have anyone his age coming, but it's better than being alone." She knew that for a fact after years of spending miscellaneous holidays semi-alone when David was on call. "Dad's bringing a guy from that hospital support group he attends."

"You're losing your psychologist poker face, Dr. Kelsey. The look on your face left nothing to my imagination. As Dylan would say, chill." Heat rushed to her cheeks even as he winked and walked out the door. "I'll be here to take you to breakfast tomorrow. With my overnight bag."

Chapter 57

Beyond occasional picnics when they were children, the Kempers had no Fourth of July tradition. Rachel washed Carrie's stars and stripes serving pieces, thinking about possible landmines. She loaded one bowl with potato salad, another with chips, guessing at how they had been used by pictures from Steve's cell phone.

Steve, her father, his friend, and the boys arrived together, carrying a cooler of soft drinks. She watched from the windows, unsure how she felt now the gathering was officially beginning. Most of her family now spent time in her home, yet having them all here at one time made her feel vulnerable.

"I visited your Mother this morning."

"You surprised me, Dad. I had the water running."

"No changes." They were silent. He went to the refrigerator and pulled out the pitcher of lemonade. "How did you get your mother's pitcher and dishes? I thought she chucked these."

"Steve brought over a box of stuff." So Katherine's influence, not Carrie's, would be at the cookout, defining how the food table looked. Rachel piled one of her own baskets with buns.

Todd and his kids were in the yard as she looked up. She opened the refrigerator for bottled water and looked up at the sound of footsteps.

"You're a brave woman, Rachel. I know I wasn't up for having everyone at our house." Kris wandered into the kitchen and offered a tray of desserts. "Of course I carry a whole lot of different baggage about this family. For the kids' sake, I wish I could be more open-minded about the Kempers."

Kris looked thinner, gray roots lined her carefully bobbed red hair. Tension or anger or sadness pulled at her facial features. She looked around her at the kitchen and sunroom. "You've made a beautiful home. Carrie threatened to sell their place and buy an old house in Crocus Hill, but Steve wanted nothing about city living." She sighed. "There's so much maintenance in these places."

"Actually, Steve says they began talking about making a move to the city. Now he owns her two riverfront condos." Rachel didn't share that Steve was beginning to look at places in this neighborhood.

"We are so appreciative of everything you and Art are doing this summer," Kris blurted. "Knowing she's here is one less worry. Things aren't going well at our place."

Rachel knew too much from hearing Cat's stories. "I'm sorry. Let me know if I can lend a hand, or an ear." She reached across the counter to touch Kris. "Really. Right now we have a backyard full of hungry kids and men." She picked up relish and a spare bag of chips. "David and Dad brought guests so there are neutral people for a nice chat about nothing important.

Afternoon sun heated the backyard, Dad's shirt stuck to his shoulder blades. He moved to a chair under the table umbrella, wiping his forehead with the back of his hand.

Rachel knew her mother never liked sitting outside during parties but her father liked the informality of people standing to talk and kids playing yard games. The air was rich with the scent of flowers and the smell of neighbors' grills. The afternoon foursome acted more like siblings than cousins.

Steve sat down across from Rachel and Dad. "The boys bugged me to take them golfing yesterday. We had a great time."

"Did you fire that Janel girl?" her father asked, obviously worried about the episode.

"I did. I might have to call on you for a few overnights. By Labor Day I'm done with this case. Two years of traveling to Boston and

New York have earned me a promotion and the ability to work out of Minneapolis. None too soon for the boys' sake."

Dad shook his head and watched Steve move on. Color rose on his cheeks. "Too late for Carrie," he said so only she could hear.

Chapter 58

There were giant sparklers at the water's edge and fireflies adding to the night. Over the water Katherine saw ghostly shapes moving in an odd shuffling dance. Sometimes stars formed halos around their heads and other times the wind blew the clouds into shroud-like outfits blurring her vision. She strained to hear what names her mother called. A litany of the dead as her sisters and brothers walked onto the pier followed by her father and relatives long forgotten. She felt confused to be sitting alone on the shore.

"Katherine, Katherine, can you hear me?"

She wouldn't listen to the stranger's voice. A common voice. Her mother was very particular about who was invited to their home. No impure girls, no men of less than impeccable reputation. So difficult to meet her mother's standards. She began examining her behavior of the past life, looking for cracks that would hold her from joining the family when the time was right. She settled on Art, thought about their whole lives in the fraction of a second, and moved beyond as if the thought were insignificant.

"She's crashing. Katherine."

"Dominus Vobiscum. Et cum spiritu tuo. Oremus."

Another figure joined her mother's group. A young girl, as lovely as any girl could be, drew Katherine's attention, then ire. The girl didn't belong with the people Katherine remembered from her mother's table and pictures. She was modern, out of sequence.

"Her lips are moving." The common voice came from behind Katherine. She tried shaking her head to stop these voices from interfering with the beauty.

"Phone her family."

Chapter 59

David flipped another four burgers onto buns, each grabbed by a kid. The adults laughed and continued debating the best way to keep mosquitoes at bay, whether a young pitcher could pull his head out of his butt in the long stretch for the Twins, how to avoid construction traffic on the way home after fireworks.

In the kitchen the phone rang with a message taken by voice mail. The same call went into voice messaging of at least three cell phones tucked into car consoles or purses.

The Kemper family was starting a new tradition and taking a break from reality.

About the Author

Cynthia Kraack is the author of four novels including *Minnesota Cold*, the 2009 Northeastern Minnesota Book Award for Fiction, and the *Ashwood* Trilogy. Her short stories have placed in competitions of *Glimmer Train, Alligator Juniper Literary Magazine* and The *Peninsula Pulse's* Hal Grutzmacher Literary Contest. She is a graduate of Marquette University and completed her MFA through the University of Southern Maine's Stonecoast Program in Creative Writing.

Acknowledgements

The opening chapters of this book earned me a place in the 2008 Literary Fiction section of the University of Southern Maine's Stonecoast Program in Creative Writing. Faculty members Lesléa Newman and Alan Davis were willing to mentor a writer with journalist preparation through the first year of a MFA program. *The High Cost of Flowers* reflects their strength as writers, teachers, and workshop facilitators.

The Kempers and their stories are purely fictional. Families are imperfect communities built to the best ability of people who gather around the Thanksgiving table or call on Sunday nights to share simple news of their week. Families are as comforting as a soft blanket on a cool night, and then flood adrenalin through the system in the same way as flashing lights on a police car in a rear-view mirror. It is natural to want the hands that helped guide our first steps to applaud the loudest during our first public recognition. The journey from infant to matriarch is not direct or without bumps. Without family, my world would be incomplete.

Many thanks to Gary Lindberg and Ian Leask of Calumet Editions for selecting *The High Cost of Flowers*. Their support and expertise are sincerely appreciated in many ways.

CPSIA information can be obtained at www.ICGtesting.com
Printed in the USA
LVOW11s0046300515

440453LV00001BB/304/P